ON THE NIGHT BORDER

JAMES CHAMBERS

RAW DOG
SCREAMING
PRESS

D1205229

On the Night Border © 2019
by James Chambers

Published by Raw Dog Screaming Press
Bowie, MD

First Edition

Cover Image: Daniele Serra
Book Design: Jennifer Barnes

Printed in the United States of America

ISBN: 978-1-947879119

Library of Congress Control Number: 2019942344

RawDogScreaming.com

Previously Published

"A Song Left Behind in the Aztakea Hills," first appeared in *Shadows Over Main Street, Volume 2*, Doug Murano and D. Alexander Ward, eds. Winchester, VA: Cutting Block Books, 2017.

"Marco Polo," first appeared in *Truth or Dare?* Max Booth III, ed. Cibolo, TX: Perpetual Motion Machine Publishing, 2014.

"Lost Daughters" first appeared in *Deep Cuts*. Angel Leigh McCoy, E.S. Magill, and Chris Marrs, eds. Evil Jester Press, New York, 2013.

"Mnemonicide" first appeared in *Chiral Mad 2*. Michael Bailey, ed. Written Backwards, Calif., 2013.

"The Many Hands inside the Mountains" first appeared in *Dark Hallows II: Tales from the Witching Hour*. Mark Parker, ed. Scarlet Galleon Publications, 2016.

"Odd Quahogs" first appeared in *Shadows Over Main Street*. Doug Murano and D. Alexander Ward, eds. Hazardous Press, 2015.

"A Wandering Blackness" first appeared in *Lin Carter's Dr. Anton Zarnak, Occult Detective*. Robert Price, ed. Marietta, GA: Marietta Publishing, 2002

"Lost Boy" first appeared in *Kolchak the Night Stalker: Passages of the Macabre*. Dave Ulanski and Tracey Hill, eds. Lockport, IL: Moonstone Books, 2016.

"Picture Man" first appeared in *Bare Bone #7*. Kevin L. Donihe, ed. Raw Dog Screaming Press, May 2005.

Acknowledgements

Endless, heartfelt gratitude is due to all of the editors who first believed in and published some of the stories in this collection, to my dear friends and honest critics in the Top Secret Beta-Reading Group, and to all my writing friends and colleagues in New York working in all genres. Special thanks to Michael Bailey, John F.D. Taff, and Rena Mason for saying nice things about this book—and especially my thanks to the ever-gracious, generous, and talented Linda Addison for lending me her encouragement and support (whether she knew it or not) for more than twenty years. Much appreciation as well to Faryn Black for her contributions to improving the text. And, lastly, my thanks to Jennifer and John for their support, friendship, and professionalism.

For Laurie

"From the thunder, and the storm—
And the cloud that took the form
(When the rest of Heaven was blue)
Of a demon in my view—"

"Alone," Edgar Allan Poe, 1829

Contents

Introduction: Movies Behind the Eyes

by Linda D. Addison

Beginnings can be tricky. It's been said, "How things begin, is how things end." Clearly author and editor James Chambers has paid attention to the importance of hooking a reader from line one. The truth is, he knows how to grab you by telling a damn good story. If you want to know how to nail an opening, read the first lines of every story here. I can tell you as an editor of anthologies myself that reading other authors' work can teach a lot about what brings the reader into a story and what kicks them out. I was all in from the beginning to the end.

The first story, "A Song Left Behind in the Aztakea Hills," has many of my favorite elements in it: Jack Kerouac, bars, musicians, ghosts, and space-time continuum. The writing style was smooth and made me feel like I was watching a movie, not reading words. Not surprising, since I've read Chambers before and always felt like I was in the hands of a pro—a real storyteller.

Chambers lives in NYC and incorporates a kaleidoscope of humans/relationships in his stories, which I particularly enjoyed, keeps it interesting. The storylines and voices are so varied I had to keep reminding myself one author wrote them (unless he's working a multiple personality thingy!). The stories take place everywhere: cities, small towns, in the country, a carnival in Oklahoma and a village in Africa. He even plays with alternate reality through journal entries where there are places called *Government Lethal Chambers* (is it my imagination or is there some hidden message in the word *Chambers*?).

He revisits the land of Kolchak (his previously published graphic novel, *Kolchak the Night Stalker: The Forgotten Lore of Edgar Allan Poe*, won an HWA Bram Stoker Award®) with "*Kolchak the Night Stalker:* The Lost Boy," another story written so visually I felt like I was watching an episode of the show.

There wasn't one story I didn't love, some warped standouts were "Mnemonicide" (yes, break down the title—that's what the story is about);

"Living/Dead" (a unique take on the concept); "The Driver, Under a Cheshire Moon" (um, you should just read this story and summarize it yourself).

The poet in me (I see you, James Chambers) was jazzed about the titles: "The Many Hands inside the Mountain," "The Chamber of Last Earthly Delights," and "A Wandering Blackness."

If you've ever met Chambers, he's such a nice, civil person; clearly someone channeling all his demons and weirdness through writing, especially this book. There's some seriously twisted tales here: turning the kid's game, Marco Polo, into a path to madness and violence; a good samaritan's innocence doesn't protect him from human-shaped demons spinning a web; being pregnant doesn't create safety either; the spirit of evil in an abusive mother doesn't just die when she does; and the unraveling goes on.

Now it's your turn to let his tales, aka movies, blaze behind your eyes... have at it!

—Linda D. Addison, award-winning author of *How to Recognize a Demon Has Become Your Friend* and HWA Lifetime Achievement Award recipient

A Song Left Behind in the Aztakea Hills

I slid the clipping of his obituary into the same crinkled manila envelope that held the handwritten pages he'd pushed through my mail slot the night before he ditched Knicksport and never came back. He had left town in '64, only five years ago, and I'd always expected to see Jack Kerouac again.

His death from bleeding and booze filled me with a peculiar blend of relief and sadness over open questions whose answers I'd feared to know and now had died with him. All this only two weeks after Gregory dumped me, and that weird grief of losing someone unseen, unheard, unknown for years entwined with my heartbroken loneliness, two venomous snakes nested inside me.

Days passed with the distraction of work. On my easel sat a landscape in progress — the Martinson estate's eroding cliffs prodding into Cow Harbor, commissioned by Saul Norris for the bank lobby — but my brush faltered upon those dark feelings of isolation and rejection. My hands wandered with my mind. Unwanted textures crept onto my canvas, lending unnatural life to sand, waves, sky, clouds, trees, and rocks as if weaves of ropy fibers writhed beneath the surface of everything. Voids in the composition reflected the absence in my apartment. Several times a day I glanced for Gregory's lanky silhouette as he brought me coffee only to find myself staring at paint stains on sunlit floorboards. The freshly vacated slot in my toothbrush holder gaped like a hole I could fall through forever. I let my beard grow because the idea of shaving with our shared straight razor, left behind in the medicine cabinet, set my hand trembling, and yet I couldn't bring myself to buy another.

I could've followed Gregory back to the city if he'd wanted that, but I didn't know if he did. Nor did I know what else I could give him if all I had to offer had left him unfulfilled and restless. I'd left Knicksport at age eighteen and stayed away for two decades, but it *was* my home. My family built the building I lived in before World War I, and I knew the town's streets, beaches, and secrets with the intimacy of childhood. By leaving, Gregory had rejected the core of me as if what he saw deep inside there repulsed him.

11

More than painting, drinking numbed my pain. I needed little persuasion to set down my brush, turn a blind eye to Saul's deadline, and take a break across the street at Raker's.

Once in a while, devotees of Jack rolled into town, mostly young, naïve, hopeful souls. The poets, the artists, and the songwriters, seeking to walk the same streets the King of the Beats had and breathe the same air as if they might inhale lingering particles of his greatness. Some of those folks knew by word of mouth that if they asked right and tipped well on nights when wind howled down Main Street and the stars wavered oddly in the sky, Spence at Raker's might talk about the years Jack spent with us. And if Spence sensed a soft touch with a fat, loose wallet, he might even call me down to tell the story of the night Jack, me, and three would-be rock n' roll stars hiked into the Aztakea hills south of town—which is how I came to meet the mathematician one evening in early November.

I strolled into Spence's place, my fingers still gloved in the scent of turpentine and oil paint despite my having scrubbed them raw-pink. Stepping from a clear, starry autumn sky and dry air into a fog of tobacco smoke, hazy light, and the miasma of saltwater, sweat, and spilled booze felt like crossing between two worlds. Spence fixed me a gin and tonic with a bright wedge of lime smiling on top and gave me a warm nod. Most folks in town thought I'd lost a roommate when Gregory moved out—or at least they stuck to that idea as a discreet and convenient fiction. But Spence knew Gregory had dumped me hard and had lent me an ear and a shoulder and dragged me home safe when I drank far too much my first night alone.

Across the bar sat a man in his late forties, a sandy crewcut, tortoise shell glasses, short-sleeved, plaid dress shirt, and a sheepskin jacket draped over his stool. Spence poured bourbon into his glass, which the man clutched protectively. Nervous eyes stared out from his soft face into the murk of the bar as if he expected the rowdy locals to sense his weakness like wild dogs and pick a fight. Not that any would. Spence enforced a strict policy of peace backed by a well-worn Louisville Slugger kept near the bar sink. Outside Raker's, though, the bay men — clammers, lobstermen, fishermen with sunbaked and wind-dried skin, perpetual squints, and calloused hands bulging with swollen knuckles — showed little patience for anyone different than them. They spent too much time alone on the Long Island Sound, dropping traps and pulling them up again, watching whitecaps rise and roll over, listening to the wind whine, gulls caw, and the sea whisper of things long swept away by its currents.

Being alone too much changes how you think. Rarely for the better.

Pool balls click-clacked under the rambling beat of Creedence Clearwater Revival on the jukebox, "Green River" giving way to "Suzie Q," and I drank and smoked and eyed the man for as long as it took to finish both. Spence replenished my gin and tonic, and I carried it over beside the mathematician and eased onto an empty bar stool beside him.

"Thanks for the drinks," I said.

He glanced at me, eyebrows raised. "What?"

"Spence has been putting my drinks on your tab."

"Oh, you the guy who knew Kerouac?"

"Uh-huh."

"You've been sitting right over there for half an hour, keeping me waiting."

"I finally decided you looked harmless."

He processed that with a frown then shrugged.

"My name's Fenton Grive. My field's mathematics. My condolences on your friend's passing."

"Thank you. I'm Salvatore Cinelli. Spot me a ciggie-boo, wouldya?"

The mathematician slid a Marlboro pack from his pocket and shook one loose for me. In the match light, his face boiled with confidence born of something outside himself. He resembled a trusted clerk on an important business trip, a scent of chalk and after-shave hanging about him, but he made me anxious. Epiphanies and lies stirred behind his face and a faint sense of menace, not from him, but from what he represented, though I didn't know yet what that was.

"I guess it's smart to be cautious. You get a lot of people asking about him?"

"Used to back when Jack lived down on Judy Ann Court. They came banging on his door at all hours, swiping books off his shelves if he let them in. Not too many these days. Life goes on, you know?"

"Time stops for no man as the saying goes. I hear you're an artist."

"That's right. A painter."

"Yeah, nice. Um, listen, I'm no good at small talk so I'll cut to the chase. I'm moving into the Martinson place after the New Year while I do a fellowship over at Brookhaven National Labs. After that Kerouac fellow died, some folks at the lab and a few I've met in town said you might know something about him of interest to me. Professionally, I mean. An incident in the Aztakea Hills back in spring of '64?"

"Can't imagine what that has to do with mathematics."

"Maybe nothing. Could be I'm wasting my time here. I can't tell you much because most of my work is classified, but you ever heard of Walter Gilman or the Keziah Mason formulae?"

I shook my head.

"Not many people have. Among other things, I research sound. Frequency, modulation, pitch. There's a lot of common ground between math and music. These KM formulae date back to the late 17th century and Keziah Mason, a character who lived up in Arkham, Massachusetts. Authorities threw her in prison for witchcraft but she vanished inexplicably from her cell into the shadows of history until around 1929. That's when a student named Walter Gilman found some of her notes in a loft he rented in an old house. Turns out what passed for witchcraft in Keziah's day may have been advanced mathematics. Pan-dimensional physics and space-time distortion, stuff scientists only started researching after Einstein. There's the outer dimensions, the multi-planar angle paradox, honeycombs of non-Euclidian geometry, and the — "

I held up my hand. "Fenton, I have no idea what the hell you're jawing on about."

His face blanked then blushed before he re-engaged with humility.

"Sorry. I get carried away. Bottom line, an acquaintance of mine acquired Gilman's notebook. This man goes by the name Redcap. Lives in the West Village and plays at magic and witchery, mostly I think to get laid, though some folks believe in him. Anyway, he collects occult artifacts. He gave me Gilman's notebook to research, thinking the KM formulae equations might be replicated in properly composed and modulated sounds. If performed at certain key dates that coincide with planetary orbits and gravitational matrices, such sounds might open the way into non-linear realities outside — "

I gripped his forearm and squeezed. "The bottom line again, Fenton."

The mathematician tugged his arm away from my hand. "I want to know about the band you and Kerouac met, the Sultans. I think they know something about this music."

"Fenton, my new friend, I've been asked some wild questions, about Jack, this town, and art, and life in general, but no one has ever hit me with the kind of mad ideas you're spinning. How many bourbons did you drink before I got here?"

Spence, pretending to clean glasses, kept close enough to eavesdrop, which I appreciated. That man had seen all of Knicksport's ugliness in one form or another, and he looked out for his friends. I finished my gin and tonic and let him replenish it.

"This is only my second." Fenton pressed ahead as if he might agree with me if he took time to think about his words. "What can you tell me about the Sultans?"

"Not much. They came from Rhode Island. They absolutely abused denim and paisley."

"They disappeared, right?"

"So people say. They dreamed of being rock n' roll stars like the Byrds or the Stones. They sure smoked grass and drank booze like it. Anything might've happened to them."

"What'd you do that night up in the hills?"

"A little stargazing, some drinking. Jack and the Sultans got high, played music, sang."

"What kind of music?"

"Psychedelic folk rock, I guess you could call it. One had a guitar. Another played the flute. The third one strummed an instrument I'd never seen before, a sort of short sitar with these asymmetrical branches and complicated strings. A lot of buzzing, popping chords. Sounded like someone shaking a wasps' nest. Not my cup of tea. Or Jack's. He liked jazz."

"You hear anything else up there?"

"Wind creaking the trees when they stopped playing."

Fenton frowned. "Rumor is your friend and those rock and rollers heard something else. Maybe you did too?"

"Jack *said* he heard something wild in their music. He called it a turbulent bubble of sound like the world breathing across the top of a million open beer bottles, but he was high and even drunker than usual, which is saying something. Anyway, I didn't hear it. We got split up coming back. I didn't find him till morning. Neither of us ever saw the Sultans again."

"He ever say what happened to him after you got separated?"

Pages cocooned in an old envelope. Ink decaying, black to blue to gray. Gaping holes in my memory, the whole world breathing across a million open bottles, and *Knicksport is full of witches*, Jack told me once in a late-night, inebriated confession. Full of witches, full of secrets, all hiding behind shadows and false faces—full of monsters, too, like me. Too ugly for Gregory. Too grotesque for the world. Too disappointing for the family I'd left and returned to only after they'd all died. *Knicksport is full of witches*, said Jack, but to me it swelled with the angry ghosts and weeping wounds of the past.

"Nothing besides what I already told you," I lied.

Impatience backlit Fenton's eyes. "How about you take me up there into the hills and show me the place?"

I drank, long and slow, clinking ice gathering at my lips, freezing them a little, and then I set the glass down and shook my head.

"Why would I want to do that?"

"I'll pay you."

"You want to hear about my wild night in the woods with Jack Kerouac and a bunch of badly dressed musicians? Fine. I'm happy to let you buy me drinks and listen to me talk until closing time. But I haven't gone up in those woods since that night, and I see no need to change that."

"So take me as close as you want and point me in the right direction. I'll go the rest of the trail alone. You can tell me the story along the way."

"What exactly are you looking for?"

"Not a thing. I'm listening. I'll know it when I hear it."

Fenton pulled money from his pocket and eased it across the bar, exposing enough from beneath his hand for me to see a hundred-dollar bill. Wide-eyed, I shook my head nervously.

"Put that away. Are you nuts?"

He did, clenching his jaw, mistaking my reaction for refusal when I only meant to spare Spence any possible embarrassment. Discreet fictions or not, people talked. Gossip about me and my lack of a wife cropped up now and then, very goddamn little of it even half true, but no need to grease the skids. Granted I'd downed three gin and tonics, but a hundred bucks and a night spent tramping around the woods appealed to me more than drinking myself numb again and fighting oil paint demons.

"Another round, then we'll go," I said. "Pay me outside."

"Oh, sure, that's fine."

"I don't know what you expect to find, though."

"Like I said, I'll know it when I hear it." Relieved, Fenton waved for Spence to set us up once more. "Say, I've never read *On the Road* or *The Subterraneans*, and all those Kerouac books. Not my thing, I guess. What was he like?"

"Not what you might expect. Came here to escape his own legend. It's like two Jacks existed. One walked barefoot through town, jingling nickels for beer in his pocket whenever his mother, Mémère, tightened the purse strings to curb his drinking. The other, forever youthful and windswept, sped over ribbons of

16

endless, dusty blacktop in cars piloted by a crazy saint. By the time he came here, though, that second Jack lived only in his books.

"The humble one, though? The one who tossed a football around the schoolyard on warm autumn days and wandered town in his slippers dragging groceries home in a beat-up, granny shopping basket? That's the Jack I knew. He hung out in my studio, playing records and reading while I painted. A lot of nights we drank here. He really came to life in the bar with the bay men at the end of the day, some still gaffed in their hip-waders, stinking of fish and sea water, Jack jawing about this or that he'd done or seen zipping back and forth across the country until they bought him a beer to shut him up.

"Once he started, sheer joy poured out of him. He was mad to talk, just like he wrote about, and he spun stories like no one I've ever heard before or since. Never about books or writing or literature but about real life, and women, and working-day sweat, which he knew as well as any bay man washing brine from his lips with beer."

"He drank a lot?"

I laughed. "When Mémère held back his drinking money, he snuck a bottle of Canadian Club in here in a valise and sipped it in the men's room. Spence found out and banned him from bringing in any kind of bag at all. That happened about a week before the Sultans came to town."

I finished my fourth gin and tonic.

"Ready?"

"Lead the way."

Fenton scattered a few more bills beside his half-touched bourbon. Spence flashed me a questioning eye, and I winked to let him know all was well. Then we waded through the crowd and the acrid smoke to the cool outdoors. A run to my apartment across the road garnered some flashlights. I guided Fenton toward the harbor, shimmering with scales of moonlight, and then along the road to the woods.

At the trailhead, I flicked on my light and handed the other to Fenton.

He gave me the hundred and asked, "Why didn't you take this in the bar?"

"Spence is a friend. It might look bad for him if someone saw."

"Look bad how? You push dope or something?"

"No, but I got a bit of an unearned reputation."

Fenton looked my skinny frame up and down, filling in blanks. "I had a sense you might be queer when we shook hands."

I glared at him. "You want me to take you into the hills or not?"

"Yes. Doesn't matter to me which way you swing as long as you don't swing it my way. I didn't come here for that."

"You got nothing to worry about there, Mister Math Whiz."

I stamped up the first rise of the trail, putting distance between us, making Fenton work. I considered running into the dark and leaving the bastard on his own for thinking I sold myself to anyone who stood me a few drinks or that I sold myself at all. My desire for Gregory to return and put things back how they were ached inside me. I should've been home in his arms, streaks of paint on my face, a glass of cabernet on the table, and no worries about the frigid, black hills and empty shadows.

Christ, how lost and alone I felt to walk back to those hills. Right then, though, I wanted to get close to Jack and the good old days we'd had, when I'd still had Gregory.

My flashlight narrowed the path in a wash of dusty, ivory brightness. Leaves crunched underfoot, and branches scraped my legs. I tromped up the steepening incline, Fenton panting and wheezing to keep up. Away from town, the darkness called me, like the unwanted shadows slipping into my painting, like words written in old ink fading on yellowing paper, like a forgotten straight razor and a cold bed, all things meant for me whether I wanted them or not.

Fenton broke the quiet. "You were going to tell me about that night."

"Right," I said. "So Jack sat moping over his beer at Raker's because Spence caught him with his whiskey, and Mémère wouldn't give him enough cash to drink how he liked. He lived with her most of his life, rushing off to see the world, always coming back to look after his mom, a good son for his all wildness. The Sultans came in, long hair, beards, beaded denim, paisley shirts and kerchiefs, psychedelic patches on their jean jackets, embroidered with angel wings on the back. Half the crowd about laughed beer through their noses at the sight of them. The other half wanted to kick their asses to the street, but Spence doesn't tolerate any dust-ups. They wanted Jack. We gladly ran up their tab while they rambled on about ritualistic trance music that brought visions and raised consciousness to enlightenment about the universe. Jack dug it with his whole search for grace in the everyday world, feeling the beat of existence kick, but it didn't interest me. They said they knew songs kind of like what you described. If played certain times in special places, the music unlocked new doors of the senses. They'd come from playing them up in Rhode Island in an abandoned house in Providence, then road-tripped down to Knicksport, chasing the next time and place. They figured it'd be groovy if we went with them."

"You remember the songs?"

"No. I heard them only once, while drunk."

We reached a plateau. From there the trail ascended steeper than before through a broken netting of tree branches and tangled brush. Sweat broke out all over me, chilling in the cold air. The town sounds barely reached us. I leaned against a tree. Fenton squatted on a fallen trunk.

"Another hundred yards, up inside that ring of pines." I pointed to dense foliage above us on the trail. A melodic whistling tickled my ears for half a heartbeat then fell to the wind. "Hey, you hear that? Someone's up there."

"Who?" Fenton said.

"I don't know."

"Well, I didn't hear anyone. Let's keep moving."

My head spun like an invisible whirlpool had sucked the breath from my body all at once. I gripped the tree.

"You okay?" Fenton asked.

The sensation left me as quickly as it had come, and with a gasp, I straightened, restored.

"Yeah, must have caught a chill."

"Maybe I ought to go on alone from here."

"No, I'll come. The trail gets tricky."

I couldn't have let Fenton go on alone, not with the whisper of that music in my mind, tugging on me, and my unexpected need to reconnect with that moment in the past I'd shared with Jack. Wind rustled the sparse leaves and dry branches as we climbed. Stars danced in the sky, as if knocked out of place and frantic to find their proper positions, ants scurrying around a boot-smeared anthill. Whistling pipe music flitted across my ears, gone as quickly as it came. I hesitated, gazing at the shadowed pines and birches atop the hill.

"What?" Fenton asked.

"Nothing. Keep going."

The air cooled and seemed to congeal as we neared the top, leaving a coppery, electric taste under my tongue. The wild drumbeat of my heart filled my chest. I wondered what world we'd stepped into when we walked out of Raker's because it didn't feel like mine anymore.

Nervous, I said, "This one night Jack got so drunk he laid down in the middle of Main Street, right on the double yellow line, and refused to get up again."

"That right?" Apprehension in Fenton's voice hinted he, too, sensed the change in the air.

"Five or six of us tried to get him on his feet, tried to lift him, but he resisted."

"What happened?"

White birches, striped by peeling bark, filled my light like posts in an invisible fence.

"Gregory came down from our apartment, looked at Jack, and said, 'Hey, Jack, does this mean you're back on the road?' Jack — always one for a good joke — cracked up, jumped to his feet, and we went on drinking — listen! You hear that windy sound?"

Fenton cupped his ear, trying to catch it, then shook his head.

"Oh. Well, this is the place," I said.

Pine branches parted onto a pitch black clearing, where moonlight and starlight never reached earth. A figure in the clearing stood how I recalled Jack standing, legs wide, arms in motion, chin tilted upward as he spoke, and then it vaporized. Jack made words of the shadows, wrote them down, shoved them through my mail slot, and ran, back to motion, back to the road, fleeing or chasing as he had most of his life, leaving me with mere words to fill the cavities in my memory. Words too frightening to read. Except I did. I read them the day Jack left town, line for line, page after page, every one of them filling me with unvoiced screams and bitter laughter until blackness overcame me, and I woke up on the couch, Gregory holding my hand, all Jack's words erased from my thoughts as if I believed I'd never seen them.

A lie I reinforced every day after that.

A monstrous lie from a monster unwanted by family, lover, or friend.

"I shouldn't have come back here," I said.

"Why? What do you hear? I want to hear it too. Help me hear it."

The music sounded like Jack said. All the mouths in the world blowing across an infinite number of empty bottles. In the vibration, and the whisper of discordant notes, and the weight of their sound swaddling my flesh and throbbing against my skull, I knew those mouths came from a place much vaster than the world. They blew not across bottlenecks, but pipes, flutes, horns, and more as alien and disordered as the sitar-like thing the Sultans had played that night.

I bolted for the trail. Fenton grabbed me, crushing my arm.

"Wait a goddamn minute!" he shouted.

He shoved me. I tumbled into the center of the clearing, hitting my head on the ground. Fenton stood over me, a spread-legged, hunkered-down wrestler, hands opening and closing.

"Hold on, dammit! I didn't mean for you to fall. I'm sorry about that, but tell me what you're hearing. Describe it. Please! I have to know. You've got to tell me. Help me listen. Why can't I hear it too?"

I tried to stand. Pain exploded in my skull where it'd struck the ground.

Dizzy, I fell.

Amber and white flashes filled my sight.

I closed my eyes tight then opened them onto the night peeling back like skin and visible waves of muscle curling up the way the edges of burning paper do. Jack's ghost stood nearby, handsome, burly, and grinning drunk. I saw right through him and found the Sultans, who had never left that hill but become part of the clearing, petrified with their instruments frozen in hand, embedded to trees and stone, fused to this forlorn place. Blood dribbled from their ears, cold-syrup slow. Their eyes stared as wide as coffee mugs, funnels of dark motion tugging on me with pinches of gravity and widening as I watched. Through them I gazed at musicians playing complex, asymmetrical instruments carved of unearthly materials, piping blistered melodies and hypnotic notes with an urgency that made my hands shake.

The musicians spun and hopped from foot to foot in ragged, arrhythmic steps. Sinuous dancers, stretching mottled skin of indigo and ebony, scaled limbs raised, pressing mouthpieces to inhuman lips, a dancing circle orbiting an immense, churning, incomprehensible confusion on the edge of wakefulness, one best left to slumber and dream. Its naked pulse bled into the music, the universe, the world and every part of it, a hidden beat beneath all things like Jack had once sought, but nothing like the grace he'd searched for all his life. He heard and saw this that night we walked into the hills. We both did. The dancers ringed around the madness at the center of all existence. The words, the beat, the drugs, the travels — they had opened Jack's mind to what the Sultans showed him while mine rejected it even in the form of words on paper given me by Jack. Rejected it until grief and loneliness shredded my barriers and opened my ears.

I rose to my feet. Fenton stood rigid beside me.

The Sultans' paralyzed faces glared. Trapped awarenesses. Not petrified but slowed to its appearance, part of this place now, simultaneously part of all places, joined to the gyrating ring and the eyeless pipers, linked through the music, and the dance, and the revel that sated chaos until some inevitable day came when it grew tired of the melody and awoke.

Jack and I didn't walk back down that hill that night in '64. We stepped through the doors the Sultans opened into the shadow of a throne made of night and stars, the cosmos molded like a mother's hand cupping the skull of her mad son filled with cyclones of conceptions and notions shredded like words on cut-up paper scattered into a maelstrom. The scraps streamed and flowed to form a brutish man, with skin as lightless as empty space and eyes like carven black obsidian. He approached us, a word stillborn on his lips that cracked like old blacktop, a name Jack and I refused to hear as we turned away from the music, sought the trail, and then —

— the maelstrom ejected us —

— and I awoke in the parking lot behind my apartment, wedged between a dumpster cockeyed against the back alley wall, and Jack returned in an odd crook of the gazebo in the harbor-side park. Nightmare's end, except here in the hills, where the song we left played on and forever as if we'd never departed and I'd never lost Jack or Gregory, leaving me to return tonight alone. A tiny, drawn-out voice, a whistle among the din of a jet engine cacophony, drew me to the Sultan playing the sitar-thing, which now seemed ancient and derived from musical traditions long dead and forgotten in other worlds. I picked out his voice, like a record slowed down to the barest spin, taking what seemed an eternity for him to whisper: "Help me!"

"I don't know how," I said. Then I closed my eyes.

Frigid breath blasted my face. A stony, cold hand gripped my chin.

For the moment between two shuddering breaths, I felt wanted again. A monster desired by other monsters.

A demon fit only to dance in madness, enslaved to hideous music.

What other planet, the sounds of an entire world now swimming through this window, and who knows but that the universe is one vast sea of indifference, the veritable cruelty and apathy, beneath all this show of compassion and yearning? Microbes warring in the innards of Mercury, microbes dreaming, and oh, the void, oh, Hozomeen, great mountain, the void to my eyes, blinded then, before the mountain Mien Mo, and the mountain Coyocan, lush with sacred darknesses, hungers, and temples burnished with gold, opened my sight, my graceless soul craving salvation, non-existence, or the winding-down of experience to having never known the infinite roads upon which nothing ahead, nothing behind, and all the false idols of life and living receding to specks in the easy leaving, unexpected, bleak, and necessary, a dreaming which ultimates outward to the endless vast empty atom of this imaginary universe, never born, ending nowhere, never significant, the hollow beat, the deceitful beat, music that hesitates death rather than inspires life, fickle, mad, desolate, and the true life of all things that dwarfs our tiny souls, so fragile, hobbled, meaningless, and lost…

Jack's words on those pages I read so long ago rushed back to me.

The cold hand's wanting died. Its fingers lifted from my face, my monstrous nature unfit even for madness and despair.

Jack's words ended. My mind refused to remember anymore.

All the doors in the universe slammed shut around me, all but one.

I stepped through and fell into absolute cold, ice, my bones cracking with impact, frigid water embracing me, and gray light stabbing my eyes. Liquid silence, sloshing bubbles and air, yelling voices, knives of winter stabbing me, hands and feet numbed to oblivion, and then finally warm grips raised me and dragged me onto hard-packed earth and rocks, a crowd of foggy masks staring down at me with gasps, prayers, and swearing, a familiar face among them.

Spence. And he said, "Holy shit, Sal, where the hell have you been?"

Then came a flurry of recovery and reorientation and questions for which I had no answers, and my body and mind aching for anesthetic booze, and then finally obtaining it after the town decided to let me be, my disappearance of more than a month and no sense of what had happened to me written off as another in a long history of occurrences without explanation in this town full of witches. My December deadline for Saul Norris had come and gone, but when life returned fully to my body, I finished painting the Martinson cliffs, with the unwanted shadows and uneasy textures, and Saul grimaced when I showed him, and Spence told me I needed more rest. When Fenton Grive turned up, banging on my door, calling to my window for me to tell him where I'd gone, how I'd simply blinked out of reality that night in the Aztakea hills, I took my painting and Jack's pages, meaning to burn them all in the kitchen sink. I got no further than piling them up and opening a window to let out the smoke before I sat drinking whiskey by candlelight, smoking with winter air trickling in, and staring at the jumble of canvas and paper, the sharp white corners losing focus as warm alcohol haze kicked in, understanding, maybe, why Jack never strayed far from the bottle after that night, and fearing if the truth of the universe at the height of the hills and the end of his search had killed him, what it might now do to me.

Marco Polo

"What if it's not there? What if someone else got it?"

"Wuss." Mark flipped Henry his middle finger. "You're chickening out."

"Am not." Henry glared at him. "It's been, like, a year, right? Anybody could've gone in there and grabbed it. Maybe it burned up. I don't want to catch shit from you if I come out empty handed because the thing isn't even there."

"It's there. My brother saw it," Nabhi said.

"When?" Henry asked.

"Last month. His crew worked there."

"Why didn't he take it?"

"His boss would fire him if he took anything. They get out the toxic stuff, that's all. What would he want with it anyway?"

"People collect that sick shit. Sell it on eBay," Henry said.

"Not my brother."

"Well, someone else could've taken it since then," Henry said.

"We'd have heard about it," Mark said.

"If it was someone we knew, maybe. But who would blab about stealing something like that? Or what if the cops took it for evidence?" said Henry.

"The cops didn't need evidence, douchebag. Grandin died in the fire. No charges, no trial. Case closed," Mark said.

"I don't know. I heard they couldn't identify his body," said Henry.

"Yeah, his face burned off, and the heat cracked his teeth," Nabhi said.

Mark frowned then punched Henry in the shoulder. "Chickenshit. I knew you'd pussy out. Don't play the game if you don't have the balls to follow through."

"Shut up, loser." Henry swatted Mark away. "I said I'd do it, and I'll do it. But if it's not there, I still did it, okay? I go in there and it's gone or I can't find it, I still did the dare."

"Fine. Whatever. But you have to go down to the cellar and hunt for it. You either come out with the mask, prove you searched high and low, or I kick your ass. Now get in there before you bore us all to tears," said Mark.

Henry faced the burned-out Super Family Mart, the big box store's scorched walls and cracked glass only ashy, lightless smudges in the night. Clouds shifted, leaking moonlight down onto red-and-white "No Trespassing" signs plastered on the boarded-up entrances. Day-Glo orange posters touted the building's condemned status. The store's name and logo—a smiling, red dollar sign in a blue cape—loomed overhead, its high-wattage lights darkened more than a year.

Henry shivered.

He had shopped here dozens of times before the place burned, often with his dad on runs for supplies to fix up the house. He had even applied for a part-time job once, and shaken hands with the store manager, "the demon of Quogue Neck" himself, Avery Grandin; and when the man's sleeve tugged back, revealing vertical scabs on his forearm, Henry barely noticed them. He had other worries then. Two days before Grandin torched the store, Henry had shopped there with a black eye and three boxes of screws to exchange for the right size ones his father needed, the size written down this time, rushing to get them home before his father got off work.

Marie's gentle hand squeezed his arm.

"Don't go in, Henry. It isn't safe. Let's go home, all right? Dad will kill you if he finds out you went in there."

Henry scowled at her. "He's not going to find out, right?"

Marie shook her head and covered her mouth with her hand, all her plastic gypsy rings glittering with moonlight. A freshman, Henry's kid sister still liked to dress up for Halloween. At her side, her best friend, Sam, a year older, zipped her leather coat against the breeze and gave an exasperated sigh. She held Henry's hand for a moment. Her touch set his hairs on end and gave him goosebumps before she let go to tighten the black scarf around her neck.

"It's too risky. The floors could give out. Something might fall on you. You could cut yourself on broken glass or rusty nails. Breathe in something poison. Forget this. Let's go back to the bonfire, okay? My brother has a cooler. Maybe he'll slip us a few beers. Who cares what Mark thinks?" she said.

Henry mustered up a smile for his sister and her friend. His friend too now—much more than a friend if he didn't screw things up. "If Nabhi's brother did a job in there, how bad could it be? Right, Nabhi?"

Nabhi flashed an exaggerated expression of disgust. "My brother wore a hazmat suit. They worked in groups of three for two hours at a time, max. They didn't even see rats, man, and they always see rats."

Henry's smile faltered. "Guess I'll have the place to myself then."

"Screw this. I'm going back to the bonfire. You lose, Henrietta," said Mark.

"Shut up, tool, I'm going already."

Henry pulled an LED flashlight keychain from his pocket. He switched it on and, aiming through a gap in the boards, speared part of a window with its cold, white beam. Light pooled on the sooty glass, faltering when it reached the darkness beyond. Henry leaned against the window, pressed the flashlight right up to the glass, and cupped one hand over his eyes.

"What do you see?" Nabhi asked.

Henry smirked. "Mark's mom, blowing a hobo."

"Asshole," said Mark. "You got ten seconds to get your ass in there before you lose and I beat the shit out of you for talking smack about my mom."

"Sorry." Henry edged along the front of the store, putting distance between himself and Mark, heading for an emergency exit rumored to be broken and unlocked. Rounding the corner, he shouted back: "I shouldn't have said that about your mom. I mean, it was your sister blowing the hobo."

Mark swore. His footfalls slapped the crumbly pavement.

Henry bolted out of sight and rushed to the windowless side door, praying to find the lock smashed as promised, wishing suddenly for more assurance than the word of Adam Hammill from computer club. The door looked perfectly intact. Henry's insides twisted in an anxious knot. He grabbed the handle, jerked it, then winced at the sharp jag of the lever biting his palm as it held rock solid. Mark skidded into sight, stopped, pushed up the sleeves of his varsity football jacket, and then, with fists clenched, stalked toward Henry.

Henry yanked the handle up and down and pulled on the door; neither budged.

"You're *so* dead. I don't even care about the dare anymore. I can't wait to beat you," Mark said.

Too nervous to censor himself, Henry said, "It'll be a change of pace for you, beating on me instead of beating off right?"

Mark laughed. "Oh, keep it coming, dead man."

Panicked, Henry thrust with all his weight and strength against the door, pushing inward instead of yanking outward. The frame creaked and popped. The door jolted, scraping open into a darkness that swallowed the moonlight. Henry stared into a perfect void across the threshold. The stink of ash and mildew, of burnt plastic and moldering drywall poured out. In the vast husk of the abandoned store, something dripped, and the walls seemed to groan with the weight of the darkness. Henry wanted to turn back, but Mark—approaching red-faced with a nasty grin—left him nowhere to go.

Behind Mark, the store parking lot seemed like an impassable stone sea, the high chain link fence along its perimeter a rogue wave, frozen as it broke on the unreachable shore of the empty street. Sodium vapor streetlamps gilded everything copper. The distance hadn't seemed so great on the way in. A paper Halloween decoration blew down the road like an enormous, orange-and-black winged moth, snagged on the fence for a moment, then tumbled away. Then the moonshadows of Henry's friends jumped from around front of the store as they caught up to Mark.

Henry picked out Sam's long, graceful shadow and that decided him. He never wanted Sam to see him as weak or frightened. Nothing would flip the killswitch on their young romance faster than Sam watching her junior, would-be boyfriend reduced to ground meat by her shithead, senior ex—and Henry didn't want to fight anyway, didn't want to be the asshole who solved his problems with his fists. The thought stiff-armed him into the blackness. He jogged several yards into the store then cut down a vaguely discernable aisle, dousing his light to hide from Mark, whose broad figure towered in the moonlit doorway.

"I'll be waiting for you, asshole. You come out without the mask, I'll fucking break you. You hear me, dead man?"

Mark's voice echoed in the darkness.

The voices of Henry's friends joined it—Nabhi warning him to be careful, Marie and Sam yelling for him to come out, but the sound of Sam's voice only urged him deeper into the dead store, where his feet scuffed debris, and a cobweb brushed his ear. He switched on his keychain light to check his location. He stood two-thirds of the way down the outdoor aisle, its shelves empty except for the dregs of melted rubber hoses and a gathering of garden gnomes with blackened beards and scorched eyes, their red and green hats miraculously intact.

He walked to the rear of the store and the stockroom entrance. The stale stench of char and wet wood and the musty odor of rot invaded his nostrils. He gagged, raised the collar of his T-shirt over his mouth and nose, then entered the stockroom and located the cellar stairs. Giving himself no time to reconsider, he started down, spotting each sagging riser with his light as he descended, expecting one to break anytime. At the bottom, he swept the cellar with his light, which suddenly seemed inadequate for anything more than finding one's keys in the driveway.

The quiet of the cellar amplified the rapid whoosh of his breathing.

He pulled out his iPhone, checked the time—he'd been in the store about six minutes—then turned the light of its display forward, kicking himself for never downloading the flashlight app Marie had showed him. He would've nabbed it now if he got any kind of signal down here just for a little extra light. Orienting himself, he recalled the diagram he'd seen in news reports online that showed Avery Grandin's hidden dungeon in the northwest corner, and then he picked his way past the burned remains of stock shelves and inventory reduced to ash, walking almost an entire block under the store before he found what remained of Grandin's false walls. They lay dismantled, probably by police and fire investigators, and stacked outside the narrow opening into the dungeon they had hidden. The news said it had once been an electrical room.

Henry confronted the doorway.

Another blank space.

Another chance to prove himself to Mark, to Sam.

To himself.

To his father.

A tiny step on a passage away from fear, a path he hoped—if he proved determined enough—would lead him far away from home. Maybe with Sam beside him, the two of them leaving Quogue Neck behind and never looking back. Sam made it all seem real—or at least possible. It still awed him that she liked him, that she'd even kissed him once. Sam, who'd quit cheer squad to take AP classes, the same as Henry took. More than anything, as silent waves of darkness swirled around him, he wanted to smell Sam's hair and feel the warmth of her hand in his again. He didn't know what she saw in him, but he wanted to be that person, the brave version of himself worthy of Sam's heart—not the version who cowered in his bedroom with tears in his eyes until his father's rages passed, or the version pushed around by Mark since the fourth grade.

He entered Grandin's dungeon and inhaled its dank air.

His light revealed rusty chains bolted to a concrete floor stained by the remnants of black, liquid splotches. A rancid odor tickled his nose. Everything turned real then—and for a moment, Henry thought he might pee himself. His heart pounded in his chest, and his muscles quivered. A voice from the back of his mind told him he didn't belong here, that he should get out, that he should've chosen to tell a truth, to answer the question he knew Mark would ask, and admit how he felt about Sam and what he wanted to do with her—but Mark would've asked it in the nastiest way possible simply to humiliate Sam.

Henry couldn't take part in that if he wanted to keep his promise to himself to be nothing like his father. The dare had been his only choice.

He flipped around his iPhone and snapped pictures to shove in Mark's face. His flash freeze-framed awful things concealed by the darkness. Chains fitted with manacles, and others rigged to overhead pulleys. A row of four rusty, heavy-duty hooks mounted into the wall. A wire box spring stripped of cloth and affixed on a hinged base, leather straps dangling from its corners and sides. A corner drain choked with detritus and haloed by stagnant water. Deep gashes in the cinderblock walls freckled with what looked like dried blood.

No sign at all of the damn mask.

The police must have taken it. Nabhi's brother was only telling stories.

Henry looked again, probing with his light, casting it under the box spring and down into the drain. He knew the pictures would shut Mark up well enough and win the dare, but he wanted Mark to look small, stupid, and frightened. He wanted to see Sam's eyes widen with awe when he returned with the trophy. He *needed* the mask so they would see him how he wanted them to and so he could see himself that way too. He toed the debris around the drain then scoured the room once more. This time he noticed a group of chains dangling from a ceiling-mounted pulley: one heavy chain fitted on its end with four thinner chains that hung loose, their shadows casting lines on the far wall. A scrap of torn leather dangled within them. Henry knew then the mask really was gone. He saw nowhere else it could belong. Reportedly made of leather and fitted with iron rings through which Grandin had looped chains, the mask had locked his victims in place, raising them off the floor, forcing them to stand on tiptoes or hang by their head while Grandin tortured them. That had to be the rig, and the mask would be nowhere else.

"Shit!" Henry kicked one of the manacles on the floor.

It clanked loudly.

As he turned to leave, a flash of red caught his eye.

He paused, brought the light back but couldn't locate it. He retraced his steps, repeated the turn, gripping the light in the same position, and discerned a tiny red scrap at the edge of his beam. He scanned the wall, exposing deep red folds of material dangling from one of the rusty hooks. Henry hadn't seen the material earlier and froze in place, suddenly terrified that someone hiding in the room with him had hung it there. But when he counted the hooks this time, he came up with six. Two more than before, the extra pair set about a foot apart from the others. He had only overlooked them—and the red thing. He released his breath then lifted the material off the hook. It felt coarse, leathery, and oddly supple.

It unfurled into a mask with frayed, black, stringy laces on the back and similar stitches sealing slits where the eyeholes and nostrils should've been. Only the mouth remained open.

Feeling triumphant, he compared the mask to the scrap of black leather in the chains and realized this one, which had no iron rings sewn to it, wasn't the one he sought. Mark could call him on that and claim someone besides Grandin had left it there, or that Henry had planted it himself. His sense of victory dwindled.

He draped the mask from one hand, spreading it on his fingertips, and snapped a picture.

It stared back at him from his screen, eyeless yet lifelike, the red much pinker, almost translucent in the image captured by the camera flash. Then he realized how the mask could save him from Mark and made his way back across the cellar.

He ascended the creaking steps and crept toward the side door.

His friends' voices murmured outside. Worried he'd been in the store too long, the girls wanted to call their parents or 911, but the boys urged them to wait. Henry spied Mark standing with his back to him, a perfect target framed in the doorway. He put away his flashlight, slipped the mask on, and tied the coarse, slippery laces. The leather hugged the contours of his face. The fabric stank with a meaty odor and sucked at his skin. The stitches in the eye positions chafed at is eyelids. He couldn't see, but he if he ran screaming in a straight line, he would run right into Mark—and scare the piss out of him. His face flushed. The mask warmed. Henry found it hard to breathe despite the mouth hole. As he charged the side door, heat filled him, spreading from the inside out, and…

…he rushed through a wall of flame.

Fire flared all around him. Smoke choked his lungs, seared his nose.

Voices filled his head. A man roared, shouting down screams of agony. Henry pumped his legs, but they felt weak, and he didn't know where he was going. The heat rose.

It built up within him, blistering his insides.

He tried to scream, but super-heated air rushed into his throat, scorching his larynx.

Pain erupted in his body. Images flooded his mind. Men and women in chains, stripped and bleeding, cut, burned, bruised, tufts of hair yanked from their scalps, eyes swollen shut, lips cracked and caked with blood, and noses funneling rivulets of snot down their chins and onto their breasts, and a man yelling: "Do you want to play a game? Do you want to play?"

The flicker of a knife blade. Skin opening. A line of blood expanding.

"Tag! You're it!"

Henry felt his stomach lurch, preparing to empty itself, and then...

...he collided with Mark, who shouted with all the shock Henry had hoped to hear.

The boys toppled to the ground, Henry's hands brushing Mark's face and neck.

In an instant, the heat vanished, cool breath inflated Henry's lungs, and he saw stars and the moon overhead. Mark screamed. The mask covered *his* face now. Its laces twined themselves tight to the back of his skull—and Henry saw then they were made from strands of hair—and the mask itself... The idea horrified him, but it looked like skin turned inside out. Dead skin he had worn. He felt dizzy and touched his forehead, wincing when his fingers stroked sore skin. Mark staggered, still screaming, his chest heaving. He lumbered toward Henry, who rolled away, then scrambled to his feet and ran to Sam, Marie, and Nabhi.

"What the hell did you? Is that the mask? How'd you get it on him?" Nabhi asked.

"I don't know," Henry said, shaking.

"Your face is all red! You're burned." Marie touched his cheek.

Henry recoiled, wincing.

"I told you to stay out of there. What happened?" Sam asked.

"Forget Henry's stupid face. We have to help Mark!" Nabhi shouted.

Mark charged toward them, flailing his hands until he struck Nabhi, who stumbled then recovered and grabbed Mark's shoulders to steady himself and Mark.

"Mark! Calm down, man. It's Nabhi! We're going to help you. Okay? We'll get that thing off —"

Mark shuddered, shook off Nabhi's grip, and then grabbed his friend by the neck.

The mask vanished from Mark's face and reappeared on Nabhi's.

Nabhi yelled as Mark let go of him, and then blindly ran several steps before he stopped and clawed at the neck of the mask.

Mark dropped to his knees. A stream of black smoke spilled from his lips; streaks of ash caked his nostrils and the corners of his mouth. His eyes watered. Tufts of hair had been seared from his head.

"What the hell... did you do to me?" he said, his voice hoarse.

Sam and Marie stared at the boys, stunned.

"What is that thing?" Sam said.

"Nabhi!" Henry called.

Nabhi whirled and barreled at him. At the last moment, Henry ducked down beneath Nabhi's hands, and his friend smashed into him, toppling them to the pavement. Marie rushed to help. Nabhi leapt to his feet and grabbed her by sheer luck, clutching her bare wrists, and then Marie's screams sliced the night. The mask snugged itself tight to her face. She darted into the vacant parking lot, crying. Nabhi dropped to the ground, coughing and hacking up wads of black phlegm, his body trembling, his face blistered and streaked with soot, smoke rising from his hair.

Henry and Sam dashed after Marie, shouting for her to stop, but Marie kept racing in a manic path around the parking lot, struggling to pull the mask from her face, unable to even pry her fingers beneath its edges.

"Oh, god, why does she keep screaming like that? What's it doing to her?" Sam said.

"Maybe we can cut it off her, but we have to stop her first," Henry said.

He called Marie's name, but it was Sam's voice that pierced her frenzy. Marie halted and leapt toward her friend. Sam braced herself and opened her arms to grab hold of her. Her bright eyes fearless, her lips set with determination, Sam displayed everything Henry loved about her. She looked beautiful, and the sight terrified him as he realized what would happen the moment Marie touched her—the same thing as when he'd touched Mark, and Mark had touched Nabhi, and then Nabhi, Marie.

"No!" Henry shoved himself between his sister and Sam, knocking Sam away. Marie's fingers scraped his raw face, drawing blood before…

…darkness filled Henry's eyes and a horrible heat exploded in his lungs, his chest, his veins. All his senses burned, except his hearing, which brimmed with a man's voice, hollering over and over, "Marco! Marco!" and others screaming, "Polo! Polo!" in reply.

Flashes of hell flooded Henry's mind. The dungeon in the Super Family Mart cellar lit by candles and red spotlights, shadows dancing on its walls, chains flashing, clanking, the box spring jolting and blood dribbling down the body strapped there, draining into the floor. A knife biting flesh. Long-nailed hands scraping against the knife hand, gouging bloody furrows along the wrist and arm, leaving wounds that would never fully heal. The knife withdrawing. Then in the flash of its blade, a reflection: a man's face turned inside out. Like the red mask.

Behind him loomed a giant shouting, "Do you want to play a game?"

The man with the inside-out face shrank to child size as he ran, frightened, and then screamed when the giant touched him. A burst of flame washed him away.

Pain surged through Henry's bones.

Walls of fire surrounded him. Angry, hateful voices cut through the fire's crackle, crying, "Tag! You're it!," and all of it growing louder and more intense, building toward the cold certainty of death, and…

…Henry smacked the back of his head against the concrete.

Nabhi stood over him, wearing the mask.

He didn't scream. Instead, he ran three steps, hesitated, listening, then lunged to his left, grabbing Mark by the face. The mask jumped. Nabhi dropped to his knees, head smoking.

Mark howled then staggered, caught himself, and mimicked Nabhi—*listening.*

He tried to snag Marie, whose burned face glistened with tears, but missed, and then he dashed in Sam's direction. She sidestepped him. Nabhi hopped back to his feet in time to dodge Mark when he came for him. Everyone scattered with firecracker bursts of footsteps.

"No! Don't leave me!" Mark shouted.

He took off after the closest footfalls—Marie—and gained fast.

Henry yelled, "Get away from her!"

He swerved across the lot, pumping his legs as hard as he could, reaching Mark as he stretched a hand toward Marie, who coughed and doubled over, unable to catch her breath, the loose skirts of her gypsy outfit tangling her legs. Henry seized Mark's arm and shoved it away. Mark followed the motion, moving like a football player, pulling Henry close, groping for his face with…

…red heat and the stink of blood and burning flesh, and an adrenalin eruption, a thrill of ecstasy unlike any Henry had ever felt before, even as his body lit up with agony from head to toe, and not even the screaming or the cutting or the power of chaining his victims and owning their terror, their despair, and their hope could salve the pain. The fire burned down his skin, excavating deeper wounds, old cuts and bruises that bit deeper than flesh. He sensed someone behind him, whirled and faced the man with the inside-out face, a knife clutched in his hands, his arms grooved with scabby ridges. Grandin's hands. Behind him stood the giant, his face inside-out as well, and a third man loomed beyond him, twisting his inside-out face to snap back into place against his glowing ember skull. The face righted itself. Henry's father's face. Lips drawn back, teeth bared, fire sparking from his mouth, and an old, weathered axe handle Henry had known since the second grade gripped in his right hand, words spewing from his

throat, *"I'm only teaching you how life is, Henry. Sometimes it punches you in the gut or blackens your eye for no damn good reason. The universe gets you in its sights and—* wham! *You best learn to roll with it because when it happens…"*

The axe handle began its descent.

Avery Grandin's knife paralleled it, firelight dancing on its blade.

"…tag! You're it!"

White firelight plumed into…

"Marco!"

…shadows swallowed Henry as he hit the ground, scraping his knees and palms. He vomited the taste of ash and burning flesh. Mark wore the mask now, and he tracked Marie, the youngest and slowest of them, by her whimpers and coughs.

"Stay away from her! Over here, asshole!"

The remnants of bile in Henry's throat garbled his voice, but Mark turned.

Henry sensed the scenes inside the mask. Having worn it, he knew it was part of Avery Grandin, maybe all that remained of him, and whatever strange fire burned within it neared its climax. His head swam with violence. All the places where his father's axe handle and fists had touched his body over the years ached as if preparing to rip him apart. Henry didn't want Marie, or Sam, or anyone else he cared about wearing the mask when the axe handle and the knife blade fell.

"This way, dickhead," he shouted.

Mark yelled and raced toward him, hands outstretched, and the boys collided, Henry trying to wrestle Mark down, get the mask off him, and figure out how…

…the world became fire and blood, a whirl of violence, a mass of hateful, crashing thought breaking into reality through the hands of a demon, his fingers wrapped around the handles of knives, and skewers, and red-hot brands, and axes that…

…Henry tagged Mark, sending the mask back to him. Mark screamed once then batted Henry with his fist…

"Polo!"

"…got you, you're it, you little bitch," a man's voice said.

Henry watched the knife edge flicker, the axe handle's shadow cut a dark arc against the conflagration filling the sky, and so little time left NO TIME LEFT…

…Mark howled as Henry tagged him, his voice breaking with despair.

Henry tried to scramble out of reach. He needed to catch his breath. From inches away, Mark groped his face. Henry leaned away and yelled, "No tag backs! No backsies! I call it! No tag backs!"

Mark's hand touched Henry's lips, his chin.

No fire came, no blades or blood. Mark released an anguished shriek. He spun in a frantic circle, searching for anyone to tag, the mask glowing, smoke leaking from the edges of its neck. Nabhi and Marie helped Henry onto his feet. They ducked Mark's wild lunges, kept quiet, and tried to slip away without Mark following them, but then Marie coughed again, and Mark came at her, fast and hard. Henry pushed Marie behind him and shoulder-checked Mark, who jolted sideways and ran stutter-step for several yards, seeking his balance. The mask flared like a jack-o'-lantern before he slammed right into Sam, who'd been running to help Marie.

His hands touched her face. The mask jumped.

Mark fell face down on the pavement. Smoke trickled from his scalp.

Enveloping Sam's head, the mask lit up like a giant candle flame.

Henry bolted to Sam's side, fingers grasping for her skin even as she sank to her knees. He reached into the ball of searing light around her head to tag her and take back the mask, then recoiled, and snatched his hand away, his fingertips blackened. Sam toppled onto her side. As she hit the ground, the edge of the mask fluttered, and its laces came undone. The odors of burnt flesh and charred bone wafted out from the hot embers of his dream, the dying glow of his first love. He didn't understand how he'd failed to protect her, how he'd let the axe handle and the knife and the flames find her.

Wind tugged the mask from Sam's head and blew it into the parking lot. Sam lay still. Smoke poured from her blackened, faceless, hairless head.

Henry doubled over and vomited again.

Behind him, Mark coughed and tried to rise.

The sound drove Henry to his feet. He surged at Mark, shoving him back, and then kicking him in the stomach. Mark fell, and Henry kicked him again. He beat on Mark with his fists, ignoring Marie and Nabhi begging him to stop. He pounded on Mark how his father had hit him, how Mark had hit him in the fourth grade, how inside-out-faced Avery Grandin had hit his victims, how the giant had hit Grandin, and how Henry wanted to hit himself for failing Sam. He struck with all the violence and pain dealt to him his entire life channeled through his raw fists, and he didn't stop until lights and sirens filled the air, and three police men restrained him and dragged him away.

Lost Daughters

Three young women in black party dresses stood by the side of the "suicide bridge" and looked into the darkness over the guardrail. Drew dropped his Audi to a crawl as he passed them then stopped, put it in park, and watched the women in his rearview mirror. His tail lights gilded them electric red. It was well after midnight and there were no other vehicles or pedestrians around, but the girls paid him no attention.

He opened the door, stepped halfway out of the car, and called against a chill wind, "You ladies okay?"

The three turned together and looked at him.

Black streaks of makeup ruined by tears lined their cheeks. Their dark hair was mussed and wild and their stylish dresses torn ragged along the hems and spotted with dry leaves and flecks of mud. They were barefoot, and their feet were scratched and streaked with blood and dirt. The youngest, who wore a beaded shawl across her exposed shoulders, held a single pink sneaker. Torn across the front, it dangled from her right index finger by a frayed lace. The women possessed the innate beauty of youth—but spoiled and bruised. They weren't much older than Drew's two daughters in high school.

"Did you have an accident? Are you hurt?"

The women didn't answer.

"Want me to call someone? The police? An ambulance?"

The women only stared. Maybe he'd frightened them by stopping.

"I won't bother you or anything. I'm on my way home from work. I thought you might need help."

Nothing.

"You want me to leave you alone? Fine. Whatever. It's none of my business why you're out here, but people sometimes throw themselves off this bridge. You're not going to do that are you? Tell me you won't, and I'll go. Tell me you're not here to kill yourselves."

Nine people in the last two years and more before then had dropped themselves onto the desolate railroad tracks more than a hundred feet below the bridge, a guaranteed lethal descent.

Times were tough, Drew knew well enough. The recession claimed its victims. Drew had worked down the hall from one for six years: Carmine Price. Drew and Carmine were analysts, and then their boss laid Carmine off from his six-figure, eighty-hours-a-week job. He came to this bridge, which Drew drove over almost every day, and leapt. His funeral remained vivid in Drew's memory. Sometimes he ran into Carmine's wife and three kids out shopping, and they always looked trapped in a state of shock, as if they'd never come to grips with their loss.

The three women would undoubtedly leave their people haunted the same way if they threw themselves over the ugly bridge's side.

Drew sighed. "Have it your way. Whatever you're thinking of doing, there's nothing that could've brought you here tonight that's worth throwing your life away. You can get help. Call a hotline. People care what happens to you. You're young. Life will get better. So, please, come off the bridge."

The women stayed still as statues, but the wind ruffled their dresses, teasing dead leaves from the fabric and scuttling them along the pavement. It embarrassed Drew how they stared at him, their dark eyes gleaming like hot coals in the glow of his taillights.

"Dammit, say *something*. All right? If you won't let me help, then whatever happens to you isn't on me. Okay? It's your choice."

Drew waited for a reply, but none came. He shrugged and got back in his car, intending to call 911 and let the police deal with it. Before he closed the door, though, the woman Drew took as the oldest stepped forward, and asked, "Are you going through Quantuck?"

Drew popped out of the car again. "Why?"

"You could give us a ride."

"No," Drew said. "You can use my cell phone. Call a cab or a friend to pick you up. I'll wait with you until they get here."

"We have no friends. We have no money for a cab."

"I'll help you, but I'm not giving you a handout."

The woman scowled. "We don't want money. We only want a ride."

"I'll call your parents so they can come get you." Drew took his iPhone from his pocket. "What's the number?"

"We can't call them," the woman said.

"Why not?"

The women exchanged glances with each other, but none answered.

Drew noticed then that they had no purses and gave them each a closer look. Their long, chipped fingernails glistened with polish the color of dried blood, and something dark stained their fingertips. Each woman wore a single piece of jewelry. A silver-weave choker with a red gem dangling from a silver chain adorned the oldest woman's neck. The one with the shawl wore sharpened hook earrings of tarnished brass, and the other wore bracelets made of rusted iron. The choker half-obscured a ring of raw, bruised skin, and the bracelets covered pink furrows of scar tissue.

"How did you wind up on this bridge?" he asked.

The second woman stepped up. "Our shitty boyfriends dumped us here because we wouldn't put out."

"Please give us a ride," the youngest woman said.

"I'll help you get home but no ride," Drew said.

Drew imagined his daughters stranded this way, and he sympathized with the women, but he saw too many unwelcome possibilities if he let them into his car. A sharp ache stabbed the back of his eyes, a headache building. They often came at the end of a long day, which meant almost every day. This one's first pangs reached back to before he'd left the office, too drained to finish the quarterly reports now sitting on his passenger seat. He massaged his temples and tried to rub away the pain.

It was so late. He wanted only to go home.

He gazed at the heavy darkness beyond the edge of the bridge. Wind whistled through it, and Drew thought of sleep.

"Listen." The oldest woman inched closer. "We're screwed if we're not home before sunrise. Our stepfather doesn't know we're out. Our little sister isn't even supposed to be with us. If we have to call him to come get us, he'll *kill* us, for sure. We'll never get home on time if we walk. All we need's a ride."

Drew shook his throbbing head. "I won't do it."

"If you give us a ride," the oldest woman said, "I'll make it worth your while. A guy like you coming home from work this late, you must be stressed out, right? You must be the kind of guy who works *all* the time, no life outside the office, hardly ever see your family—your *wife*. When was the last time you were alone with her? Maybe you tell yourself you do it all to give them the life

38

they want, but really, isn't it easier for you when you're not there? Then their problems aren't your problems, and you already have so much stress at work, you don't need more at home too. The worst part is how afraid you are of losing your job even though you hate it. Maybe you know someone like you who jumped from this bridge. Maybe *you've* even thought about jumping. It would be so easy, falling into the darkness, escaping all the bullshit. What kind of life would you be leaving behind? Not much of one. Someone should be there to make you feel good. So if you do something nice for us, I'll do something… *nice* for you."

Drew retreated, stunned speechless.

A wicked glint in the woman's eyes made him shiver.

So did the black space behind her, the emptiness beyond the bridge.

Composing himself, Drew said, "Don't embarrass yourself. I'm old enough to be your father. You should show some respect for someone who stopped only to help you."

The three women rolled their eyes and snickered.

"We know what you want," the youngest said.

"Forget it," said Drew.

He crouched to get back in his car, but the oldest woman grabbed his shoulder, her touch cold and stiff. "Give us a ride."

Drew opened his mouth to say no, but he couldn't move.

The woman looked too weak to hold him, yet he was unable to break her grip or change position. She plucked his iPhone from his hand and dropped it on the road. The other women joined their sister.

"Give us a ride," all three said.

Their voices echoed in Drew's head: *Give us a ride.*

He didn't want the women in his car, didn't want them anywhere near him, but when the woman let him go, and he found himself capable of movement again, instead of getting in the car and driving away, Drew straightened his jacket, opened the driver's side back door, and let the sisters slide onto the backseat. The youngest paused before she got in and hurled the torn pink sneaker off the bridge. It spun into darkness. Drew waited for the noise of it crashing below, but if the sound came, it was too faint to hear. He shut the back door and then settled in the driver's seat and latched his seatbelt. The quiet in the car emphasized the nearness of the women. They brought with them a scent like smoke and fresh mud, sea salt and wet dead leaves.

Drew licked his lower lip. His mouth dried out.

"Where in Quantuck?" he heard himself say.

"Start driving. We'll tell you," the oldest sister said.

Drew tapped the gas. The car finished its interrupted crossing, and Drew drove east along a connecting road.

"Don't you know that bridge's reputation?" he said.

"We know," the youngest woman said.

"Of course, we know," said the second woman.

"How could we not know?" the oldest said.

All three giggled.

"Why were you really there?" Drew asked.

"Like we told you. Our boyfriends dumped us," the oldest said.

"Like that, in the middle of the night? Where'd they go?"

"Who cares? They're pigs," she said.

As Drew drove, the two older sisters whispered over the head of the youngest, sitting between them. They sounded like hissing snakes.

"At least, tell me your names," he said.

The youngest raised her eyes to meet Drew's stare in the mirror. "I'm Venge."

The second sister said, "I'm Grudge."

"I have no name," the oldest told him.

Grudge and Nameless resumed whispering.

Venge leaned forward and touched Drew's arm.

"Do you have any food? I'm so *hungry*," she said.

Drew pointed to a gold foil bag beside his briefcase and reports stacked on the passenger seat. Metallic, red ink formed a heart-shaped store logo and the words: Gwendolyn's Gourmet Chocolates. "There's some candy I bought for my daughters."

Venge snatched the bag and dragged it into the back seat. It rustled as she removed one of the boxes it contained. She undid the ribbon tied across the top, opened it, and then peeled away the crinkly paper under the lid. Drew watched in the mirror as she popped a chocolate into her mouth and chewed. Right away, she made a sour face and then spit the half-chewed candy onto the floor and gave a disgusted groan.

"No good!" She chucked the open box against the dashboard, spilling chocolates around the front of the car. She pressed her face close to Drew's and sniffed him. "You know our names. What's yours?"

"Drew Cahill." The words came before he could stop them.

"I'm so hungry my stomach aches, Drew." Venge ran her finger along Drew's neck, scraping him with her nail. Then she licked her fingertip. "Before we go home, we're going to eat you up."

She smiled and pulled her shawl tighter. Glimpsing her in the rearview mirror, Drew thought he saw rows of sharp teeth in her mouth, but she closed her lips as she sat back in the shadows. He wished he'd gone home early that night. He should've never stopped on the bridge, should've ignored the women. They weren't his responsibility. He should've rationalized his indifference and driven by without slowing down. A year ago, he would've, but not tonight— not once he saw them leaning on the rail, their faces pale against the ready darkness over the side.

He *had* to stop.

He had to *know* they weren't going to jump.

The moment he noticed the women, he'd thought of the last time he saw Carmine. Leaving his office, his personal belongings collected in a cardboard box, a framed picture of his family face down on top—and his face so pale Drew had worried he might faint. He had wanted to walk him out to his car, maybe even drive him home to make sure he got there safe and sound. But too many people were watching, and no one ever stepped forward to help the *losers* who lost their jobs; Drew didn't want to get too close, afraid he might be seen as one of them. Afraid it might be true, that all his work and time were wasted, and he would be discarded too.

Yet if he'd helped, maybe Carmine would've made it home.

Home.

It seemed so far away to Drew now, and the night so late.

He had to be back at work in only a few hours.

…home…

A nagging question sprang to mind: Whose torn sneaker had Venge tossed from the bridge? He doubted it belonged to any of the sisters. He should've looked over the side, where the women had been looking when he first saw them. Maybe it was better he hadn't.

"What do you mean you're going to eat me?" Drew asked.

The older girls stopped whispering and leaned forward between the seats.

"She means what she says. We've been out all night. We're hungry. We want to eat. But not until after you take us home," Nameless told him.

"That's nothing to joke about," Drew said.

"I never joke about eating," said Venge.

Her two sisters laughed.

"You're all crazy. Get out of my car. Now!"

Drew tried to swerve to the shoulder and stop the car, but the women's command—*give us a ride*—resurfaced in his aching head and forced him to keep driving. He couldn't lift his foot from the gas, or turn the car, or move his hands on the wheel.

Nameless leaned between the seats. "Take us home."

"I don't know where your home is," Drew said.

"I told you. Go to Quantuck."

"Where in Quantuck?"

"Turn left at the next traffic light," Grudge said.

"No, go straight," said Nameless.

"I want to go the back way."

"It will take too long. We'll go the right way."

"Right, wrong." Grudge gave a dismissive wave. "They both get us there, don't they?"

"No, no, no, he should take the road that passes by the cemetery. That's the fastest way—*and* it goes by the cemetery," Venge said.

"Hush, the cemetery is way out of our way," said Nameless.

"The cemetery *is* nice at night, and it's such a dark night. I say we go that way too," Grudge said.

"No. Go straight," Nameless told Drew.

"I know Quantuck. Tell me the address. I can find my way there," Drew said.

All three of the sisters replied, almost in unison, "Shut up! Drive where we tell you."

Venge whispered to Drew, "We have to find our own way home. If Father knows we snuck out, he'll stop us from wandering again."

Drew clenched the wheel and followed the road. Traffic was sparse even for this time of night, and all the shops closed. Even the all-night diners and fast food restaurants looked dead and full of vague shadows. There wasn't even a cop on patrol as there almost always was on this road at night. Not that it mattered. Drew couldn't have asked for help even if there was any to be had. The second he thought about stopping, the pain in his head spiked, and the women's words filled his mind again, locking his body behind the wheel.

They passed three more lights. Nameless told Drew to take the next left. Grudge argued, and her sister clamped a hand over her mouth to silence her.

Drew turned left, and they came to a fork in the road.

"Go right," Nameless said.

Grudge shoved her sister's hand from her mouth. "No, go left!"

"Let's go by the cemetery," Venge said.

"Morning comes fast. You want to get home before sunrise or be punished?" said Nameless.

"I don't want to be punished."

"Then forget the cemetery."

"But I'm *soooo* hungry…," Venge said.

"We'll eat later. Go left," Grudge said.

"No, go right," said Nameless.

Drew stopped at the crux of the intersection.

"Left," said Grudge.

"Right," Nameless said.

"Go back a block and take the left to go by the cemetery," said Venge.

"Shut up! Don't listen to them. Go right," Nameless said.

Grudge snapped at her sisters, and Venge complained again that she was *so hungry*. The pain behind Drew's eyes spread to his whole head. Pangs of nausea squirmed in his stomach. The car idled. If only he could move he could've taken the keys and run so they couldn't use the Audi to chase him. He would have a good head start, and he ran five days a week. His legs were longer than theirs. They would never catch up running barefoot—except he couldn't unwrap his fingers from around the wheel. He couldn't unfasten his seat belt or reach for the door handle. His body simply refused.

"What are you?" he said.

The women stopped arguing. Their deep, cold eyes and sudden smiles filled the rearview mirror. Now there was no mistaking the rows of jagged teeth hidden behind their soft lips. Drew didn't want to believe it. Maybe their teeth were filed, a body modification thing, or they were fake, custom vampire fangs like those Drew had worn one Halloween in college. He could buy that if not for how large their teeth were—and that he no longer controlled his body. Had they hypnotized him? But that didn't feel right. His mind veered toward darker answers and groped for the right word—*demons, ghosts, monsters*. Except Drew believe in none of those things.

Venge said, "We are spiders, spinning our web."

Grudge said, "We are lovely shadows breaking your heart."

Nameless leaned between the seats so her breath brushed Drew's neck. "We are lost daughters."

They all laughed then.

"You know about daughters, don't you?" Nameless asked Drew. "I smell your daughters on you. Leah and Gabby. Good daughters. They ask you for only one thing above all the things you give them. Do you give them that one thing? Hmm? Do you, Drew?"

Drew couldn't answer. His thoughts disintegrated into the pain swirling in his head.

"No, you don't. Do you know what that one thing is? I'll give you a hint: It's not fancy chocolates," said Nameless.

In his mind, Drew heard echoes of Gabby and Leah scolding him for working so late, for spending so much time at the office, for always coming home and leaving again while they slept. He heard Heather lecturing him: "No one gets to the end of their life and wishes they spent more time at work." He'd told them he'd try—he'd *promised* them, and as often as he had he'd broken those promises.

"Oops, guess not." Grudge giggled. "Now you'll never know. You'll never see Leah and Gabby again, never know what's going on in their lives, and you won't be there for them when they really need you most. All daughters have a dark side, Drew. They have secrets, and secrets always turn toxic sooner or later."

"*Hungry…,*" Venge said.

Drew found his voice then, only a whisper. "How'd you know my daughters' names?"

Nameless inhaled, flashing her jagged teeth. "Their scent is all over you. I could follow it to your house and pay them a visit. Would you like that, Drew?"

Drew shook his head.

"Then turn right."

Drew stepped on the gas and took the right fork. The sisters resumed bickering. Every turn generated an argument, every intersection a dispute. Drew trawled the night while the sisters fought. They cruised around a residential neighborhood of winding streets, steep hills, and dead ends. Beyond reach of the car's headlights hung a deep, patchy grayness only a shade removed from black by the ambient light reflected off the overcast sky. It passed 3 a.m. Heather would be worried. Drew hadn't called or answered his phone. He turned down another desolate road.

"You're taking us the wrong way," Grudge said.

"What do you know?" said Nameless.

"What I know is we *should've* gone past the cemetery. My stomach is *growling*," Venge said.

"Oh, will you *please* let it go. You could stand to miss a meal or two," said Grudge.

"Like you're so smart. Can't even find our way home. Our stepfather will have the door locked up tight by the time you get us there. Then what'll we do?" Venge asked

"Shut up. Everything will be fine," Nameless said.

Time slipped away faster now, and the fuel gauge fell below a quarter of a tank. Drew had meant to fill up on the way home. He didn't know where he would find a gas station open this late, and he wondered what the sisters might do if he ran out of fuel.

"Here! Turn left here," Nameless said.

Drew sensed that in spite of the sisters' arguing and all their misdirection, every turn took them closer to home, a place Drew didn't want to reach. Mustering all his will and concentrating on Leah, Gabby, and Heather, picturing their faces, their voices, he silenced the sisters' words in his head long enough to turn right instead of left. He felt triumphant. His skull throbbed like it might split apart, but he'd defied the women and broken their control. Then Nameless smacked him in the back of his head so hard he jolted forward and cracked his nose against the steering wheel.

"Drive where I say!" she shrieked.

Drew rubbed his sore nose with the back of his hand. It amplified the pain beating inside his skull. He found a tissue in the console and wiped snot and blood from his upper lip. His turn had taken them into an industrial area. Sprawling old buildings and fences topped with barbed wire coils lined the road, casting complicated shadows.

"Go straight then take the next right, and we'll be back on track," Grudge said.

When the turn came, though, Drew focused on his wife and daughters, and once more broke the sisters' hold; he forced himself to punch the gas straight through the intersection.

The intensity of his headache exploded.

The sisters attacked him, spilling into the front seat, pinching him, drawing blood with their fingernails, screaming in his ears—and blocking his view of the road. The car swerved and jerked. It jolted over a sharp bump. Drew hit the brakes for a shuddering halt halfway up the curb, only inches from a telephone pole. The interior of the car swam with shadows, and then Nameless occupied the passenger seat, while Grudge and Venge returned to the back. Nameless held her finger against Drew's neck. Her nail dug into his skin like a saw tooth.

"You're wasting our time! Drive where we say or we'll eat you here and now," she said.

"You're going to eat me anyway," Drew said.

The woman let out a low hiss then sniffed around Drew's neck. "Drive, or one night we'll go visit *Heather*. She's sitting up with the TV on, wondering why you aren't home yet, why you haven't called. She smells so sweet. And after we see her, we'll visit Leah and Gabby—unless you drive *now*."

Drew felt near exhausted. The sisters' voices roared inside his head. He couldn't raise the energy to resist them again, so he drove. They directed him along crooked routes that detoured and overlapped until they came to the edge of the industrial zone and passed rows of run-down houses.

"Go left up that hill," Nameless said.

Grudge and Venge said nothing.

Drew accelerated up the slope. Thick trees and unruly brush lined the road. They grew denser and more scraggly as the car ascended.

"Park by the house at the top of the hill."

The higher they drove, the more cracked and pitted the street became. The car jounced as it strained up the incline and rolled to a dead end. Ensconced among pines and elms tall enough to blot out the sky stood a three-story Victorian in an overgrown yard filled with wild shrubs and rangy weeds. Not a single light glowed inside or out. The house's black windows were grimy and cracked. Its shingles and shutters hung askew, and paint peeled from its trim in papery strips. A weedy, gravel driveway faded into the shadows beside it. Drew parked at the entrance and shut off the engine. The sisters exited the car. Venge opened the driver's side door and yanked Drew out. She dragged him onto the front lawn. Drew struggled but he couldn't get free. Venge didn't look even half strong enough to pull him around how she did, but Drew felt as if she hadn't only grabbed his body but had reached inside and latched onto some intangible, essential part of him.

The front door of the house swung open.

Impenetrable darkness filled the entry. A burning odor drifted out on a wave of heat and haze. A musty, earthy scent followed, and then the doorway exhaled stray winds.

Grudge smiled. "See? Father doesn't even know we were gone."

"I'm so hungry." Venge looked at Drew and parted her lips, uncovering her teeth.

"There's no time." Nameless pointed east. Glimmers of dawn already brightened the sky, deepening the silhouettes of trees and houses. "Drew made us late. Let's go while the door's open."

"No. I'm hungry, and I *want* him," Venge said.

"Then you shouldn't have argued so much about which way to go. Now the sun's almost rising," Grudge said.

"You argued too. *Both* of you! If you'd listened to *me*, we could've gone to the cemetery and gotten here in plenty of time." Venge pressed Drew against the ground and knelt on top of him. Her mouth widened; her teeth protruded as if they might pop loose from her jaw. "I'm going to eat."

"No, stop!" Drew shouted.

Grudge pulled Venge away and spilled her onto the lawn. "Me first!"

"Why are you doing this?" Drew said.

Nameless shoved Grudge aside with Venge and bared her teeth.

"Because small crimes get punished too," she said.

"What did I do?" said Drew.

"What you did, what you didn't do, what you're going to do, it's all the same thing. You weren't there when we needed you. You let us go. You let us die, *Father*." Nameless slapped Drew. "You let us fall into the darkness, and you'll do it again and again and again."

"Please, I don't know what you're talking about," Drew said.

"You think helping us tonight makes up for anything? Makes anything better?"

Nameless's fingers dug into Drew's chest. Her nails tore his shirt and stabbed his skin.

"You'll stand there and stare into the blackness one day. I know you will, because you could see us, and we could see you. Who can say what will happen when that day comes?"

Her head jolted sideways. At first, Drew thought she was leaning in to bite him, but her head bobbed as if her neck was broken, and then it snapped back into place. The raw streak of scarred skin on her neck peeked out from beneath her choker. Grudge knelt down beside him; blood streamed from the scars on her wrists and dripped off her hands. A trickle of blood and foamy, white saliva trailed from the corners of Venge's lips. Nameless lifted Drew until her teeth gleamed inches from his neck. Her mouth split so wide and looked so deep, Drew thought she might decapitate him with a single bite. He thought of the darkness over the side of the bridge. If he jumped, he would only be breaking a machine, a construct of organic gears, tubes, and wires that would scatter on the ground and wait to be collected and repaired. But that wasn't right, that wasn't true. Something horrible waited down there in the darkness. He pictured Leah and Gabby, faces drawn and haunted like the faces of Carmine Price's children. Worse yet, Leah and Gabby standing on that bridge themselves like the three sisters. A reservoir of darkness he'd barely known he possessed broke inside him. It leaked out and stained his thoughts. Nameless seemed to savor the exact moment.

A fierce burst of searing wind blew from the open door of the house with a rumble like a long, low growl. Shocked, Nameless glanced at the open door. The odor of burning intensified and mingled with the stench of something ancient and rotten.

"No! Not yet!" Nameless said.

"We're sorry, Father! We didn't mean to stay out all night. It was so hard to find our way home," said Grudge.

"They made me go with them! I didn't want to, but they made me!" Venge said.

Nameless let go of Drew and dashed toward the door. "Please! Don't punish us. We made a mistake, that's all. We promise it'll never happen again. Give us another chance!"

Grudge and Venge followed their sister, rushing to the house.

Drew wriggled onto his belly. He rose onto hands and knees in time to see the first ray of morning sunlight break through the trees and touch the gaping black entrance of the house. It lit up the door saddle and crept inside, and then the door slammed shut with the sisters still several steps from the front porch. A burst of shadow erased the dawn twilight, blinding Drew. From inside the house, a low, deep laughter reverberated. Then the stink faded. Drew's sight returned. His mind cleared, and his headache subsided. Where the sisters had been running stood three gnarled and stunted trees bowed toward the house. Torn, black leaves adorned their gnarled branches. On the smallest tree fluttered the weathered remnants of a knit shawl. The others bore twisted scars in their bark. They looked like they'd been growing forever out of the cracked front path. In the light of the rising sun, the trees cast moving shadows that groped toward the front door of the house. They made sounds like whispers and groans when the breeze rustled them.

Drew leapt to his feet and ran to his car.

He drove fast into town, filling up at the first open gas station he found. The morning paper fresh on the news rack showed a headline about another suicide at the bridge: a young woman who'd jumped last night around the time Drew left his office. He stared at the article, afraid to touch the paper, terrified of learning that the dead woman had worn a pair of pink sneakers. He paid the attendant and sped away. He reached home in time to cook a special breakfast for his wife and daughters, who were surprised and happy to see him. After his daughters left for school, he called in sick and skipped work to be with them that afternoon.

He wanted to make the most of whatever time they had left.

Sum'bitch and the Arakadile

Let me tell you about the Arakadile and how Sum'bitch thought he killed it, because that pretty much says all anyone needs to know about me. My doctors argue there's a lot more to me than that, but what the hell do they know?

They never met the Arakadile. Or my mother.

She had a favorite word, my mother. *Sum'bitch*. She could use it six ways in the same sentence. My older brother got his name because Mama called him "sum'bitch" so often everyone forgot his real name, except for me with my knack for recalling names, faces, favorite colors, and details like that. Sum'bitch was Evan. Then we had Louie and Dougie-boy, my younger brothers. And me, Jillian, except most call me "Buzz" because I stepped in a fallen wasps' nest one summer and spent a night in the hospital. Nasty little critters stung me thirty-two times.

Thirty-two times.

Every sting burned how a hot cigarette eats a hole in your skin then itches when it scabs over and heals, but all at once instead of over days. My eyes swelled shut so tight my tears puffed out my eyelids like water balloons. When I came home, Mama stopped calling me Jillian and just laughed and made a buzzing noise whenever she saw me. Said she needed to remind me to look where I stepped, and it stuck hard. I was six then and passed my twelfth birthday before I heard myself called Jillian again. That same year Sum'bitch met the Arakadile.

Way Mama talked, the Arakadile sounded like the fiercest, ugliest beast that ever lived, one with a habit of coming down out of the deep woods, hunting for food, and like Mama put it: "That sum'bitching monster loves the taste of young flesh. Don't matter what kind as long as the sum'bitch's fresh. Calves, cubs, pups, fawn, but especially *children*."

That last one kept us up nights. When one of us broke a dish or left the wash on the line after dark or forgot to close the barn doors, none of us could sleep for worry. Mama said the Arakadile rooted out misbehavers, smartass wisecrackers, and no-good wastes of space because they tasted better than anything else.

"You little sum'bitches sass me, you lie, you duck your chores, it'll know. The rottenness comes right off your skin. Once it gets a whiff, it'll come miles in the rain to find the little sum'bitch putting up the stink."

Many nights we crept from bed when Mama's snores rattled up through the floorboards and took turns keeping watch by my bedroom window, the only second-floor one that overlooked the woods. All of us glimpsed signs of the Arakadile on those vigils. Evan said it skulked through the woods like a fat old bear, a hump of shadows pressing pines with its tree-trunk shoulders and shaking needles loose into the wind. On full moon nights or when Mama smoked weed behind the barn with Noreen Goody or our "Uncle" Walt Palmer, the moonlight or the spark of their lighters glinted off the creature's eyes as it watched our house. In the summer, warm breezes delivered dead skunk stenches through the window screen, the Arakadile's breath billowing from a mouth full of rotting scraps of young'uns flesh stuck in its raggedy teeth. Whiffing that odor after sunset sent us scurrying inside, to heck with catching fireflies. We rushed to bed, pulled the covers over our heads. Every time Mama saw us running scared, she laughed so hard she hocked brown blobs of phlegm onto the dry grass.

"That's right, you chickenshits! Haul your asses inside. The Arakadile's on the prowl. Gonna eat you sum'bitches whole, he catches you."

Tell you something true, it pissed me off how she never tried to protect us. I guess she figured since the Arakadile didn't eat grown-ups she had no worries.

Three weeks after my eighth birthday, Mama took us out hunting squirrels and raccoons with "Uncle" Walt: me, Sum'bitch, Louie, and Dougie-boy, with Cougar, our retriever. We passed the creek and snaked into the loneliest stretch of woods, where the trees stood as thick and old as god's beard and scratched the sky. We didn't see many animals, but we heard them in the brush or scampering across overhanging branches.

"Uncle" Walt carried my daddy's shotgun. It upset me how Evan stared at that gun in Walt's hands with his brow knit tight, his lips flat, eyes burning. My daddy and Walt grew up together and worked construction till Daddy died. His pickup troubled him two, three days a week, because he kept spending the money socked away for a new alternator on happy hour at The Fox's Den. At least that's what Mama claimed. Then one morning running late for work at the Hackett sewage plant going up in the next town, he rigged the jumper cables to Mama's old Buick, hopped in to turn the engine over—and never stood up again. Massive heart attack. Sum'bitch found him in the car, eyes wide open, hand still on the ignition key, and that old song about afternoons and skyrockets playing on the radio. The doctor said he'd been born with some kind of nasty, fancy-named heart trouble that hides itself right up until it drops you dead.

Mama cracked the whip after that, and "Uncle" Walt came around a couple days a week. Then every day. Then he started staying over with Mama and new sounds came up through our floorboards at night. Pretty soon Walt lived with us all the time. Mama spent more and more time out back of the barn, smoking with him, Noreen, and their friends, playing cards, drinking beer by lantern light around a splintery redwood picnic table. Some nights strangers came and went, chatting up Walt, handing him envelopes, and taking away tiny packages. Long as we did our chores, Mama left us kids on our own. She smiled at Cougar more than she ever did at us. Cougar had been our father's dog, taken from a litter birthed by Walt's old bitch back before I was born. I guess he reminded her of Daddy better than his own children did.

That day hunting, Cougar led us down a rocky hill into a clearing, sniffing and wagging his tail, and there it lay: the Arakadile. Dead on a bed of fallen leaves and pine needles, its fur and flesh rotted away, leaving only pale, soiled bones. It looked kind of mannish except for having too many fingers and ribs, and its pumpkin-sized skull with knife-teeth and horns all tangled and gnarled sticking out from the top. Thing would have been seven or eight feet tall standing. Laying there lifeless like some old burned out barn, it set my skin crawling. Dougie-boy grabbed Mama's waist and hid behind her. Evan wrapped his arm around me to stop my shivering while "Uncle" Walt circled the carcass with my daddy's shotgun aimed at it as if it might jump up and grab him. Louie gave a wild, unexpected whoop like his birthday had come early.

"The Arakadile is dead! Oh, yeah! No more Arakadile 'round here, that's a fact. Can I get a Amen!" he yelled, imitating the tent preacher Mrs. Lewis, who lived down the road, took us to some Sundays.

Mama smacked Louie in the ear. He fell and rolled over in a cloud of dust.

"Shut up that caterwauling, you dumb sum'bitch. Ain't no one said the Arakadile is gone. This here is just one of her sum'bitching pups, strayed, and got killed. Sum'bitch looks like a runt, too. If you were wondering what's got a hunger for you, well now you know what it looks like. Now, let's get your asses back to the house. Almost supper time and I'm sum'bitching hungry."

We all followed Mama, except for my big brother. He stared at the remains of the Arakadile pup, then in a growly, shaking voice he said, "Fuck you, old lady. That ain't no Arakadile. Ain't no such thing as a Arakadile. That's a pile of old bones and antlers you and Walt gathered up and tied together."

No one ever gave Evan much credit for tact. He came as hard-nosed as dried pinewood. "Uncle" Walt shook his head and raised the stock of Daddy's shotgun to belt him, but Mama waved him off and slapped Evan instead. Took four hits before his eyes filled up with tears, but Evan didn't swing back. Thirteen then, he already looked like he might grow up bigger and stronger than "Uncle" Walt or even my daddy. Louie, Dougie-boy, and I saw the changes in him. We noticed Mama hitting him less and less, too, but she still cursed him out and called him names plenty. That night Evan would sleep in the Well, no doubt about it. Can't swear at Mama and Walt like that and expect to skip your time in the Well. Evan got the whole night out there, down in that ten-foot-deep hole Walt dug beside the barn. Right about midnight the heavens opened up and poured down rain through the barbwire mesh cover. Nothing worse than trying to sleep in a muddy hole filling up with cold water.

Evan never again swore at Mama, though. Not even the next summer when she took us all walking back through the woods, down that same old hill, past where that dead Arakadile had laid, no sign of its bones remaining, and out to the streambed, dried near to dust by the August drought except for a pissy little trickle of silty water.

"Now, how about that?" she said. "The Arakadile tracked through here and not too long ago I'd say from the look of those sum'bitching footprints."

Indentations trailed along the exposed, mucky stream bottom for about fifty yards, cut across the rivulet, and disappeared up the far bank. Older now, my brothers and I showed less fear though it churned like boiling water beneath my skin. Three nights ago, shaking treetops and ragged howling from the woods woke us up and reminded us of what lived nearby. We hid under the covers until the noise died down and then listened to Mama, Noreen, "Uncle" Walt, and some of Walt's friends laughing it up behind the barn, happy because maybe one or two less mouths to feed didn't strike Mama as an awful proposition. The monster must have walked off by way of the streambed on its way back to the deep woods.

Evan didn't believe it, though. He pointed out how everything we knew of the Arakadile could've been made up by Mama, the footprints more of the same. How horrific for me and my little brothers to consider that Mama had lied so much to us. A crazy notion, one of several Evan whispered about away from Mama, like how Walt had no right to Daddy's shotgun, and how once Daddy slammed down the phone and called Walt a "fair-weather friend." Well, at least Evan had sense enough to keep his mouth shut and nod when Mama jabbed an elbow into his side.

"You ain't too sum'bitching old to wind up chow for the Arakadile," she said.

"I sure hope that don't happen," Evan replied.

Dougie-boy and I let loose with a sigh of relief. We had all taken our lumps for breaking Mama's rules, but she always dealt Evan worse than the rest of us. She wanted him, as the oldest, to set an example. If Evan cried or yelled during a punishment, Mama doubled it because he needed to show us how to take whatever we had coming. Argue right or wrong about Mama's steady hand, but none of us ever yelped or cussed or whined about a punishment. By the time Evan turned seventeen, people in our town knew him as one tough and stony-hearted young man, which Mama praised because it meant no one would dare fool around with him or try to cheat us.

Growing tough helped Evan work up the nerve to finally go into the woods after the Arakadile. One October afternoon, my brothers and me jumped from our seats at the kitchen table when Mama came running in from sitting outside with Walt and Noreen Goody, stinking of whiskey and smoke, and yelled, "Grab your sum'bitching guns, the Arakadile is near!" We did as she said, picking up our hunting rifles, but something sat sour with me. Mama kept a sober eye on Evan, and the corner of her lip half-curled, kind of smirky like. We got out into the dusky yard and the twilight made it near impossible to see more than a few feet into the woods. A clatter of snarls and growls greeted us, along with thrashing in the brush, and the crack of branches snapping. We backed toward the house, Mama, Evan, and me, with our rifles raised, and trembled.

Mama teased us, called us crybabies and no-good wastes of space, and said we had nothing to fear if we didn't stink of bad behavior. Taunted us about who'd acted up the worst and which of us the Arakadile had come sniffing for. Evan let out a long, heavy breath and then strode out from the house's shadow straight across the grass toward the trees. Mama hollered at him not to walk off with his rifle like a moron, but he ignored her and vanished into the dusky woods. She chased after him right up to the tree-line then stood there yelling curses and awful names, calling him weak and sorry, shouting real loud about how he ought to get outta the woods before the Arakadile saw him.

Right then, Cougar barked, his voice coming from the trees, kicking up a fuss like he'd cornered a stray cat under the front porch again. Then two rifle shots came, followed by a howl of pain that raised goosebumps all over my skin. The woods quieted and the trees stopped shaking. Stamping feet drew our eyes to the trailhead by the barn. I watched for Evan, thinking the Arakadile had got past Cougar and chased him. Only, instead of Evan, Noreen Goody and her cousin Nina blustered out, waving their hands and yelling "Don't shoot! Don't shoot!" Mama cast a string of nasty names at them before she told them to shut up and make themselves scarce. Then she planted her feet and waited.

Before long Evan walked out of the woods cradling a bundle too little for an Arakadile carcass. Bloody smears darkened his cheek. He stepped out of the shadows, revealing Cougar pressed to his chest.

"Aw, no, Sum'bitch, you killed Cougar!" cried Dougie-boy.

"Thought he was the Arakadile. Poor dog deserved better, don't I know it." His cold eyes staring at Mama's, not blinking. Her face lit up red like a taillight in the dark, but she said nothing. Cougar followed her everywhere after Daddy died, waited by her feet for scraps, and if Mama kicked him in the ribs or shut the door on his tail now and then, he only sulked off for a while before he forgot about it and came back. My mama surely loved that obedient streak. Stupid dog didn't know any better than to love her back.

Finally, Mama spit, then said, "You killed my dog on purpose, Sum'bitch."

"I told you I thought he was the Arakadile," said Evan. "Said yourself the damn thing was in the woods. I probably scared it off. Good thing, too, what with Noreen and Nina messing around out there."

"Don't sass me, Sum'bitch. This is more trouble than you ever brought me before in your entire, piss-poor life, and I'm sum'bitching sorry to say, I don't think the Well is going to straighten you out this time."

Mama leveled her rifle at Evan, bracing it against her waist, pointed low, like she didn't want no chance of missing if she fired.

"I'm going to tell you what to do now, and you're going to do it," she said.

"I don't think so, you dumb, pathetic, tired, alcoholic old bitch," said my brother.

Mama gasped—and then the gloom exploded. Trees quivered. Branches cracked. An awful shriek ripped itself from the woods, and something came snarling and jabbering toward our yard. Louie and Dougie-boy ran screaming for the house. I almost went with them but my feet refused to move. I needed to see. And when the Arakadile burst from the tree line with its horns swaying above its head, howling, almost trampling Cougar's carcass; when two more gunshots erased every other sound, it took me long, horrifying seconds to realize that Evan had fired his rifle again. He had kept it hanging easy in his hands after setting down Cougar's remains. When "Uncle" Walt came running out from the trees, waving his arms and flailing bare branches over his head, hooting and hollering like a beast, Evan pulled the trigger twice.

Mama cried and wailed, but I couldn't hear her. Heavy ringing filled my ears. She dropped to her knees beside Walt. Evan crouched down on the other side, on his face that mean grin he used to scare folks in town. Dying light gathered in Walt's eyes. Mama's darkened and filled with coal hardness and bear claw spite. She pointed her rifle at Evan, but he snatched it away from her then clocked her in the face with the stock, knocking her to the ground beside Walt. Her screams pierced through the ringing, faraway and fuzzy as she laid into Evan and said if he didn't have that gun in his hands, she'd teach him a thing about respecting his elders, that the Arakadile would eat him up for real, and then he'd be sorry.

Evan slung Mama's rifle from one shoulder as he straightened up, raised his own gun, and aimed it at her face. My stomach tied itself in knots. I wanted to yell at Evan to put the rifle down and leave Mama alone, but my throat closed, choking off my voice.

Mama's eyes changed as she stared up at the gun barrel. The hardness drained out of her. At the same time, Evan's eyes turned stony as if he'd sucked all her meanness into himself. He lowered the rifle and grinned. Then he chuckled and it snowballed into belly laughs so big and uncontainable he doubled over, shaking until it died down. He put his hand on my shoulder.

"You gonna be all right, Jillian. This shit is done. Those shitheads—," he pointed at Louie and Dougie-boy watching from my bedroom window, "Who knows with them two? But you're a good kid, don't I know it, and you got a head on your shoulders. You got a chance now. The Arakadile is dead and gone for real."

Except he lied.

All the ugly I'd seen swimming around in Mama's eyes now danced in his, and I understood how much more it took to kill the Arakadile. Bony hardness and razorblade spite that had shaped how Mama spoke to us, looked at us, and raised us since Daddy died now filled up Evan's eyes, replacing his bright stubbornness.

Shivering and crying, I backed away from Sum'bitch, letting his hand slip off me, trying to recognize the boy who'd been my big brother. His smile faded.

He offered me his hand. I flinched.

"Well, fuck it, then," Sum'bitch said, looking sad.

He dropped both rifles and ran into the woods. The shape of antlers and a black-haired hump moving among the trees made my heart pound. I got my courage up and snatched my brother's rifle and—

—well, I don't recall what I did next. Everything after my hands wrapped around the gun turned into a swirling blur of teeth and antlers, bone and mud, and black, bristling fur, and howls crashing against the snap of breaking branches. The doctors try to explain and tell me stories. I don't believe them. The girl in their stories doesn't sound at all like me. Anybody can fake a photograph by acting and tossing around a little fake blood and mocking up a scene like they do on television. I remember the police lights, the flashing red and blue that washed away the darkness. A woman with a badge took the rifle from me then led me by the hand to a car and closed me up inside, a firefly trapped inside a jar, wondering what kind of world existed on the other side of the holes in the lid.

They split up me and my brothers that night, and I haven't seen Louie or Dougie-boy for ages. Don't know what happened to Sum'bitch with that hard, jagged darkness fresh in his eyes. Police never found him, though they spent a good long time hunting. Found a camp out in the deep woods with a few spots of blood around the ground. Not far away, they saw tracks in the mud like some big old bear had tromped its way through the trees. All down by the bank of the stream, which had flooded hard and overflowed when the rains came in November.

I have an idea what happened to Sum'bitch. I can't say for sure, of course, but I'll never tell anyway because I know what waits for misbehavers and wastes of space and I know where the Arakadile lives and it's not only the deep woods. My doctors say I'm safe from it now I'm growing up and it's okay to talk about it, but my doctors are full of shit.

Maybe I'm getting too old, maybe *not*.

Mama, Walt, and Sum'bitch all believed that part of the myth but they're gone now—and sometimes I see some of Sum'bitch's hardness in my own eyes when I look in the mirror. I do what I'm told. I keep my room neat. No one ever really does know do they? I miss them all, I truly do, but I miss Sum'bitch the most.

Mnemonicide

Angie holds the gun while you tie a humiliating memory to the chair.

You bind his hands behind the wooden back, fasten his ankles to the chair legs, the coarse rope scratching your fingers. An August breeze flows through the open garage door and tickles the sweat on the back of your neck. The memory's name is Robert. He stares at you with wide, watery eyes, terrified Angie will shoot him if he makes a sound. Dirt and grime streak his crooked tie and tailored suit. Blood trickles down his face from a gash where his head cracked against the hood of your trunk. His face is your humiliation, his eyes witnesses to your shame, his existence a lifeline for a cold shadow from your past, a distant moment you want to erase.

With the memory secured, you step outside and collect the padded moving blankets that dropped from Robert's body when you and Angie walked him in from your car. You toss them back in the trunk. Spots of Robert's blood shine on the edge of the hood as you shut it. You roll the tension from your shoulders, take a deep breath. Maple leaves flutter above you. Bulrushes sway at the edge of the clearing around the old municipal garage, an ivy-covered, brick building no one has used in years. A weedy dirt road leads away into the thin shade of the tangled woods. The lapping of surf lilts through the air. Somewhere a seagull caws. From across the bay on the far side of the trees come the broken-down hum and groan of the old city, the buzz of helicopters flitting past tired skyscrapers. It's so good to live in the moment, in the bright, wonderful present, even if only for a few seconds before the past drags you back to it.

It's a taste of the life ahead of you.

You return to the garage, pull down the door. Sunlight drops from Robert's face, leaving him pale with terror in the gloom. A trembling memory. Too scared to speak.

Robert, who you described as "never at a loss for words."

His eyes beg for answers.

You tell him, "You can talk now."

Angie lowers the gun and paces. Her attention jumps between you and Robert, who eyes the gun like it's a trap waiting to spring.

"Don't worry about Angie," you say. "She's here to remember for me."

Quavering, Robert says, "Why… why are you doing this? We're friends for god's sake. We've known each other for twenty fucking years. What did I ever do to you… to deserve *this*?"

You grab a battered folding chair propped against the wall, open it across from Robert, and sit, wobbling on its uneven legs. "We *are* friends." You squeeze Robert's shoulder, reassure him. "You're a good friend. But you remember the night Mary dumped me."

"Mary?" Robert says.

"Mary Lawson. Junior year."

Robert's face puckers. "That was so long ago."

"You remember," you say. "I heard it in your voice when I called you yesterday. The first thing that came to mind when you heard me on the phone, wasn't it? That night she dumped me? How could you forget, right? She shattered my heart. Dumping me in front of all my friends then naming off all the times she'd cheated on me, boasting about what she'd done—shit, I nearly killed myself that night."

"That was so long ago. I had no idea," Robert says.

You shrug. "I can tell you now because you won't remember it for long."

"What the hell does that mean?" Robert asks. "Please let me go, please, please, whatever this is, whatever you need, say the word. I can get you help, okay? Doctors. Or a lawyer. I know the best. I swear. You need a job, right? I can get you a good job. I can give you money. Just don't take me away from my kids. Please."

"I climbed up to the observatory on top of the student center that night. I knew the lock was broken from volunteering there with the local kids in the enrichment programs. I stood by the telescope for two hours trying to talk myself into jumping into the alley. A hundred-foot drop, at least. But I couldn't do it. I wanted to forget, not die. If I could've pushed a button in my mind and reset everything how it was one day before, I would've. I'd have pressed it over and over to scrub the humiliation and the *hurt* from my mind. But nothing can ever unhappen. We can't bury anything deep enough to ever really forget it. You know why?"

"I'm sorry," Robert says. "Shit, man, whatever I did, *I'm sorry*. I should've been there for you that night—is that it? I felt awful for you, but you ran from Pria's room and disappeared from campus for three days."

"Stop," you say. "Answer my question. Do you know why we can't forget?"

Robert comes up empty, shaking his head. "No."

"Something always reminds us," you say. "I can forget, but then what? A song, a picture, a place, or a smell dredges up the memory. The hurt comes rushing back as fresh as it was that night. Songs, pictures, places, *things*, though—their power dies, but people *know*. They keep memories alive. You were *there* that night, and even if I make myself forget like it never took place, *you* sustain the memory when *I* suffocate and kill it. I see you, or talk to you, or think about you or the others, it surges back to life in me. You, Eduardo, Selena, Pria—especially Mary. You won't let me forget that pain."

"I never brought it up after that night," Robert says.

"You think about it, though," you say. "You thought about it when I called you. You're thinking about it now."

"No, I swear I'm not," Robert says.

"I *want* you to think about it now," you tell him.

You reach toward Angie. She sniffles as she hands you the gun, warm and moist from her sweaty palm, its weight solid, deadly. You rest your hand and the gun on your leg and slide them forward till the barrel bumps Robert's left knee, and he flinches.

"Remember it," you say. "Right now. *Think of that night.*"

"O-okay. Pria's lava lamp was on. It was late. We came back from the bars. We were drinking—"

"Don't talk. Remember."

Robert nods, slips into the memory, and the parasite you share with him— that you shared with the others—consumes his face. A memory that senses it has nowhere left to hide. You've killed it inside yourself over and again, until you realized the only way to stop it growing back was to kill it in everyone else who remembered it. Eduardo. Pria. Selena. *Mary.* Only you and Robert remember now.

"That night was awful for you," Robert says, his voice rising out of the muddled, shifting shape of the memory eclipsing his face. "I felt so bad for you, man. But *Mary* hurt you. *She* was wrong. *She* was a total bitch. *I* didn't hurt you!"

"But you won't let me forget the pain," you say. "We each have our own memory of that night, diverging from the same point in the past, but mine shaped by pain, yours by compassion. We're the last two reflections of what happened. You know what formed the others' memories? For Eduardo, contempt. He was one of Mary's lovers. Pria pitied me. The whole scene disgusted Selena. And Mary—she *wanted* to gut me. We all saw and heard the same things but we kept the memory—*a memory I want dead*—alive inside us in our own ways. Memories live as long as we let them. You're the only one left keeping this one alive."

In Robert's face, the memory lashes like the tail of a whirlpool, desperate to flee the boundaries of his expression, which cracks as panic sweeps in and forces fresh tears from his eyes. His lips tremble.

"You *killed* them?" he says.

"No one else can be allowed to remember what you want to forget. As long as someone else remembers a thing, it happened. If no one else remembers then the memory dies. Everything bad in my life is your fault. Yours and everyone else's for not letting me forget what I want to. It'll get easier now I've worked out how to kill those memories. What Mary did to me isn't the worst of what I need to get out of my head."

You stand and press the gun barrel to the top of Robert's skull, aiming down. The memory squirms in his face.

"Wait, *wait!*" Robert says. "What if I forget too? Wouldn't that get rid of it?"

You shake your head. "How could you ever forget it? Especially after all this."

"No...." Robert's voice strains; his chest heaves. "Don't... kill... me... *please!*"

"I'm not," you say. "I'm killing a memory. I'd spare you, if I could, but it doesn't work like that."

The memory writhes. It wants to lash out at you, cut your throat, punch a hole in your heart, or rip open your scars from that night and wither you with sadness. Its shadow twists in Robert's face like a cornered, wild animal. Robert is barely there anymore—suppressed by the memory. It saddens you they have to die together, but there's no other way. A bad memory is like an invasive tumor. After this, the cancer will be gone. You'll never feel this humiliation again, never shiver from the crippling, cold, lonely sensation it wells up inside you.

"Angie?" you say.

"Got your back," she says. "I'll remember for you. I'll be your final memory."

Now Remember why you have to pull the trigger, I say.

Do it this time. Please.

"Thank you," you say.

A squeeze of the trigger. The report of the gun and a spray of hot blood remake the world in a flash of acrid heat and raw violence. The dying memory bleeds from Robert, screaming as it flickers in the air like ball lightning, struggling to survive, then gives out while the echoes of its cries fade away. Robert's ruined face becomes his own again. You thrust the gun into Angie's hand then rush to a corner, double over, and heave, ejecting more than bile, coughing up the last, red remnants of something dead inside you that you once shared with Robert and four others. The pieces twitch on the ground before they dissolve, leaving behind a dark, foamy stain. When your guts settle down, you take another look at Robert. Angie stands beside him, her face and shirt spotted red, gun in her hand.

"I killed him?" you ask.

"Yes," Angie tells you.

"Who was he?"

"A memory to be forgotten."

"I had to kill him?"

You killed a memory.

"Yes."

"I don't remember why."

Because you're weak.

"That's right. That's very good," Angie says. "I'll remember for you."

Angie sips the Cure from a green glass bottle. You've given up riding her about how much of it she drinks, but you still don't like it. You lay on the lumpy hotel bed, drying from the shower, the TV news humming like a distant beehive. You tell Angie the gaping space the bad memory once filled in your head itches like the edges of a healing wound. It feels good, feels right. Angie nods then drains the bottle. She switches off the lamp because the Cure widens her pupils to twin eclipses blotting out her irises.

She stands, sways.

You say, "You look like a cat when you're high. All the harshness leaves you."

You follow her into the bathroom, watch her undress and run the shower. Steam appears in the tub, fogs the edges of the mirror above the sink. Angie slips under the spray. Water strikes her body and races off her skin in frantic zigzag streams made by her scars. Their tough surfaces shine in the water. Her thighs and torso glisten. Keloids form a constellation on her belly. Whorls of thick tissue clutch her right breast tight to her chest. Lines of it stretch up the right side of her neck. Pink webs. Cracks in reddened skin. The signature of torn metal and shattered windshields, broken pavement and fire, the odor of gasoline. And screams. Of children. Of a man. Angie says she drinks the Cure because it all still hurts, inside and out. She can never forget what's etched into her flesh and bone. There's no killing a memory like that. She remembers—keeping them alive in an instant of terror and pain—like she remembers for you.

This is what happened, I say. I remember for you all.

"My father beat the shit out of me once in front of my cousins. He usually didn't hit me when other people were around, but that time was different," you say while she washes her hair. "He bloodied my lip, broke my nose, almost broke my arm, all because he thought I lied to him."

Angie arches her back, rinsing away shampoo. "Did you?"

"No."

"Why didn't he believe you?"

"That's how he was. Couldn't find his wallet so he found someone to blame. My cousins were with us for the weekend. One of them said he'd seen me hide it from him for a joke. I had no idea where it was, but Dad was paranoid about things like that. He wanted to beat the truth out of me. My cousins even joined in, kicking me when I fell down. Then Dad's wallet dropped out of Nick's coat pocket. *He'd* taken it and then lied. Dad didn't lay a finger on him or his brothers. They weren't his kids. Dimmi, Marco, and Nick teased me about that for years."

"Did you hit your father back? Or your cousins?"

You shake your head. "I was only a kid. I was too weak."

"Shall we kill that memory next?"

You expel a long sigh. "I think so."

"How many?"

"Dad died years ago. Cancer took Dimmi last summer."

"Two, then."

"Nick and Marco."

Soapsuds running off her body, Angie's eyes seek yours, but you only stare at her scars shimmering in the water, at your final memory gestating in her face, driving her own horrible memories down deep so she can escape them for a little while. She spreads her arms, invites you into the shower, opening her body to you like she did her soul the night you met in the shelter and she agreed to be your final memory.

"One or two good memories between us wouldn't hurt things, would it?" she asks.

"It would ruin everything," you whisper.

You retreat from the bathroom to peeling wallpaper and a television ten years out of date, to a worn-out mattress with yellowed sheets and walls so thin you hear snoring from the room on one side and lazy moans of pleasure from the other. Angie leaves the shower, dries off, watching you as your legs bump the edge of the bed, and you fall backward into sleep.

You surprise visit Marco, introduce Angie as your girlfriend, get him drunk on wine, then leave him in his car in the garage with the motor running and the door closed. His ex-wife finds him five days later after he misses a court date over their child custody dispute. The police rule it suicide because the divorce depressed him. You wonder if the memory of your father beating you that lived inside him knew it had been tricked before it died.

The presence of your mother, in a black dress and a small, black hat with a veil, keeps you away from Marco's funeral. You watch from the shadows of trees across the cemetery then after almost everyone leaves, catch up to Nick, and explain how you didn't want the family to see you since you've been out of touch so long, but you're so sorry about Marco. He takes in your threadbare clothes, dirty shoes, and hungry face, and then invites you to his apartment in the old neighborhood. You get together late one night, making sure no one sees you and Angie arrive, and Nick breaks down, crying over his dead brothers. Behind his tears, though, his face is boyhood Nick's face, thirty years younger, and it wears a mask of scorn where your father's shadow still lives, kicking your small, child's body curled up on the ground. A pulsing vein in Nick's forehead matches the *thump thump thump* of your father's foot striking your stomach. Nick drinks until his face becomes a window to that day. Stealing your father's wallet. Telling the lie. The memory burns in him. A serpentine coil of fire taunting you with a hissing laugh, stoking its reflection inside you.

Nick follows you and Angie out, "for a walk, for some fresh air to sober up," so drunk he doesn't realize it when you lead him onto the East Side railroad tracks. The memory surges in his eyes, though, livid to escape, wanting to hurt you like it has so often before. You watch its angry, panicked throes in the light of the approaching freight train as it realizes Nick is far too drunk to make his way off the tracks, and its fury explodes from his face.

Nick disappears into a black streak of motion and dark metal.

Horrible sounds of metal striking flesh. The scent and spray of blood in the air.

His memory of the day your father beat you lingers like a toxic cloud before it disperses into the wind and nothingness. You clutch your stomach, double over, and vomit crimson chunks into the weeds.

Brakes squeal as the train slows. Angie leads you into the shadows of a run-down shed then away into the night. You don't remember why you're in the old neighborhood—but Angie does. She knows why; she knows your way home.

She's your final memory.

"Your cousins are gone," she says.

"I never had any cousins," you say.

Angie smiles and leads you to the motel room, to the next town, to the next memory.

))●((

Your third-grade best friend, Archie, who knows you wet yourself on the second day of school and reminded you of it almost daily until after high school.

Jeff and Lance, bullies, who made your life hell all through middle school; the teacher, Mrs. Carter, who blamed you for it.

Mr. Williams, down the street, who asked you to help him carry bags of leaves to the curb then groped you in his backyard and lied about it when you told your parents.

Your high school homeroom teacher, Mr. Connolly, who mocked how you dressed, or talked, or combed your hair every day; Andrea and Tomas, classmates who piled on with him.

Your pothead roommate, Fallon, and his brother, Nestor, who beat you up and sent you to the hospital freshman year because he thought you hit on his girlfriend.

Helena, who laughed when you asked her to marry you.

The waiter, who snickered as he overheard Helena say no. He proves hard to track down, but you find him, Carlos Ruiz, living in a crumbling tenement on the edge of the meat-packing district. It's frightening how vibrant the memory remains in him. It twists his face, makes him into a monster as it struggles. But it's only a memory. Its power dies when you tighten the noose around Carlos's neck. The memory leaves a rank taste in your mouth as it rises and spills past your lips. Afterward the man hanging from a hook in his closet puzzles you.

Angie remembers. "You put him there to kill a memory."

She gathers your dead memories and holds them in her ossuary soul.

You feel lighter and freer after erasing each one, while her burden grows, but she only leads you further along the barbed line of your past.

The job interviewer, Forbes MacNeil, who cut you down question after question, made you feel worthless, called you "ridiculous," before you walked out of his office into a depression that lasted a month.

Your co-workers, Rita, Sandra, and Sam, who stole your work, badmouthed you behind your back, and screwed your promotion.

Your boss, Mr. Eisenstein, who fired you to cover his mistakes.

Your friend Kevin, who stole a box of valuable old records from you.

The landlord, Mr. Lopez, who evicted you.

Kristin, your ex-girlfriend who dumped you while you stood in her doorway with all your clothes and belongings shoved into two suitcases and a backpack, asking to crash with her for a few days. She told you to "start over and get a new life without her" then slammed the door in your face. One more boot pushing you back down into a hole you could never figure out how to climb out of, a darkness that kept you lost.

"I wanted to start over," you say the night before you kill the Kristin-memory. "My old life got in my way. My memories made me sick."

You tell Angie you surrendered to the streets then, ashamed to let your family remember you that way. You wound up in a shelter full of people like you—poisoned by memories—and saw only one way to ever exterminate them.

"I realized it the night I met you," you say. "You were high on the Cure, but I knew you were right. The only thing you said would ever free you from your own bad memories could free me as well, but I could still live."

Do it this time, I say. Please, do it.

Pull the trigger.

I still remember.

Time and again, the police question you, but you know nothing of the deaths of people you don't remember. You show genuine confusion about their suspicion.

You cooperate, pass polygraph tests. Angie coaches you how to talk to them. She knows their techniques. She's made sure neither of you left behind any evidence where you killed your memories and few clues to connect any of them other than they all happened to know you at some time. Before Angie found the Cure and followed it to the highway where she destroyed her life, she was a good cop—a good person too. Some people—weak, helpless ones—let that slip through their fingers. Others have it ripped away from them. Their old lives, their good days flayed until only bad memories remain. Angie knows how to make deaths look like accidents or suicides, how to make the police see things to make them turn elsewhere for answers. After a while they stop talking to you, give up tracking you.

Still, you're careful no one ever sees you with Angie.

It's not hard. No one misses her.

You left the shelter together after the first night you met.

No one connects you two.

Months pass while you wipe clean your past's dark geography piece by piece. Existence becomes a patchwork of motels, stolen cars, and sleeping parked in alleys and abandoned places around the city. Vacant lots. Shuttered factories. Neglected parks. You drift along the life-flow of the streets. Steal food when you can. Rely on library computers to track down your memories. As your mind empties, Angie's bloats. She never again opens her arms to you, but she takes the Cure more often, except when you hunt. As each memory falls, the space it held opens in you, revealing an end to the shadows though the darkest ones still wait.

The last memories prove the hardest for Angie. Memories of your own mistakes. She never cried when you killed memories of people hurting you, never hesitated over recollections of others mistreating you, victimizing you, humiliating you—but she cries for those you wronged and betrayed.

Those memories have to die too, though, because their shame weighs the heaviest.

Your high school girlfriend, Lisa. You lied to her, said you loved her to take her virginity then broke up with her. Your sophomore year roommate, Len, whose money you stole, and Tara, his friend, whom you convinced him had taken it. Your co-worker, Parnell, who you envied so much you spread nasty rumors about him and got him fired. Half a dozen others you deceived or screwed or hurt. The hardest is your mother, the last of your family. She remembers more about you than anyone else and will never forget any of it, never let it go. Mothers never do, because as mundane and painful as some memories are, mothers keep their children alive inside them at any cost, any suffering.

Angie refuses to remember this for you.

She disappears for several days. You think she'll never come back, but she does because all your shared plans fall apart if your final memory is incomplete, and only Angie can be your final memory now because only she remembers. She finds you sleeping in the car behind an abandoned hospital, knocks on the window, and tells you how you'll kill the last memories on your list.

The next day, you clean yourselves, buy cheap, new clothes, and then go that evening to your mother's house. She's aged much in the years since you last saw her, and she stares at you like she's seeing a ghost when she opens the door. Her joy beats out her uncertainty, though, and she welcomes you into her house—your childhood home. Memories live in every wall, door, and piece of furniture, but they'll all fade and die with the memories in your mother.

You introduce Angie as your fiancé, and tell your mother you're starting a new job soon, getting your life back on track, starting a family. All she could ever want for her son, you tell her it's happening. She's overjoyed. She makes you coffee, puts out cakes and cookies, tells you to visit more often because she wants to be close to you again. The memories swarm in her face, her eyes, her lips, her touch, so many things from your past, good, bad, light, and dark, things you might cherish if they weren't interwoven with the rot that has weighed you down for so long.

After a second cup of coffee, you excuse yourself for the bathroom, and then, while your mother talks with Angie about future grandchildren, you slip down to the basement and rig the furnace how Angie told you. Half an hour later, you give your mother a last kiss, the warmest hug you've ever managed for her, and wish her goodbye. You and Angie drive away, circle back, then park down the block, and watch the lights go off on the first floor of your mother's house. The single light on the second floor soon follows. You watch the darkened house for two hours before you drive away. Sometime in the night, you wake in the back seat, no idea where you are, Angie watching you from the passenger seat.

She says, "Tell me about your mother."

"I don't remember my mother," you say.

Snapping open the door, you jump out of the car and throw up into sand and gravel. Your body quakes; pain tries to tear you apart. A flood of glistening, red blobs pours from your throat, heaves and flows, pools on the ground, until you fall back against the car exhausted. Angie helps you crawl back inside.

"Angie," you say.

I got your back, I say.

I remember for you because you're too weak.

"Yes?" she says.

"Do you remember?"

"Yes."

"Okay," you say, then fall asleep.

The next morning Angie makes an anonymous phone call; the police find your mother in her bed, dead from carbon monoxide poisoning.

Your final memory sits across from you on a bed in a dingy motel room off the highway, where the walls reek of cigarette smoke, and the rumble of traffic vibrates through the building. Tears streak down her face. All your shame and hurt swell inside her.

Your final memory speaks all the things you've done, all the memories you've killed, and how, and why. She remembers all your dead memories for you. She speaks your past. She sips from a green bottle. She moans. Her eyes darken. Your memories swim inside them then twine across her face. She peels away her clothes and sits naked on the bed, her tortured flesh exposed.

"See my scars," she says. "Understand everything you're going to kill. Not only your memories, but mine too. You'll be free to live, and I'll be free from the hell I made of my life."

She hands you a gun, presses your finger around its trigger.

"I'm your final memory. You won't remember when you're done. You'll walk out of here, and the memories I've held for you will never grow back. I give you my life because it's worthless to me, and because you're a pathetic, pitiful excuse for a man who couldn't pull his shit together. People get over all the petty crap in their lives and move on, but you wallowed in self-pity. Defined yourself by your failures. Clung to your depression. Blamed everyone else for your weakness. I saw it all in you the night we met. I've hated you our whole time together, but I don't deserve to die for any better reason than to give a piece of shit like you a second chance at life. Perfect punishment for the lives I ruined. Maybe you'll find some good. I hope so."

Don't be confused, I say. I remember for you. I got your back.

Please, do it now. Don't make me wait any longer. Don't make either of us wait.

I'm your final memory. All your darkness, sadness, hate, shame, regret, failure, loss, pain—all of it is collected inside me, nested beside my own pain and horror, for you to kill once and for all.

Do it. This time, please.

Kill our memories.

Squeeze the trigger.

You shudder as Angie sighs. She opens a fresh green bottle and sips.

She grips your tired hand and raises it, re-aiming the gun toward her.

Resigned, she begins again: "I am your final memory. You tie a humiliating memory to a chair. You bind his hands behind the wooden back, fasten his ankles to the chair legs, the coarse rope scratching your fingers."

You have to squeeze the—

The Many Hands Inside the Mountain

Whatever guilt Zach Reynolds felt as Tamara Porter's warm, naked flesh slid against his disintegrated when he opened his eyes to his ramshackle bedroom. Tamara kissed and caressed all his cautions away, but his dingy room behind the auto garage — left to him by his father — reminded him of what justified all they did behind Katrina Van Bollin's back. Grasping Tamara's waist, he pulled her heat tight to his, and released his body to the rhythms of pleasure. Neither spoke. The time for talk lay well behind them, and after this last secret tryst, each would have their heart's deepest desire.

Later, sweat drying on their skin and the setting sun impelling golden bars through the blinds, Zach slid from the sheets and assembled his Halloween costume. Tamara followed suit with a sigh, pausing with her shimmering, translucent gown around her waist to pepper kisses down Zach's bare back. Then, dressed and ready, Zach saw her to the door and shut it without looking back.

Outside, the two shared a lingering, last kiss, ended with reluctance.

"Tell Cord not to foul this up," Zach said.

Tamara rolled her eyes. "Cord will do what I tell him. You do your part."

"You can count on me."

"I know." Tamara slid one hand down Zach's back to his butt and pressed him against her. "You could still come with me."

"I'm pretty sure Cord would have a problem with that."

"I can dump Cord here or when I get to New York City. No difference to me, especially if I get you in the bargain."

"Nah. I owe this town too much, and I'd like to own it one day."

"You think too small."

"That's the first time you ever accused me of being small."

Tamara laughed, slapped Zach's rear, and then pushed him away.

"Suit yourself. Is Bollin's Creek the only thing you love?"

Zach blushed.

"You're *really* in love with Kat?"

"It's not her fault who her father is."

"Promise me you won't have a change of heart before we do this."

"Kat had nothing to do with what Arthur Van Bollin did to my father, but she and I can't have a life until I settle scores with him. Do it how we said, everyone gets what they want."

"Mostly." Tamara ran a fingertip down the side of Zach's neck. "Have a nice life with that fancy bitch and her ice queen aunt. Maybe I'll send you a postcard from the city."

Zach watched Tamara walk away in her opalescent faerie gown. Silk and cellophane wings bobbed on her back. Where the path through his oil-stained yard hooked right out the gate, she looked back and blew him a kiss. Her smell still lingered in his nostrils, her taste on his tongue. A high price, losing her, but he deemed it fair trade for obtaining what he'd longed for since third grade. For half a heartbeat he considered accepting her offer to shuck his past and all its burdens in exchange for a fresh start far away. But he *did* love Bollin's Creek. After Arthur Van Bollin ruined his father's business and drove him to suicide, the people here took care of Zach like one of their own children. They fed and clothed him and hired him to repair their cars when he reopened his father's garage. He owed them, and breaking the Van Bollins' hold over the town and its people would settle the debt.

No one knew exactly how the Van Bollin family earned their money, but nor did anyone object to them spending a fair chunk of it on the annual Bollin's Creek Halloween Masquerade Festival. A town tradition dating back to the Depression, Zach had joined in the party as long as he could remember, starting with the children's Trick Or Treat March before graduating to the Haunted Horse and Buggy rides through the graveyard then moving on to the Corpse and Corn Maze and the bonfire behind the high school football field. Now, only a few years out of school, he'd devised his best costume ever and been invited to the Festival's exclusive last hurrah at the Van Bollin house—the Midnight Masque.

Hell or high water, he intended to make it a night to remember.

Katrina Van Bollin deserved no less.

Her father deserved no better.

"Oh my god, Zach, it's brilliant!"

Katrina squealed as she grabbed his shoulders and planted a kiss on his lips, tickling them with the tip of her tongue. She stepped back for a better view of his costume, which consisted of a navy blue silk shirt bought from the consignment shop and a breastplate hammered from sheet metal scrap and painted with a unicorn head sigil. Snug, black pants and battered, leather boots completed the overall look to which he'd added a low-slung belt strapped with a short sword at his left hip and a blaster at his right, the prop weapons fashioned from odds and ends around his shop. On his sleeves he'd sewn gold bands of his rank as Prince Vinn Northstar, Commander of the Algernon Rift Fleet, meticulously designed from descriptions in Katrina's favorite series of fantasy novels, *The Northstar Saga*. His touch of genius, though, lay in his shirt's collar, which projected color sequences onto his face. Reflected by the polished breastplate, they created a cloud of light that mimicked the personal auras essential to the saga's characters.

"I *love* the aura! Promise you'll do one for me next year, okay? We can go as the King and Queen of House Northstar with the brightest, most perfect auras."

"You bet."

Katrina spun to show off her red-and-black gown, slits rising to her waist, accentuating her long, lithe legs. A ring mail shawl draped across her shoulders hid much of what the gown's plunging neckline revealed yet exposed a temporary tattoo centered below her breasts, a thorny vine twined into a heart shape topped with a black rose.

"What do you think?" she said.

"Absolutely stunning," Zach said. "Lady Asanander, right? Aren't she and Prince Vinn enemies?"

Katrina replied with a salacious grin. "You haven't read book four yet."

"Maybe I should jump ahead."

Katrina laughed then pulled Zach by the hand. "Come on! See the costumes. Everyone looks wonderful. This will be the best Halloween ever."

She led him through the house, every room decorated. The parlor resembled an enchanted woodland, the den a spaceship command bridge, the dining room a tableau of grinning corpses set to feast. Clever wall hangings and projected light transformed the halls into torch-lit tunnels. In the kitchen, cooks and waiters in skimpy, gothic outfits worked among black-and-white tiles with serving dishes smeared with faux blood. Zach had grown up like everyone in town listening to rumors of the Midnight Masque's excesses but the rumors fell far short of the reality.

They stepped out onto the back veranda, overlooking a yard where the party's heart beat to a four-piece band playing on a skull-shaped stage surrounded by a dancing crowd. Guitars, drums, and voices filled the air with a rockabilly cover of "The Monster Mash." Tables alongside offered heaps of food lit by candelabras draped with cobwebs, and at each corner, bartenders in skin-tight, black-and-white skeleton suits served drinks from behind gravestone bars. Candles, bonfire barrels, and wrought-iron braziers provided the only light. Beyond that, stars glimmered above the dead-black peaks of the Nasquaiga Mountains. The partygoers all wore masks, some integral to their costume, others ornate leather sculptures tied on with decorative silks.

Katrina handed such a mask to Zach, House Northstar blue and gold, the eyeholes cut in the peculiar, trapezoidal shape of the Northstar race.

"Daddy insists."

Zach let Katrina tie the ribbons around his head and then he did the same for her, a blood-red mask with cat's-eye tips.

"You're supposed to put it on before you come, but I wanted you to see me," Katrina whispered. "I hated the idea of you dancing with other girls all night trying to find me. Go fetch us drinks. I'll tell Daddy you're here."

Katrina hurried off and submerged into the crowd.

Zach worked his way to the nearest bar, where he discovered the bartender wore body paint, not a skin-tight suit. Goosebumps rippled her flesh, and he pitied her working in the chill night, but if the cold or her nakedness gave her any serious discomfort, he saw no sign of it. He ordered a pumpkin spice beer and a glass of Malbec for Katrina then crowd-watched while he waited for her to return.

A text from Tamara buzzed his phone: *We're here.*

Setting down the drinks, he texted back: *Don't c u.*

U will.

He glanced around for Tamara's faerie outfit amidst a living collage of pirates, wizards, football players, werewolves, nurses, and super-heroes.

Cord's a gladiator. Rog and Kevin took the pickup up the service road. Everything's set.

All good here.

U sure u don't want to come with?

I'm sure.

Ur loss. U really love her that much?

I do.

More than me?

I never loved you.

Jerk.

Before Zach could reply, Katrina gripped his arm. Startled, he tried to shove his phone into his pocket, but his blaster blocked it. Katrina turned him to face a burly man in a tuxedo of forest green and a porcelain jack-o'-lantern mask engraved with scrolls of fine, archaic writing and secured by flame-colored ribbons.

"I'm truly happy to see you here, son," Arthur Van Bollin said.

Shaking the man's hand, Zach nodded. "I'm honored you'd have me. Everyone in town dreams of getting an invitation here."

"People here and pretty much anywhere else they've heard of our Festival. Folks come from all over these days. The Festival has become quite the tourist attraction. Good for business, good for the town. Lots of money coming in. The bad old days are far behind us. Of course, no tourists ever score invitations to the Midnight Masque. Can't have that. This is only for those of us who call the mountains home. You should see the emails we get, begging and pleading. Make no mistake, Zach, you're right to be honored, but the invitation is only icing on the cake. The true honor is you'll be family soon. Family outshines everything. We don't bring young men into the Bollin fold idly. But you make Katrina happy. I know I could never fill your father's shoes, of course, but I hope I can fill an empty part of your life."

Zach swallowed then stammered, "My father…," but only angry words and accusations came to mind, so he held his tongue.

"He'd be proud of how you've made his business a success. I hear folks come up all the way from Albany for your custom car services. That true?"

"Bollin's Creek is so out of the way, those customers are few and far between. I do a lot more oil changes and brake jobs to pay the bills."

"Why not take your talent elsewhere? Get yourself a reality TV show. I've seen that Jeep you made over like a *Star Wars* fighter ship for Force Insurance in Hackett. It's good enough for the big time."

"Leave Bollin's Creek? No, doesn't feel right."

The changeless expression of Van Bollin's pumpkin mask rattled Zach; he couldn't tell if Katrina's father smiled or sneered behind it. "Wise words. And, believe me, we'll be glad to put your creativity and skills to work for the Halloween Festival. Here, let me snap a picture of you and Kat."

Zach's heart jumped as Van Bollin took the phone from his hand, and Katrina sidled in close to him. Every last drop of moisture in his throat dried up. He prayed the text window had closed. Then the camera flash blinded him while Katrina rubbed the back of his neck, and her father returned his phone.

"You kids have fun. I've got people to entertain. See you at midnight for the unmasking."

"Daddy likes you a lot," Katrina said.

She sipped her wine, while Zach downed half his beer to soothe his dry throat.

"Guess I'm lucky," he said.

"We make our own luck. I see how much you love this town. You'll fit in perfectly with our family. You'll hardly remember all the years you spent without one."

Zach withdrew from Katrina, too reflexively to stop himself.

"I'm sorry," she said. "What a dumb thing for me to say."

"Forget it."

"No. Growing up alone is part of what made you the man I love. So is what happened between our fathers. I don't want to ever forget that, but I want you to be happy with us."

Finishing off his beer, Zach tossed the bottle into a recycling bin and took Katrina's hand.

"I can't imagine why I wouldn't be," he said, pulling her toward the music.

They eased through the crowd, close to the band, now rocking through Screaming Lord Sutch's "Jack the Ripper," and they danced.

As the night grew long, Zach spied Tamara in her iridescent gown, always with Cord in tow, and she ignoring the lascivious looks men cast her way when the light caught her right and gave glimpses of her body within her wispy costume. She ignored Zach, even when they passed close on the dancefloor. Her indifference chilled him. She had planned tonight for more than two years, from before she and Zach ever spoke, before she introduced him to Katrina, maybe even longer.

The band finished off Michael Jackson's "Thriller" then announced a short break.

Katrina seized Tamara in a manic hug. Zach caught up and gave Cord a nod.

"Can you believe we're all here together?" Katrina said.

"It's like a dream come true," said Tamara.

Katrina pulled Zach to her side.

"Cord, take a picture of me with my best friend and my fiancé."

Cord dug out his phone and snapped a shot.

"Take one with mine," Tamara said, digging into the folds of her dress.

Katrina play-swatted her arm. "Forget it. Cord can send it to all of us, right, Cord?"

"You bet," said Cord as he hit send. He put his arm around Zach's shoulders. "Hey, amigo, let's grab a fresh round."

They walked to the nearest bar and ordered. While the bartender poured, Cord leaned in close and said, "You better be ready, Reynolds. That pussy costume of yours doesn't give me a lot of confidence. A fucking unicorn? That's some *My Little Pony* shit."

"Kiss my ass, Cord. We wouldn't even be here if not for me."

"If not for Tamara, you mean."

Zach put his hands around two drinks, but Cord squeezed his wrist, hard.

"As long as it plays out how Tam said, everything will go fine."

Cord squeezed harder.

"I mean it, Reynolds. Kat's told Tam stories about this since her first sleepover here in the second grade. No one outside the Van Bollin family knows more about the mountain vault or the Many Hands inside the Mountain."

"You really believe they killed the men who built the vault then butchered and buried them up there to keep the secret?"

"Why not? The family goes up there once a year to pay homage or some bullshit. This year, we're going too. We got one shot at this so when Rog and Kevin arrive you do your part. Understand?"

"Fuck off. This isn't high school," Zach said. "I'll convince Van Bollin to go along about the vault. *You* make sure whatever you do to him looks like an accident. And *don't* hurt Katrina, or I promise I'll rip you in two."

Cord snorted. "Like you could take me."

Zach held his gaze steady on Cord's eyes until the flicker of doubt he desired appeared. "You really got a thing for Katrina, huh. How sweet. Hasn't stopped you from boning Tamara behind my back, but sweet. Yeah, I know all about you two—and I don't care. She's using you, she's using me, she's using Kat, and I'm using her, and so are you. We're all using each other, because that's just how things get done, ain't it?"

Cord took his and Tamara's drinks.

Zach watched him shoulder a path through the crowd. His phone pinged. The picture from Cord popped up onscreen: Zach between two smiling women dressed like things that didn't exist.

He downed a long swallow of beer then rejoined the party.

The effigy heralded the unmasking.

Part piñata, part balloon, part latex foam, it stood twenty feet high, swaying like a parade float, all flowers, crepe paper, and colored streamers. At midnight, servants in orange and black robes wheeled it out from the woods on a rolling platform. The crowd fell silent. All eyes turned to the towering figure, which featured an exaggerated phallus and prominent breasts. An almond-shaped orifice tapered from its cleavage to its waist, sealed with a translucent membrane bulging with piles of jewelry, watches, gold and silver chains, boxes wrapped in orange foil, bags of gold coins, and even rubber-banded stacks of cash. A massive jack-o'-lantern, etched with obscure writing, like Van Bollin's mask, bobbed on its shoulders. Fires flickered in its eyes and mouth, streaming aromatic smoke.

The party staff cleared the skull stage and the party debris, damping the candles and braziers, leaving only the bonfire barrels lit. Their black body paint blending into the dark and their white bones reddened by the firelight, the bartenders passed out sticks, each about six feet long and tipped with an iron bulb. Workers hurried a five-foot-high platform with stairs on either side in front of the effigy. After preparations ceased, the night existed for a moment only as wind, shadows, fire, and the crowd's collective, withheld breath.

Van Bollin ascended the platform and raised his arms.

"Thank you for celebrating this special time with us!" His voice resonated from behind his mask. "Your presence means a great deal to my family, but more importantly, to Bollin's Creek. We have a wonderful town here. May it never change, and our traditions keep us forever prosperous. Tonight we share the wealth!"

The crowd applauded. Van Bollin waved them quiet.

"Soon, we'll play that special music we hear but once a year, on this very evening. When the first notes sound, all who wish to may don a blindfold and take three swings." Van Bollin gestured to the effigy. "Three strikes only. The first to break the seal gets pick of prizes. When all are taken and the music ends, we'll light this on fire and the unmasking will commence. If no one breaks the seal before the music stops, all this treasure goes up in smoke. Remember to kiss the person next to you when you remove your mask. If it's not your boyfriend, your girlfriend, your wife, or your husband—well, I hope they're the understanding type."

An outburst of laughter and applause covered his descent.

Hidden speakers played organ music, dolorous and low, a pulsing rhythm for a melody of reedy pipes and discordant strings. The tempo lumbered. The notes wove a hypnotic sound web as the partyers lined up. The effigy's membrane vibrated to the music. A woman in a black cat-suit tried first, blindfolded, spun three times, and ushered up the steps by a robed servant. She hit the figure's arm, leg, and phallus, which shook up and down, eliciting laughter, but missed the membrane with all three swings. Loose bits of paper, flowers, and embers showered down. Next, a man in a knight's costume tried, and a Mad Hatter waited his turn, along with dozens of others.

Kristina took Zach's arm. "Time to go," she said.

They slipped away, scooping Tamara and Cord out of the crowd, then joining Van Bollin on the edge of the woods.

"Everyone here? Good," he said. "Let's go."

They walked a gravel path among the trees. While the voices from the party faded, the music traveled along, replaying itself in Zach's mind. The gravel glowed faintly, especially when Zach looked at it sidewise. Eventually, the path ended at a hard-packed dirt road and a Jeep.

"Get in!" said Van Bollin. "Zach, sit up front with me."

Katrina climbed in the back with Tamara and Cord. The engine growled. Van Bollin hit the gas. The Jeep shuddered then rolled into the night. Its headlights revealed the service road up the nearest of the Nasquaiga Mountains, then reduced the woods to a shadowy blur as the vehicle accelerated. A sharp turn sent them up a steep incline. The lights in Zach's collar played across the dashboard. After a time, when the ground leveled again, the mountain range lay splayed out in every direction beneath stars twinkling high in a cloudless sky. On each peak, a pillar of flame burned, overlooking the valley behind the Van Bollin land.

"What is all this?" Zach asked.

"We aren't the only ones who celebrate tonight," said Van Bollin.

The Jeep lurched as it renewed its ascent.

Bonfires came in and out of view on the far peaks. Shadowy figures passed in front of them, some dancing, others jumping, some playing with what looked like large dogs. Zach swiveled to check Katrina and spotted headlights lurching far down the rough service road, sticking steady behind them. Soon the Jeep stopped in a clearing at the base of a sheer rock face. With child-like excitement, Van Bollin dashed out and lifted a branch with rags coiled around one end. He took a lighter from his pocket, touched fire to cloth, and the rags erupted in flames.

Zach and the others exited the Jeep. The aroma of kerosene lingered in the air.

Van Bollin lit the wood pile with his torch. An abrupt conflagration swallowed the logs and boards. The night chill fled and heat licked at their faces. Van Bollin mounted his torch in an iron brace on a tree beside a stone ring, eight feet in diameter and two-feet high, surrounding a pool of utter darkness. He glanced over the low wall.

"What's in there?" Zach said.

Katrina touched his lip. "Ssshhh."

Van Bollin dragged a footlocker from the brush, opened it, and pulled out gear. Soon the dreary music for the effigy played on a portable speaker linked to his iPhone. He dropped two bulging burlap sacks from the locker at Zach's feet, then handed him a leather case the size of a book.

He winked. "Don't open that yet."

"Katrina, what's going on?" Zach said.

Ignoring him, Katrina tapped on her phone. Zach's pocket buzzed. He checked his alerts and found a text from Tamara's number.

Ur not really a jerk. I love u 2.

Zach stared at empty-handed Tamara, but Katrina waved a phone, sheathed in Tamara's familiar pink, leather case. She keyed in a new message. Zach's phone vibrated, another text from Tamara's number.

Trick or Treat!

"Why does Katrina have your phone, Tam?" Zach said.

"What are you talking about? My phone's right here." Tamara reached into her pocket. Her face crinkled with surprise then worry. "Where the hell did it go?"

Katrina giggled.

An engine's low grumble echoed from the valley. Zach scanned the mountains, the fires too distant for him to see much besides the ecstatic shapes gathered by them. The crunch of dirt and rocks beneath tires joined the engine noise. Brightness sprang from the road as Rog's pickup truck jolted to the edge of the clearing and then squealed to a stop, headlight beams pale against the flames.

Cord drew his Roman short sword, exposing it as a long hunting knife, grabbed Katrina by the waist, and pressed the blade to her throat.

"Cord! What the hell are you doing?" said Van Bollin.

"Shut up, you old prick! Do what I say or I'll cut Katrina."

"Shit, that's Rog's truck," Zach said.

Van Bollin smirked at Cord. "What's this about?"

"You and Zach are going to open your mountain vault for me."

"Shit. That's all? Do you believe every half-assed rumor you hear around town, Cord? There's no cave. There's no vault. Why would I stash a fortune out here in the mountains? You think the 'Many Hands inside the Mountain' would watch over it? The ghosts of a bunch of dead workers who never existed?"

"Don't fuck with me, old man. Rog and Kevin will wait with Katrina. You and Captain Unicorn open the vault. Then I'm out of here with the money and Tam. Either of you pulls any shit, Kat dies." Cord jerked Katrina against his chest, creasing her neck with his blade. "I've got your daughter, and I've got backup."

"No, you don't." Prudence Van Bollin, Katrina's aunt, stepped out from the driver's side of the pickup. "Unless you mean me. But I don't help douchebags who threaten my niece."

Dressed in a blood-soaked wedding gown, hair matted, face streaked deep red, Prudence reached into the truck and pulled out an axe, its blade dripping. Firelight turned the blood nearly black. She wiped at it with the back of one hand, only smudging it around.

"Trying to scare me?" Cord said. "I don't fucking scare!"

"What's Halloween without a few good scares?" Van Bollin said.

"Rog, Kevin! Get your asses out here *now*!" Cord shouted.

"Don't waste your breath. Pru, show Tamara how her boyfriends are doing." Van Bollin nudged Tamara. "Go on. It'll clear things up."

Reluctantly, Tamara followed Prudence around back of the truck. Prudence lowered the tailgate then yanked off a canvas sheet. Tamara screamed and recoiled then bumped Prudence and fell to the ground. Struggling to rise, she landed on her knees, shivering, and then threw up.

"What? What is it?" Cord asked.

Blade tight to Katrina's throat, he dragged her to the truck.

When he glanced into the bed, all the color and bravado fled his face, and his knife hand drifted from Katrina. Prudence's face lit up, and she swung her axe. A spray of blood flew off the blade before the flat of it thumped Cord's head, snapping it sideways and silencing the cry he'd opened his mouth to release. He dropped the knife then toppled, missing Katrina by inches.

"What did you do to them?" Zach asked.

Van Bollin's hand came to a fatherly rest on his shoulder.

"Only what's needed. Understand, Zach, marrying my daughter is all or nothing. We do this for the good of Bollin's Creek. My great-grandfather started it in the Depression to keep the whole town from dying. We've kept the tradition ever since, so we take the lion's share of the profit. I believe you love this town. I believe you love my daughter. Her little game with Tam's phone was a test—you passed. Now you have to pass one for me. Go and look."

Stomach clenched and churning, Zach inched toward the truck, hoping what he imagined proved far worse than the reality, only to feel his hopes shattered when he saw Rog and Kevin's mutilated bodies. Naked, side by side, hacked dozens of times, throats cut, and skulls opened—and from chest to groin, they lay split apart, with piles of candy stuffed in among their organs. Plastic wrappers and colorful logos glistened with blood. Hershey's bars. Skittles. M&Ms. Laffy Taffy. Life Savers. Twix. Bubble Yum. Rog and Kevin looked as if they'd fallen into a thresher alongside a candy counter. The stench of their innards flooded Zach's nostrils. He felt a quiver in the mountain, and the sky swirled, the stars becoming fiery, golden streaks spiraling toward the flames on the other peaks. Multi-colored flashes sparked before his eyes. He switched off the lights in his collar and steadied himself against the pickup.

Prudence and her brother carried Rog's body to the pit then made a second trip for Kevin's.

Katrina, clutching Cord by the armpits, dragged him there.

Wind swirled the dirt, and the dour, oppressive music flowing from the portable speaker resonated in Zach's mind, awakening his senses in an unfamiliar way. He took a step and almost tripped over Tamara lying in a fetal ball beside him. Katrina came back, helped her onto her feet, and walked her to the pit. She tried to break free, but Prudence whacked her with the flat of the axe, and they laid her out stunned beside Cord.

"Bring those sacks over here, would you, Zach, sweetie?" Katrina asked.

Zach did. The music made him want to comply. He looked inside one sack, filled with brightly wrapped candy, and then dropped both by Katrina.

Gradations of shadow whirlpooled within the darkness of the pit.

An enormous hand emerged, bony fingers tipped with crimson talons on an arm at least nine feet long. The hand scrabbled in the dirt until one talon sank into Rog's throat and dragged the candy-stuffed corpse to the wall. Three similar hands came to pull Rog up and over the stone ring into the pit. Looking at them hurt Zach's head. One second they all looked bony and hairy and then scaly and plump the next, then fur-covered and cat-clawed, then charred, rotten, and tipped with bone-needles, then chitinous and coated with sharp bristles, then…

Zach shook his head and looked away.

"Hurts the eyes. You get used to it," Van Bollin said. "We have to break the membrane to earn the treasure. This one night of the year it weakens enough for us to breach it as long as we follow tradition. "

"Tradition?" Zach said.

"Five sacrifices and all the candy they want. Satisfy the Many Hands inside the Mountain and they'll fill our real vault, safe in the basement of my house, with riches by morning."

"We have to do this together so we can be married, Zach," Katrina said.

"I… I don't know what to do."

The music tamped down Zach's rising hysteria and eased his rejection of the impossible. Its elegiac melody restrained his fear.

"We prepare the offering. I'll do Cord. You do Tamara."

"How…?"

Katrina unwrapped a Jawbreaker and popped it in her mouth. With a smile, she rammed Cord's knife into his chest below the neck and carved downward.

Blood sprayed her face and ring mail shawl.

"Inside that case, Zach, is the blade of my great-grandfather," Van Bollin said.

Zach undid the snap, revealing a silver knife.

"You want me to… to do this to Tamara?"

"Not like she doesn't have it coming," Katrina said, still sawing at Cord. "Little hussy's been plotting against me ever since I screwed her brothers in the eighth grade."

"You did what?" Zach asked, but Katrina only shook her head.

"Let it go, sweetie. *You* get to marry me," Katrina said.

More hands reached from the pit, each with a changing number of joints, their skin and features in constant flux as if, unable to comprehend their reality, Zach's mind shuffled possibilities like a deck of cards, hoping one might stick. He looked away when they clutched Kevin's body.

"You said five sacrifices. Who…?" he said.

"You don't mean you didn't know?" said Van Bollin.

Katrina chuckled. "You and Tam have been boning like rabbits for months. What'd you think would happen? We were worried she might be barren the way you two went at it, and her as regular as can be. It was such a relief when she told me a few weeks ago, not that she said who the father was. But I know it's you."

Zach sank to his knees beside Tamara, placed his free hand on her belly, and watched her chest rise and fall as she breathed.

"She meant to get rid of it in New York. Bitch never could keep a secret worth a damn."

Sticky sweetness touched Zach's tongue, a caramel Katrina pushed into his mouth, her fingers leaving salty blood on his lips.

"Here, it's easier with a piece of candy," she said.

A grasping muddle of hands emerged from the pit. A dozen. Twenty. Forty. More. Zach couldn't count unless he looked at them, and he couldn't bear the pain of looking. The sight of the effigy filled his mind, its burning pumpkin eyes enmeshed by ancient writing, its engorged sex aspects, its treasure-bloated womb, and the earthy scent of the smoke from its eyes.

Break the membrane.

The music rode him. Katrina smiled. Even bloody and deranged her smile made his heart race. She had shown him the real Bollin's Creek as only the few who knew it could understand. All his dreams of saving this town disintegrated in the mad swirl of night and fire.

Katrina's great-great-grandfather's knife weighed heavy in his grip.

Giant, inhuman hands bristled from the pit, horrid flowers writhing in a terrible vase.

Zach bit the caramel, releasing a creamy center tinged with woody bitterness.

He swallowed, and it filled him with sweetness and light.

What's in the Bag, Dad?

"Come one, come all! Gather around and let the ancient secrets of the Persian desert mystify you. Powerful magic dwells in the hot sands of Persia, magic known only to those sons of sheiks who are the hermits and mystics of the outlands. I, Alhazarda, rogue disciple of the ancient Mesopotamian seers, have not only studied this magic but have harnessed its power and brought it here for *you* to witness! Gaze upon this magic bag! It grants power over life and death, over the very fabric of nature herself. Within its enchanted cloth hide the mysteries of the ages, the secrets of the universe, and wonders unseen in our modern times. Do any among you dare pit your wits against the magic of the distant past? Do any feel lucky enough to make three guesses and look into the bag?"

Alhazarda gestured to a coarse sack large enough to hold a person. It hung beside him suspended by rope from a nine-foot, wooden tripod, dangling four feet above the stage boards. Its once brilliant colors, now faded to dusty pastel greens, yellows, and reds, shimmered in the dim light. A repeating zig-zag pattern woven into its fabric framed intricate embroidery depicting the phases of the moon. The sack danced as if hungry badgers wrestled inside it, a melee of strained wheezing and whistling leaking out through the fabric. To an educated eye, the textile spoke not of desert sands but of lush, Mesoamerican jungles. To the small crowd gathered, most of whom had never left Oklahoma, it became whatever Alhazarda told them.

"Do no courageous, clever souls stand before me on the midway tonight? The meager price of only twenty-five cents buys you three chances to win your fortune, three guesses at the contents of this lively bag at my side. Not one, not two, but three! The one who guesses correctly shall not only take home your choice of prize from all the carnival—but shall also be granted a single wish. Your heart's most fervent desire! An opportunity to change the course of your life, to glimpse the future, or perhaps revisit the past. Who will take a chance and test their wits? Step right up. Don't hesitate. Fortune awaits!"

The name of Alhazarda's act, "What's in the Bag, Dad?," emblazoned the painted cloth banner strung up behind him. Colorful minarets illustrated its edges. A man sitting cross-legged on a flying carpet flew through the "a" in "Bag." In a flowing, royal blue robe and a bejeweled, white turban, Alhazarda's gaunt height and long, narrow beard deepened his wizened, sinister appearance and distracted from the threadbare fringes of his costume. The crowd listened to him bark, pondering his exotic, yet vaguely familiar, accent, their eyes on the wriggling bag, all wondering the same thing: *What the hell is in there?*

None looked eager for the chance to find out.

"Come now, folks," Alhazarda said. "What could it be? A pack of coyotes? A ballerina from the hallowed halls of the Peking Opera? A feral child from wildest Borneo? The dread Tasmanian devil?"

"Last week's laundry!" shouted a man in the crowd.

Laughter erupted. Alhazarda took it in stride.

"Entirely possible that it's yours, sir. From the looks of you, it's been quite some time since you washed your clothes." Another burst of laughter. Alhazarda sensed energy growing, the crowd's interest intensifying. "Please, though, absolutely no guessing until you've paid for the privilege. Hand me your quarter. Make your guesses. Look into the bag. As easy as falling off your chair. Guess right and your wish will be granted. Who is brave enough to try?"

A man in a red flannel shirt held up a quarter. "I'll give it a shot, wizard. How do I do it?"

Sweeping the money out of sight inside his robe, Alhazarda ushered the man onstage.

"Easy, easy, sahib. Simply step right here and declare your guesses. I'll lower the bag so you can look inside. Guess right, you win! What is your name, sahib?"

"Leonard."

"Are you ready to guess, Mr. Leonard?"

"Ready as I'll ever be," he said.

"Excellent!" Turning to the crowd, Alhazarda stretched his arms wide. The stone in his turban glistened in the midway lights. "Now, I ask that you all remain still and silent for the next several moments. What Mr. Leonard shall attempt requires concentration, consideration, and concatenation. Don't fret if you don't know what those words mean. They're Mr. Leonard's problem now, not yours. Mr. Leonard, please, share with us your attempt to pierce the mystic veil and win your fortune. Tell us your guesses."

"The way that sack is bouncing around, I figure something alive is in there. My guesses are a pack of kittens, a pair of monkeys, or one of them midget folks I saw walking around by the sideshow."

"There you have it!" Alhazarda retreated from Leonard. "Kittens, monkeys, or one of them midget folks. Would anyone else like to join Leonard on the stage and guess? No one? All right then. Let's test Leonard's choices."

The mystic untied the rope from the iron hook that tethered it and then lowered it an inch at a time. The tripod creaked.

"Kittens, monkeys, midget folk!" he called. "Could one be right?"

The bag came to rest on the boards, still shimmying and thumping.

Alhazarda lifted the top and loosened the knot that bound it closed.

"Mr. Leonard, before you look, I'm obligated to warn you that the powers of the ancients can be unpredictable and spiteful. There is a risk—a small but very real risk—that even if you guess correctly you will be *cursed* rather than rewarded. I should've said so earlier, but it's such an infinitesimal chance, likely with only the unluckiest of souls, hasn't happened in years, and there's so much you stand to gain. Knowing this risk, do you still wish to look into the bag?"

The man laughed. "Unless you're giving me back my quarter, I'm playing the game."

"No, no, I'm sorry, sahib, there are no refunds, so you must forge ahead. I shall pray for the safety of your soul and the souls of your sons and your grandsons."

Alhazarda furrowed his brow and muttered strange words as if casting a spell over the bag. Finished, he raised his head and handed the untied cloth to Leonard.

The crowd pressed against the stage, everyone straining to glimpse inside the jerking bag.

Leonard spread the opening and looked.

A blast of air whooshed between him and Alhazarda, mussing his hair and repelling him. The audience gasped and flinched. The sack went limp. Alhazarda gripped it, peeled it inside out, raised it in the air, then shook it.

Empty.

"It seems you guessed wrong, Mr. Leonard. But don't be upset. You gained no wishes or prizes, but nor did you gain the curse. Would you like to guess again? You've eliminated kittens, monkeys, and midgets. What else might this magical bag contain?"

"Nothing! You just showed us it's empty."

"Is it really, though?"

Alhazarda pulled the bag right side out and tied it shut. He hoisted it back into the air, securing it to the hook. Once in place it filled with weight, snapped to life, and resumed shaking and hopping on the line, rippling its dusky colors and moons.

"Ah, go on, it's just a gag," Leonard said.

He jumped down from the platform and walked away.

The bemused crowd broke up. A few remained, eyeing the bag.

Alhazarda caught them in his gaze and resumed barking. "Who is next? Who shall test their wits against the ancient mysteries of the Persian sands?" He cast his voice over the midway, working hard to draw a fresh crowd, waiting for his hook to set once again, haunted by better days when his ominous, silent presence on stage drew double the crowd he now hawked and hollered to attract.

At the other end of the midway, the calliope played.

All throughout Garde and Rockfern's Traveling Exhibition, where smaller crowds than ever roamed the sawdust paths, the aromas of hot dogs, popcorn, and cotton candy mingled with the scent of desperation.

Gabriel Garde, Last of the True Wild West Sharpshooters, listened to Alhazarda's spiel trail off as he walked the midway and lamented for the days when people lined up three deep with quarters in hand in front of Alhazarda's stage. Back then, the mystic collected $30 or $40 on a good night, and for a long time they had all been good nights. Now he pulled down $5 or $10 at best, his heart gone from the hustle. Garde would've fired any other act that dropped off so much, but he sure as hell couldn't fire the great Alhazarda, aka Juan Sanjulian, formerly of Mexico City, formerly of Pancho Villa's guerilla army, and presently Garde's father-in-law.

Still, not all the blame lay with Alhazarda's lackluster showmanship. No doubt about it, the Depression hit the circus circuit as unmercifully as it did everything else, replacing a bounty of money and joy with dust and unfulfilled hungers of all kinds.

Garde sensed it in his bones, the world drying up.

A far cry from the days and nights when he had to push his way through the midway's elbow-to-elbow crowds, tonight he walked it with ease. Whether the seeds of the circus's loss sprouted from a bum stock market or the same curse that had stricken his dear wife Luna, he didn't know. Maybe the old man's bag held the answer. Three guesses and a peek inside. What if he saw nothing too? Or, worse, something he didn't like? His belief in Alhazarda's magic kept him struggling to squeeze every red cent he could from all the Dust Bowl burgs they passed, but he wanted as little to do with it as possible.

He kept the circus rolling for Luna. She had wrangled his guns and posed with a cigarette protruding from her pouty lips for him to shoot clear down to the nub. She had kept the business afloat when it overwhelmed him and inspired their performers and their crew. He missed seeing her in the frilly, red-and-black saloon girl outfit she wore for their act. He missed her dusky skin and shiny black hair, missed her warmth, her soft touch, her sweet breath.

With a sigh, Garde entered the sideshow. He waved to Sardon, the Snake-Man, his scaly, dry skin riddled with the cracks and scabs from the painful disease that earned him his name. He tipped his hat to the Bearded Lady, Angelica, who blew him a kiss, and then acknowledged the ushers, watching from the shadows, ready to intercede with any unruly visitors. One could look but not touch, nor taunt, nor throw food at the freaks. That policy—and the absence of a burlesque tent—had earned Garde and Rockfern's a reputation as a family circus. A devoted but swiftly diminishing audience awaited their return each season. Garde passed the others in the "Freak Show" without pause. To him, they were workers, friends—and family.

In the back of the tent stood the sideshow's main attraction.

Garde wrestled with the urge to call the glass box a coffin.

It stood vertically in a wooden frame, a seven-foot-tall cube of glass and iron. Lights mounted on top shone down on the interior. Another set lit the box from below.

Resting inside, Luna looked peaceful and as gorgeous as ever. The brown heat of her skin had cooled, bluing her lips and fingertips, and her hair had turned a crisp, silvery hue, but not a speck of rot had touched her. She looked ready to open her eyes at any moment. She wore her saloon girl outfit and black leather boots up to her knees, just as Garde had dressed her. Even lifeless and still, Luna charmed people. She was their top sideshow attraction most nights—Luna, the Living Porcelain Doll.

He wished she knew how popular she was.

Garde opened the box and held her cold hand.

He willed its warmth to return.

He reached in and rolled her head to one side on her pillow. Her wound remained, as if cast in wax and varnished to a glossy, wet sheen, unchanged since the bullet struck her skull. The silk pillow fringe hid it well. If the rubes ever saw that gaping, bloody hole in the back of her head, it would spoil the illusion of her perfection.

He told her how bad things were, how he was losing hope. If only she would tell him it would be all right, the way she used to do with her fingers brushing his cheek, he could find a way to keep going.

One year ago, four men tried to steal the gate money after closing.

Garde, on his way back to his and Luna's wagon after drinking with the freaks, surprised them with his irons. Two robbers died, two escaped. One's stray bullet clipped Luna solid in the back of her head.

What happened after that, Garde still couldn't explain.

Alhazarda had come running with his magic bag. Tears streaming from his eyes, he slid his daughter, Luna, into it, whispered words Garde didn't know, then did—well, Garde didn't know exactly what. Luna should've died that night, but she didn't. Nor was she exactly alive. But Old Al promised he could restore her if only they found the man who had shot her.

Another reason they played these podunk towns for bread and pennies.

Searching a year for the man who had shot Luna.

Garde assumed the robber had fled to another state by now, never to be seen again, but Alhazarda insisted the bag told him otherwise, that the man remained near. Despite his natural skepticism, Garde believed in the bag's magic. How could he not when Luna lay so perfectly preserved even after months gone by?

A fresh wave of gawkers neared. Garde kissed Luna's hand and then closed her box.

Almost show time.

Marybeth, daughter of one of Garde's clowns, assisted him with his act. The girl knew the routine well and worked liked a pro, but it felt wrong and dull without Luna. After Garde fired his final round for the night, a cloud of depression settled over him as it always did at that time—and with only the proceeds from another slow night, counting the gate failed to lift his mood.

If they stayed through the weekend, they'd take in enough to make it to the next town. He stared at the meager stacks of cash on his desk. His great-grandparents had founded the carnival; Rockfern had been his great-grandmother's maiden name. They had lived full, satisfying lives, a sharpshooting team like him and Luna, and that was all Garde had hoped for from life ever since childhood. From the moment he laid eyes on Luna when she and her father joined them outside San Antonio, Texas in the roaring days of a more prosperous decade, he had wanted her as part of it. He wondered if his great-grandparents ever faced hard times like this, if their life together ever seemed on the brink of extinction.

Sardon pushed into the trailer with a knock on the door.

"What's the good word, boss?" he said, then without waiting for an answer, "Don't tell me. I already heard this yarn, and it goes down better with a touch of liquid courage."

He set a whisky bottle on the desk and opened it.

"Maybe time to reconsider that buyout offer from Tom Mix."

"Mix only wants my trucks. Even the damn rail's too expensive these days. He'll take our gear, some of our animals, maybe a few acts he doesn't already have, and send the rest begging the WPA for jobs while he rides off with my family's legacy. Hell, I can outshoot that son of a bitch blindfolded and drunk but put a man in those damn movies, and everyone thinks he's some kind of special. Why people waste time watching pictures on a screen when they can see the real deal up close and personal, I'll never understand."

Garde produced two glasses and watched the snake man pour. Sardon's scaly skin ran all up and down his arms, over most of his torso and neck, and even on his legs. Little shiny patches of it dotted his face. Garde knew the name for it—eczema, psoriasis, something like that. Sardon had it worse than anyone ever should. The way he drank, Garde figured the man's liver looked as hard and crusty as his skin. A black-and-green snake looped itself around Sardon's neck and shoulders. It flicked its tongue at Garde.

He stared back into the black beads of its eyes.

"Old Al's pretty broken up being back here. You must be too, I reckon." Sardon refilled their drinks and swirled whisky around his glass. "At least you're not cracking up, though."

"How's that?"

"Old Al, he's been talking to himself all day, muttering under his breath, weird nonsense, like what he says when he's acting all wizardy. I saw him dragging that ugly sack of his out into the woods. What the hell's in there, anyway?"

"Damned if I know," said Garde. "Where was he heading?"

"West."

"Reason we didn't skip this town is the old bastard thinks we can find the guy who shot Luna here, and if we do, we can save her."

Sardon frowned. "Well, Garde, what do you think about that?"

Garde drained the rest of his whisky and pushed the glass away. He shrugged.

"No one likes to talk about it, boss, because we all loved Luna, but it's damn weird how she's, y'know, so well *preserved*."

"Don't I know it? At least, you ain't married to her."

"Aw, boss, I didn't mean nothing."

"I know." Garde stood and strapped on his gun belt.

"Heading west, you said? I ought to make sure Al's all right. Get him home okay."

"Al will be fine. He's a tough one."

Garde crossed the room. Sardon called him back.

"You think there's anything to all that ancient powers of the Persian desert bullshit?"

"Naw. Alhazarda's from Mexico City. He's never even been to Canada, let alone Persia. He bought that bag off some old street shaman in Mexico City. Used it to con Pancho Villa by making predictions about his battles. Lucky guesses, was all. Except maybe when he warned Villa about being assassinated. That panned out. But, hell, he could've known other ways, and that's why he fled to Texas to escape revenge. When my family met him and Luna, he went by John Chihuahua and worked as a traveling salesman with two samples cases. One held Spanish Bibles."

"What about the other one?"

"Not Bibles."

Alhazarda had been half in the bag by closing time and hadn't wandered far. His low, furtive voice drew Garde deeper into the dark woods.

Among the trees, a lantern flickered.

Garde crept up on a small clearing crisscrossed by several fallen trees. There, Alhazarda stared into the open bag.

"Dwellers in Mictlan, servants of Mictlantecuhtli, oh, Xolotl, who rules death, attend your faithful, answer my plea, and grant me audience." Alhazarda repeated the chant in Spanish then again in English, cycling through it four times before he flinched from the bag as a pale light shimmered around its opening.

"Ah, blessed be Xolotl! All thanks to Mictlantecuhtli!"

A low voice answered from inside the bag, its tone familiar to Garde.

"Yes, tell me, are we close? Is the time right?" Alhazarda said.

The thing in the bag murmured its reply.

"You're sure?" Alhazarda said. "Here? Now? I never thought the day would come."

Garde inched closer. Alhazarda crouched on his haunches, blocking the interior of the bag from Garde's sight.

"I will do it! I will find the truth. I will punish the man."

The other voice sounded like wind through dry leaves.

"I'm sure if he knew the reward, he would—Yes, yes, okay, I understand. He must agree of his own will and without promise. A sacrifice of the spirit. Then the truth shall be revealed?"

Garde crept nearer. A dry stick cracked underfoot.

Alhazarda cinched the bag shut and shot to his feet. "Who's there?"

Garde stepped into the lantern light. "Only me, Al. Sardon said you'd walked off this way. Figured I'd make sure you got back safe and sound. Reckon maybe you had a bit too much to drink tonight. Hell, Al, you're white as a sheet and shaking. You better get to bed."

Garde gripped Alhazarda's shoulder and pointed him toward the carnival. He slung the closed bag over his shoulder.

"Whoof! What the hell you got in here?" he said. "Weighs a ton."

Alhazarda let Garde guide him. The old man looked frail and troubled as only the elderly can, as if possessed by a loss beyond the grasp of any younger man.

"Be careful with that," he said.

"You go it, Al."

When they reached Alhazarda's trailer, the old man snatched the bag away from Garde, dragged it inside, and slammed the door.

The next night, Garde put his all into his act.

He plugged a hole in every coin he aimed at, shot playing cards at remarkable distance, and then did it all over again while swinging a lasso. He even did the cigarette trick, blindfolding Marybeth, poking a lit Lucky Strike between her lips, and then knocking it free with a single, quick-draw. Marybeth beamed at his energy.

The crack of the shot and the crowd's applause made it feel like old times.

Better times.

Between performances Garde walked the midway, listening to the whirl of calliope music and chatting up the rubes. People lined up for cotton candy, peanuts, and hot dogs. They played all the games. A crowd watched Lester, the Geek, hammer nails up his nose, and a steady stream of gawkers flowed into the sideshow. Everyone seemed in good spirits for a change.

Inside the sideshow tent, Sardon slipped Garde his flask, and Garde took the first of many drinks that night. He carried on with a warm feeling in his gut. When he passed Luna's glass box, the mob of enthralled people gathered before it pleased him, and then he moved on.

From his dusty platform, Alhazarda's voice crackled with life Garde hadn't heard in it for a long time. The old man sure knew how to spin his patter. His energy swept up Garde's interest, but the way the bag hopped and bobbed at the end of its rope filled him with dread.

"You, sir!" Alhazarda pointed at Garde. "A gunfighter of the first stripe, a man of action, possessed of corded muscle and panther-like reflexes, won't you take the challenge? Guess the contents of this bag and have your heart's desire granted!"

Heat burned in the old man's eyes. His stare melted into Garde, whose face flushed when he realized Alhazarda really wanted him to play.

Garde tipped his hat. "Sorry, Al, old pal, I got another show to do." Garde drew his right pistol and spun it twice before shunting back at his hip. "But you ever need a man who does his guessing with his guns, you let me know."

The crowd laughed uproariously.

The circus ran late.

An hour before closing, people still lined up at the box office. Garde knew he risked a fine going past permitted hours, so he sweet-talked the mayor and sheriff on the midway, treating them to drinks at the beer cart, letting them beat him in a round of sharpshooting. Then after his last performance, he drifted, keeping an eye on business, his mood lighter by degrees but a ghost of how Luna had made him feel. He could barely see Sardon under the pile of snakes writhing around him. Perched in her high cage, Patrice in her feathered costume sang in the high-pitched trill that made her the Bird Girl. Angelica flirted with a group of admirers, mostly teenage boys less concerned with her beard than what her low-cut, spangled blouse contained.

Excited and whisky-buzzed, Garde found himself passing Alhazarda's platform again, although he'd intended to avoid it. Again the old man seized on him.

"Here, now, folks," he said. "Admire the stance and confidence of the last of the Wild West sharpshooters, Mr. Gabriel Garde. Would you like to guess what's in the bag, my friend? We've had many attempts tonight, from the ridiculous to the sublime, but not one single correct guess. Not a one. Might you not be the one to finally get it right?"

"No, not me. I got no idea what's in that sack."

Garde backed away.

"Nonsense! If anyone could know, it's you."

The edge in Alhazarda's voice stopped Garde cold.

"Don't underestimate the bag's power. Woven by blind acolytes of the greatest magicians who ever lived, blessed by mystics of the Persian desert, this bag wields life, death, and truth. It may stave off one, endow the other, or reveal the third—but only for those who play by its rules, and its rules are simple: three guesses then look inside. Only a quarter. Simple, simple. Step right up. Twenty-five cents. Guess correctly, win your heart's desire. View the future—or the past. Find answers to the questions that bring you sleepless nights. Now, Mr. Garde, I ask again, would you like to play the game?"

Garde struggled to sort his booze-clouded thoughts. Old Al meant something he wouldn't come right out and say. About the bag, the past, the truth—could he mean… Luna?

Garde caught his toe and tripped as he stepped onto the boards beside Alhazarda.

"What are you pulling?" he whispered.

Focused on the crowd, Alhazarda ignored him.

"The power of life and death lies in control of the soul. Save a soul, save a life. Condemn a soul, end a life. He who controls the bag, may do either. Now, sahib, have you decided on your guesses?"

"I'll guess whatever you want, Al. Just tell me straight out what you're getting at."

"Sahib, please, there are rules!" Alhazarda extended his open hand. "First, your quarter, the price of participation."

Garde laughed. He fished a quarter from his pocket and slapped it in Alhazarda's hand.

"Thank you! And, now, I must warn you that the bag brings a risk of cursing those who choose to guess. It is a slim chance, but sometimes what the heart most desires can be a curse. The truth too can be a curse."

"I always heard the truth shall set you free," Garde said.

"So be it! Your guesses, sahib?"

"Fine, fine, I'll go along. Figure you got a boxing kangaroo or a trio of trained poodles in there."

"Careful! I tell you that life and death hang in the balance, but you make jokes. Well, okay, sahib, that's two guesses, one more to go. You want to guess correctly, don't you?"

"Sure, Al, whatever you say."

"That's the bargain, and a bargain against the magic bag must be kept. One year ago I promised the bag the soul of the man who shot my daughter if only it would in return preserve and one day heal her."

The voices of the crowd lowered. The people remembered the robbery, the shooting, and the two dead robbers, but none of them knew about Luna. Most had heard her wounds had been superficial and assumed her sideshow appearance a new act.

"What are you talking about?" said Garde.

"Surely, sahib, it's obvious even to one of your questionable cognition what your third guess must be if you wish the truth, if you wish to be set free, to set us all free."

"No." Garde eyed the crowd, the worried expressions of the mayor and the sheriff among the confused onlookers. Alhazarda's spiel had turned from entertaining to disturbing, and no one dared look away.

"Do right by Luna. My daughter. Your wife. Make your last guess the right one."

"You expect me to guess Luna is in that bag?" Garde whispered.

"Sahib, I cannot advise you on what to guess. That would be cheating."

"You're a lunatic. I should've given you the boot years ago."

"Life brings regrets. Now, please, guess."

"Fine. I'll guess, old man, but the moment you open that empty bag, I'm throwing you out on your ass. My third guess is… Luna, my wife."

Alhazarda whirled to the crowd, nearly screaming, spittle flying from his lips. "There you have it, folks! A boxing kangaroo, trained poodles, or his mortally wounded wife. Could he be right? Could he be our first winner of the night?"

Alhazarda unknotted the rope and lowered the bag.

The sack creaked its way toward the boards.

People gathered from all over the carnival, drawn by the tension, all of them taut with anticipation. The sack struck the boards and hopped around.

Alhazarda opened the knot that kept it closed and passed the edges of the cloth to Garde. The last son of the Wild West sharpshooters took a deep breath—and then looked.

From the blackness within the bag, Luna's glowing face peered back at him. The face of a tormented angel.

Garde gasped. "Luna…?"

"Oh, Gabe, I'm so sorry. I wish you two fools had simply let me die," she said.

"Where have you been?" asked Garde.

Before Luna could answer a fierce, hot wind swept out of the bag and blasted Garde in the face. He stiffened and then fell over onto his back, open-eyed and utterly still. A scene from the past formed before his staring eyes—

—the night of the robbery. Luna walks the midway. The robbers wave pistols. The circus folk scream in fear. Garde draws his revolvers fast and fires. Gun smoke. Blood. Shouting. Two dead men. And the bullet that strikes Luna's head—fired by an unsteady hand, Garde's own. Too drunk, too drunk, too drunk by far from drowning his sorrows with the freaks, his vision blurred, his aim untrue. A shot meant for the third robber takes Luna instead—

—Garde's heart broke as the truth released him. White mist speckled with ivory lights flashed out of the bag. It flowed through the night, across the midway, into the sideshow tent, where it entered Luna, the living porcelain doll. Freed from his body, Garde rode there with it. He lingered like a ghost as a dead woman returned to life with a scream on her lips.

Everyone at Garde and Redfern's heard her horrible shrieking answer to her husband's last question. *Where have you been?*

"In Hell!" she cried. "Gabe, I've been in Hell!"

The white mist recoiled sweeping Garde's spirit with it into the bag. Weary and hoarse, Alhazarda tied it closed and hoisted it high, where it jumped in the air.

The crowd stood stunned. The bag shimmied and bounced on its string.

"Who shall guess?" Alhazarda cried. "Are there no souls here tonight brave enough to pit their wits against the ancient magic of the Persian desert?"

The sheriff stepped onstage to examine Garde's body.

In the sideshow tent, Luna, her wound healed, her flesh and hair returned to vitality, stepped from her glass box and wept.

The Driver, Under a Cheshire Moon

"Here's another one," the driver said. He flipped through the pages of the jammed-full scrapbook, and let it fall open to a newspaper clipping with the headline: UNBORN BABY STOLEN, MOTHER CRITICAL. "The mother pulled through but not the child. A boy. Got a respiratory infection and lasted about ten days. He died before his mother got out of the hospital. He's buried in the woods behind a recycling plant. Only three people know that."

He lifted a paper cup from the tray beneath the radio console and sipped coffee. "Getting warm in here, isn't it?"

The driver's-side window lowered as he pushed the button on the door. Soft, sweet-smelling air breathed into the car. The driver liked that about these remote places: the clean taste of the air and how clear the sky turned on a cloudless night like this one. He saw stars he'd never known existed when he lived in the city, stars spattered on the night like raindrops slamming against his windshield frozen in place by a lightning flash. He favored the quiet, too, because it helped him spill all the clutter from his mind.

He riffled the scrapbook, seeking another article, and then spread it flat for the woman in the passenger's seat. "Another one like that." He pointed to the headline, MOTHER KILLED IN BABY GRAB. "She died at the scene. Bled out into the snow outside her trailer. Her little girl was due in two weeks. Family posted a reward for tips. Five grand, I think, but they never had to pay it out. You mind some music?"

He flicked on the radio and hit scan. Three-second bursts of sound cycled through, talk and news, hard rock and rap, which he didn't like, and Latin music, followed by country, electro-pop, and then an oldies station, and he punched the button again, letting a song first popular in 1964 pour out of the speakers. He couldn't remember the name, but he recognized the melody, the jangly guitars, the upbeat rhythm, and the harmony. His ex-wife had requested the song at their wedding, but when the band played it, they were taking pictures and missed their chance to dance to it.

"They've gotten better with security at hospitals," he said. "One time I was there when the whole maternity ward locked down because one of the mothers stepped outside the security zone with her baby. They put bracelets on the babies, got sensors in them to trigger the alarm. Had to wait twenty minutes to get it sorted out and get the doors open again. I've never seen another woman so red in the face. The staff was nice about it, laughed it off, but it was uncomfortable laughter, you know?"

The scrapbook pages fluttered as his fingers tripped through them again and then stopped at another article. "See, this one here. A few years back, a woman pretending to be a nurse walked right out of the hospital with a baby and kept her for almost a week, so that's why they have the high-tech systems now. That girl was reunited with her parents, and the woman went to prison. She taught us all a lesson, though."

The song faded out on the radio, and a new one started. The driver lowered the volume. A serious expression came over his face.

"We're never more vulnerable than when we're infants or toddlers, and you'd think, logically, that kids should be safer as they get older, but it's kind of the opposite. I got sections here by age. Look."

The scrapbook creaked as the driver jumped around from page to page, holding each one close to the woman's face, so that she couldn't avoid it. The words and pictures showed clear and bright in the glow of the dashboard and the dome light. The headlines screamed without sound, crisp, black-and-white cries of children kidnapped, or beaten, or sold, or molested, or worse, and alongside each one a picture cropped from a snapshot or a school photo, a happy image incongruous to the extreme with the story.

"This kid was eight, and here's one who was twelve. This one was nine years old, this one sixteen, this one thirteen, and this one five. Maybe they grow smarter and more capable as they get older, but they become more exposed, too. See? All it takes is one bad decision. Walk down the wrong street alone after school—gone. Trust a lying stranger when you should turn around and run—gone. Wander away from your parents at the mall—gone. And kids, I mean, come on, kids make bad decisions *all the time*. That's a huge part of growing up, so you can count on it. Like sunrise and sunset."

The woman sniffled. Her wide eyes flashed white in the dark. Tears filled them, welled up, and rolled down her cheeks, streaking the edges of the duct tape stretched over her mouth. She twisted a little in her seat, but more duct tape held her tight, leaving only her left arm partly free. It held a quiet bundle nestled there: a baby swaddled in pink flannel.

"So, you read about all this awful stuff people do to kids, see it flashed all over the headlines, the stories covered for weeks, over and over, freaking anniversary specials for the unsolved cases every ten years, and you start to wonder. Know what I mean?"

The driver smiled. His passenger stared back at him, silent and fearful. He twisted around and looked at the injured man in the backseat.

"How about you? You know what I mean?"

The man didn't answer. He could barely manage to blink. Blood matted his hair to his scalp, and he looked wide-eyed and disoriented. He'd cracked his head hard against the steering wheel when his car ran into a ditch and probably had a concussion.

"What I'm getting at is they give the most play to whatever sells the most papers, pulls the highest ratings, or gets the most clicks, right?" said the driver. "What the hell is wrong with people who flock to these stories like they're prime-time entertainment? A kid goes missing, get the word out, put the picture everywhere right away, send out the Amber Alert so everyone sees it. Yeah, maybe it helps find the kid. That makes sense. *That's logical.* But this, on and on for weeks, and sometimes years." He tapped the cover of the bloated scrapbook. "This goes beyond the pale. I have seven or eight more books like this one, all as full of the same kinds of articles clipped from the papers, printed from the Internet. Makes me wonder if people have an unhealthy preoccupation with crimes against children. Or is it all those parents out there feeling relieved because they figure as long as they're reading about it happening to someone else's child, their children are safe. Really, though, no one is safe."

The driver studied the woman, waiting for a response. Maybe if he lowered her gag, she'd answer, but he doubted it. Her eyes glowed with terror so intense that he knew she'd never felt anything like it before in her life. He'd seen the look often enough. He knew the man in the backseat would've been equally horrified, if he weren't drifting in and out of lucidity, too addled to know the situation. Not that the driver really expected answers to his questions. Early on, starting out, he'd believed maybe he could learn from the people he took for rides, pick up some insight that would help him understand. When they did talk, though, they all said the same things, every one of them, as if they'd been scripted. They begged. They pleaded. They bargained with promises they couldn't hope to keep. They called on higher powers who offered only a stone ear.

"How can a healthy society see this shit in the news day in and day out and not turn permanently sick to their stomachs and insane with outrage? Why is it tolerated? Why aren't people gathering up the proverbial torches and pitchforks, rounding up the posse, and breaking down doors. Why aren't we marching on all our elected officials until they put a stop to it?" He was almost shouting, spraying saliva into the woman's face. He snapped through the scrapbook pages. "But no, you make it so easy. Look!"

The headlines riffled one after another, a bullet point history of cruelty and violence, of perversion, of grief, of lost children, of betrayed children, of children used and abused like beings less than human, of children made over into painted grotesques, of faces so young it hurt the soul to think of them any other way than happy. Hard words surrounded the pictures of the bright-faced and the vulnerable, pictures of faces that no longer existed, of innocence obliterated with all the force and certainty of a nuclear blast by brutal, subhuman adults. Only artifacts frozen in time remained now, faces and smiles that remained only in pictures and would never grow up, smooth and perfect faces that would never become wrinkled and gray. The woman twisted away from them, but the driver wrenched her face around and made her look.

"Look. It's so easy," he said.

The baby started crying, woken from its nap. It made soft, feline whimpers that grew into a full wail; her little hand poked out of her blankets and wiggled a pink curl of tiny fingers.

"Shhh," the driver said. "Sorry. It's okay, little one. I'm sorry."

He placed the scrapbook on the woman's lap, propped open against the dashboard, and took the baby from the crook of her arm. The woman jerked and wiggled, but she was bound too tightly to move. The driver cradled the girl against his chest and held her close to his face so he could see her delicate, dark eyes, so eager and filled with the awe of new life. He rocked her a bit and hummed a lullaby. The infant settled down again and drifted back into sleep. She was four months old.

"That's it," he whispered. "Everything's fine, little bird. There you go. No worries for you tonight."

He held the girl for a while and savored the cool air spilling into the car. He listened to the night sounds of insects and nocturnal animals rooting through the brush and to the woman's sputtering breaths punctuated by whimpers. The man in the back seat gasped in shallow huffs and didn't stir. The driver thought he must have been hurt much worse than he looked.

He nodded at the scrapbook. "Seen enough?"

He could tell she was trying to nod or shake her head, but she didn't know what he wanted to hear, and she couldn't focus enough to answer. Her whole body trembled, and she sobbed behind her duct tape gag.

"I always wished for a daughter," the driver said. "My wife and I, we tried. Damn, we tried. For a lot of years. We thought we could never give up hope. Went to see doctor after doctor, spent so much money I can't even say how much. Got us nowhere. Nothing worked for us. The doctors couldn't really tell us why. Sometimes, it's just like that, they said. That was that."

Peeling back a fold of the baby's blanket, the driver kissed her on the forehead, and then opened his door and stepped out of the car with her. He opened the driver's-side back door then leaned in to place the girl into the car seat fastened there. He shoved the wounded man's pale, rubbery hand clear of the straps and then snapped the girl into place without waking her. He closed the door and climbed back behind the wheel.

"Snug as a bug in a rug," he said. "I have a special feeling about her. She's going to grow up to be someone important, someone who makes a difference in the world. You must feel it, right? How wonderful is it having a child like that?"

A fast song came on the radio. The driver tapped his fingers against the steering wheel in time to the rhythm. His thoughts wandered and his gaze strayed toward the blackness of the trees and the midnight blue of the sky behind them where a Cheshire moon sliced clean and white among the endless pinpoints of stars. He emptied himself for several seconds, as if his mind had skipped a few beats or his soul had wandered off, but then he snapped back into the moment, and turned to the woman.

"I guess we could've adopted," he told her. "I wanted to, but we didn't have a dime left to our names by then. Plus, I think the whole process had taken too much of a toll on Lila. She left me. What she really wanted was a child to grow inside her, and she felt she might have a chance at that with another man. I can't fault her for that, can I? I wanted her to be happy. Always did. Still do, in fact."

The driver reached over and opened the glove compartment. He groped around among half a dozen discarded cell phones and a few pairs of sunglasses and then pulled out a notepad and a pen, exposing a wide hunting knife as he shifted things around. The woman saw the blade and squealed behind her gag.

"Hush, now," he said, snapping the glove compartment closed. "Don't wake her up again."

He twisted around to make sure the baby still slept and then righted himself in his seat. He handed the pen to the woman and held the pad where she could reach it. "Write down the address for me."

The woman's hand quivered so much she couldn't grip the pen upright or keep the tip pressed against the paper.

"It's okay. Take your time," said the driver. "Anyway, this all began about six months after Lila divorced me. Started with the clippings. Something drove me to start collecting them. Three years, and I've filled eight scrapbooks already. There were limits at first. Things had to be taken gradually. This isn't something you can leap into without thinking it through. It takes consideration and planning. Not that I ever had a choice. Not that I ever even had any doubts. But it pays to do things right."

The pen tipped sideways in the woman's hand. The driver reached out and righted it. "That help?"

She forced the tip over the paper, scrawling an address in long, shaky lines, and when she finished, the driver lifted the pad and took back the pen. He keyed he address into his iPhone. A map appeared with the route traced along it in yellow.

"You're not lying, right? I'll find out if you are. It won't do you any good, anyway."

She shook her head.

"Okay, I believe you," he said. "It helps to have good directions."

He tore the top sheet off the pad, folded it into his shirt pocket, and then he slipped the pad and pen into the driver's side door sleeve. He glanced once more at the map on his phone before propping it in the cup holder at his right.

"Excuse me for a second," he said.

The driver left the car. He walked around the other side and opened the rear, passenger's-side door. The man in the backseat spilled halfway out, and the driver caught him under the arms and dragged him along the ground and into the darkness in front of the car. He came back, closed the back door, and then sat down again behind the wheel, leaving the driver's door open. An irritating alarm chimed, announcing the key still hung in the ignition.

"There was only so much I could do at first," he said. "But once word spread they started pooling their resources, started keeping watch, tipping me off sooner and sooner, and now, well, as long as I'm in the area, I can pretty much act right when I need to. That's why I keep on the road, keep driving. They can kind of anticipate where I need to be and steer me in the right direction. They're not so good with the specifics, but I can usually piece things together.

"I figure I'll be making headlines soon. Eventually someone has to notice. Maybe that'll start something up. Maybe one day I'll be clipping a different kind of story, more and more, until, well—who knows? So, you want to see them?"

The woman shook her head. He didn't think she understood the question.

"I see them all the time, hear them all the time. It scared the hell out of me at first, but I got used to it. They'll show themselves to you, now, because our business is almost done. In fact, they kind of insist on it. As innocent as kids are, they can be cruel. They don't know any better, at least not until they grow up and learn different, but then with this bunch, that's never going to happen. And cruel is too good for some people."

The driver switched on the headlights.

In front of the car, the dazed man lay on the ground, propped against a boulder at the end of the dirt road, pale and dusty in the intruding brightness. Thick trees and brush cradled the road's end, forming a cove like a cupped hand. After a moment others stirred in this lonely, shadowed place—and children filled the little clearing and surrounding woods. Kids of all ages, sizes, and types, and dressed in a variety of clothing. The older ones held infants and babies in their arms. Some of them wore clothes decades out of style, while others looked like any kid who might be playing in the street today. They looked like kids everywhere do, except for how still they stood and how their haunted eyes stared at the woman through the car's electric light. Their gazes reached through the windshield like living threads of cold. They tightened their circle around the car.

"Wait here," said the driver.

He walked over to the dazed man and paused while he thought something over or maybe listened to a faint sound. Turning in lazy circles, he searched the ground.

The children watched him, their eyes like snuffed candle flames.

Three boys broke from the group, stood to the driver's left, and looked down. He glanced toward their feet. A heavy, grapefruit-sized stone sat there in the dirt. The driver lifted it, and then without hesitation, he slammed it against the man's head. The driver hit him again, a third time, a fourth time, pummeling him to the ground and bringing the rock down over and over until there was no part of the man's skull left unbroken, and the man didn't move.

The driver set the stone on the boulder and walked back to the car. He took the knife from the glove compartment and sliced the duct tape holding the woman to her seat. He dragged her to the rock, where he sat her down beside her man. She didn't resist. She looked at the corpse and the small faces fixated on her. Angry faces, though here and there a touch of pity lingered.

"You did the right thing, giving me the address," the driver said. "You damn well know her father is going to think it's some kind of miracle. And maybe it is. Who am I to say? I'll never meet him. He'll have to find out about you and your boyfriend from the police. Shit, all that sick crap in the trunk of your car ought to be more than enough to tell them who you are and what you had planned for the little girl. I can't believe you were fucking stupid enough to keep the mother's purse after you killed her. It's not like this was your first time. Anyway, they'll find it all back where I ran you off the road, and you know what?"

The woman didn't answer.

"When they find your bodies down here, no one in their right mind will give a shit that somebody beat your heads in with a rock and dumped you in the woods."

The woman made no sound when the driver hit her with the stone; she simply fell over onto her dead boyfriend and lay still while he bashed all shape from her skull.

The driver got back in the car, washed his hands with clean wipes, and checked on the little girl, who was still sound asleep. Her tiny closed eyes and parted lips held a tremendous beauty. Her warm, rich baby smell filled the car. All the kids who'd come as witnesses, the ones who'd helped and guided him, gathered around the car to see her.

They smiled and reached toward her with pale hands as if to pick her up, but cold and ethereal, they lacked substance if not something like love. The driver saw more and more of them each day. Word really spread fast and wide about what he did and how they could help him. He had a feeling one day his travels might even take him across oceans and around the world. That suited him fine. He had no desire ever to stop moving again.

A few of the kids got in the car and rode along as the driver backed up the dirt path and drove back on the highway. They watched the baby sleep, and they glanced out the window as they passed the smashed up car of the people the driver had killed. They watched as, half an hour later, he parked before a quiet house on a suburban street, lights on inside.

The driver emerged, unlatched the car seat from the back, and carried it up to the front porch. The baby woke up and stared at him without making a sound, seeing him for the last time, exploring a vague face she would never remember. The driver liked that she would grow up to forget him. It felt right. He set the car seat outside the front door, then returned to his car and started the motor. He sat on the horn until the front door opened.

When he saw a man step out, fall to his knees, and throw his arms around the child, the driver floored the gas and roared away into the night.

The cold, strange kids rode with him, staring out the windows in the idle way kids do on a long trip. One held her hand out, waiting for wind to lift it up and down like a wave, but the air found no purchase there.

Without taking his eyes off the road, the driver said, "So, where to next?"

Living/Dead

"Shit, Phil, I'm over here dying, and you're rubbing it in you've got a girlfriend to lie to about stuff," Gustav said, frowning.

"I'm not rubbing in anything, and you're *not* dying. You twisted my arm to come with you, the least you can do is cover for me with Lana. Tell her we caught the Tarantino revival at the AMC if she asks. She finds out I went to Everlasting Love speed dating at Mercer's—even for your benefit—I'll be sleeping on the couch for a month if she doesn't throw me out."

"She'll *forgive* you, though, right? Because she still *loves* you, doesn't she?"

"That's not the point."

"What's the point then? That at least *you've* got someone to lose?" Gustav's voice rose an octave in pseudo-near-hysteria, a trait that amused me—and apparently only me, although it had made me laugh since we first met as college roommates. "All I have is an empty apartment waiting for me at home. I don't even have a cat. Or plants. My phone only rings when my mother calls. And I might die any day! Alone! With no one to raise me from the dead!"

"Chill, drama queen. I'm doing you a favor tonight. Don't make me regret it."

Gustav sighed. "Fine. Can I say we went to see *Star Wars XXIV*?"

"No, you cannot. Lana knows I hate those movies. Say what I told you to say, and drop this death's door crap. You tell the women in Mercer's you're dying, they're not going to check the little box next your name on their romance bingo cards."

Gustav stopped walking. "Jesus Christ, Phil, you're my best friend. Some concern would be appreciated."

"Some concern would be appropriate if you were actually sick or dying. What exactly is it you think is wrong with you this time anyway?"

"I'm not sure. I get aches and pains. Chills. Shakes. Headaches. Stomach cramps. Flashes of light before my eyes. It might be a brain tumor. Or a blood disease. Maybe a nervous system disorder. I've ruled out malaria and trypanosomiasis, but the doctors have to run more tests. An MRI, maybe a CT scan."

"How many MRIs have you had this year?"

"I lost count."

"You know, I've never seen you truly sick a day in your life. Not even a sniffle. You're one of the healthiest people I know. How about I go with you to your next appointment and order your doctor to stop feeding your hypochondria under threat of a severe ass-whooping—"

Gustav gasped. "Don't talk like that about Doctor Cardigan!"

"—because you need to drop this nonsense and get on with your life. The only reason I'm here with you tonight is because if you meet someone, maybe you'll regain your senses and start living again instead of obsessing over dying."

"Easy for you to say. You have Lana."

"And you should've married Carrie the second she said yes instead of nitpicking and obsessing over everything and driving her crazy."

"She ignores my e-mails now. Won't even take my calls."

"Would you if you were her?"

"I guess not. But what if—well, what if deep down she still loves me? That might be enough to reanimate me, right?"

"You're not dying." I slapped Gustav on the back. "You're in perfect health. Look both ways before you cross the street, don't play with guns, avoid skydiving, and you've got all the time you need to find the love of your life."

We rounded a corner, almost colliding with a living/dead couple hurrying in the opposite direction, an olive-skinned brunette in her thirties and a man who looked a couple of years gone, his flesh not yet decayed to the leathery wrinkles that eventually came to all the loved dead. They rushed past us as fast as the man's stiff joints allowed, glancing back at a mob of protestors down the block across the street from Mercer's Pub.

More than two dozen men and women marched in a circle, some waving poster board signs that read: "Love Life Not Death," "Just Say No to Necrophilia," and "Stop Molesting the Dead!" All of them wore green and red T-shirts printed with the familiar sealed coffin logo of the Society for the Preservation of Natural Death. SPOND. The "old school burying brigade." Or, as I referred to them: douche bags. That people so full of fear and hate needed to worry about reanimating against their wishes made no sense. I mean, who loved these fools? Maybe it's true there's someone for everyone, but it's hard to imagine. This group wore crimson baseball caps and arm bands, tagging them as corpse burners who wanted to deny all rights to the living dead. The kind of assholes who fire-bombed re-awakening centers and date night funeral parties.

At the opposite end of the block, two living/dead couples, gray-haired ladies with their long-dead husbands, decked out in suits and dresses for a night on the town, turned the corner, halted when they saw the protest, then rushed back the way they'd come. One of the protestors hurled a rock in their direction then rushed them, giving up the chase after a few steps and rejoining the protest.

Gustav eyed the protestors. "Maybe if we hurry we can still catch that Tarantino revival."

"What? No. Don't let these ignorant morons rob you of a chance for true love. They're all bark and no bite. Stare them down and move on."

"I don't know if I'm up to it. Between doctor's appointments and tests and Caitlin getting on my case every day, I'm red-lining this week."

"Caitlin's still ripping into you?"

"She kept me till eleven four nights this week to run through our West African malaria stats again and triple check Guatemalan DTP vaccination field reports—and found not a single error. Then she reminded me I need to treat working for the World Health Organization like an honor not a job. She's fishing for an excuse to get rid of me, I'm sure of it. If she axes me I'll be unloved and unemployed. Let's just go to the movies. I can't face the rejection."

"No, no, no, don't think about striking out. Think about how good you'll feel when one of the ladies wants you to ask her out on a date. Focus on that. Relax. You can do this."

Gripping Gustav's shoulder, I guided him across the street toward Mercer's, giving him no chance to drag his feet. I kept us moving to hide how nervous the SPOND scum made me—so jittery I jumped back two steps when a woman in a SPOND shirt popped out from an alley, blocked our path, and shoved photocopied pamphlets at us. She looked about twenty-five, with chestnut hair pulled back in a bushy pony tail. Her oversized T-shirt hung down over a pair of jeans.

"Life is for the living. Let the dead die. Don't you think it's a selfish sin to love the dead? We're born mortal. We should die mortal. Love *shouldn't* conquer death. Stay away from this den of iniquity!"

Gustav stared at the woman, wide-eyed and pale.

"It's only a pub. Try it sometime. You might like it. I'll even spot you a round," I said.

"Don't be fooled! The people in there only want to prolong their earthly existence, but that's not what love is for. We all must meet our maker one day. Nothing should come between us and ultimate grace."

She pushed her pamphlets, printed with the headline "The Dead Must Die," at our hands. We refused them. Gustav looked rattled, so I steered him around her.

"There's nothing more natural than love enlivening people," I said.

"No! It's the Devil's work!" she said.

Gustav glanced back at her, frowning, growing paler.

"Why do those people want everyone to die when they die? Why do they want *me* to die? They're all healthy. That's why! They're not dying like me!" he said.

"You're not dying either, you raging hypochondriac."

Gustav stumbled and clutched his chest. He panted for breath, emitted a gakking noise, and sweated bullets. His eyes bulged, and he shuddered. I yawned and shook my head.

"Deep breaths, amigo. In and out. Let it go."

I squeezed Gustav's shoulder. He trembled and coughed some more while mopping his brow with a handkerchief from his pocket. The SPOND woman watched him, shameless, her pamphlets fluttering in her hand. I gave her a "see what you did" glare that sent her scurrying.

"Don't worry about these blockheads. They're misguided and ignorant. Bullying people and poking holes in other people's happiness makes them feel good. It gives them a false sense of security. It's freaking pathological."

"Yes, yes, you're right. Of course, you're right."

Gustav tucked his handkerchief away. Before he could voice any further doubts, I opened the door of Mercer's and shoved him inside.

The voices of the protestors faded as the door closed. Air conditioning blasted us. The aromas of polished wood and beer filled my nostrils. Men and women furred the bar like bristles on a hairbrush, anxious, avoiding each other's eyes. Some sipped frothy pints, others technicolor cocktails. A few held steaming mugs. Bob Marley played over the speakers, continuing the reign of yesteryear's mellow rock. It was always Marley, or the Stones, or U2, or, god help me, Van Morrison at these things. Echoes of simpler times before the Reanimation Revolution, when matters of the heart were less life and death, and it was okay to die lonely. The music of a dead generation seemed like a stamp of approval for singles mixers and community matchmaking socials of all kinds these days, as if a secret love spell hid woven in their chords and melodies. I'd been to more than a few such events before I met Lana. When I stopped going, my life and music choices improved immeasurably.

Rejuvenated by the pub atmosphere, Gustav led us to the dating hostess, a knockout blonde in a snug blue dress with reckless décolletage. She smiled, and Gustav finger-combed his hair and stood a little straighter, as if he had a chance with a woman like that.

"Welcome, gentleman. I'm Barbara Ballard. Dating with us tonight?"

"Yes, Gustav Marino and Phil Kowalczyk. We signed up last week," Gustav said.

Barbara leaned over to find our names on her list. Her low-cut dress draped away from her body, and Gustav locked eyes on everything her loose clothing revealed: the edges of a lacy black bra shaping ample cleavage and perfect curves of smooth flesh. I kicked Gustav in the shin, but he didn't get the message. Barbra caught his clumsy gaze as she checked our names off and straightened.

She raised an eyebrow. "I don't have to remind you to behave yourselves tonight, do I? This isn't about getting lucky. It's about finding true love."

Gustav continued ogling. I elbowed him in the ribs, and then the light switched on in his brain. He finally met Barbara's stare, but she shook her head at him.

"Gustav has been off the dating scene for a while. He's a little rusty," I said.

"I remember what it's like between relationships. No one likes to go unloved too long. Accidents can happen anytime." She peeled a pre-printed nametag and handed it to me to stick on my shirt. She peeled one for Gustav and slapped it askew on his chest, pushing him back two steps in the process then turning her hand to make sure he saw her sparkling engagement and wedding rings. "But you'll get nowhere treating women like that, Gus."

"It's Gustav," he said.

Barbara handed us our dating cards, and said, "Have fun, *gentlemen*."

Gustav and I honed in on the last free spaces at the bar to await the dating rounds. Chairs and tables, set with timers, scorecards, and pencils stood ready for us, closed off on one side of the pub. A crowd of people filled the other side, the two sections separated by the bar. Several living/dead couples, men and women, women and women, men and men, even a trio or two, intermingled with an equal variety of living/living couples in the open dining area. With one's return from the dead riding on the outcome, the dating and mating game qualified as a spectator sport, especially among those who'd already taken the plunge. Their weirdly sweet interest gave me an uneasy twinge, compounded by all the people in the crowd who'd died young. Corpses with no signs of trauma, disease, or other obvious cause of death who looked like they'd been in their twenties or thirties when they kicked the bucket. Some people chose death over marriage, with one partner killing themself and then by reanimating, proving both partners' love and cementing their commitment. Suicide weddings. Lana and I had discussed it, but we hoped to have children one day. The presence of so many living/dead explained the protestors' presence: Mercer's was a living/dead hotspot.

A waiter passed bearing a tray laden with plates of bar food—burgers, Buffalo chicken wings, French fries—as well as dishes piled high with meat so raw trickles of blood ran through its folds. That gave me a quick shiver. Out for dinner on our anniversary last year, Lana and I sat beside a living/dead couple locked in an all-out nuclear armageddon of a lover's quarrel. The man broke up with his dead girlfriend then and there. The second he renounced his love for her, Lana, I, and everyone else in the dining room tensed like cows outside a steakhouse. The dead woman overturned the table, lunged at her boyfriend, missed, and then whirled and came at me, mouth wide, teeth bared, snarling, lips frothing with putrid spittle and remnants of merlot. All her self-control and sense of identity eradicated by heartbreak, no love left to keep her sane, her natural craving for live flesh seized her. The maitre'd, who'd been watching the fight escalate, shot her in the head before she reached me. The restaurant comped our meal and slapped her ex with the standard break-up and disposal charge, then sent the prick home.

The dead never recover from rejection. The dark side of true love in action.

The bartender slid us a couple of beers Gustav had ordered.

I raised my mug, said "Cheers," and waited for Gustav to clink glasses. He rolled his eyes as he did it, and then we drank.

"Gustav? That *is* you. What in the hell are you doing here?"

A voluptuous redhead with a modest, lyrical brogue, about our age, and on the short side approached us. Her hair hung in waves of curls around her fair-skinned face. A pair of thick eyeglasses that should've looked geeky only emphasized her crystal blue eyes. She wore a white blouse, a hip-hugging gray skirt, and high heels. Gustav lowered his mug, half-choking as he swallowed wrong.

"Caitlin…? Um, wow, yes, hi! Funny to run into you here."

"Funny, yes, especially since you e-mailed me you had to leave early tonight for a doctor's appointment. I can't believe you *lied* to me." She punched his arm. Not gently.

"Oh, well, my appointment was canceled, and then my friend, Phil—have you met Phil? Phil got nervous about this whole speed dating thing and asked me to tag along, and—"

"You're such a terrible liar. This is Phil, the same Phil of Lana and Phil, about whom you complain endlessly when you should be compiling dysentery statistics. Did you break it off with Lana, Phil?"

"Nope," I said.

"See? Now why would Phil be here unless it's the other way around who got nervous?"

I looked at Gustav. "You complain about us?"

"No, I—"

Caitlin cut him off before he could defend himself.

"About how lucky you are, about how happy you are, about how lonely it is being a third wheel around you and Lana, about how hard he has it, and you don't understand, and won't you be sorry if he dies alone, unloved, and yadda yadda yadda." Caitlin tapped her index and middle fingers and her thumb together, the universal sign for jibber-jabber.

"What gives?" I asked Gustav.

Gustav downed a slug of his beer. "She's exaggerating."

"I hope so, man. I never complain about you to my crew in the studio."

"The only thing he goes on about more is how he's at death's door from some disease or another, a different one every week. I never had anyone on my staff take so many long lunches for doctor's appointments," said Caitlin.

"That I believe," I said.

"It doesn't affect my work or interfere with anyone else's. Despite my health problems, I do my job well," said Gustav.

Caitlin's annoyed expression softened to one of admiration. "You do it beautifully, brilliantly, even. You're an artist with your stats and analysis, and you know the diseases better than half the doctors we use in the field. But you shouldn't lie when you need time off. I'll let you slide this once but never again."

"I'm so sorry. It just seemed easier to say it was another doctor's appointment than to explain… all this." Gustav gestured to the speed dating tables. "It won't happen again. But why are you here, Caitlin?"

"Same reason you are. Maybe we'll be matched."

She grinned with a twinkle in her eye and squeezed his arm, and all the late nights and extra attention Gustav bitched about suddenly made sense to me. Gustav remained too pigheaded to see it, though, and the prospect of dating his boss—even for five minutes—left him opening and closing his mouth as he grasped for a response. The music faded out on the PA system then for Barbara Ballard to speak, saving him from having to produce one—and mercifully sparing me the Aerosmith ballad starting. Ballard called for everyone's attention, her vivaciousness capturing the excitement in the crowd. Every face in the room turned her way. Even the people in the dining section of the pub fell silent.

"Thank you for joining us tonight. In a couple of minutes, we're going to get started, and I'd like to cover the rules. Most important, you're here to find someone to love, someone to love you back—someone who'll hold your life-after-death in their hands. Don't waste time lying or pretending you're someone you're not. Life's too short, and death is forever. Be yourself. Be honest. Let the connection happen. Everlasting Love has an enviable 72 percent success record, making us the third-ranked matchmaker in the state. Our motto is: 'In death do we join forever!' And we take it to heart. You're in good hands."

I pointed to Caitlin, her back to us while she listened, and whispered to Gustav, "Your boss is into you."

Gustav's mouth gaped. "Not a chance. She's constantly on my case."

"When I had a crush on Donna Jones in the sixth grade, I pulled her hair and mocked her shoes," I said.

"It's not like that."

"She called you an artist."

"Ugh, sarcasm. See what I'm dealing with?"

"Why do you see everything in the most negative way imaginable? You're hopeless."

Barbara carried on, stating the rules. Women sat at the tables. Men rotated from one to the next, according to the rosters on our dating cards, five minutes per table. The ladies always spoke first, and they chose who they might want to see after the event. Barbara urged everyone to replenish their drinks before we began. A man entered through the front door, letting in the protestors' chanting voices. I couldn't make out their words, but the emotion came through loud, clear, and unpleasant. The door swung closed and shut them out again.

The next second a front window pane shattered as a rock hurtled through it.

The crowd around the bar flinched and sent up a jumble of screams. Only Barbara stood her ground. The rock landed, tumbled across the floor, and stopped by her feet. She snatched it up, stamped to the front door, opened it, and then hurled the rock back outside, shouting, "Hey! I'm trying to work here!"

When she slammed the door shut, the crowd burst into applause—nervous, uncertain applause, but applause nonetheless.

"I apologize for the disruption. The manager has called the police, and if any of you want to leave now I understand. Contact my office tomorrow, and we'll arrange for a full refund."

A handful of people, mostly older living/dead couples but a few of the speed-daters, too, paid their tabs and slipped out the side door. Barbara waited till they left.

"Ladies, if you'd take your seats by number, please," she said.

The women sat, and a minute later the men seated themselves at their starting tables. The women flipped their hourglass timers and launched their first date.

A pretty woman, around twenty, wearing a pink blouse, her blonde hair styled in a wave off the left side of her head, offered me an eager, hopeful grin and introduced herself as Nina. Her sweet voice and innocent face made me feel like a heel for participating under false pretenses. I glanced at Gustav, paired with an older woman, her impatience for his awkwardness apparent in her long fingernails rattle-tapping the table.

Nina talked nonstop about her college for three minutes, then said, "Oh, I'm so sorry, I'm rambling."

I smiled. "It's all good. Only you're so young to be doing this. You must meet tons of guys in college. Why are you wasting time with geezers like me?"

"Oh, come on. What are you thirty, thirty-five? You're not old. At least, not too old for me. Wait, that's not what I meant. The thing is—I probably shouldn't say this—but... I suck at relationships. My first love came when I was thirteen, and it only lasted six months. Once your first love comes your parents' love won't reanimate you anymore, and now I'm afraid of dying unloved and not reanimating. I've had, like, a thousand boyfriends, and none of them stuck, and I really worry about being dead, you know? That makes me sound desperate, doesn't it?"

I eyed the last grains of sand spilling into the bottom shell of the hourglass. "No, it's all right. You're beautiful, you're sweet, and you're young and healthy. One day, you'll find true love."

"You seem so sure."

"I'm positive. True love comes when you least expect it."

Nina smiled, beaming at me then scribbling notes on her card as I shifted to my next dating station. One down, nineteen to go. I swallowed the last of my beer and ordered another—with a shot of whisky.

Although they were too polite to call me out, my next three matches sensed my lack of genuine interest. But I kept up my side of the small talk while I watched Gustav strike out with date after date. His fourth woman actually stopped talking and sat with her arms crossed on her chest, staring at the ceiling while the sand ran out. By my ninth date, it hurt to smile. I shared none of the nervous energy or need buoying everyone else through the grueling ritual. I was in love; I was covered by Lana at home, where I belonged, and I wanted to get up and go. Then Gustav—sitting near enough for me to hear him say "mystery blood disease" and "malignant ennui"—crashed and burned with an Indian woman with striking, deep-set eyes. Like he did each time before, he looked to me for support to keep going, and I knew if I wasn't right there in the thick of it with him, setting an example for him to follow, he'd have bailed out after that one.

I was sliding into my seat across from lucky number thirteen when the front of the pub erupted with a blast of heat and light that transformed the wall into a storm of wood splinters and glass shards tearing through the air. An oven-blast cyclone pummeled me to the table, tumbling me and it onto Shaniqa, a divorced mother of two with her own computer security business, who proved surprisingly muscular as we crashed to the floor.

A roaring filled my ears for half a second before deafness overcame me. A jumble of table legs and chair backs, glasses, dishes, and wood fragments, even Shaniqa and her oversized handbag punched and buffeted me until abruptly the movement ended and a terrifying stillness descended.

I lay entangled with Shaniqa long enough for the throbbing in my head to subside and to confirm that all my limbs remained attached. When I sat up, the dim wail of sirens cut through the muted screams and commotion broiling around me. Smoke stung my nostrils. Fire flickered around the shattered front windows. I groped my way onto my knees then checked Shaniqa, who, aside from shock, seemed unhurt.

I spotted Nina crying across the room and dragged myself over to see she was only stunned. Damn lucky. People lay on the floor or slumped in chairs all around the pub, many bleeding, their clothes torn or singed. At least none looked dead or dying.

Dying…

"Gustav?" I called. "Where are you, man?"

I saw Gustav's last date, a Japanese woman in a silver dress, helping another woman pack a napkin to a wound on her forehead. I scanned the room again, nothing, then looked lower and saw Gustav's shoes. He lay face down by his last dating station.

"Oh, no, Gustav!" I rushed to him.

Being so accustomed to watching the dead move, it's easy to forget how deeply disturbing an utterly still body can be. Gustav lay spread-eagled, a splintered piece of window frame and several shards of glass driven into the back of his neck at the base of his skull. I knelt beside him, reached for the spike, then drew my hands back, knowing I could do nothing. The wood had penetrated into his brain or his spinal cord. Blood welled up around it and spilled onto the floor. I sat with my head on my knees, trying to shut out the chaos.

A hand fell on my shoulder. I looked up into the eyes of Lana. My Lana.

Scratches across her forehead dripped beads of blood, and her mascara ran in streaks with her tears. She favored one leg and leaned on a man I didn't know. For several seconds, I waited for the hallucination to clear, for Lana's face to vanish or give way to another woman's. Instead, she knelt and hugged me.

"Thank god you're alive. I couldn't live with myself if you'd died tonight," she said.

Wrapping my arms around her, I eyed the man. "What are you doing here, Lana?"

She leaned back and glared at me. "What are you doing here speed-dating?"

"I came for Gus. Moral support."

I pointed to Gustav's corpse. Shock in Lana's eyes told me she hadn't recognized him lying face down.

"Oh, god, Gus!" More tears flowed down her cheeks.

"Why are you here? I thought you were staying home to get some extra work done."

"I've been meaning to tell you. I really have. You said you were going to the movie with Gus, so I called Anderson, and we met here for drinks. We've been seeing each other. Not for that long, and I didn't mean for it to happen this way, but it did, and I was planning to tell you soon, and—oh, Phil, I'm so thankful you didn't get killed tonight."

"Because you don't love me anymore."

117

"Phil, I—"

"Don't say anything. Just leave me with Gus."

"Gus!"

Lana and I both turned when Caitlin cried out his name.

Aside from a few rips on her blouse, she seemed unhurt, but tears gushed from her eyes, and she trembled. Her beautiful, fair face and sparkling blue eyes twisted in such a show of grief and shock that I felt my own heart break a little more. I'd teased Gustav about his anxieties, but he'd been right all along. Death could come anytime, and love could be fleeting. I'd taken Lana for granted, trusting my life in her heart, and a few feet to either side might've proved that the worst mistake of my life tonight. Turning my back to Lana, I put my arm around Caitlin and cried along with her. Crazy as Gustav was, he'd been a good friend, as loyal and generous as he was neurotic. I wished platonic love possessed enough passion to ignite reanimation, but every study ever done had concluded that it simply didn't have the fire to bring the dead back to life.

My hearing gradually improved, and outside Mercer's, more sirens wailed. Ambulances, maybe. They couldn't possibly arrive in time. On the street, the sounds of fighting erupted as the crowd from Mercer's rushed to confront the SPOND scum and police reached the scene.

Caitlin shoved me away and then punched Gustav's shoulder.

"What the hell?" I said.

She did it again. And again. Then her petit fists launched a flurry of blows upon Gustav's prone body, and she muttered under her breath: "Stupid, stupid, stupid…"

I grabbed Caitlin's hands and stopped her. "Whoa! Hold it, before you hurt yourself."

Caitlin glared at me, her face tear-soaked. "How stupid can one man be? All those times I practically threw myself at him. Tight skirts and stopping by his office day after day. Keeping him late until we were the only ones in the office—*alone*—night after night. He never got the damn hint! Not once. I came here tonight for him. I saw it in his e-mail, and I came, hoping…" She slipped a hand loose and hit Gustav once more. "What does a woman have to do to get a… a… brilliant, oblivious jerk to ask her out?"

Caitlin pressed her face against me and sobbed into my chest.

Behind her, Gustav stirred. My heart skipped a beat.

Gustav rolled over and winced as he lowered his head, thunking the wooden spike on the floor. He looked the palest I'd ever seen him. He frowned at my tears. My heart ached for him, but at the same time, a slow-growing joy blossomed in it. What I'd told Nina had been right: *True love comes when you least expect it.*

Gustav sat up. "What happened?"

I squeezed his shoulder. "There's bad news, good news, and terrible news."

"Tell me already!"

"The bad news is you have to cancel all your doctor's appointments because you're dead. The good news is someone loves you enough to reanimate you."

"Oh, god, I'm dead!" Gustav's eyes widened. "Wait, who… who loves me? Is it Carrie?"

"It's not Carrie."

Before I could say another word, Caitlin broke away from me. She hugged Gustav, kissed him on the lips, and then buried her face against his bloody neck. He looked up at me, his face a cataract of confusion.

"I told you, man. She called you an artist. You need to learn how to listen to women."

Moving hesitantly, Gustav took Caitlin in his arms. A moment of awkwardness passed before he settled into the embrace. Caitlin raised her head. He stared at her for a second, then, as if wondering how she tasted, he kissed her—and in death Gustav looked happier and more relaxed than I'd ever seen him in life.

"What's the terrible news?" he asked me.

I made a face and nodded at Lana, taking comfort in Anderson's arms. Demonstrating uncharacteristic insight, Gustav read the situation and gave me the kind of pitying stare I usually directed his way.

"I'm so, so sorry," he said. "But, listen, it's like you told me, you're young and healthy and you've got all the time you need to find the love of your life."

"Fuck you, man, stop rubbing it in you've got a girlfriend now."

Anderson led Lana away. Gustav settled into Caitlin's fervent embrace.

I sat on the floor beside them and wondered if Nina or Shaniqa might check the little box next to my name on their date card.

The Chamber of Last Earthly Delights

July 13, 1921

For now, I can only record here that I write this on the pages left unused in my son's journal, recovered from his personal belongings while I processed his decapitated body for disposal last night. The law forbids funerals to those who surrender their lives to the Government Lethal Chambers. I may mourn him only here.

July 14

My son's life and last days deserve whatever meager memorial I may provide, but tears overcame me yesterday morning and forced me to set down my pen. In supporting the passage of the progressive public euthanasia statutes, a feat accomplished only a scant fourteen months past, I never considered that the flesh of my flesh and blood of my blood might find his life so utterly abhorrent and torturous he would choose to end it. I believed my family contented, blessed with a modest but comfortable degree of financial security due to inheritances and investments, and free of the depression and moral ills that often inspire individuals to self-murder. Only a short time ago, my wife, Eliza Mary, and I proudly anticipated our son, Ronald, and our daughter, Sarah Jane, starting families of their own one day.

Mercy alone shaped my views on the wisdom of the lethal chambers. Daily I witnessed the plight of those with debilitating afflictions, mental disorders, and moral weaknesses that stranded them in the gutters, where they suffered from the elements and the abuses of men and women who treated them worse than vermin. The lethal chambers offered a painless means of salvation for these wretched folk. When my district's city councilman, Mr. Winslow Nebbins, an ardent champion of the program, offered me a supervisory position in the inaugural lethal chamber last summer in gratitude for my efforts toward the cause, my eventual rise through the ranks of the city's civil service appeared quite secure.

I foresaw no hint whatsoever of Providence's sharp reversals that soon stripped away these cherished futures. Eliza laid to rest in the churchyard six months thence, her life claimed by a fever. Sarah Jane unseen and unheard since her mother's demise, lost, abducted, or worse.

Now Ronald, too, has departed. Alone, I catalog the items removed from him before I consigned his headless corpse to the crematory furnace: my grandfather's pocket watch, which I gave him on his sixteenth birthday, part of an heirloom set that included gold earrings, passed to Sarah Jane, from my grandmother, and a gold and ivory brooch given to Sarah in trust for her first daughter; Ronald's incomplete diary in which I write; a copper amulet enameled with a citrine design of unknown meaning; and a copy of *The King in Yellow*, an infamous book too easy to acquire despite municipal seizures of its reprintings in Paris, Boston, Rome, and other cities. I presume my rakish nephew, Tyson, who studied art for a year in Florence, brought the damn thing back from Europe.

My only comfort comes from having been spared the sight of Ronald's lifeless face, a sour boon granted by the nature of the lethal mechanism within the Terminal Chamber.

But I cannot bear to think of this any longer today.

July 15

Mr. Nebbins arranged for me the favor of a few days' release from my duties. I'm ashamed to admit I spent the hours since in the company of a whiskey bottle cached in a hat box before our nation embarked upon its great experiment in prohibition.

It occurred to me upon rousing from my alcoholic stupor that the means of euthanasia utilized within the lethal chambers remains widely unknown despite their growing popularity. Should anyone ever chance to read these words, some insight into these procedures may benefit their understanding. The lethal chambers strive to offer tranquility, comfort, and an air of dignity and affirmation to all those who enter. I cannot speak to the chambers operating in Atlanta, Boston, Chicago, and Washington, D.C., nor those soon to open in Denver, Milwaukee, and half a dozen other cities, but New York City's chamber presents a bronze entrance framed by Ionic columns preceded by a sculpture garden of the "Fates." A juvenile Clothos, eagerly spinning the fabric of life, greets one upon entering, smiling, a lifelike light in her marble eyes.

Next, Lachesis, mature, statuesque, a steady gaze, like the eyes of a carpenter setting beams, fixed on the measured cloth draped on her fingers. Lastly, one encounters Atropos, a vision aged in ideal fashion to suggest the promise of life fulfilled, earthly duties completed, and rest well earned, a pair of long scissors in her hand. Cleverly carved and attired, the androgynous figures appeal to all.

Upon entering the chamber proper, patrons gaze upon frescos and mosaics in each of the three interior stations. These murals depict vibrant and inviting scenes of the next world as a place of ease, equality, good health, and material abundance. Conceived by Mr. Nicolas Rice, a protégé of Thomas Hart Benton, they overwhelm the eye with beauty and calm agitated arrivals. In the Declaration Chamber, patrons sign the register and swear an oath that they undertake their final passage freely and of their own will. A supervisor clandestinely witnesses and warrants this oath. I undertake this duty myself many nights, but Maurice O'Neal, a burly, red-headed Irish man from the other crew, did so the night Ronald died, sparing me the ignominy of vouchsafing my own son's suicide. Next, one enters the Chamber of Last Earthly Delights, which offers rich wine mixed with a soporific in a chalice kept always full and assorted sweets and delicacies to help mask the opiate aftertaste. Soothing music plays on a hidden Victrola. The murals show paternal and maternal figures who appear to long for union with the patron. In the Terminal Chamber a luxuriant day bed surrounded by fresh flowers replenished daily invites one to repose. There patrons drift into their final dreams. After sufficient time for restful slumber to take them, a specially crafted guillotine ends their life in seconds, a means of execution globally accepted as precise and painless in spite of its horrific reputation. Two crews tend to the remains, one to enshroud and remove the head, and the other, which I supervise, to wrap and prepare the body.

I recognized Ronald by his hands and clothing. A coworker, Stefano Luciano, who met my son several times, viewed his face to confirm the terrible truth. "Why would your son choose this?" Stefano asked me, teary-eyed and shaken. I hoped to avail myself of the answer from Ronald's journal, but, having now read through it many times, it feels no closer. All seemed well with him until he read *The King in Yellow* gifted him by his scoundrel cousin, who never spared so much as a "Good Day, Uncle," without expecting something in return. What Ronald wrote after that refers to the book frequently but offers only a confused and baffling muddle.

I believe *The King in Yellow*, with its notoriously affecting second act, infused in my son a spiritual toxin, leading him to total despair that warped his perception of reality. I must read it again to understand.

July 16-17

I finished the first act of *The King in Yellow* this morning then slept through the stifling daylight hours. In the evening, I left my apartment to replenish my whiskey. The sweat of others clung to me as I pressed through the herds seeking relief from summer heat in the evening's relative coolness. I sidestepped a stream of urine pooling outside an alley abused by the street wanderers. The city stank with a nauseating mélange of garbage, horse manure, roasted peanuts, and the exhaust of infernal automobiles. Drawn by lachrymose trumpet tones, I crossed Washington Square. Throngs of dirty, diseased street dwellers bathed in the park fountain, turning the waters greasy with a film of pus and filth rinsed from their tainted bodies. They peeled scabs from their sores and let them float on the polluted water.

Why did they who had no future persist in their existences while one such as my Ronald, with so much promise and so many prospects, cast it away? I regarded them with hatred for the circumstance's unfairness. The lethal chambers offered an easy end to suffering yet these wretches insisted on prolonging it, even extending it to all those around them confronted with their rank character, their infectious effluvia, and their shameless begging. I covered my nose and hurried to Broome Street where my political connections allowed me to obtain a jar of whiskey from a local speakeasy.

Returning home by another route to avoid the park, I perceived someone trailing me. When I lingered by my place of employment between South 5th Avenue and Wooster, just below Washington Square to study its empty sculpture garden, my follower loitered nearby. Clotho's long shadow melded with that of Lachesis while Atropos cast a lonely silhouette on the bronze door. My pursuer remained a discreet distance away, masked by the crowds, and trees, and the arabesque streetlights, though I felt his presence drawing inexorably closer. Had I not lived so near and attained my apartment lobby swiftly, my stalker—a cadaverous man of six feet or more, clothed in tattered linens stained yellow with a soiled white rag tied across half his face—undoubtedly would've assaulted me in the street for my life, money, or spirits.

Such is the city in which we dwell.

No doctor or philosopher has yet unlocked the enigmas of the human beast that sire our violence against others and self. Avarice, envy, ignorance, lust, hatred, and apathy remain, as they have all through history, fertile ground for the seeds of many horrors. Unnerved by my encounter, I poured myself a glass of what passed for whiskey these days, a coarse concoction that lit bonfires in my throat and chest, and sat by the front window to watch the street while I perused the pages I assumed had provided the last words my Ronald ever read.

Eliza Mary's lace curtains swayed in the weak breeze. On the opposite sidewalk, hidden poorly in the alley's gloom, lurked my stalker, betrayed by his height and his garments' light color. A metallic bauble on his ragged shirt glimmered in the gaslight whenever he shifted his position. Whether he spied on me or waited for another ripe mark to pass by, I couldn't say, but there he stood till well after midnight and into the small hours.

By oil lamp, I read the words of *The King in Yellow's* second act. The words engaged me with such totality, I lost all sense of time, drinking and reading until exhaustion overcame me as dawn crested the city's eastern skyline.

July 20-21

Mr. Nebbins came this afternoon to express his kind sympathies for my loss. He also conveyed his belief that my return to the routine and distraction of the lethal chamber should expedite my mourning and spare him the inconvenience of promoting Stefano to my position. I agreed to resume my regular shift that night then asked him if anyone had followed him to my apartment. He regarded the question curiously, almost eagerly, so I described the recent encounter with my stalker and explained my concern for Mr. Nebbins's safety. Reluctantly, because he held no small measure of pride in our neighborhood, he concurred, "Our district has grown sadly more perilous than usual of late thanks to the boiling summer and the indigents and immigrants clogging the streets. Be patient with them and show them kindness, I always say. After all, one never knows which beggar today may be a bureaucrat next week. Nevertheless, I shall raise the issue with the City Council. We can't have undesirables flouting their social duty by refusing the benefits offered in the lethal chamber. Perhaps compulsory usage might be enacted." Promising to keep me informed, he thanked me for my civic concern then left.

From my front window, I watched him cross the street and confer briefly with a tall figure who peeled himself out from the alley shadows. My stalker in rags and white cloth. The two leaned their heads together for several seconds, seeming to regard my window at one point before Mr. Nebbins hurried off toward Bleecker Street. The encounter confused me as the two acted quite familiar with each other, but I presumed my stalker, recognizing Mr. Nebbins as a man of means, had most likely pleaded with him for a few coins. Mr. Nebbins, always conscious of his relationship with the public, likely offered the wretch some encouraging words, nothing more.

I should have slept then to prepare for my night's return to labor, but my nerves refused me any rest. I sat by the window, watching the ragged man who'd settled in the alley. I lifted *The King In Yellow*, having revisited the second act many times since first completing it. Hardly rousing from my chair, captivated by words I comprehended no better than I did my son's suicide, I read it yet again, my mind grasping the superficial facts, the death of Ronald on one hand, and on the other the tale of Cassilda and Camilla in lost Carcosa, a city of unearthly qualities, and the Lake of Hali over which twin suns burned before the Hyades, where a King in yellow tatters reigns. Or reigned. I'm unsure. He controlled the minds of his subjects, I think, or at least deceived them by leaving an awful truth in plain sight so they chose to rationalize and deny it rather than accept it. When Camilla asks the King to remove his mask and he declares he wears none, the terrible truth unravels. What any of it means for me or Ronald remains elusive, but I'll keep reading until I catch on.

At half past ten, I left by a side door to avoid the alley across the street, carrying the book and this journal in my pockets.

I arrived at the sculpture garden shortly before 11 p.m. The streets, though less densely filled than in the evening, still teemed with life. Steamy weather persisted, and the city's gelid stench made each breath an exercise in willpower, a sensory insult lessened by aromatic flowers, such as rose, lavender, marigold, and lilac which perfumed the garden's air. I stood by the gate for a moment bracing myself for my return to the scene of Ronald's death. A teary, disheveled man brushed by me and traversed the garden, hesitating at the door where the latch indicated the chamber already occupied. He glanced back. I took his expression for annoyance that I should witness his arrival, but after a moment's unease, I saw his stare fall upon the cadaverous ragman who stalked me. His face still half hidden by the soiled, white cloth, he took no notice of me, his attention fixed on the young man, whose weeping intensified. His hand shook on the brass doorknob. He reminded me of Ronald, being about the same age, and I suppressed an impulse to snatch his hand from the door and walk him around the city until he found reason to go on living. The law strictly prohibits anyone, especially lethal chamber employees, from interfering with a would-be suicide. Once they enter the sculpture garden, they walk alone with destiny. The latch reset. The man sobbed again then rushed inside. I looked to the road to observe the tattered man's reaction but saw no more sign of him.

Puzzled, I rounded the building to the employee entrance, arriving in time to witness the removal of a body from earlier in the night, wrapped in sheets, its shrouded head resting upon its chest. The men of the earlier shift guided it to the crematory adjoining the chamber, a facility that vented smoke and ash into the sewers to spare the city the macabre sight of a gray plume rising from what was intended as a reassuring and socially beneficent installation. As I entered, the muted thud of the guillotine resounded through the building, marking the man's final escape from his tattered pursuer.

In the staff room, Stefano greeted me with a bittersweet smile. We changed into our uniforms then took our posts as the previous shift workers departed. I monitored the Declaration Chamber, prepared to alert the crew when someone entered while they tended to maintenance, blade-sharpening, and cleaning. For nearly an hour, no one came, until shortly after midnight a girl arrived. Fifteen or sixteen years of age, wearing a frayed and sooty blue dress, her round face bruised, bleeding, distorted beyond recognition, her blue eyes ringed with indigo, belly swollen large, obviously pregnant. I saw reminders of Sarah Jane in her lips and hair, and my heart sank. I despaired for anyone so young to enter our doors, a sadness deepened by the unborn life she bore—but her face told a familiar story, her wounds the work of an outraged father, or a jealous boyfriend, or an inconvenienced procurer of prostitutes, or worse the very father of the child inside her. When she hesitated before signing the book, my hope grew that she might change her mind, but several drops of blood rained from her cheeks onto the back of her hand, jarring it to action. She scrawled her name and then spoke the oath, which I witnessed in my log. I switched on the ready lamp then prepared my removal team.

The death of the young mother-to-be dampened our spirits. Noting my deep melancholy for her, the others offered me words of kindness and support, a gesture I returned. Sometime later, we rolled her body in the bedding and placed it in a cart for the crematory. Lifting her, my hand grasped her belly, and a spasm from within brushed my palm, her baby kicking. I jerked away, unable to stop myself from wondering if it was a boy or a girl. Then Stefano rolled the cart away to supervise the cremation.

Disturbed by the stirrings of life within the woman's cooling womb, I followed him, only to spy an unsettling occurrence. Stefano rolled the remains not to the crematory entrance, but out of sight into shadows around its side. I awaited his return, but only a faint light came from deep in the night dark beyond the crematory. Its diffuse illumination wavered, but its hold rendered me unable to look away, my eyes engrossed trying to discern its source and meaning.

After a time, it faded, releasing me. The remainder of my shift brought two older men, both of whom appeared infirm beyond recovery, and a tearful, middle-aged woman with the air of heartbreak about her. Sad in all cases, but their ends went smoothly, and the rest of the night passed without occurrence. In the staff room, I asked Stefano, "Why didn't you take the pregnant girl to the crematory?" He feigned irritation and answered in a burst of Italian, conveying his frustration if not his meaning. Uncertain why he evaded my question, I chose not to press the matter, wondering if perhaps my emotional state had induced me to misinterpret events.

July 21-22

My stalker returned to the alley. I spied him as I readied for work. I'm certain he stares at my window, though I have no idea why. Again, I left through the side door and hurried along the most direct route to avoid him. A new supervisor, Mr. Abner P. Garland, greeted my shift at the Chamber and announced changes for the night's duties, most distressingly my transfer to oversee the head crew. Mr. Garland refused all questions about our previous supervisor with a shrug and a smile intended as reassuring, I'm sure, but which instead conveyed a patronizing indifference. Denied knowledge of who entered the Declaration Chamber by this change, it came as a severe shock when, at 3:30 a.m., I entered the Terminal Chamber after the guillotine's fall to retrieve the suicide's head and looked upon the face of my ragged stalker.

His uncovered right eye lay gently shut from poppy sleep. Blood pooled beneath his severed neck, soaking the bed fabrics crimson-black. I froze, gripping his shroud, until a frenzied need to see beneath his white rag broke my paralysis. I tugged the dirty cloth away, revealing the hidden half of his face. A ridge of cicatrices formed a design of curves and lines from his left eye to his chin, filling most of his cheek. It resembled a brand, but closer inspection hinted the scars had formed after removal of some mass gouged from beneath his flesh. A lemony hue, his nearly transparent skin showed a network of veins and arteries, from which blood flowed only outward now. Its lid fused to his brow, his eye protruded from its socket as if squeezed by the malformed tissue that encircled it, an egg crushed upward from its shell to spill yolk over his face. The sight summoned in me a pang of guilt at my earlier lack of compassion toward him, but it quickly segued to horror as I saw life remained in the mutilated organ. Its misshapen pupil dilated and focused on me, setting my skin crawling and my heart pounding.

It watched me unfold the shroud and then the dead face sprang to life with a wrinkled expression of utter, hopeless fear. Thick, yellowish tears dripped from its damaged eye. They mingled with his blood, forming multi-pronged, coiled swirls of milky amber and glistening crimson that amazed me with their near-perfect reflection of the mental shapes and maps conjured in my imagination by the words written of distant Aldebaran, the Hyades, the Lake of Hali, and lamented Carcosa. The spreading bloody pool and rheumy, mutilated eye became black suns in a night sky comprised of thoughts leaking from the severed heads of dreamers in a world baked yellow and dusty by unknown hands. I touched the face. A cold burn forced my finger to twitch and my nail to nick the edge of his left eye, which lifted like a scab and floated away on a draft of air. Beneath it lay a plunging abyss funneling to a bespoke golden point at its nadir, a point that writhed and churned with hideous, inhuman life in spite of its miniscule size. Air wheezed from between my stalker's lips then, and his jaw moved, distracting me from his eye. His open throat bubbled as he tried to speak. Unable to deny my curiosity, I leaned close as the faintest of breaths formed the words: "Your son loved you and wished to make you proud. No one can read each other's words. We can only know our own." A gurgle came, followed by a faint, final expulsion of air suggesting "yellow sigh" or perhaps "sign," then life departed.

I stared at the face, now only a death mask, the shroud dangling from my hand. Stefano—sent on behalf of the crew who feared to approach me, he later said—helped me cover it. Breaking the eye's spell permitted me to lay the shrouded head in the cart beside the body, which seemed now so familiar and fragile. I would mourn the man's absence on the streets. A copper medallion clung to his tunic, a rough-hewn simulacrum of the one I had recovered from Ronald's corpse. To the horror of the others, I tugged it free and pocketed it.

Maurice O'Neill challenged me, asking "Why's that nasty thing so important you've stooped to corpse-robbing?" I told him I didn't know it's meaning, but I intended to learn it.

I sensed tension among the others as we returned to work. Even my sympathetic and loyal friend, Stefano, seemed anxious in my presence. I feared the body of my stalker found its final rest beyond our crematory walls as I witnessed him wheel the cart alongside the building into the dark where the inexplicable light returned. At dawn, I detained Stefano beneath the "Fates" and asked him, "Why do the others view me so harshly?"

"Your reaction to the man's disfigured head was unnatural. Your disposition has been worrisome for weeks now," Stefano said.

"I was only curious about the man's odd scar," I explained, "Don't forget a severed head may show signs of life for thirty seconds or more after decapitation."

Thanks to the opiate sedatives given before death, we rarely observed the phenomenon but for one who possesses a high tolerance for alcohol or narcotics, it's possible for the decapitation shock to awaken them. Stefano swore in Italian then castigated me for taking the man's medallion with "the forbidden mark." Insulted by my loyal friend, who perhaps forgot I had retrieved a similar item from my son's remains, I demanded to know why he sent some corpses elsewhere than the crematory.

He only barked at me in Italian again, waved his hands, and then stomped from the garden.

July 22-23

After the last night's incident, Mr. Garland returned me to the body removal team. I reclaimed the post by the Declaration Chamber, where Mr. Nebbins came to visit me, an unusual loosening of protocol. We conversed for some time, pausing when my duties required my attention, and after a discussion of the political prospects for our district and party, he admitted Mr. Garland had asked him to assess my fitness for further work in the lethal chamber. He asked me a series of questions: "Do you understand the nature of suicide? Can you envisage the societal progress the lethal chambers embody and the future they presage? Does death bother you? What do you believe regarding life after death?" I answered in detail that seemed to satisfy him, though I confess some passed over my head. Afterward, I inquired as to his considerations on the same matters. Smiling, he said simply: "The man who kills a man, kills a man. The man who kills himself, kills all men. As far as he is concerned he wipes out the world." I recalled the words, written by G.K. Chesterton, in a book I'd once read. I asked Mr. Nebbins to expound upon this allusion. Instead he invited me to quit work and come to his home where we could speak in comfort. Mr. Garland approved my early departure and assigned a visibly relieved Stefano to assume my post.

Mr. Nebbins resided a short walk from the lethal chamber in a MacDougal Street brownstone above Houston Street, where jazz music from nearby clubs enlivened the night. He ushered me to his study, a narrow room finished in dark wood and lined with bookshelves, where he offered me a drink from his secret liquor stash, harvested from a smuggled case of Canadian whiskey interdicted near Niagara Falls. I complimented him on its taste. The dry heat rolled in on summery drafts through the open windows, and we resumed our talk of suicide, particularly of my son's, which Mr. Nebbins appeared to have taken very much to heart, further endearing me to him. At one point, he asked, "What do you know of *The King In Yellow?*" I said I had read its words several times but did not yet comprehend its meaning. He nodded, lamenting the book's troublesome nature then settled into his wing-backed chair with a stiffness I hadn't observed earlier. The pale moonbeams streaming through the windows and the flicker of the lamps gave his face a plastic quality. His eyes sunk into their sockets. His cheeks and brow appeared sculpted and immobile. His lips remained rigid and inexpressive, reminding me of a ventriloquist's dummy in a Vaudeville theater, when he asked, "Do you grasp what it means to wipe out the world?"

I scoffed at the idea of one man doing such a thing. Again he nodded, his face sliding as his head moved. He conceded that *no man could know*. Then he handed me a sheaf of papers, some typewritten, others scrawled by hand, and indicated I should read them.

They dated to six months back, each written by a coworker, supervisor, or subordinate of mine at the lethal chamber. I had, it seemed, overlooked their anxiousness and discomfort with me for many months. They had written repeatedly to Mr. Nebbins and other higher ups to complain of my behavior and instability. Most expressed deep sympathy for the incident believed to have sparked my downturn—the arrival one night six months ago of my beloved Eliza Mary in the Declaration Chamber. The letters applauded my unwavering execution of my duties, dedicated to the point of restraining myself from making any attempt to alter my wife's suicidal intentions. They all claimed to have comforted me when I broke down wrapping her headless body for burning and made efforts to boost my spirits when I insisted on coming to work, taking no time to grieve. As the picture formed in my mind, I lowered the sheaf of papers and smiled at Mr. Nebbins to show I had a sense of humor about this morbid joke. His lips bent to a grin but no trace of humor touched his eyes. He gestured for me to continue reading.

Doing so, I discovered that this elaborate prank included a rationale for my dear wife's suicide so disturbing as to shatter any man's good sense. According to this abhorrent and ludicrous scenario, an incestuous conception between Sarah Jane and Ronald supposedly drove Eliza Mary to end her life after I disowned both my children and cast them onto the streets.

At this point, I threw the pages at Nebbins in disgust, and demanded explanation. "Why do you mock me with these insane lies?"

He laughed without mirth and let the papers fall about his study. He then directed me to follow him to the cellar, where he would clarify everything. Out of respect for all the good he had done me over the years, I consented. In the cellar, he lit several lamps, and I shuddered at what they illuminated. The pallid flesh of her brutalized face, the waxen quality of her dead, naked figure with her abdomen drawn taut around her swollen belly inspired such an intensity of dread and curiosity, I found myself speechless, nearly breathless. Nebbins kept on a slab the corpse of the pregnant suicide. Beside her on a second slab lay the corpse of my ragged stalker. Beyond him, shrouded in shadows, I sensed others in a makeshift morgue that impossibly fit in a single home's cellar. Their odor nauseated me.

Nebbins then asked, "What baubles do you carry in your pocket?"

Thoughtlessly, I showed him the copper amulets I'd collected, displaying their sign of yellow enamel. He grinned like a birthday boy then, took a matching item from his coat and held it next to mine.

"It is the Yellow Sign. You see?" he said.

"What does this mean?" I said.

"Did you think it mere coincidence our lethal chambers began operation so soon after publication of *The King In Yellow*?"

Nebbins roamed to the other side of the girl's corpse, her sallow, broken face propped beside it. From there he spoke to me of a place across the Hyades where filamentous shadows drew men's thoughts from their minds and knit them into ebon balls of chaos that graced the night sky. A bright King once ruled there under twin suns and beneath those black dream stars. I recognized the story—and yet still did not comprehend it. Nebbins ranted about Cassilda and Camilla who'd dared ask a forbidden favor and thus learned a terrible truth.

"Do you recall the day I came to visit you how I stopped in the alley across the street to speak to your son? He begged me to put in a good word with you to welcome him back into the home that once cherished him, yet you persisted in denying him."

"My stalker not my son," I said. "My son died days before."

"No, that was your nephew, Tyson. Do you not recall lifting the white rag from your son's face tonight to expose the eye socket where you mutilated him with a fireplace poker after discovering what he'd done to Sarah Jane? The same poker branded the Yellow Sign into his skin. He did all he could for his sister while they wandered the streets, but the time had come for stable circumstances, which he hoped I would help to provide by persuading you to reconcile."

The assertion—so far removed from reality—left me dumbfounded.

Nebbins's face rose and fell when he spoke, not in its expression but in its rigid entirety. I relinquished the copper ornaments to his open hand. He laid one on the woman's chest between her small, alabaster breasts, and one into the empty eye socket of my stalker.

"You are confused," he told me. "You have read only your own words. No one can read another's words even if the words are the same. Do you see? Though the play itself may never change, each reader changes it. You share understanding only when the Pallid Mask lifts from your face. Be consoled. You have played a part in a magnificent performance, a celebration of the rise of the new son of Hastur, the herald of an unprecedented age. The King in Yellow may remove the Pallid Mask from those he favors, rich or poor, man or woman, elder or child, or even an entire world should its peoples prove grateful. Or he may let them suffer behind its façade. Who suffers when a god commits suicide? All suffer, yes. But also, in lost Carcosa, we all shall be found. You see? Simple, yes?"

He pressed the dead girl's belly, causing a ripple of motion within. A glutinous ripping sound came as her turgid skin split below her belly button. A tiny hand emerged, dripping mustard-hued fluids. Nebbins crouched so close the little fingers struck his cheek, streaking it yellow, and knocking his face sideways on his skull, affording me a glimpse of rotted, worm-infested flesh, black pits, and jaundiced eyes beneath it before he put it right again.

132

The fissure in the dead woman's stomach widened. Tossing off his jacket, Nebbins then rolled up his sleeves, exposing arms riddled with black spots and pus-filled blisters. He thrust his hands into the woman to excavate an infant boy.

The stench and sight overwhelmed me, and I vomited.

When I regained my composure, Nebbins stood close to me, the horrible pale infant wrapped in tattered, yellowed silks, its face a pale void, veiled in a shimmering golden fog, yet signifying some reality beyond my grasp. The face gleamed, and as Nebbins thrust the child at me, its glow glinted off the copper medallions, which reflected the light into my eye—

—and at last I saw the faces of the dead clearly.

My dear son, Ronald, and his precious sister, Sarah Jane. My prodigal nephew Tyson. I searched among the others but did not see Eliza Mary, grateful for her absence. Ronald stirred, the copper sinking into his eye as his hands lifted his head upon his neck. Sarah Jane prodded rotting fingers into the gouge along her belly. Her eyes opened on her severed head. She and Ronald regarded me with anticipation and an unknowable emotion, a question I could never answer, and behind them, Tyson and the other dead stirred, restless.

Nebbins thrust the child at me again, insisting I cradle it to my chest. The boy mewled wetly and waved its hands, brushing my arm with moist fingertips. Taking his copper medallion from his pocket, Nebbins moved to lay it upon the baby's chest. The coin, I realized, would reveal the infant's true face, which I knew I could not bear to see.

With an inarticulate cry, I fled.

I raced along MacDougal Street, ignoring the voices of the late-night parties and the jazz club melodies now so harsh to my ears. What had happened in the six months since Eliza Mary left this world, I could no longer say. Had she died of a fever and gone to rest in the churchyard? Or had she given herself to the lethal chamber, her remains rendered to ash and blown into the sewers? How did I lose my children? All possibilities hung clear and vivid in my mind. I feared each, in some maddening way, stood equally true.

I slowed to eye the Fates as I passed the sculpture garden and wished killing myself might wipe this entire world from existence, as Nebbins had said, leaving it barren and bleak as Carcosa. It deserved no better than to be rendered a ravaged, empty place where dread thoughts became black stars charting the sky, where lakes of crimson-indigo blood sucked yellow suns into them each night like the eyes of a drowning man sinking for the final time, and the ghost of a self-murdered god walked alone. He belonged there, not here. Not where people lived, yearned, and struggled. I wished I believed in Nebbins's idea and possessed the courage to test my belief. Instead I staggered to Washington Square, where I immersed myself in the water of the fountain, desperate for a baptism of humanity, of squalor, filth, rot, and life's end as it should reach us all, not after some unnatural extension. I thrashed the water, frightening the street dwellers, drawing the police, who rushed me, chasing me as I clambered up the fountain's central structure, my gaze transfixed on the sky full of black stars streaked by wisps of yellow like the rotted cloak of a king who defied earthly bounds to look down upon us with eyes of putrefactious eternity...

July 30

I offer my final words. After days I spent shouting myself hoarse and thrashing my room, my doctors allowed me Ronald's journal and a single writing implement to calm me. Nebbins comes to visit me daily. I refuse to see him. At night the infant with the face of a golden enigma, his body dripping yellow afterbirth into torn, citrine silks, whispers to me, crying in my dreams until I awaken and see the night sky alive with golden streaks passing voids like rotting bone fingers grasping black and withered brains. To rid myself of this burden, I have arranged with one of the guards to facilitate my escape. I hear him unlocking my door to enter now. Though his face bears the same unusual plasticity I saw in Nebbins's that night in his house, I have no other choice but to put my trust for salvation in him and the means of soothing troubled minds used in European hospitals for the deranged. I pray my dreams and awareness end when he thrusts the icepick through my nose into the frontal lobes of my brain.

Odd Quahogs

Big Gene shook from the top down.

The quake started in his head, which twitched, before it enlivened his face with tics that made his eyes jump and his lips quiver. His shoulders rippled, launching shivers down his torso and along his arms, so that his hands jiggled while he clenched and unclenched his fists. When the tremors passed his waist, his legs vibrated like he might start dancing, except any partner Gene chose when he got that wound up had a date with the nearest hospital. I first saw Gene shake like that at the Chosin Reservoir in Korea, winter 1950, when the People's Volunteer Army surrounded us two to one, and Gene's fight-or-flight reflex lodged itself firmly in fight. The second time came before he launched himself at three shithead baymen who called his wife a spook and a prostitute when she met him at the dock with a picnic basket on their two-week wedding anniversary. Gene walked off with a bloody nose; the three baymen had to be carried.

He always walked away solid. He didn't know how to back down or go along to get along, and his strength and grit backed up his attitude. Gene lived in a different world than me, and I didn't always understand it, but whatever had him shaking that way when he broiled into Raker's, I figured it to end with an explosion.

At least until I saw the tears brimming in Gene's eyes.

I poured him his usual Rheingold as he took a corner of the bar.

The Tuesday-night crowd greeted Gene with a lull in their chatter and a few glances through the cigarette smoke swirling around the lamp above the pool table. Most saw what I did when Gene walked in: a friend, a veteran, another bayman shedding the day's sweat. The ones who saw a man who didn't belong in the same bar with them, let alone clamming the same waters—they knew better than to speak their bullshit in Raker's. Anyone who did earned a sweet invitation out the door courtesy of the Louisville Slugger I kept behind the bar.

Gene steadied his mug with both hands; beer still sloshed over the rim as he sipped.

I couldn't read his expression.

Not fear; Big Gene wasted no time on fear. But not pure anger either. Something deeper than both exposed itself there. Something raw and drilled down to Gene's core, down to the pulse of his blood and the beat of his heart. When the answer dawned on me, my stomach shriveled to a nut.

"Aw, shit, Gene," I said. "What happened to Bethie?"

For a second, fury burned in Gene's eyes, and I imagined tanks, turrets blasting, lined up in his pupils like in a *Popeye* cartoon, but then his stare softened. He dragged the back of his hand across his eyes, smearing tears on his face.

"How'd you guess?"

"Never seen you tear up, except maybe laughing."

Gene nodded. "I made a bad mistake, Spence. Real bad."

"Is... ?" I exhaled, almost whistling. "Is Bethie all right?"

"Truth is I don't know," Gene said. "I took that job. I know I shouldn'a. I shoulda turned it down flat like you said, but I needed the dough, and I... I took it. Now Bethie... I don't even know how to say what's happened to Bethie 'cause of it."

"Aw, no, man." I shook my head. "Told you not to mess with those south-end freaks, didn't I? Living down by the power plant, keeping to themselves, they're real bad news. god knows we should've run them out of Knicksport when they came down here from Massachusetts in '30."

"God ain't got nothin' to do with these folks," Gene said. "Not the god folks 'round here visit with on Sunday."

I braced myself on the bar. "Did they hurt Bethie?"

Gene shook his head.

"Well, where's Bethie now?"

"Home."

"Safe?"

Gene shrugged. "As can be."

"What'd they hire you to do?"

"Rake quahogs."

"Couldn't you sell them some off your regular catch?"

Gene shook his head. "I had to rake 'em up special at night. They insisted. They picked the nights going by how the stars and planets lined up or whatever hoodoo they like. Had to rake 'em from that stretch off the tip of the Martinson estate that no one works. Hardest raking I ever done. Swear the muck down there tried to suck me and my rake right down. But I hauled up bushels of 'em. Oddest damn quahogs I ever seen. Shells sort of star shaped. Sprouting stalks pocked with suckers that puckered to my fingers. I brought 'em in before dawn and delivered 'em over on the south end. Came home with better than two weeks' take. Did it five times over the past month or so. Got damn near three months' pay socked away. Easiest dough I ever made, but then Bethie… oh, lordy, Bethie."

"Gene, for mercy's sake, what happened to Bethie?" The thrum of my pulse thundered in my ears, shutting out Jerry Lee Lewis's "Great Balls of Fire" on the jukebox and the snick-snack of pool balls—everything but the whoosh of Gene's breath as I waited for his answer.

"Bethie…." Gene's head hung. "Bethie ate some of them odd quahogs. I must'a dropped a few in with the hard shells I pulled for supper and Bethie didn't know no better. Didn't notice when she dumped them in the pot, I guess. They're poison, Spence. Real poison."

"Did you call an ambulance? What are you doing here when she's been poisoned?"

"Ambulance can't help. This ain't like arsenic or cyanide. It's poison for your soul. Never saw anything like it." Gene raised his eyes to mine. "You gotta come with me. I got an idea how to fix this, but I can't do it by myself. Can you do that? Can you help me?"

I pounded my hand on the bar and hollered over to Phil Maroni.

One gander at Gene and Phil asked no questions when I pressed my door keys into his hand and made him bar captain for the rest of the night. I'd known Phil since first grade, and he backed me up at Raker's as often as I covered his butt at his marine supply shop across the road. I grabbed the keys for my Chevy Bel Air and hustled Gene out back. His shaking jostled my car as I drove us up Main Street, past the movie theater with *Touch of Evil* on the marquee, and Dewey's General Store, both closed. Ten o'clock at night and hardly a soul on the road. I gambled on Petey the Cop napping behind the post office as per usual and tipped the speedometer near 50, bull-roaring past winking porch lights and quiet yards behind low picket fences and azalea hedges. When we reached the turn for Gene's neighborhood, he clutched my wrist and forced the wheel straight.

"South end," he said. "The Marish place."

"What? Why?" I eased down to 30, uncertain.

"They got something I need."

Gene directed me past the power plant to a street lined with slouch-backed, three-story houses that dripped shadows. Built in the 1860s by a whaling captain for his crews, the houses had nearly died with the whaling industry before the turn of the century.

I hated this part of town. Avoided it. Wished Gene had done the same.

He didn't know Knicksport how I did, having grown up here. He came to town in '53, following me home from Korea because his girl in Motor City had sent him a "Dear John," and he had no family or job waiting. I set him up as a bayman, working Knicksport Bay and the Long Island Sound. Watched his back when locals who didn't like black folks kicked some shit his way. I had a lot of friends in Knicksport and that made them Gene's friends, too. Not that he needed us. Gene knew more about dealing with all that hate and venom than I would ever understand. He never let it show how much it dogged him, and after a few years, most folks treated him like any other bayman. Then he met Bethie and settled down. When it came to avoiding the south end and the waters off the Martinson estate, though, Gene laughed off my warnings as "old wives' tales."

Those ghosts either lived in your blood or not, I guess, and Gene wasted less time on superstition then he did on fear. Couldn't blame him too much, with television and Sputnik and nuclear ICBMs eating up what room remained in the world for mysteries. But if you grew up in Knicksport, you knew some parts of town stood rotten and best left alone. You knew the south-end people followed strange traditions and got up to business with the Martinsons and William Wintermill, who owned the land adjoining the estate and brought god-knows-what back from his world travels. Rumors swirled about improper acts in the woods and on the cliffs overlooking the bay—and sometimes, people disappeared. Not often, no, and usually strangers, sure, but more than seemed usual for a fishing town on Long Island's sleepy north shore where even New York City only fifty miles west seemed a world away. We never connected anything solid to the south-end people, but we suspected.

Gene pointed out the Marish house, and I parked my Bel Air by the curb.

"What are we doing here?"

"You're here to keep me level," Gene said. "I need something from these people. They don't give it to me, I might take 'em apart. You can't let me do that till after we help Bethie."

"Bethie needs medicine. They got an antidote here?"

"They don't, I don't know who will." Gene kneaded his trembling fists together. "You keep me even, got it?"

"I don't get anything about this."

Gene flashed some anger my way.

I rolled my eyes. "I got your back. Whatever you need, let's go get it."

Trailing Gene to the front door, I prepared to insert myself between him and whoever answered. No one did, though. Not right away, at least. We knocked for fifteen minutes before the door creaked open and a man appeared. Darkness hid most of his face, but his wide, round eyes glistened with the faint light coming off the street.

"Jonah," Gene said.

"What do you want?" Jonah sounded sick, congested.

"I want to undo it," Gene said.

"You were warned. You didn't listen," Jonah said.

"I listened, I swear!" Gene slapped his open palm against the doorframe. "It was an accident."

"No difference. She's eaten what was ours."

Gene wrenched the outer screen door open, snapping its hook-and-eye latch right out of the wood then shoved the inner door hard, entering the house. Jonah fell into the foyer. Gene towered over him, his body wired, trembling.

"Wrong answer," Gene said.

Stepping inside was the last thing I wanted, but I kept my promise. I sidled in beside Gene, into a veil of dampness that saturated the air, and I gripped his arm.

"Remember, we're here to help Bethie," I said.

"Can't help her. You should've listened." Jonah's voice gurgled as he scuttled back till he bumped the foot of the stairs then pulled himself up by the newel post. He struggled to catch his breath.

Gene's fist closed, and his arm coiled to strike. "Give me what I need."

I braced myself to run interference, but then something thumped on the floor above us. One, two, three quick thuds, then two more. Gene hesitated. We all glanced at the gloomy ceiling.

Jonah said, "Wait here," and then he limped upstairs.

Gene seethed.

Deeper in the house, water dripped. Footsteps shuffled and bumped overhead. Burbling voices filtered through the boards. A faint cry like the echo of a whale song came through the ceiling. Gene and I exchanged questioning glances as the sound faded. I wanted to run outside. But I stood by Gene how he'd done by me when our lives had been on the line in '50. Minutes ticked away before Jonah returned. He handed Gene a burlap sack loaded with something heavy.

"Take this and your woman to where you harvested." Jonah's clammy, pale complexion glistened with sweat. "Go tonight. Read what's written on the paper inside. Don't ever come back here."

Gene glanced inside the sack. "If this doesn't work, you better believe I'll be back."

In the car, after we passed the power plant and turned for Gene's neighborhood, I asked, "What's in the bag?"

Gene exhaled. "I didn't tell you everything. Wasn't only right place and time I had to harvest those quahogs. They made me put one of these on my clam boat and say some words over it."

Gene drew out a football-sized, bronze sculpture and held it up for me to glimpse in the flicker of passing street lamps. A cluster of four semi-human, fish-like heads facing the cardinal directions, rising from a star-shaped wave, and carved all over with ugly writing I couldn't read.

"You actually did it?"

"Saw no harm. What's a prayer matter if you don't believe in it? 'Sides, people pay me to do a job, I do it right. Except, now, maybe I have to believe...."

"What's that mean?" I asked, pulling into Gene's driveway.

He leapt out without answering before I even killed the engine.

I caught up to him in his kitchen, and my stomach shriveled up again.

Bethie sat at the kitchen table, still set for dinner, the meal almost untouched. I'd seen men lost in a thousand-yard stare before, but Bethie seemed to stare off a million miles as if she looked into another world. Hazy light glowed in her eyes, shifting like star-shine reflected on bay waters, tracing milky webs of brightness in her dilated pupils. Words I couldn't reckon danced on her lips. Rhythmic, half-whispered utterances. Chanting, cycling, circling back over and again.

Gene took Bethie's left arm and coaxed her to stand. She sat still.

"Help me, Spence. Take her other arm," he said.

The thought of touching Bethie while that light glowed in her eyes made my skin crawl, and I burned with shame for it. Bethie had been good for Gene and kind to me. She had a sweet singing voice, and a sharp wit, and every once in a while, she baked me an apple pie. I clutched her right arm, flinching at the icy damp oozing off her skin. Gene and I helped her to her feet, walked her out to my Bel Air, and sat her in back. The whole drive, she stared at some horizon only she saw while she chanted those words, back again and again to the one that punctuated all the others. *Dagon.* I didn't know what it meant, and by the time I parked at the marina, I never wanted to know—or hear it ever again.

We ushered Bethie down the dock, helped her into Gene's dinghy, and then clambered in with her.

"Steady her," Gene said.

He cast off and rowed us out to his clam boat.

Gene hoisted Bethie on board. We tied the dinghy to the mooring then motored out by flashlight to where the bay brushed the shore below the Martinson estate. When we reached the place, trees on the cliffs stole our moonlight, and darkness surrounded us. The waters stilled; the surface turned glassy.

Gene dropped anchor then cut the motor.

"We shouldn't be here. This feels wrong. Look how smooth the water is," I said.

"It's how the current runs here," Gene said.

"Been on these waters since I was six. No current does that. Listen, Gene, let's go back. We'll drive Bethie straight to the hospital in Huntington. They'll help her."

"Look at me." Gene aimed the flashlight at his still-twitching face. "I'm not afraid. This'll work, and Bethie'll be all right."

"You can't trust the south-end people. You simply can't."

Gene sat Bethie in the center of the flat deck then placed the fish statue by the prow. He knelt beside it, Jonah's note in hand, and began to read. The words sounded like Bethie's. Coarse. Guttural. Soon her words matched his, and the two fell into one rhythm.

A mile away, the lights of downtown Knicksport sparkled, a patch of brightness nestled against a mesh of dreaming shadows. The neon Budweiser sign in the window of Raker's glowed red, and I hoped Phil would remember to turn it off when he locked up. I spied the shadow of the church steeple at the top of Main Street and remembered the town picnic scheduled for next Saturday with Raker's supplying the beer. Then the breeze shifted, carrying a pungent, briny scent like the first whiff of low tide. Gooseflesh rose all over me.

"Gene," I said.

Gene kept reading. Bethie's gaze settled on a spot in the dead water.

"Stop, Gene. We shouldn't mess with this. Let's get out of here."

Gene and Bethie chanted faster, harder. Awful words. Horrible names I'll never repeat.

Beneath Gene's clam boat, the water shifted. The boat bobbed on swells created by something unseen. I considered cutting anchor, hitting the motor, and heading in to dock, but I couldn't let Gene down. Then something scraped the hull and rocked us.

"Gene, please, let's *go*."

"It's going to be all right," Gene said.

"How can any of this help Bethie?"

A prolonged, muted wail rose from the water, a dizzying vibration rippling the surface.

Bethie hollered that damn name then stuck her hand in the water. I searched for the thing playing with us. I saw nothing, but I felt… well, I felt *noticed*. Something down there, aware of us, of me, like how my dog half raised an eyelid if I walked into the room while he was sleeping. Something down there slept. And we'd disturbed it.

My knees folded. I dropped to the deck.

Aqueous light swam in Bethie's eyes.

"*Dagon!*" she shouted.

Gene shook so hard his teeth chattered.

He fished around in the water but came up empty. Only Bethie rightly saw whatever swam there. Her stare never wavered. Gene dropped the paper, which fluttered over the side, and then pulled a knife and a clam from his pockets. Before I knew to stop him, he shucked it and sucked it down raw. The shell hit the deck and skidded to me—star-shaped, like none other I'd ever seen.

Gene clutched his stomach. I reached for him, but he swatted my hand away.

His eyes turned watery bright like Bethie's; his gaze found the same patch of water as hers.

The boat rolled on wild arcs. Waves swamped the deck.

A vast, black solidity broke the surface and rose, dripping, beside us, lifting Gene's boat higher on the growing swells. Water rained down from it, soaking us all.

Bethie reached for it, arms wide open.

Moving faster than I could react, a lash of the blackness broke loose, encircled Bethie, and dragged her off the deck.

I froze, my mind reeling from the sheer size of the thing.

Gene clutched the sides of his head and screamed.

Now he saw what Bethie saw, and for the first time, I heard fear strain Gene's voice. As much as I wondered, though, I thanked my luck I couldn't see what he did. It all appeared to me as shadows and vague shapes in motion, enormous forms cresting the water then splashing back down. Don't know if I could've withstood looking at something capable of making Gene feel such raw terror.

The darkness shifted and tossed the boat. I clutched the wheelhouse to hold steady.

Gene pitched overboard. He cried Bethie's name as he vanished into the water.

The black thing submerged only to surface again, rising higher and higher, blotting out the stars and the lights from shore, a night leviathan that dwarfed my world. Gene and I had stood together against war, against hatred, and we'd walked away solid, but this—this made me feel like a worm pushing back against a rolling truck tire. Its call sang in my mind, and I believe if I'd eaten one of those odd quahogs, I'd have thrown myself into the sea with Bethie and Gene. I swung one of Gene's rakes from the deck, knocking the statue overboard, pointing the sharp tines toward the shape, but something clutched the other end and yanked it from my hands. Maybe I imagined what I saw next, but I swear I glimpsed Gene high up in the darkness, clawing his way across the thing, crawling toward Bethie, standing solid once more. Then the monolith…

…crashed water…

…submerged…

… nearly swamped Gene's boat.

I fastened myself to the wheelhouse with a line and waited for the end.

The sun came instead.

The early baymen out of the harbor found me around dawn, tied to Gene's boat. I spent the next month in bed. Missed the town picnic, but, thanks to Phil, I found Raker's just as I'd left it when I returned.

I'll never know what Gene and Bethie saw out in the bay. No more than I can ever fully understand the life Gene lived or where he found his fearlessness. I let people assume the three of us had been drinking, and he and Bethie fell overboard, drunk. I never told anyone all that really happened out there, but I shared enough with the right few to make sure no bayman ever again worked that stretch off the Martinson estate, no matter how much money anyone on the south end put on the table. And every day after, I hoped for Big Gene to rumble through the door at Raker's, order a cold Rheingold, and tell me how he'd stood his ground one last time.

A Wandering Blackness

Some people rely on talent to live their dreams, and some make it through hard work; others cheat and steal to get there, and a fortunate few know the right people or fall into the right place at the right time. Too many people never even come close, and a few don't even know what they crave. Consider the heart's truest desire. Can anyone ever know theirs for certain, even when they hold it in their grasp? Has anyone ever attained that desire then stopped, *forever*, wondering what it might be like if they had something different or could live someone else's life? And then there's Robert Blackapple, a complicated man with a simple dream, who knew with rare clarity what he wanted and pinioned his hope of obtaining it on the most unlikely avenue of all—Blackapple believed he deserved it. Promised him by doting parents and the electric oracle of his childhood living room, by every girl he'd ever seduced and every jealous enemy he'd ever suffered. It was his right.

The wondrous sprawling home with antique charm and a history, the kind of house that slick magazines covered in splashy pictorials detailing its painstaking restoration. Women of arresting beauty whose presence would silence the rowdy, drug-fueled, celebrity-filled parties Blackapple would attend. A waterfall of money running through his fingers. And the adoration of millions of proud fans who lived only to see what Robert Blackapple would do next. His favorite fantasy: a Beatlesesque romp through the halls of a five star hotel. He's traveling incognito when an envious bellhop blows his cover and his breathless admirers hound him from floor to floor, penning him finally in a linen closet; he submerges beneath the fawning throng, but not before throwing a knowing aside toward the camera, a resigned smile and jaunty shrug that says it's all just the price of being Robert Blackapple.

These things Blackapple knew, deep in his soul and with every muscle of his body, were destined to be his, were, in fact, already at large in the world, awaiting his fashionably late entrance to make it all real. Yet despite this Blackapple had no idea how to activate it, how to make people take notice and realize the incompleteness of their lives without him as part of them, however small or superficial. Thus he found himself utterly inconvenienced and resentful bordering on enraged the day he turned thirty-five as an out-of-work record store manager with a lethal hangover. Fourteen years out of college and nothing had changed.

That morning the sun woke him, baking the slender trail of saliva laced from his lips into a patch of filmy varnish on his cheek. He'd left the heat on too high, and his mouth felt like charcoal. He'd been out until nearly dawn, not that it mattered without a job to get up for, and he could thank Clarissa for that, the damn whiner who couldn't keep her mouth shut. And after he'd spent the last three months fixing her mistakes and showing her how to do her job right. *All for the best*, he told himself in an attempt to remain philosophical. The job had been a crutch, an obstacle like every other thing he'd ever done to make his rent and feed himself. This wake-up call from the universe ordered him to stop wasting his time and start being Robert Blackapple.

He splashed water on his face, tried to remember last night, but dredged up nothing more than a jumble of hazy impressions of smoke-clouded darkness and pink neon, wet streets and murmuring crowds, and thought he recalled leaving the third bar, but wasn't sure. The phantom taste of vodka danced on the back of his tongue, the flavor of his favorite painkiller. He shrugged off the blackout like he had so many others. Anything not worth remembering didn't matter, he decided, at least until he hit the shower and numbing fear lanced the base of his spine at the deep, eggplant-shaded bruises on his left thigh and hip. What the hell had happened to him? A big black nothing squatted where he expected to find the answer. He couldn't even recall how he had gotten home, if he'd stopped on the way or if he'd arrived alone.

He wrapped a towel around his waist and sat down on the edge of his mattress, amidst the flotsam of his bedroom. Pillars of books and CDs stacked on the floor. A computer piled under leaves of paper from the latest screenplay he hadn't finished. A disheveled arrangement of hard drives storing the demos he'd recorded. The dusty shuffle of his headshots sat on his nightstand next to three empty beer bottles and an unwashed glass. All the scraps that added up to his life, missing only the evidence of his repeated dismissals, the steady pulse of rejection letters he received and discarded immediately, unread past the point where the message was clear. Stale air lingered in the room, made him sleepy again. He needed to eat, needed to get out. He needed some company.

Blackapple dialed the phone and hung up when the voicemail answered. Voicemail disgusted him. He mustered lukewarm contempt for Wilson Graham for not being there to answer his phone. *Wil, my man, where are you when I need a little reassurance?* In truth Wil, the last of Blackapple's friends who kept up with him, hardly came around at all these days. The others had all moved on, gotten married, had children, bought houses, settled down and dropped out of the lifestyle Robert insisted on living. No more staying out till the small hours, no more combing overheated bars looking for something less than romance, something more than a one-night stand. Now Wil headed on his way down the same old road, engaged to be married and on the way up in his job, preparing to buy his share of middle class mediocrity, 401K and retirement in the Sunshine State included.

"Fuck all that," Blackapple mumbled.

After he had dressed and ate what food lurked in his vacuous refrigerator, he took the subway into the city to lose his thoughts in darkness in front of a movie screen for a few hours, but the special effects looked phony and the hero—shorter and less good-looking than Blackapple—could barely spit out his corny, tough-guy lines. But he got the girl in the end, a doe-eyed beauty with bust and waist that could not have occurred naturally on the same body. It depressed Blackapple. The whole thing strained his suspension of disbelief, and it didn't help that he'd once met the actress a few years ago on the street in Times Square before she hit the big time. She'd spent half an hour talking to him on the corner, encouraged him a little, said she liked him, asked him to write her through her agent, gave him the card, kissed him on the cheek when she finally slid into the cab Robert hailed for her. But Robert never wrote, unable to think of the right words to put down on paper or in an e-mail without sounding foolish.

He slouched in his seat until the credits finished rolling, then spilled out with the crowd onto the streets draped in fresh night, and felt the familiar plaintive aching for a drink at the back of his throat. It sent him across town to the Barrow Street Ale House, a college bar serving NYU students, where Blackapple felt right at home and received looks of naïve admiration when he called himself "a screenwriter, a singer." Nobody there cared how much he drank, and he could always find someone to keep the party going. He dressed the part, his looks presenting younger than his age, and maybe something in his soft blue eyes put the college girls at ease when he smiled at them.

Screw Clarissa. If she won't put out, I'll find someone who will.

After five pints of amber and losing six games of darts in a row to a bulbous film student who claimed to have "some real Hollywood connections," he did. Later, though, he wished he had never spoken to the raven-haired witch who took him home that night. Rena wasn't the first witch Blackapple had slept with, but she was the first one he'd ever met who practiced her craft like the fabled wicked witch of whatever point on the compass you care to name—not all that "Earth-Mother, living in harmony with nature, herb-gathering, retreat-from-reality, Goddess-loving crap they shove down your throat to look respectable," as she had put it. Rena practiced black magic, sorcery, necromancy, anything you wanted to call it as long as you didn't ask her to mix you a love potion or frolic skyclad around the Maypole on a chipper spring day.

"The art of the big long-distance fuck you," she called it, and then recited a laundry list of all the painful, stomach-twisting fates she could dispense without ever leaving her Thompson Street studio. Blackapple laughed, missing half of what she said in his intoxication. He thought her crazy, but he didn't care when she started pulling off her clothes and kissed him with lips that caressed his mouth like scented steam. At that moment nothing mattered except the way he felt, and he felt awfully damn good. It was nearing dawn when they fell asleep. Robert woke up with a pounding head, alone in Rena's narrow bed, feeling like all the life had poured out of him in his sleep and wishing he hadn't passed out and stayed the night. He tried to focus his eyes by picking out the water stains on the ceiling from the spots of broken blood vessels floating across his vision. He wanted a shower and to be home.

Rena emerged from the kitchenette covered in a wash-worn T-shirt and handed him a steaming mug as she coiled beside him on the bed in a feline pose that exposed her sleek, pale legs.

"The perfect hangover remedy. Drink up," she said.

"How'd you know I was hung over?" he asked, accepting the drink.

"I see it in your eyes. I see everything in your eyes."

Her mouth curled in a kittenish smile.

He tipped the warm ceramic to his lip and sniffed at the pungent tea, then sipped. The hot brew hit his dry mouth like gasoline, bitter and harsh and with an unusual oily quality to it, but it soothed his raw throat and he drank it down. It filled his stomach with fire, and his gut squirmed nauseously, but he could not stop drinking. His hand felt locked in place, his throat constricting by reflex, drawing the heavy liquid into him, gulp after gulp, until he choked on the chalky leaves at the bottom of the cup and managed then to pull it away. He sputtered for breath, his tongue stinging and tears rolling from his eyes. His heart jumped as he realized he was crying not in pain but because he couldn't help himself as a wave of despair crashed and flooded inside him. He scrambled from the bed, stumbling over a plastic storage crate, upending a lamp and Rena's jewelry box, flattened himself against the wall and tried to slide away. His legs ignored him. The crying strained his body and pain shot across his pectoral muscles.

"What...? What'd you do to me?" he asked, gasping.

"Shh, hummingbird. It's okay. Really, it's all right," Rena said, and she came toward him, folded him into her arms and stroked the back of his skull. "I'm gonna do you a big favor, hummingbird, if you let me. All you have to do is tell Rena what you need. Share all your little secrets. That's not so hard, is it?"

Blackapple's entire body quivered and he wanted to collapse, but Rena helped him to the bed, never taking her arms from around him or her lips from his ear, coaxing, urging, ordering him. Whispered promises of release from all that pained him, all his worries and his longings. Blackapple lost the fight, and everything gushed out of him, his entire life spewed forth like wads of dry phlegm, everything offered up to Rena, his ambitions and needs, the wall of rejection and humiliation that had left stillborn his screenwriting career, woman after woman who had broken his heart by not giving herself to him, the ones who had clung to him after he had gotten what he wanted. His parents who scorned him for not growing up like them. His one-time friends who moved on in their lives and never returned his calls. The record executives who insulted him and hung up before he could say a word. The police who had dragged him to the hospital the night he drank so much he almost died. The losers at work who ridiculed him behind his back. The owner of the Mercedes he had broken into one night, drunk and angry, to steal a radar detector. All the rotten secrets he kept, and now couldn't stop from flowing out of him.

An epic of failure.

A terrorist plea for sympathy.

Rena had felt it in every inch of his body tense like cured oak as they moved together in the night. She told him so as she took him in her arms and massaged his wracking confession.

"Hummingbird, you've been wronged," she said when his tears dried to arid heaving. "I know it and I can fix it. All you need is a little something to help you straighten out, let you show people just what kind of diamond in the rough you are. All you need is your chance, isn't that right? Is that too much to ask for? I don't think it is."

He hadn't really noticed the shelves of odd things beside Rena's window the night earlier. He'd been too drunk and uninterested in the short rows of books and the little bone jars with cork stoppers or the black ceramic box that sat alone at the center of the top shelf. But he watched closely now as Rena reached from shelf to shelf, pulling down the things she needed, clearing a space on the table to set them together in a tidy collection. He waited as she skimmed through three of the old books before finding the right one, and he wondered when she reached into the shiny obsidian container that jingled with its secret contents and removed a small, shiny, and very special thing.

That afternoon Blackapple left with his backpack full of everything Rena said he needed to make his dream life happen and the feeling that it had been she who'd picked him up last night and not the other way around, though it hadn't seemed so at the time. He wasn't sure he liked the sensation, but he was too muddled to give it much thought. The book and candles and the pouch of herbs and the little plastic Ziploc of crucial, blue powder weighed surprisingly light in the pack. Rena looped a jade key around his neck on a strand of silk, so it would not get lost or damaged, and kissed him in the doorway, flashing her dark expressive eyes at him. Was that a spark of pity he saw there?

"Why?" he asked her.

"You deserve it," she said.

She shut the door gently. He thought, as he turned his back and started down the stairs, that he heard faint laughter coming from the other side, but in an old building with thin walls and doors that never shut quite right, the sound could have been coming from another apartment or perhaps from his own thoughts.

He called Wil when he got home, voicemail again, and decided to wait and call him at home that evening. He lay down to nap. In his dreams Rena towered over him trying to help him find his way home. He reached to hold her hand but she stood too high and when he had followed her a ways, he looked back and saw that a great sea of crashing red waters had carried away all he had left behind. The roar of thick surf drowned the world and abruptly Robert was surrounded by it, entrapped on a small patch of swiftly eroding land, the sanguine waters rising, lapping at his legs. A storm cloud formed above, and in the void something laughed and Robert knew he must dive into the sea, plunge deep and not worry about coming up for breath, but he couldn't make himself move even as the water kept rising and the darkness above drew down and the air grew cold....

The bundle of Rena's gifts sat atop Robert's desk like a coiled snake and stared back at him when he awoke sluggish and hazy after dark. His fingers found the key still hanging from his neck, warm from being pressed against his chest. He should call Wil but he felt so tired he wanted to stay in bed and sleep through till morning. He could call Rena, return her things, forget all that had happened between them, but he'd never gotten her phone number, and the forty-five minute subway ride to her apartment discouraged him. It was tonight or never, she had said. Something he had drunk in the tea she gave him would no longer work after tonight, putting it all to waste. He knew it couldn't be real, knew Rena was playing some freakish head game with him whether she believed it all herself or not. He'd been tired and hung over and depressed for days now—no wonder he'd broken down in front of her. Power of suggestion, nothing more. He'd been a switch ready to be flipped.

When he looked around at the ruins of his life draped carelessly across his weathered one room apartment, he couldn't see what harm there was in giving it a shot.

He dialed Wil and smiled when his friend's voice came on the line after three rings. Half an hour later he left for Graham's apartment, carrying the backpack with all the things Rena had given him and the key around his neck. He stopped at a bodega on the way and bought a six-pack of stout, something heavy with a thick taste Rena said worked best. He felt a little better walking through the streets, stronger and less self-conscious. The mild night lifted his spirits. Thoughts of Clarissa faded, taking with them his icy hatred of her and the dark notions that had loitered at the edge of his consciousness for days. He labeled himself a fool for buying into anything Rena had tried to tell him. *Should've left this junk at home for all the good it'll do me. Just dead weight.*

By the time he reached Graham's apartment, he'd almost forgotten Rena's instructions. Wil looked beat when he opened the door. "I hope you don't feel like going out, tonight. Work's been brutal. I'm wiped," he said.

"I thought we'd go to a club so I can meet my future wife," said Blackapple. He handed Wil the six-pack and slung his coat over the back of a chair in the entryway.

"You met her outside the Angelika last week. Actually, I think you stared at her while she waited on line. You're going to make all your other future wives jealous."

"You just don't want me to be happy."

"Damn, you've found me out. And here I thought I'd done so well keeping my cover since high school. What tipped you off? The time I dragged your stoned ass out of the street after you jumped out of my moving car?" Wil opened two beers and handed one to Blackapple. He stashed the others in the refrigerator.

"I don't remember that."

"You don't remember a lot of things. It's why you keep me around. I'm your memory," said Wil.

"Absolutely," Blackapple said. "You gave yourself away when you told me you were marrying Karen."

"I knew I should've kept that to myself."

They sat in Wil's living room with music playing and joked back and forth as their way of talking had always gone, random, tangential, the long way around to any point or conclusion, and eventually Blackapple told him about losing his job because Clarissa had complained about him and how she had lied about what he'd said to her but no one there would listen. No one believed him. He talked about how he was getting nowhere with his writing or his music, and he told him about the blackout from the other night and the mystery bruises and reminded Wil that he had missed his birthday. It had been years since they had remembered each other's birthdays. Blackapple had known Wil a long time, but it had been different years ago when Wil had looked up to him, and now their positions had switched and Wil had so many things Robert wanted.

Why did he even bother to keep him around?

To amuse himself, to measure his own accomplishments against my failures. To flaunt his fiancée and career in front of my isolation, and to Hell with the fact that we're supposed to be friends.

Wil finished some somnolescent story about his job just as they downed the last of their second round, and this time Blackapple went into the kitchen for the last bottles. His crumpled backpack sat on the kitchen table. Inside were Rena's things. *Why not?* He opened the zipper and unloaded the bag. *Why the hell not?*

He pulled the cap off the beers and poured the fine blue grains Rena had supplied into Wil's bottle. They sank into the brown murk and dissolved, fizzling for a moment, then gone, leaving a trace of a rich earthy scent like bay leaves around the open bottleneck, barely noticeable mixed with the powerful aroma of the stout. Minutes later Robert watched Wil drink. When they finished the beer and Wil showed signs of a gentle buzz, Robert brought the contents of his backpack to the coffee table and asked Wil if he believed in magic.

In the morning Graham's neighbor across the hall called the police when she noticed the creeping blossom of wet blood staining the carpet from beneath his door. The cops broke it down, splintering the frame and popping the chain. Inside they found most of Graham's body, though one of his hands turned up on the fire escape outside the shattered window and they never located part his left leg. It appeared Wilson Graham had exploded or a wild animal had torn its way free from within him, flailing and clawing, ripping flesh, snapping bone, spraying blood, now dark and stiff, onto the furniture and walls as if his organs had revolted and fought a war of attrition for their freedom. The uniforms shuffled through the scene in uncomfortable silence. No signs of forced entry but two sets of footprints remained in the damp rug, one certainly Graham's, and the kitchen window had been shattered outward. A number of tall blue candles stood arranged around the room on the points of a star, the remnants of a leather pouch found near Graham's head, its drenched and coagulated contents unrecognizable by sight. They recovered a book, also heavily stained, lying butterflied on the floor where someone had discarded it. The night doorman told the cops that Blackapple had arrived about nine, but he didn't remember him leaving again.

"A real patronizing son-of-a-bitch," he called him. "Always dropping by here to see Mr. Graham, expecting me to let him up unannounced."

"Like last night?" asked Detective David Colán.

"No. Last night he was invited. Mr. Graham called down ahead of time to ask me to let him in. You think Blackapple did this?"

"Well, it's really too soon to say, but thanks for your help." Colán closed the interview, and returned upstairs to the crime scene. He waited until the evidence unit completed their work and went away, and walked through the apartment, avoiding the taped areas and the places coated with blood. He kept his hands in his pockets and touched nothing and looked through the broken window at the gray bones of the city cresting against the pale sky. No person could have fit through the hole in the glass, not without leaving a lot of blood on the jagged edges and the fire escape outside, but there was none. The detective walked back and forth through the apartment several times, trying to visualize how the killing had occurred, what might have happened to leave such a slaughter, what the candles and the book could have meant, and when, on his fourth pass, the sensation of little fingers tickling the underside of his skin did not leave and he felt no closer to the desired epiphany, he surrendered and made a call on his cell phone.

"Dr. Anton Zarnak, please," he said to the politely clipped English voice of the woman that answered. He felt silly waiting and found his fingers fidgeting with the buttons on his coat. He glanced in the mirror and saw tiny sprinkles of perspiration on the dark skin of his forehead. When the doctor came on the line, the detective continued, trying to steady his words. "Doctor, my name is David Colán. I'm a detective with the NYPD. Captain Thorner gave me your number before he retired. I believe the two of you were close friends. Well, he said you're an expert on the unusual, the weird, the occult, said I should call you if I ever came across something like… well, something like what I'm looking at now. Is there any chance you could meet me here?"

))●((

Several hours later Anton Zarnak entered the Barrow Street Ale House, his appearance conspicuous to the point of comedy among the crowd of college-age patrons drinking cheap beer by the pitcher and displaying their tattoos and body piercings. Though still strong and more than capable, Zarnak looked at least eighty years old, though in truth he was much older. His dark, custom-tailored suit, and the lightning bolt streak of silver that improbably managed to remain visible in his graying hair clashed with the tight T-shirts, baggy jeans and acid blonde crew cuts that surrounded him. He paused in the doorway and leaned on his slender walking stick, a scarecrow framed by the late evening sun, skimming the crowd for one man. He found him sitting at the bar with slumped shoulders and a pint glass in his hands, as out of place as the one who sought him. The youthful appearance Robert Blackapple worked hard to maintain had crumbled, and he looked thin and pale and old despite the fact that he dressed as though he were the same age as the students who surrounded him. Fear rippled from his body like a heat mirage.

Zarnak wound his way through the mob, pushing into the line of clamoring people three deep at the bar and placed a powerful hand on Blackapple's shoulder. Robert spun around, and spilled beer on his shirt. Puzzlement replaced expectation as he absorbed Zarnak's appearance.

"I'm Doctor Anton Zarnak. You and I must talk," Zarnak said.

"I don't think so," Blackapple replied. He shrugged the doctor's hand loose from his shoulder, and thrust his glass toward the harried bartender, demanding another drink.

"I've just come from Wilson Graham's apartment," continued Zarnak. "I've seen what you've unleashed. If you want to live past tonight, you and I must talk."

Blackapple never wondered how he could hear Zarnak so clearly over the din of music and babble. "Get lost," he said. He took his drink, threw some bills down on the sticky bar, and sipped at the cold stout.

"Mr. Blackapple, lying to yourself will not protect you."

Blackapple inched the glass away from his lips and gave Zarnak a second, slower look. "How do you know my name?" he asked.

"Unimportant," stated Zarnak. "My proposition is this—let me buy your next round in exchange for a few minutes of conversation. Is there somewhere here we could talk more privately?"

Blackapple eyed his glass, already two-thirds empty. He scanned the overcrowded tables against the far wall, and then rose from his bar stool. "Downstairs."

They found a small booth recently unoccupied, its table littered with filmy beer mugs and ashtrays mounded with the detritus of cigarettes, and Blackapple sat with his back against the wall, flagging an indifferent waiter to order the promised round.

"I don't know how much you understand of what you've done," Zarnak began. "You've unleashed forces better left alone. Dangerous, otherworldly powers. They may very well claim your life and the lives of uncounted innocents. You've already gotten Wilson Graham killed."

"I didn't kill Wilson," snapped Robert, then after too long a beat, added, "He's dead?"

Zarnak studied Blackapple's eyes. A small surprised sound came from his throat. "No," he said. "I believe you didn't kill him, at least, not intentionally. How interesting. But you hardly seem shocked for someone hearing for the first time that his best friend has been murdered."

The waiter delivered Blackapple's drink and he slurped it eagerly. His eyes grew glassier with every mouthful. "We're done when I finish this."

"Let me be direct, then," said Zarnak. "Something is hunting you, and it's something terrible you don't want to find you. It's something you never meant to let loose, but you did and now you're afraid—mortally terrified would be more accurate—that you can't escape it. It killed Graham, and perhaps it's killed others since you freed it. Perhaps you've seen what it can do and it's driving you mad with fear. Am I getting warm, Mr. Blackapple?"

Robert said nothing but sipped his drink as his eyes darted around the room, from corner to corner and always back to the narrow entrance by the stairs, searching for someone.

"There are only two people alive who can help you, Mr. Blackapple—me and you. You know what you've done, but you don't have the knowledge or the experience or, quite possibly, the intelligence to understand it or properly deal with it. I, on the other hand, have all these things, but I don't know what you've done, not exactly, anyway."

"How did you find me?" asked Robert. "I mean, why aren't the cops after me?"

"I assure you the police are rather eager to meet you. They seek information as I do, though I can't suggest that they'll be in as helpful a frame of mind as I am," explained Zarnak. "It was simple to locate you before they did—I traced the stink of your fear. Graham's apartment was thick with it. You left a distinct trail across the city. Psychic energy this intense can take days to completely dissipate. This close to you it's like locking myself in the closet with an open bag of week-old trash."

Robert grabbed the waiter, asked for another drink. In the moment it took to order, his eyes—Zarnak counted—scanned the doorway four times.

"You're looking for someone," he said. "Who?"

"Someone I met here last night. A girl."

"I see," Zarnak said, then striking where he hoped Blackapple might be vulnerable, "Tell me what happened in the subway."

Blackapple snapped around and his gaze fixed on the wizened doctor's penetrating eyes. He turned pale and a few drops of beer breached the rim of his glass and dripped down onto his shaking hand. "What are you talking about? Nothing happened."

"I felt a very strong sensation there of your fear, Robert. Very strong." Zarnak reclined in the booth and did his best to look bored and clinical. "Maybe, I'm wasting my time. Maybe you're beyond helping."

"Look," said Blackapple. "Maybe something did happen. So what? Maybe it scared the hell out of me, but it makes no sense, do you understand? What's happening to me—it's crazy! It can't be real. She did something to me and now my head is all messed up."

"Who?" asked Zarnak.

Robert shook his head. "No one. Nevermind."

"Crazy is pretending it isn't happening," Zarnak said, modulating his voice to a soothing tone, bordering on mesmeric and commanding. "You can trust me, son. Be honest with me. I've heard it all before. I know how it works and I can really help you."

Robert laughed a sick, joyless chuckle. For the second time in two days a complete stranger wanted him to bare his soul, assuring him his future might depend on it, and here he was again, unable to hold back. Something about the deceptively strong-willed, grandfatherly figure opposite him had wormed its way into his skull and wriggled loose all the things he wished he could take back from the night before and the torturous day he had passed since then. Robert Blackapple had no secrets anymore. He couldn't hold onto them.

He started with the subway.

"It tore the homeless guy apart like confetti," he said. "After I left Wil's I ran to the train. I figured I would make it, but it was late and the platform was empty. There was a train coming, and I thought if I got on it, I could get away, but then it came sweeping down the stairs, flowing past the turnstile, plowing towards me. I stopped breathing and tried to close my eyes. I couldn't stop looking at it. There was something to see inside it, black shapes shifting, rolling, falling, and spinning as if every part of it were alive. When the homeless guy crossed its path, it wrapped him like a blanket. It wanted inside him, to be in his mind, but something was wrong, and it couldn't get in, couldn't get what it wanted, and that angered it, so it lashed out. It squeezed him, closing like a snake and then snapped open, shredding him and spitting the remains onto the track. I felt its need and its rage, the sucking black hunger it carried. I jumped on the train just as the doors closed and got away, but it's still out there, isn't it? It wants me. It's looking for me."

"It could kill others like that man, Robert. It may already have done so. You have to tell me more," Zarnak urged.

So Robert told him about Rena, about her witchcraft and the strange drink she served him, about the book, candles, and blue powder she'd given him and how he'd used them at Wil's. He described the ritual in detail, slipping the blue powder into Wil's drink, the candles in the pattern shown in the book, looping the fetish bag around Wil's neck, reading the words. He did everything just as Rena had said, and felt like a fool as Wil laughed at him, going along with what he thought a joke, until Robert took the jade key from inside his shirt, clutched it in his moist hand and completed the words of the incantation. That's when Wil's skin split open like an overripe fruit. Blood, Robert remembered. Blood everywhere, spraying from Wil's wounds, whipping around the room as his body convulsed. He saw Wil trying to scream, but something filled his throat and bulged it outward, something dark like India ink dried to a fine powder or a cloud of smoke from burning rubber. It had shape, though none Blackapple recognized and it was fighting its way free of Wil's body, killing him in the process. It was meant to be his salvation, but he wanted no part of it. Robert dropped the book and ran for the kitchen. He threw open the window and leapt to the fire escape, slamming the window shut behind him to slow the thing he already knew with deadly certainty was coming for him, traveling down the side of the building, along the street, into the subway tunnel. He fled and spent the night wandering the city, never stopping for too long, taking a dizzying path of random turns and switchbacks on the subways and cabs, never straying far from where there were people until it was late enough in the day to come to the bar and wait, hoping Rena might return.

Zarnak asked to see the key. Blackapple, still wearing it around his neck, slid it from his shirt. "I tried to throw it away, but I couldn't."

"I'm not surprised. It's not through with you, yet," Zarnak said.

"She promised me everything. Promised me the life I deserved. The life I should have."

"Did you envy Wilson Graham?" asked Zarnak.

"That prick was supposed to be my friend, but you'd never know it from the way he blew me off all the time." Blackapple's voice rose. "I was meant to have everything that was his. He should have been like me, and at least if we were both living shitty lives, it would've been like it always had been."

Rage took hold and Blackapple wrestled with the idea of running from the bar, fleeing before the thing had time to find him, but he sensed that if he tried to leave, Zarnak would do nothing to stop him, and somewhere a tiny voice from the trenches of his mind screamed out that maybe this time he was in over his head and should just for this goddamned once do something to help his own sorry ass and listen to someone who might know more about things than he did.

"Do you know that this key is not even supposed to exist? I can't begin to guess how it came into the possession of your girlfriend," said Zarnak.

"She's not my girlfriend," Blackapple said. "Do you know what it is?"

"Theron's Key. An educated guess, mind you, but I'm reasonably confident. It's a piece of legend that even those whose vocation is to believe in legends don't believe is real."

"What does it want with me?"

"Nothing. Theron's Key has no will. It's what you set free with it that wants you. Think of this jade bauble as a skeleton key to the universe. Want to open a door between dimensions, a passage to Heaven or Hell, a window into someone's soul? You can do it with this."

There was more but Blackapple's growl cut him off. It came from low in his chest, and he burst from the rickety booth with enough force to send Zarnak twisting to avoid the small eruption of cigarette butts and ash flying up in his wake.

"You!" he shouted, and in three steps reached the doorway by the stairs, grabbing Rena by the arm, wrenching her around to face him. "Take it back. Whatever you did—take it back!"

Rena saw Robert and her shock evaporated. "What are you doing here, hummingbird? Shouldn't you be busy with your new life?"

"I don't want it," he said.

"Sure you do, hummingbird. It's everything you *ever* wanted. Everything you ever cried for. You and every other loser like you, too weak to go out and get it for yourself, too caught up in waiting for it to happen all on its own, waiting for someone to tell you it's your turn. You wanted the world to come to you and I brought it, ready and willing. Now, go be a big boy and take what's yours."

Blackapple shook her, and raised one hand to hit her, no longer thinking about anything but the fact that it was all Rena's fault that Wil was dead, that the black hungry thing that wanted to devour him, that had minced the man in the subway, was loose in the world.

"You did this to me!" he said.

"You did it to yourself, hummingbird."

Zarnak stepped between them, pressing his walking stick against Robert's chest, pushing him away. "Enough! This is pointless. We must leave, Robert. I can't help you here."

Robert turned rubbery and staggered back, propping himself up in the doorframe. The room quieted as the crowd gaped at the bizarre scene.

Zarnak turned to Rena, held her gaze with his steely eyes. "You know who I am?"

The witch shrank away, a touch of humility softening her face. She nodded.

"Your part in this is over. I've no idea what selfish wrongs you hoped to avenge by this, but you'll pay the price for your rashness when less urgent matters are at hand. I won't forget you."

The doctor seized Blackapple by the shoulder and rushed him away. Upstairs they fought their way rudely to the front door and emerged onto the sidewalk. Blackapple's will had deserted him. He followed wherever the strange doctor led. At the corner Zarnak waved and moments later a black car that had been double-parked on the next block pulled alongside them. Zarnak opened the door and shoved Robert into the backseat, entering after him. The dark sedan sped away from the curb, driven by a tall, muscular woman with hair the color of white sand tied back in a rigid ponytail. Zarnak called her Midra.

"Oh, god, oh, god, I can't escape it, can I?" Robert said.

"Shut up. You're alive and you'll have my help, but if you convince yourself you've already lost, there's little I can do for you."

"What is it?"

"What you released is the darkest part of a man's soul. Everything that made Wilson Graham the man he was. All the pain and fear and insecurity, all the veiled greed and hidden ambition and contempt that shaped him, all the misery and isolation he never shared. All the things he did and suffered to be where he was in life, to be *who* he was. The ritual ripped him apart to free it all for you, and once it becomes yours, it can do exactly what the girl told you. It can give you your heart's desire."

"No. What came out of Wil was evil. It had nothing to do with him. It *killed* him."

"He died for losing it, Mr. Blackapple. The reality is you killed him by summoning it forth. Denying it cannot unmake it. You didn't know your friend as well as you thought, but you do now, and you did last night when you saw what it really was he had that you didn't, when you decided it was more than you could bear even to make your dreams come true. This thing craves the connection it can have only with you. If you don't finish it tonight, it will take on a life of its own and continue to kill anyone it contacts. Shred them like the man in the subway. Like Wil."

"What can I do?" asked Blackapple.

"Accept it. Take the gift you so jealously sought. It won't bring Wil back and it won't cleanse your soul, but it will prevent further wrong, and it will be punishment enough for you to live the rest of your days with that blackness inside you despite the gain it will also bring, for in the end, Mr. Blackapple, we are all stripped down to that part of us which is not purely of this world."

"I don't want it anymore. I don't want any of it. Can't I kill it? Or take back the spell?"

"Theron's Key opens many doors, Mr. Blackapple, but it has never been said to close them. You can claim your prize, or you can kill yourself. The only thing holding it here, the only thing allowing it to exist, is your desire, and if you die, it dissipates. I won't allow it to run free another night."

The car slowed and stopped at the curb. After getting out, Midra opened the door on the passenger side and waited. Robert tried to shrink into the leather seat, but Zarnak's glare urged him onto the sidewalk outside 13 China Alley.

"Thank you, Midra," Zarnak said. "Now if you would park the car, then call Detective Colán and ask him to meet us here. I doubt we'll be going out again tonight."

Midra said nothing, but returned to the vehicle and rolled away in it. Zarnak ushered Blackapple to the door of his home.

The air inside the foyer smelled musty and a thin layer of dust dressed the furniture in the anteroom. The quiet shocked Robert. None of the city sounds, the rushing traffic or emergency sirens or interminable voices from the street reached them here. Zarnak took his coat and looped it over a hook by the door.

"I would offer you some refreshment, but I'm afraid my assistant Singh is no longer with us, and I'm rather inept at such social niceties. But I trust you had enough at the bar. When Midra returns, I'll ask her to put on some coffee."

They entered Zarnak's office, a chamber overwhelmed with a clutter of books and papers and items whose purpose or origins Blackapple could not guess. The volumes lining the book shelves appeared quite old and rather the worse for wear in most cases, their dry spines cracked and loose or marred by antique water stains. Artworks of madness, weapons of past centuries, a small collection of clay tablets engraved with foreign writings, and the images of unearthly winged beasts adorned the walls. Sculptures crowded the top of the bookcase behind Zarnak's desk, figures of bronze and marble, of plaster and a nacreous material Blackapple had never before seen, and leering down from the space directly beyond the doctor's high-backed leather chair was the most ludicrously appalling mask Blackapple had ever seen, a wicked thing with horns and the coloration of a clown who had dozed off at his dressing table and fallen facedown into his makeup. Blackapple wanted to laugh at it, but the face proved more unsettling than he would've expected, especially when its empty eyeholes followed him, and he managed only to release a nervous whine.

"Ah, I see you're admiring the Mask of Yama. A terrifying visage, indeed. Again, I must apologize. The state of my quarters is not what it was under Singh's charge. I fear Midra does not share his meticulous spirit. But I make do."

"What happened to Singh?" Blackapple asked.

Zarnak leveled a fierce gaze at him, his expression a study of sharp angles and hard lines hewn from granite. "You're not the first fool to toy with powers beyond your comprehension, nor are you the first whose ignorant actions have claimed the lives of your betters."

An awkward moment passed as Zarnak took his seat. When he again faced Robert, his expression had softened, and Blackapple dared to ask, "So, what do I do?"

"Open yourself to the darkness. Call it. It won't find you on its own, not here," the doctor said.

"I don't know if I can."

"Of course you can. It's your fondest wish, Robert," Zarnak said in his persuasive way. "Tell me—why do you want the things you do?"

Blackapple shrugged. "I want what everybody wants."

"Really? But so many people manage to be content with the lives they have."

"It's who I really am, who I'm supposed to be."

Zarnak knew Blackapple believed his words. Some part of him would never be fulfilled without the things he'd spent his life wanting. That was the man's personal darkness, his arrogant desire for all those things he believed life owed him. Zarnak felt a twinge of conscience for his harsh treatment of the man for he saw some facet of himself reflected in his hubris and thought of those days long ago in another part of the world when he had demanded knowledge from those who understood he knew not what he asked. The doctor, though, had never since shirked the damning road that was the only path to becoming the man he was meant to be.

"The key gives you the power," he said. "Hold it in your hand and call. I'll do what I can to bolster your strength, but you'll mostly be on your own."

Blackapple took the key and closed his eyes. Its power thrummed through his body, warm and stinging, and he felt pins and needles in his limbs. The air grew stifling. A voice called from far away. He couldn't understand the words, but he knew it was speaking to him, like a worried parent shouting for a child lost in the woods. He became aware of a space beyond Zarnak's cramped office, a vast openness where distance functioned as a factor of perspective and desire and the world of streets and buildings, traffic and great masses of people flowing like blood through arteries, was more dream than reality. He felt very small and exposed. The voice called again, closer, and he knew if he turned and peered toward the amorphous horizon, focused his will and wanted it enough, that he would see its source, the dark thing that stalked him.

The office snapped into sharp clarity as he dropped the key and opened his eyes. "It's... so huge," he said. "My god."

"The distance means nothing. Call it," said Zarnak.

Retrieving the key from his lap Robert closed his eyes again and returned to the big empty place. He heard the voice immediately this time, singing his name like a chorus of whales, crying out to him across the depths and the nothingness, and he replied, faltering at first, his words cracking in his throat, but then rushing out from him with power he had never known dwelled within him. They crashed through the stillness, shook the strange desolation, and the dark thing appeared at the limits of his vision, roiling across the plain, a black fog blowing on an unholy wind, ramming straight for him.

"It's coming," he said, and he opened his eyes. The power of Theron's Key charged through him. "It sees me."

Something thundered in the night. The walls shook and the ground trembled. Robert's heart fluttered then began racing. Zarnak sensed it, too, and raised one eyebrow in anticipation.

The thing called his name.

"Do you hear it?" Robert said.

He stood, walked toward the front door, the key clutched tightly in his hand, waiting. He sensed it outside now. Something knocked on the door, an irregular tapping, and then again in a flurry of thumps that quickened and grew harder with each blow. The door rocked on its hinges, bowed inward, and blasted open into the anteroom, as if forced wide by the wild shrieking that followed it. The desperate sound consumed the room, blocking out all other sensations, dizzying and painful. Robert slipped to his knees. Wind seized the contents of the anteroom and Zarnak's office and tossed them violently, thrashing them with determination.

The black thing entered, flowing like chemical smoke, probing, inching forward as it searched for the one who called it, the one who wanted it more than any other, whose need rivaled its own ravenous, insatiable appetite. Light flashed in Blackapple's mind, explosions, lightning, a cascade of electrical bursts and flashfires ignited as his synapses fired out of order and too fast. All at once a consuming dread spread through him, and he wanted very badly to be anywhere else in the world. He tried to shut it down, tried to send it away, tried to remember his mother's face but couldn't summon the image. His chest seemed so small and insufficient to contain his throbbing heart and he trembled as he faced the substance of all he had ever wished for. It recognized him, greeted him. It slid its oily mass around his shoulders, his chest, enveloped his legs and snaked up his neck. Robert arched his back with the incredible pain shooting through his torso. He threw back his head and howled. The thing lunged an anxious tendril down his throat, plunging home. It was inside him, now, and its black cilia caressed his heart.

An hour later Detective Colán arrived at Zarnak's office, and found the doctor calmly seated behind his desk, sipping coffee from a porcelain mug, the mess of his office hastily reorganized and carelessly tidied up. Midra had let the detective in, taken his coat, and offered him a cup of coffee. He refused since it didn't seem right to him to drink coffee while he was standing over the motionless body of Robert Blackapple, his skin ashen, his eyes eternally glassy, the jade key clutched irremovably in his waxen hand. He crouched, touching the man's pale neck in hopes of finding a pulse, but there was none nor did he breathe, and so Colán softly closed the lids of his eyes.

"He's dead, yes," said Zarnak. "It couldn't be helped."

Colán trembled as he faced the elderly doctor, though he wasn't sure if it was from fear or burning frustration. "What happened?"

"I can't be certain, not without an autopsy, but I'd guess his heart burst," Zarnak said.

"Just like that? For no good reason?" Colán pulled a cell phone from his pocket, dialed. He called for an ambulance and a CSI unit.

Zarnak asked Midra to find a sheet to cover the body, and when the detective had finished his call, he led him into another room where he told him how Robert Blackapple had been, in the end and with all he ever desired within his grasp, stopped by that which had held him back his entire life.

"I expect his heart burst from fright," Zarnak said.

Kolchak, The Night Stalker: The Lost Boy

"Missing?" I said.

"Get the wax out of your ears, Kolchak." Gus Thomson, Sergeant, LAPD, and pot-bellied donut connoisseur of the first rank spoke around a mouthful of chocolate glazed. It was March 8, 3:37 p.m. We were standing by his desk at police headquarters. "*Missing.* That's what I said."

"Well, yes, Gus, and I heard you," I said. "But the kid's sitting there on his mother's lap. Shall I fetch you a dictionary so you can reacquaint yourself with the meaning of the word? Or do you find yourself in such a state of shock over actually having solved a case you've forgotten to close it?"

"Don't be a wise guy." Thomson frowned as if he regretted not simply letting me leave with the police reports I'd come to pick up. "The mother says the boy's a phony, a replacement, like in that movie, with the space pods and the dog with the guy's face."

I shook my head. "Pod people. Really? You're bringing me pod people."

At a detective's desk across the station, a woman sat with her back to me, her young son bubbling in her lap. The detective looked like he had a throbbing headache. The boy, who was maybe three years old, had the detective's stapler and was trying to staple his mother's ear to her head. She plucked the stapler away, but the child snatched up a pen, spilling the detective's pen cup onto his desk blotter, and then tried to impale the detective's hand with it.

"Forget that B-movie nonsense. The lady is one of Harold Sunderland's mistresses, who maybe is enough off the rails to break the omerta these princesses all stick to. Of course, if dirt on Sunderland doesn't interest the *Hollywood Dispatch*, I could take it to the *Times*."

"Ah, now, don't be like that, Gus. I appreciate you telling me, but what exactly are you saying? Is this supposedly substituted youngster one of Sunderland's rumored lovechildren?"

"You catch on fast, Carl," Gus said.

"Well, why didn't you get to the point?" I asked.

The great Harold Sunderland—age 54, the City of Angels' slick-as-oil, impeccably coifed answer to the Big Apple's Donald Trump, thrice divorced, and clinging to twenty-three-year-old trophy wife number four—was the driving force behind more than half the major construction projects in and around Los Angeles and had been for two decades. Rumor was Mr. Sunderland also had a number of smaller, *livelier* achievements around town, little bundles of joy he preferred not to tout in the *Times* social register or at the mayor's annual Cinco de Mayo celebration. He—*allegedly*—paid their pretty, young mothers quite well to make sure potential paternity suits never saw the inside of a courthouse and that the fourth Mrs. Sunderland in twelve years never met her extended family. The reporter who exposed Harold Sunderland's secret life would write his own ticket in this town, and that was one piece of writing I'd wanted to do since the first day I set foot in La La Land.

"What are the police doing for her?" I asked Gus.

"In the department's eyes, no crime was committed, so we're taking no action," he said.

"Always an effective response."

"Ease up. The kid's prints match his birth records. He's the same boy. His mother's got a screw loose. Who knows what she might tell you about Sunderland? You interested or not?"

"Sure, I'm interested. If anything pans out, it'll be chocolate glazed for a week, on me. Now do this lady and her son have names, Gus? An address? A phone number perhaps?"

I glimpsed mother and son leaving the detective's desk, the mother crying quiet tears that may have been a result of how hard the boy was yanking on her hair. The relieved detective put his desk back in order.

"Her name's Angela Martin. Her son's Jeffrey."

Gus kept chewing as he told me the rest. I tried to catch Ms. Martin outside, but she was already gone, so I went back to the *Dispatch* and called her half an hour later. When I got off the phone, I had an appointment to speak with her that evening. I hoped it wouldn't be a waste of time. Ms. Martin sounded nice enough, but she also sounded desperate, and experience told me that desperate mistresses tended to be the epicenter of their own private earthquakes.

Regardless, that evening, I guided my Mustang, top down, along streets so clogged with cars that only the miraculous intervention of Our Lady of the Angels allowed traffic to move at all. At 6:46 p.m., I arrived, a mere fifteen minutes late, at the Del Sol Estates, a conglomeration of high walls, manicured lawns, and restrained palm trees with so much security on display I almost mistook it for a ritzy prison. The gate guard squinted and eyeballed me and my car until I offered him my camera and suggested he take a picture for his scrapbook. He acted shocked when he found my name on the guest list.

I navigated the perfectly landscaped curlicues that passed for roads at the Del Sol and drove past the gaudy, spot-lit suburban castles of lawyers, financial traders, and corporate bigwigs. At the police station, I'd gotten only a glance of Ms. Martin half-hidden behind an armful of wiggling toddler, but I found it hard to work up much sympathy for her. Against the backdrop of the Del Sol, I couldn't imagine any version of Angela Martin who wasn't a soulless gold-digger or a scorned mistress determined to give hell a run for its money teaching Harold Sunderland about fury. Worse, I figured her for a possible crackpot more in need of little green-and-white pills and regular visits to the psych center at Cedars-Sinai than the aid of the police. But being shallow and crazy didn't disqualify her from potentially handing me a blockbuster story on Sunderland. Visions of Pulitzers danced before my eyes as I rang her bell.

My little dream went up in smoke when Ms. Martin answered the door. Neither of us spoke as we adjusted our expectations. The woman in the doorway, Ms. Angela Martin, age 30, former art dealer and gallery owner, was classically beautiful with warm, kind eyes, dressed modestly with her hair pulled back from her face, and barely a speck of makeup or a link of jewelry on her; she looked haunted by worry and sadness, a far cry from the gaudy, bauble-laden harlot I'd pictured. It was a distinct and intriguing improvement. Ms. Martin, I'm afraid, adjusted her expectations in the other direction after a glance at my rumpled suit, pork-pie hat pushed back atop my thinning mane, and the notebook and ballpoint pen clutched in my hand. If I hadn't seen that deflated look so often before, it might've taken the wind right out of me.

I smiled, and said, "We don't send Anderson Cooper and a camera crew unless something blows up. Carl Kolchak, at your service."

Ms. Martin blushed. She accepted my extended hand and then invited me in.

"I'm sorry. I didn't mean... I mean..." she said. "I didn't know what to expect. On the phone you sounded..."

"More handsome, dashing, and full of *joie de vivre*?"

"Well, no, you sounded younger."

"I have a young voice," I said. "You haven't exactly lived up to my expectations either."

"Oh?" She looked worried.

"No. I was expecting an overdressed Barbie doll with fake boobs dripping a perpetual shower of loud, spangly jewelry, and here I find instead a woman possessed of elegant beauty, who is also clearly well-educated, warm-hearted, and possessed of a winning sense of humor."

Ms. Martin laughed. She tried to suppress it, but she failed. Miserably. Minutes later we were seated in her kitchen, sipping coffee, and talking like old friends.

"Harold built the Del Sol," she told me. "He put me up here after Jeffrey was born, and he's taken care of us ever since. But I'm no freeloader, Mr. Kolchak."

"Carl, please," I said.

"I had a career when I met Harold. I didn't want or need his money. It might be difficult to understand, Carl, but I wanted Harold. He's charming, romantic, fun. He knows something about everything. His great love after construction is art. We met through my gallery, and then—well, then there was Jeffrey, and the economy put the last nail in the coffin of my gallery, so now I'm a full-time mom, except…"

Ms. Martin tried to hide the tears brimming in her eyes, but I saw them well enough. I handed her a tissue from a box on the table, and she pressed it to her face.

"Except now, you think someone's taken your son," I said.

She sobbed and nodded. "I know how it sounds, how crazy and ridiculous—"

I held up a hand to stop her. "You may not believe it, but I've heard crazier. And if there's one thing I've learned, one achievement I'll take to my grave never having doubted, it's that I know when a damsel is truly in distress. So, let's say I'll believe—or at least keep a very open mind about—everything you tell me until I have all the facts. Sound all right?"

She nodded.

"Then let's hear your story."

"It's easier if I show you."

Angela led me through the house, which was decorated with paintings, statues, and sculptures of impeccable taste and expensive pedigree. The place was opulent and bigger than any four apartments I'd ever rented combined. I tried not to notice. Or get lost.

"Harold promised to leave his wife for me, and I believed him. I was foolish. Once Jeffrey came on the scene, he didn't want me anymore," Angela said. "He may not be faithful, but in some ways he's honorable. He makes time for Jeffrey when he can. He supports us."

"In exchange for your silence about your son's father," I said.

I felt guilty when I saw how my words cut her, but Angela only nodded.

"The change happened about five weeks ago." Angela led me upstairs. "I knew in my heart that the boy in Jeffrey's bed that morning wasn't him, no matter how much he looked like him. I didn't know what to do. I told myself he was only ill. I took him to doctor after doctor, and they said nothing was wrong, it was only a phase, the 'terrible threes,' but I know it's not. I've called the police four times, but all they see is a woman with too much money and time on her hands, a single mom looking for attention."

Angela stopped at a door decorated with a blue-framed sign with the name "Jeffrey" spelled out by animals contorted into the shape of letters.

"Thank you for listening to me, Carl. However you make up your mind, at least you've done that much for me tonight."

"I've had a lot of practice."

Angela gripped the doorknob, took a deep breath, and then opened the door.

"Jeffrey," she said. "Come say hello to Mr. Kolchak."

I peered into a typical boy's bedroom, sky-blue walls, bed unmade, plush super-heroes and plastic racecars scattered on the floor among rumpled pajamas and the odd sneaker or shoe. I saw no sign of the boy. Only my quick reflexes spared me a poke in the eye from a small, blue, wooden train painted with a smiling, rosy-cheeked face that sailed straight for me. I ducked, and the train chunked against the wall.

"Jeffrey, stop it," Angela said.

Jeffrey emerged running from the shadows of a closet, kicked me in the right shin, and then darted away with a laugh. He jumped onto his bed and bounced on the mattress like it was a trampoline. Then he stuck out his tongue, and gave us the old Bronx cheer.

"That's enough, Jeffrey!" Angela shouted.

Jeffrey snatched up a plastic dump truck and hurled it at Angela. She batted it away with weary precision. The boy leapt to the floor, grabbed a toy racecar, and tossed it against a lamp, knocking it over. Angela righted the lamp like it was second nature. Jeffrey zigzagged around the room, kicking toys and clothes into the air, hollering at the top of his lungs like a junior Tarzan practicing his jungle calls. A flying shoe knocked my pen and notebook from my hand. They spun into the hallway behind me. Angela, embarrassed, dashed out to pick them up. The moment she left the room, Jeffrey ceased his rampage, pointed a tiny plump finger at me, and in a voice that would've sounded too deep and gruff even coming from a fifty-year-old trucker dangling a cigar from one corner of his lips, said, "Kolchak, Kolchak, stay away from me you old hack!" A soft, electric tingle ran through me, and a sugary–coppery taste filled the back of my mouth. Both sensations lasted only a moment.

Angela returned with my pen and notepad.

Screaming in his little-boy voice, Jeffrey went full swing back to raising hell.

"Did you feel that? Did you hear that?" I asked Angela. "Does he talk like that a lot?"

"He's always yelling and shouting," she said.

"Not the screaming. That voice! Like Barry White with a hangover. How could such a small mouth make that kind of noise?"

Angela's blank expression told me she hadn't heard what Jeffrey said. She hadn't yet experienced this particular part of the boy's oddity. Maybe he'd never done it while she was around, I thought. I jotted the phrase he'd spoken in my notebook and let it go. Angela shut the door and we went downstairs. To highlight Jeffrey's change, Angela showed me some videos from his third birthday party three months ago, sounds and images of a decidedly calmer and more pleasant child than the toddler of terror cooped up in Jeffrey's room. They looked exactly alike. Maybe half a dozen medical conditions could explain such a dramatic personality change, but my gut told me they weren't the answer. And neither was possession. No, I believed Angela Martin. Something had replaced her son. The weird, deep voice—so alien to any normal child—persuaded me. At that moment, my desire to dig up dirt on Harold Sunderland abruptly took a back seat to getting to the bottom of what had happened to little Jeffrey Martin.

I made a few wrong turns on my way home from the Martin house. It was rare that my beat brought me to wealthy enclaves like the Del Sol Estates. Driving back, I found myself on unfamiliar roads that seemed strangely isolated and uncharacteristically dark for a city that prided itself on sunlight and vanity. I drove past gated communities and small mansions hidden behind thick hedges and security fences. It was 8:49 when I turned down Coronado Street, which looked almost abandoned, and my car began to cough and sputter. Tall palms and heavy scrub growth lined either side of the road, overgrowing plywood fences along a construction zone. Beyond the fences, tall cranes and burly machinery rested in shadow like escapees from the La Brea tar pits. As I reached the middle of the block, my faltering Mustang coughed louder and lurched twice. The dashboard needles flicked left then right like a happy dog's tail. My headlights flared, and the volume of the radio shot to maximum. Then all at once, my trusty old chariot gave up the ghost and clink-clunked into unwelcome silence. I popped it into neutral and coasted to a curbside stop. I turned the ignition key to restart the old girl, but it only clicked. I pumped the gas, tried again, and—nothing.

Someone flashed a light at me.

I raised a hand to shield my eyes. I expected a security guard from the building site or a member of L.A.'s thin blue line armed with a flashlight and questions about why I was parked on a deserted road at night. But there was only the light. Floating in the air, shining onto me, onto my car, onto the oddly glittering pavement. It wasn't alone, either. Other small lights floated behind it, and still more danced along the sides of the road, moving in and out of the shadows. I heard voices then. High and reedy. Talking fast. Conversations I couldn't follow, words that sounded almost English but not enough that I could make them out. The speakers broke into song, a chorus, of thin, mouse-like voices following a lilting, whimsical melody. Faint music played and more lights came. They flocked to my car, swarmed me like thirsty mosquitoes. I swatted them, feeling weak electric jolts whenever I made contact. It was the same tingle I'd experienced in Jeffrey's room. My skin crawled. The scent of flowers and warm sugar filled the air and lingered on the back of my tongue. I felt eyes watching me, but I saw no one around.

The lights scattered apart then formed a miniature parade in three parallel lines, bobbing toward the construction site's main entrance. They passed through the locked, chain-link gates and continued on the other side, flickering into the curtain of night over the work zone. Grabbing my camera, I slipped out of my car and ran to the gate. After a glance around to see I was still alone, I pulled myself up the chain link, over the top, and dropped to the other side.

A huge sign informed me that the Coronado Dale development—a luxury townhome community to be completed by next May—was a Harold Sunderland project. At the bottom of the sign was the Sunderland logo: a photo of Mr. Sunderland's face smiling out from the center of the letter "u." The lights drifted deeper into the site. I tailed them. They gathered in a circle ringed by trees marked for removal with spray-painted Xs. Only a handful had been felled. The ring was far back from the road, a place that felt calm, peaceful, and—somehow—very, very old. No foundations had been laid there, no building equipment waited nearby, and no signs of work were visible. The lights flashed. They pirouetted to the rhythm of the phantom music. I tried to snap some pictures, but the power switch on my digital camera was useless, the screen blank, the lens cover frozen tight, dead like my car. Then light flashed around me and something knocked me from behind, tipping my hat from my head. I heard laughter as I bent to retrieve it, and when I straightened up, the lights were nearly gone, the last of them vanishing into the center of the open ring.

Seconds later, I was in the dark.

A car engine growled to life.

My car engine.

I raced back to the entrance. The Mustang idled by the curb, headlights bright. I clambered over the fence and hurried into the car, threw it in drive, and floored it, eager to put Coronado Street far behind me. Whatever I'd witnessed, I had no doubt it was connected to Jeffrey Martin; the now familiar sweet-metallic taste in the back of my mouth convinced me.

My cell phone rang from the passenger seat, where I'd left it. I answered.

"Carl!" No one on earth said my name quite the same as Tony Vincenzo, my longtime friend and editor. Despite the noise of the rushing wind, I moved the phone an inch away from my ear. "Where have you been, Carl? I've been trying to reach you all night."

I reminded him about my meeting with Angela Martin. "Besides," I said. "The night's still young."

"What are you talking about?" Vincenzo's voice downshifted from yelling to shouting. "It's half past midnight! I needed you to cover a crime scene tonight. I had to send Updike. To a double homicide. Updike, Carl! If he tosses his cookies again, it's another dry-cleaning bill I've got to pay. Plus I thought maybe you'd had an accident or been arrested again. You don't need bail, do you?"

"Uh, no, Tony, no, I'm fine," I said.

I checked my watch. Then I punched the brakes and swerved off the road and jolted to a stop. My watch confirmed Tony; it was almost 1 a.m. I'd left Angela's around 8:30, driven ten or fifteen minutes, spent fifteen or twenty watching the lights, which left approximately three hours unaccounted.

Calming from shouting to snapping, Vincenzo, said, "Where the hell have you been?"

"Tony," I said, "I don't know. I honestly don't know."

Like many of my old friends, Brenda Nicole Harper was happier to see me than she liked to let on. I know because when I turned up at her book signing at the local Big Books shop, she grimaced but she didn't call security. She was signing copies of her latest paranormal self-help book, about using crystals, spirit tunings, and angels to lose weight and fight depression. You can imagine the people on line for her autograph. What I needed, though, was real information. Despite her penchant for pandering to the holistic hordes and weekend mediums, Brenda was a genuine expert on many things from the far side of normal.

She pretended not to know me when I handed her a tattered copy of her first book, *Vampire Lovers: Tips and True Stories,* and asked her to sign it to her "good pal, Carl." She scribbled on the title page and returned the book. Smart girl, though, instead of her autograph, Brenda wrote "Meet me at Grinder's Heaven, 5:30." It was a coffee shop next door. A cup of coffee was exactly what I needed so I went there and got us a table.

Brenda wandered in around 5:45.

"Carl," she said. "How did you know I was here?"

"I subscribe to your e-mail newsletter."

Brenda sat down, ordered, and after the waitress walked away, she put her head down on the table. Her dark hair spread around her, muffling her voice.

"Do you enjoy torturing me?" she said.

"What on earth are you talking about?" I asked.

"I told you after Phoenix I never wanted to see you again. It wasn't that long ago. You couldn't have forgotten, could you? Are you really that dense?"

"No, of course, not. I didn't forget. I just didn't think you *meant* it," I said. "When you said that, you were angry—"

"I had good reason to be."

"True, but you were also upset—"

"Again, with good reason."

I shrugged.

"The reason in both cases was *you*, Carl. You've done enough damage to my reputation. It's been hard work to win back my readers—"

"*Readers?*" I reached into a shopping bag under the table and pulled out a copy of Brenda's latest book, which I'd bought on my way out of the store and skimmed while I waited. "People don't actually read this, do they? If they think this is real, we ought to show them a few things that would really put some hair on their…"

I stopped as Brenda raised her head with fire in her eyes. It was an old dispute of ours. After years of writing articles about supernatural events that the world ignored or covered up, I'd found new hope when I first met Brenda. Pretty, smart, *media-friendly* Brenda. For a while we'd thought together we could convince the world that the supernatural things we'd experienced were real. We hadn't counted on the world not caring about long-legged beasties and things that went bump in the night, on the public preferring to believe that guardian angels could help them eat less chocolate and still be happy. I'd taken it harder than Brenda.

"What do you want, Carl?" Brenda said.

"Information."

"What could *I* possibly tell *you*?"

I dropped the book back in the bag and set my notebook down on the table. "Something weird happened to me last night."

"Something weird happens to you almost every night."

"Well, I do live in L.A., now," I said. "But this was different, like a UFO abduction encounter, with strange lights, my car stalling, and missing time, except it wasn't that at all."

"How can you be sure?"

"No UFO, no aliens, no abduction." I placed a folder next to my notebook then slid it across to Brenda. "I spent most of the day trying to figure it out. I've got an idea about what it was, but it seems impossible. Even to me."

Brenda listened to me describe my encounter on Coronado Street. She deserved credit for that. No matter how much New Age, pop-psychology, feel-good nonsense she wrote to eke out a living, she never lost what made her such a great investigator and writer. When I finished, she glanced inside the folder and flipped through reference pages I'd printed from online sources.

"You're right," she said.

I hesitated then asked, "Are you only saying that so I'll go away and leave you alone?"

"No. You're really right."

"I was afraid of that," I said. "But in this day and age, in a city like Los Angeles?"

"They didn't go away when the cities came," Brenda said. "They only made themselves harder to find. They're all around us. We only see them where the veil is thin, or where their magic is strong—or where someone mucks with their turf. They really hate that. You saw them because meeting the child and making contact with his energy sensitized you. Throw in a wrong turn or two, a little of the Kolchak luck, and there you go. But if everything you say is true, especially about the boy's behavior and voice and the lights around the circle, I don't think it could be anything else."

"Then the boy's almost as good as lost," I said. "There's no easy way to get him back."

"You could beat the fake," Brenda said.

I frowned. "Torture. I read about that."

"I know. It's awful. And there's no guarantee it would bring back the real child. The only other choice is for the one who made the bargain to unmake it. Do you know who it was?"

The picture of Harold Sunderland smiling at me from the Coronado Dale work site sign sprang to mind. "I've got a pretty good idea who to ask. I doubt it will be easy to convince him to go along."

"You'll think of something. You always do."

Brenda asked the waitress for her coffee to go.

"Coffee's on me," I said. "And thank you."

"It's okay. There's a child involved, so I'm glad you came to me." Brenda took out a business card, wrote on the back, and then handed it to me. "I don't want to be in the field anymore, but I'm still doing research. This URL will take you to a private part of my website, where I store raw data for things I'm working on. You'll find some information there that might help you. It's even indexed."

"Wow, you're good. Thanks again." I slid the card into my pocket.

"One thing, though, Carl."

"Name it."

"If you write this one up for the *Dispatch* or anyone else, keep my name out of it."

Brenda proved as good as her word. Her online site provided a trove of information pertinent to Jeffrey's disappearance, including various remedies, warnings, and traditions she'd collected from folklore around the world. It did little to lift my spirits. The odds were against Jeffrey Martin ever being reunited with his mother. As often as I'd faced down vampires, demons, aliens, werewolves, ghosts, and all other manner of mystery and horror, it never once occurred to me that something so insidious could exist in a form I'd always thought of as...*cute*. After comparing Brenda's research to my experiences, though, I had no doubt who had taken the Martin boy.

Or rather, who had accepted him as a bribe.

Given time, I would've dug around until I found proof of what I suspected Sunderland had done. But time I didn't have. The longer Jeffrey was gone, the less likely it was he could ever come home. That is, if it wasn't too late already. I stayed up all night studying Brenda's research and learning what I could about the Coronado Dale development.

I hoped it would be enough.

))●((

At 10:02 the next morning, I arrived at Angela Martin's house. I started a fire in the gas fireplace and asked Angela to get Harold Sunderland over there. It took her four phone calls and some well-timed hysterics, but she got him on his way. Angela opened every window on the first floor.

"It's 82 degrees. Is a fire really necessary?" she asked.

"Yes, it is. Also I'm going to need some beer, half a dozen eggs, and a pitcher of water." I hefted the fireplace poker. "Is this iron?"

"I think so. It's an antique." Angela gave me a blank stare. "What's this all about?"

"You won't believe me if I explain."

Upstairs, the thing-that-wasn't-Jeffrey stomped circles on the floor of his room, shaking a chandelier that hung over us. Muffled crashes and shrill screams came through the ceiling.

"You'd be surprised what I'd believe," Angela said.

She left for the kitchen. The doorbell rang. Then the front door cracked open, and Harold Sunderland stepped partway in and called for Angela. He was a fit, stocky man on the far side of his prime, but hair dye and judicious cosmetic surgery took ten years off his age. I invited him to warm himself by the fire.

"Who the hell are you?" he said.

"Carl Kolchak, *Hollywood Dispatch*." I offered my hand. "A friend of Ms. Martin's."

"What the hell is this?" Mr. Sunderland pushed past me. "Angela!"

"Now, Mr. Sunderland, just a question or two if you don't mind. Is it true your Coronado Dale development experienced a series of dangerous accidents when work began, that in fact you were almost forced to shut down?"

Sunderland stared at me as if I were an insect. "Angela!" he called.

The lady appeared. Everything I needed was piled in her hands.

"Hello, Harold. The truth is I'm not sure what we're doing here," Angela said. "But it's about helping Jeffrey."

Sunderland's expression softened. He gripped Angela's shoulder. "Angela, dear, the change in Jeffrey is awful, I know, but he needs medical attention, medication, therapy."

"I tried all that." Angela shrugged free of Sunderland's hand. "It didn't work."

"You have to give it some time," Sunderland said.

I took the things Angela had gathered and placed everything on the hearth. I cracked the first egg then dumped the yolk and white into an ash pail. I cracked a few more, then balanced each empty half shell on the phony logs at the front of the fire.

"Angela," I said. "Would you please bring Jeffrey here?"

Once she left the room, Sunderland approached me, red-faced and confused. "What on earth are you doing?"

"Isn't it true," I asked, drawing on information from news articles I'd read last night, "that a dozen of your men on the Coronado site were hospitalized with injuries in the first two months of work and that you lost half a million dollars worth of equipment to accidents?"

"What does that have to do with Jeffrey?"

"Isn't it also true that the accidents, which became daily occurrences, ceased four weeks ago—around the time Angela says Jeffrey *changed*—and construction has gone smoothly ever since?"

"I hired a new foreman, one with a better safety record."

A dotted line of sweat beaded on Sunderland's brow. I couldn't be sure if it was the heat or the pressure. Angela carried Jeffrey—wiggling, kicking, yanking her hair—into the room. I opened the beer and poured each eggshell half full, added some water, and then used the poker to nudge them deeper into the flames.

"Put Jeffrey down," I said.

The change in the boy was instantaneous. He stared at the eggshells and the flames.

"What's that?" he said, in his little-boy voice.

"Nothing," I told him. "Wouldn't interest you."

Jeffrey inched closer to the fireplace. "What are you doing?"

Steam rose from the shells. The beer and water popped and bubbled as they came to a boil. Jeffrey gasped and clapped his hands.

"Remarkable!" Jeffrey dropped his little-boy voice for his grizzled, truck-driver voice. "Why, I've lived 800 years and yet I've never seen anything so marvelous and odd! Brewing beer in eggshells! How is it done?"

The boiling beer and the bright shells mesmerized the thing that would be Jeffrey. He clapped again then danced in a circle, giggling. When he stopped, he no longer resembled Angela Martin's little boy. The thing beside me on the hearth was ugly and misshapen like a gnarled tree trunk come to life. Pointed ears. Straggly hair. A mouth full of crooked, uneven teeth. Unaware of the change in his appearance, he stared at the boiling beer and giggled some more.

Angela gasped and dropped onto the couch.

Sweat streaked the sides of Sunderland's face.

"Jeffrey," I said.

The boy glanced at me. "What do you want, Kolchak Old Hack? Don't distract me."

"You've forgotten your glamour."

Jeffrey glanced at himself, realizing that the magic that had disguised him was gone. He peeked at the stunned faces of Sunderland and Angela.

Trembling, Angela said, "What are you?"

The stand-in for Jeffrey jumped full around and pointed a knobby finger at Sunderland. "It was his idea! All his idea! He put us up to it! He made the bargain!"

"Harold," Angela said. "What is that thing? What is it saying? *What… did…you…do?*"

The expression on Harold Sunderland's pale face will remain etched in my memory forever. Ah, I thought, how the mighty have fallen. Sunderland spun us half a dozen lies, even suggesting Jeffrey's transformation proved he wasn't his son. He looked as if he was about to make a run for it.

"Get away from that door, Sunderland," I said. "Or so help me, if you don't put things right, I'll make a bargain of my own and set your little friends loose on every construction project you've got going or ever will have going."

"You wouldn't," he said. "You couldn't."

I gestured to the fireplace where the hideous changeling child was back to staring at the boiling beer. "I did this, didn't I? All it'll take is some silver and gold, a little milk and honey. The little folk are easy enough to handle when you know what they like."

Not that I knew much more than the eggshell trick, which I'd learned from Brenda's research on an old Welsh legend. That it worked amazed me as much as Sunderland. And who knew why it worked? Maybe it was the same reason wooden stakes destroyed vampires, silver harmed werewolves, and a mouthful of salt could stop a zombie. I didn't understand it all, but Sunderland didn't know that.

Looking deflated, he flopped himself beside Angela.

"Harold," she said, her voice tight with anger and fear. "*What is that thing?*"

Harold hung his head. "It's…a *fairy*."

He told us everything after that. As I'd surmised, the great builder of Los Angeles had disturbed a fairy ring when he broke ground at the Coronado site. In retaliation, the fairies had harmed his workers and sabotaged his equipment. The little folk have raised spite and nuisance to an art form, and Sunderland couldn't afford the delays. When you're supporting three ex-wives, half a dozen mistresses, and a jet-set lifestyle with wife number four, any break in cash flow induces panic. Sunderland did the only thing he thought he could: He bargained with the fairies. He accepted a changeling child, a deformed fairy reject, in exchange for one of his children, who went to live in the land of the Fey. In return the fairies lived and let live at the Coronado project. It amazed me how well Angela reacted. She couldn't have been prepared for Sunderland's story, but I think getting Jeffrey back was the only thing that mattered to her. When Sunderland stopped talking, she slapped him.

"What are you going to do about it, Harold?" she said.

I interceded before Sunderland could answer. "He's going to do whatever it takes to get Jeffrey back."

By 12:02 p.m. we were at the Coronado Dale development. Sunderland cleared the work site, gave his workers the afternoon off. The three of us walked the changeling, wearing a hoody to hide his inhuman features, to the fairy ring. I had the fireplace poker in one hand, and I hoped I wouldn't need it. The fairies, it seemed, were expecting us. Lights glittered around the circle, faint in broad daylight. The small voices were there too, speaking in bent squeaks and chirps that sounded almost like words. The lights gathered around Sunderland as he approached the ring. He pleaded and begged with them, promised to return their land, to shut down the Coronado project if only they'd let his son go. Negotiations dragged. Angela held onto me for support, tears streaming from her eyes.

The lights flipped Sunderland's tie into his face, mussed his hair, tied his shoelaces together, undid his belt buckle, and filled the pockets of his suit jacket with gravel. He ignored the tricks and taunts. As I looked closer, the blurs of color and brightness came into focus. I made out tiny people with delicate features, dressed in fine, miniature clothes, and each with wings of some kind—dragonfly, butterfly, bird, even bat and fly wings.

Angela squeezed my arm. "Can this really work?"

"I hope so," I said. "If Jeffrey has eaten or drunk any of the fairies' food then he can never come back. But, time passes differently in their world. To you, he's been gone more than a month, but it may only be a day or two he's been with the fairies. The rest depends on how good a negotiator Harold is."

Angela took some comfort in that. Sunderland hadn't become one of Los Angeles' greatest builders without learning how to cut a deal. The bargaining and pleading concluded when half the lights flitting around ushered the changeling child to the circle's center. The empty air shimmered. I glimpsed brightness and colors through an oval fog of ripples like those of a heat mirage. The changeling vanished into it, giving us a quick wave before he was out of sight.

The oval began to shrink.

"No!" Sunderland shouted. "They're double-crossing us!"

I raised the poker and ran into the circle, thinking of stories from Brenda's website about iron harming fairies, about folktales of people prying open fairy mounds with iron daggers and swords, and then I plunged the tip of the poker into the ground at the ring's center and said a little prayer. The prismatic oval widened.

"Jeffrey!" I called. "Are you there?"

The swirling colors in the oval hurt my eyes, but through them I glimpsed another world—the world of the little people. It looked like a storybook painting come to life. Before I could stop her, Angela dashed by me and crossed into it. I lost sight of her when she passed through a cloud of green and orange light. Beside me, Sunderland fell to his knees, speechless. We were frozen by uncertainty. Then almost as if she'd never been gone, Angela returned, leaping from the oval with Jeffrey in her arms. A squeaky uproar came from the fairy side, and red light started gathering. I pulled the poker from the ground and threw it out of the ring. The oval irised into clear air, and the fairy sounds ceased.

I gave Angela a few minutes with Jeffrey before I drove them home. We left Sunderland on his own in his fairy-disheveled clothes. I figured it would be a long time before he got back to business as usual. In fact, he never did.

They say behind every great man there's a good woman, but what the proverb ignores is that great men aren't necessarily *good* men. Enraged and insulted that Sunderland had broken their bargain, the fairies carried out my bluffed threat all on their own. After that day, every Sunderland project suffered nonstop, fairy sabotage. It took three months for Sunderland's house of cards to collapse, and when the great man fell, all the good women he'd kept behind him—their lovechildren in tow—came out to tell their stories.

Excluding Angela and Jeffrey Martin, that is.

With Jeffrey returned, Angela wanted nothing more to do with Harold Sunderland. She sold everything he'd ever given her, took the money, and left town for a fresh start in a city far away. I wrote her story as it happened and delivered it to Vincenzo—who killed it out of mortal fear of a libel lawsuit from Sunderland. When the Sunderland story broke wide three months later, at least I got to tell Tony, "I told you so."

Picture Man

His eyes troubled me. They refused to take shape in my mind or on paper, and without eyes his face loomed blank and anonymous in a gray fog that hung over my memory of that night. It ate away at me knowing it was there yet unable to picture it. So, over and over again, I drew the subway platform at the York Street stop on the F with its stained pavement, long rows of steel columns painted blue, and wide, tiled pillars; sketched in the bodies draped with soiled white cloths; suggested the spatters of blood as they had fallen in the photo that ran on the front page of the *Post*—and I hoped he would emerge to take his place. But the picture remained incomplete. Without his eyes I couldn't bring him to life or fit him into the scene, and without him my own place in the composition remained a mystery.

I swept the page from my drawing table. It fluttered onto a pile of crumpled failures full of black and white lines and charcoal smudges, all unfinished and useless. Outside, the darkened streets whispered with the late-night din of the city.

Last week I awoke in the hospital to my grumbling stomach and cotton sunlight drifting through the window. That was Wednesday morning, and by then everyone in the city knew my name. They knew my face, too, from a picture Nicolette shot years ago in better days on a warm afternoon in Washington Square Park. The *Post* ran it that Monday, bloated and grainy, on the front page, and the *News* printed it inset over a shot of the subway platform crime scene where the bodies waited to be sealed into black bags. It sat atop a column in the *Times*. Later the networks latched onto it and reduced me to a sardonic graphic over the shoulder of their talking heads. In the picture I'm smiling and wearing my Yankees cap, a little drunk and stoned on a day in June that I remember more clearly than I'd like to.

The city sent a balding lawyer to see me. I couldn't understand what he said because the morphine drip kept me foggy and the cold, hospital light gleamed on his pasty skin. His hands shook as he adjusted his cheap tie while he prattled. He wanted me to sign a paper crowded with small type, but I couldn't hold the pen straight. I giggled each time it slipped loose and fell to the floor, forcing him to crouch and retrieve it. His voice warbled like a worn-out tape playing at the far end of a long tunnel. I heard him say "gun" twice before I drifted back to sleep, only to awaken alone hours later.

Harlow came that evening with all the newspapers I hadn't yet seen; he had saved them for me like he had saved Nicolette for a surprise at the party the night of my attack, though god knows what he'd expected from bringing the two of us together. After two years I wanted to forget Nicolette had ever lived. Harlow stayed until he saw I was still angry with him.

At night the doctor lowered my medication and said I'd feel more alert after a good night's sleep. He wore a tuxedo and surveyed my chart like a maître d' searching his list for a name he knows won't be there. His wife was going to kill him if he made them late for the opera, again, he told me. It was *Fidelio* and her birthday.

"Tell her happy birthday from me," I said, and then I laughed because I had never met his wife and it seemed like the funniest thing I had ever said.

The doctor replied with a patient smile. "I will."

His narrow blue eyes flashed cold, appraising, and deep, and I wondered if he could see right through me, like an MRI, reduce my body to digital slivers of color-coded biological data, and heal me with his eyes.

Others entered my room that night, creeping through like lost ghosts who'd wandered away from their haunts. Nurses and orderlies came and went with efficiency, but others lingered, strange men who moved with conspiratorial slouches and held furtive debates in whispers and gesticulations above my broken body. Their voices hissed like the monsters under the bed come out to argue over the best way to divvy up the meat. How much was dream and how much real, I couldn't say. Days later I sketched my impressions in pen and ink wash on Bristol—loose figures with empty features, hollow eye sockets, generic noses, traces of mouths without lips, the kind of chins that might fit a thousand jaws.

In the morning my head felt like it had been scrubbed clean inside and sterilized. All the pain I'd registered in a dim way the day before became a garish lamp dragged out of the attic and left unexpectedly in the middle of the room burning a two hundred watt spotlight. I glared at the orderly when he crashed my breakfast tray down at my bedside and glared at him again when he clanked it away untouched. His grin sparkled with a giant gold tooth. He flashed a backhanded peace sign as he curved left to make sure his cart jarred the foot of my bed. TV chatter thrummed through the wall from the next room. I tried to remember being brought here but couldn't.

I dozed a while, dipping into cool blackness that made the pain bearable, and when it later subsided to a steady throb, I found the strength to page through the papers Harlow had left.

It's disorienting to read about yourself in the news, stranger still when every word reads like fiction. For example: "…controversial artist noted for his paintings of street people and the homeless is the city's latest avenging vigilante after Sunday morning's subway shootout…" How the hell do you react to that when you don't even know what they're talking about? Every paper and all the news channels carried the same story. Depending on which one I read or heard, I was a hero or a monster. Either way, two teenagers were dead, and I'd spent several days in the hospital unconscious. The *Post* called it the "Subway Showdown." A *Times* editorial dubbed it "the York Street massacre." Outside City Hall, supporters in NRA T-shirts faced off against protestors crying racism because two black teens had been shot dead. If it hadn't been my name in the article, my picture below the headlines, it might have made some sense instead of feeling like a sick practical joke. I dredged my memory for any detail or sensation to stitch together what had happened after I had left Harlow's party, but the fog between then and now hung thick and heavy around me.

I slept the entire afternoon and opened my eyes that evening to Harlow reading a book in the bedside chair. My anger had burned itself out, and I took comfort in how his eyes brightened as I awoke.

"How you feeling, kiddo?" he asked

"Gonna run the Marathon. Dumb question."

"Ethan, I'm sorry, you know. I really am. I shouldn't have lied about Nico being there, but I wish you hadn't left the party so angry like that. The doctors weren't sure about your chances when you came in here."

I waved a weak hand at him. "Screw it. Don't beat yourself up. Buy me a beer when I get out of here. I'm just glad to see you."

He reclined, satisfied. Even if I was the kind to carry a grudge I couldn't have held one against Harlow. He'd done too much for me, helped me with connections and advice, taught me my way around the city. He'd put me up when I ran out of money and lost my Lower East Side apartment. He'd gotten me work when I needed it.

He'd introduced me to Nicolette.

Harlow had lived in the city all his life, his family for generations. I'd never met anyone who knew it better. We met when I took his class at the School of Visual Arts the year I moved out here from Columbus. Harlow painted covers for the *New Yorker* and had his work exhibited in galleries. People knew his name. He was a good contact for a young artist. I never understood why he'd become so fond of me until Nicolette told me I reminded him of their kid brother who'd been murdered in a robbery fifteen years ago.

"I don't know what to make of all that stuff in the news," I said.

"Those prick reporters. They've been calling me night and day, asking about you, what kind of guy you really are, if you're psycho or some kind of thing. I told them to fuck off." He reached beside his chair and produced the tabloid-sized portfolio I'd brought to the party A dusty footprint marred the black leather. "Retrieved from the damn police after two days of screaming at bureaucrats. I thought you'd want to know it was safe."

I unzipped and opened it. Hink's portrait greeted me.

His lazy eyelids drooped in charcoal strokes that suggested the air of crushing weight that surrounded him; a filthy hunter's cap sloped off his head. He had stunk like whiskey and rotten meat and the sewer, but I'd forced myself to get near enough to record his face and the defeated slump of his shoulders. I had found him sleeping on the subway on my way to Harlow's that night, and Hink had woken as I finished. He stared at me until he decided I was safe then asked me for a buck. I handed him a ten, and he looked at me harder.

"Oh, you da pitcher guy. Tanks, man. I put dis inna bank, save it for my bus ticket home. Going see my daughter down in A'lanta." He tucked the money into the folds of his greasy coat, sniffled, coughed, and then blew his nose into one of his gloves.

"Hink, right? Sorry I didn't recognize you asleep."

"S'okay. Hey, hear about Julio? Dead. Cut up or some shit. Cut right up."

Old Julio hung around a dumpster on 31st street near the corner of Eighth Avenue, and claimed he used to be a bullfighter down in Mexico. Some people believed him.

"Sorry to hear that. What happened?"

"Fuck should I know? One day Julio's okay, next day he's cut up. Cops took his body. Where dey take it, man, huh? To bury it? Nuh. Cops needs bodies like dat, even a shriveled old bag of bones like Julio."

"They take bodies to the morgue," I said.

Hink laughed, then pulled a bottle from his jacket and took a long slug. "You all right, pitcher man. Fuckin' morgue. Heh."

He offered me the liquor, but I passed. I slung the portfolio strap across my chest as the train braked into my stop.

"Stay warm, Hink. See you around."

"That's right. You see me around. This my line, now, pitcher man."

As the doors closed, he'd slumped in his seat and seemed to doze off again.

I closed the portfolio on Hink's portrait and grinned at Harlow. It felt sweet to have my work back in my hands.

"The damn police recovered it from the platform. You must have dropped it in the attack. That decorative boot smear is courtesy New York's finest. Otherwise, apparently, it's clean of evidence, which is the only reason I was able to get them to part with it."

"Thanks. I don't remember any of it. I feel like I should, but I can't."

"The doctors said that might happen. They had aluminum baseball bats. Pulled a fucking Reggie on you, kiddo. Worked you over real well."

"Papers say I shot them. They were just high school kids."

"They would've beaten you to death if you hadn't. And not so innocent, these two. Couple of gangbangers from Fort Greene, wanted for vandalism, suspected of rape, and earlier that night kicked out of The Tunnel for a fistfight. So, probably drug dealers, too."

"I've never even fired or held a gun. I don't even know how to switch off the safety or aim," I said.

"Sometimes we do what we have to, right? Doesn't matter in the heat of the moment if we know or not. Reality takes a nose dive, and we just learn real fucking fast and try to keep up. You took the gun off one of the thugs and you used it."

Harlow filled a paper cup with water from the plastic pitcher on my bedside table and offered it to me.

"Here, drink this. You sound like a cricket."

The water soothed my throat. I downed another cup right after it. Hunger flared in my gut. "Feel like I haven't eaten in days."

"Nothing solid, you haven't." He pointed to the intravenous drip plugged into a vein in my arm. "Shitty hospital chow ain't even food anymore."

"When can I get out of here?"

"Maybe a few days. Maybe more. They want to run some tests, check for brain damage. I told them to skip it. 'Too late!' I said, but they're fucking sticklers here, right?"

I forced a smile. "Someone came to see me yesterday. A lawyer, I think."

He nodded. "Suit and tie from the city. They want to schedule a hearing. Appointed you representation."

"I won't be able to tell them much. Shit, could I go to jail for this?"

"You were fighting for your life. What can they do?" Harlow hesitated and cleared his throat. "Listen, I hate to bring this up. I don't want to upset you, but my sister wanted me to ask if she could visit you. She's very concerned."

I felt hollow thinking about Nicolette, like a kicked dog when I visualized her face, but part of me wanted to be near anyone who might help me, was willing to do anything to not be alone. "I don't know. Not just yet."

"I understand."

Harlow stood and stretched. Although he always dressed stylishly and in clean, well-pressed clothes, he looked as if he had gone two days and slept in his open-collar, button-down shirt and flannel slacks. Dark rings underscored his eyes. He took his overcoat from the wall hook and shrugged into it.

"Thanks for looking out for me," I said.

"Trust me, Ethan. Everything will be all right. Sometimes things get bigger than you want to know about around this town. It's best you let them work themselves out. Don't fight. You've got friends who'll take care of you."

"What do you mean?"

Harlow seemed on the verge of continuing when the small-eyed doctor, his tux replaced by pale green scrubs, entered. Harlow, looking grateful for the interruption, said goodnight, and then left. The doctor, whose named turned out to be Packer, flashed a penlight in my eyes and asked how it felt when I flinched. He detailed my injuries as he worked, but I couldn't translate his explanations into the relentless aching that clothed my body.

"You're a very lucky man, Mr. Kammerer. This could've gone quite differently, and we wouldn't be having this conversation."

His probing stare stirred an old memory of when I had seen eyes like his on a pale, manic man who haunted Times Square, perched on a milk crate, screaming obscenities at the crowd. Every day the police chased him from corner to corner, but he always returned to shout horrible things and bark perverse demands at passersby. His eyes had blazed like needles of sky ready to pin you where you stood if you were too slow, as though he could read your hopes and dreams in your face—and wanted to piss all over them.

Once, when I had a freelance gig in the neighborhood, I borrowed Nicolette's camera and used a zoom lens to photograph him from across the street. Close-ups of his apoplectic face and flailing arms. People rushing by or cowering back. A French couple who stopped to argue with him. The cops threatening him. Through it all his eyes remained sharp and terrible.

The doctor's eyes penetrated me the same way.

"We'll run a CAT scan in the morning if you're up to it," he said.

"Hey, doc, how was *Fidelio?*"

"She loved it. It was a good night. We had a lovely dinner afterwards."

The hospital discharged me a week later. I tried to work on the assignments I'd left untouched during my stay, but my incomplete vision of the York Street station obsessed me. I spent hours drawing it, discarding each half-done piece as I found myself blocked by the empty face of the man I knew should be in the scene but couldn't visualize. I called Harlow about it and told him memory slivers from that night kept bobbing to the surface when my mind turned to sorting the mail or buying a cup of coffee at the corner bodega. The fog was burning off. Three kids had attacked me that night, not two, and I was certain a fourth person had been there—the man with no eyes.

Harlow suggested I get out for a while, so I met him for lunch in the dining room at the New York Association of Illustrators building off Lexington Avenue. We filled our plates from the buffet and ate beneath a Wyeth painting. Sketches of the Association's past presidents watched over us from the back wall. Halfway through our meal, a man in an immaculate, black suit and yellow, silk tie entered. Harlow waved him over to us.

The polished man swept a hand through his neat-cropped, sandy hair as he approached. A gold watch dangled from his wrist. Harlow introduced him as Mr. Jones, "an old friend interested in your work," and he took a seat with us.

Jones claimed he was an artist, but he was lying.

I think he knew I didn't believe him, but he didn't care. He possessed the indifference of a cunning predator that ignores potential prey when its belly is full and its ravenous needs are sated, but god help you if you're around when its stomach grumbles. Taking occasional sips of water, he asked me how they treated me in the hospital, if I was I happy with my city lawyer, and did I still like living in New York after ten years. He wanted to know if I had much family, and if I ever considered a more lucrative profession than art? A sense of dark symmetry crept over me as the tone of his voice hearkened back to the fevered shadows plotting in whispers above my hospital bed. Harlow quietly ate his lunch.

"Tell me how you started using street people in your work," Jones said.

"They're more interesting than other people," I told him. "Their lives are etched in their faces. They have nothing to hide because no one ever really looks at them. I was coming down Thirty-First Street from the Garden one night, walking past a group of men gathered along the wall of St. Francis of Assisi. Most of them were asleep, since it was two o'clock in the morning, but a few clustered around a heating vent for the warmth. It was October, and the weather had turned chilly. One of them asked me for change. I realized when he looked at me that he didn't expect me to see him. I mean, he knew I would hear him, notice him, probably ignore him, but no one ever really perceived him. His face captivated me. The lines caked with dirt and grime. His bright, watery eyes. The gnarled sneer he tried to pass off as a smile. I gave him five dollars to let me draw him there and then by the glow of the streetlights. After I finished, I felt like I'd discovered a new country, the home of the cast-off and forgotten, the discarded and meaningless. That was right after Nico left. I think part of me believed maybe I belonged down there, too."

"It's a very bountiful country you discovered," Jones said.

"What do you mean?"

"You've found your niche, your idiom. Like one of those people who paint nothing but pictures of cows, always the same cow, but with different settings or different colors or textures. A cow with wings. A cow with horns. A polka dot cow, a plaid one. Maybe a cow reading the paper, but always just dumb cattle with a pretense of intelligence or the divine. Variations on a theme, but your themes are pain and disillusionment and dehumanization. And it's your best work. It's earned you some recognition, hasn't it?"

"I suppose."

"Do you find it dangerous?"

"I've learned to be careful and stay away from the really crazy ones and the crack-heads. Most of them are like you or me, just lost. I've met a few who have a sense of purpose as if they could get themselves off the street if they chose to. I can tell who'll make a good subject."

The tilt of Jones's smile hinted that I had answered the wrong question. His cell phone rang, then, and he turned aside to answer it.

A few moments later, he said, "I'll be there in twenty minutes. Thank you."

Jones stood, patted Harlow on the back, and offered me his hand. I shook it.

"I'm sorry I have to leave. I've enjoyed meeting you, Ethan. Maybe I can stop by your studio sometime. Thank you for inviting me, Harlow. We'll chat later."

Jones snaked among the tables and out of the room. Harlow shoved his plate away, food unfinished.

"He's no artist," I said.

"No," said Harlow.

"You don't need a pretense to introduce me to your friends over lunch."

"He's not exactly a friend."

"No? What's going on, Harlow?"

"Trust me, Ethan."

"I do. Or I wouldn't have sat here answering very personal questions for a total stranger."

Harlow nodded his concession while I sipped hot coffee from a yellowed ceramic mug.

"I'll remember sooner or later. Every time I draw it, I get closer to the missing parts. I believed it for a few days, you know, what they said in the news, but they're wrong. Maybe I'll remember before my hearing. What might happen if I tell the truth, then, I wonder."

"Mostly unpleasant things, kiddo, because the city fathers seem content with the story as it stands. Clear-cut self-defense is hard to hold against a man, especially when he used his attacker's weapon to protect himself. You change the story, they have to bring the damn police back in, re-open the investigation, stir up the protestors. What you ought to do is concentrate on getting your work back on track."

"The *New York Press* said those kids died of broken necks, not gunshot wounds, and the coroner's office covered it up."

"Don't swallow that fucking crackpot stuff. Sheesh."

The waiters began clearing the other tables. We were the last guests in the room.

"I have to go, now, too. Stay and finish your coffee, then go home and work. And listen, Nico is going to call you tonight. I've been holding her back, but she won't wait anymore. She wants to talk to you. She has some serious things to say. Maybe you should take the call. What harm can it do to talk?"

"You're hiding something, Harlow. You're my friend, and I appreciate you trying to protect me, but I can only play along with this for so long. The truth is going to come to me on its own, sooner or later."

"Ethan, you see a lot of things other people don't. See them differently, too. That's one of the reasons I've always liked you. Sometimes it's possible to see things you shouldn't, and when you do it's smart to look away. Well, okay then, we'll do it your way, but I hope you like where it leads."

Harlow left. When my coffee grew cold I walked downstairs and wandered into the first floor gallery and an exhibit of turgid paperback covers, Sunday magazine political illustrations, and trim little editorial cartoons. Nothing at all that put itself on candid display so that I might catch some glimmer of my own reflection. I left, plunged down the subway entrance steps on the corner, jumped on the downtown F, closed my eyes, and waited for York Street.

Despite living only three blocks from the nearest stop, I had avoided the subway since leaving the hospital. When my train emerged from the long dark ride below the East River, I stepped onto the platform and froze. The early evening commuter crowd streamed around me. The station looked no different than it ever had and utterly disassociated from the grotesque of the crime scene photos. The stale air carried the odor of piss and garbage. Voices rattled around the tunnel like a bad recording, capped by a teenager shouting in Spanish at his girlfriend who walked backward toward the stairs while flipping him the bird. As the crowd emptied out, I glimpsed here and there a familiar face, artists like me who had moved out to the industrial neighborhood down under the Brooklyn-side of the Manhattan Bridge seeking cheap space to live. All of them looked away when they saw me. No sign of the killings remained where the bodies had fallen, no bloodstains or cop drama chalk outlines, no overlooked shell casings, just dirty concrete flattened and smeared by the passage of the countless feet of unknowing travelers, tarred with discarded chewing gum and littered with lost papers and crushed food wrappers.

I had left Harlow's party drunk and angry and without a word of goodbye.

Better I had walked out as soon as I saw ashen-haired Nicolette, so at least I would've been sober coming home. But I had stayed to show my indifference, ignoring her endless glances from across the room until they pricked too deep. Then, wounded and inebriated, I had grabbed my coat and portfolio and fled, desperate for fresh air and solitude, heading downtown along Fifth past the darkened shops and closing restaurants while cabs blared their horns and slalomed down the street.

I had never loved another woman like I had Nicolette. Our time together had been intense and electric as we plundered each other for secret treasures. For six months we were hardly ever apart, drawn to each other physically as though we each possessed a special gravity that forbade the other to travel too far for too long. We spent seemingly endless hours together making love, working, exploring the city by night. And then one day she was, very simply, no longer there to fill the cold hollow her absence left in my existence. After that I never wanted to see her again unless it was to take her back for good.

I don't know what time it was when I got on the F that night.

The three teens boarded at Delancey Street with their sweat-jacket hoods up and pulled tight to hide their faces. Tarnished silver bats swayed in their hands.

I should have gotten off at East Broadway, waited for the next train with the pierced-nose blonde who fled the teens' lewd comments, but I was drunk and cocky enough to think I could go one more stop unbothered. As we rumbled under the river, though, one of them sized me up and then slapped his two companions and gestured in my direction with his bat. I pulled on the door to the next car, but it was locked, and the trio came at me. Dull pain exploded in my back. I fought to stay on my feet, bracing myself against the wall as they took turns swinging at me in the enclosed space. The train braked abruptly, rolling into the York Street station, jarring us off-balance. Two of the teens slipped to their knees in a puddle of malt liquor dribbling from an old bottle. I lunged past them and out the door, stumbling along the platform, the slapping of their sneakers pursuing me. A bat smacked my legs and I folded to the floor, cracking my jaw against concrete. A follow-up shot crashed against my shoulder and another ended at my forearm where I'd thrown it across my face. My portfolio spun loose and skittered away. The wet smacking of their bats filled my ears. I tucked my head in, but they came at me from different sides, their bats flashing down in dull streaks that terminated in flares of angry pain, probing their way to my skull. The darkness began to swirl. I clambered over the filthy ground, and then—

—the beating stopped.

I cringed, anticipating the next blow, the one that might kill me.

The steamy air quivered with a scream, hollow, tinny, and trilling with fear.

Frantic voices howled and bodies scuffled. A bat soared across the track and clanged against the tunnel wall, chipping tile. A rumbling filled my ears. I took it for an approaching train before realizing it was the throaty snarl of a beast enraptured with its ferocity. I lifted my head but shooting pain forced me down. I wanted to vomit. A hand flapped against the ground, blood painted across its palm and the gold ring stretched across two fingers. Then it slid away, inch-by-inch, dragged by something unseen.

One of the kids wrestled me onto my back. His hood had been ripped loose and tears streamed down his cheeks. His young eyes pleaded with me.

"Please help me! Sorry, I'm sorry! You gotta help me!" he shouted.

The boy's eyes stand clear in my memory, wide and brown and glistening with life and fear, but in the time it took me to suck in a deep, painful breath, transformed into glass artifacts as a snarling thing seized him from behind and twisted his body. It's the eyes of my savior that elude me, the face I glimpsed when—driven past my pain by the raw, rending sounds rising from the platform—I raised my head and witnessed him.

))●((

How long had Hink stood there watching me while memories unreeled through my mind? How long had I sat on the bench clutching my head as I remembered?

"Saw you from the train, pitcher man. You all right?" he asked.

"It's a lie, Hink. Nothing happened the way they say it did."

"Tha's life, but I figger a lie's as good as the truth as long as you believe it. Most time anyways."

"I didn't shoot them. Someone else did. After they were dead. I think it was a cop. I heard the gunshots. Someone stopped them from killing me, but I can't remember who."

"Don't matter, pitcher man. You alive. S'good enough," Hink shuffled his feet and wrung his soiled cap in his hands. "Hey, you wanna draw me? You got a couple bucks?"

I handed Hink a five. "Take it. I don't feel like drawing right, now."

Hink snatched the bill and tucked it into the recesses of his stained coat. "So what if it didn't happen like they say? So what? You gotta know that bad?"

"It's chewing me up. I can't work, can't think straight."

"Cause, see, I was there that night. I seen them hit you with bats. Felt real bad, too, but what could I do alone? Saw that guy with black eyes, like glass or sumthin' when he climbed up from the tracks and pulled them kids off you."

"Up from the tracks?"

Hink nodded. "Don't know what he was doing down there, but yeah, I can't forget his eyes."

"Black like oil or obsidian. His mouth livid with jagged teeth. An eel's mouth."

"Yeah, I guess. He took that kid. Slashed him up real bad with his fingers, like, and dragged him into the tunnel. When the cops come, he told them what to do, and they lissen'd to him. You right about the gun. I seen 'em shoot those kids whose heads was twisted sideways, and then they left the gun in your hand, took some pitchers. Took everyone away."

I stared at Hink. "Oh, god, I remember…"

The fog broke all at once.

I pushed past Hink, out of the subway, and rushed home, where images flowed from my fingers faster than I could draw. The bodies tumbled into place, the shadows unfurled like wind-borne sails, and at the center hung the eyes that had escaped me, shining and abyssal like fluid-filled potholes. They stared at me from the page, the face growing around them from the blunt tip of my charcoal, its lips pulled back to bare sharp teeth varnished with blood, and a jiggling tag of flesh dangling from an exaggerated canine as it rose from the torn neck of a dead boy. Drops of dark fluid stained its white shirt. I recognized the dangling gold watch, the familiar line of the jaw, the close-cut hair.

Jones.

The phone rang in the other room. The machine picked up, and Nicolette's voice spoke.

Fear and desire collided within me. Nico could be a safe haven.

Images erupted in my mind like fireworks—Nico's hair spilling onto my face as her lips brushed mine, a half-moon above the Brooklyn Bridge as she squeezed my hand, the fathomless depths of her eyes as our bodies locked together in shadows. I needed a friend, and I didn't trust Harlow anymore. I grabbed the handset before Nicolette finished and blurted out everything.

At the end, I said, "Nico, you're the only person I trust. Whatever's behind us is done, I know. Maybe there's a future for us, maybe not, but I have to deal with this now, and I need your help."

She said nothing at first, and I thought she might hang up on me.

"I'm sorry about how I left you, Ethan, and, of course, I'll help you."

Her words brought me a wave of relief.

"I came to the party that night to apologize. I never should've walked away like that. I'll send a car for you, and we can be together tonight."

We spoke a little longer, reassuring each other that we should be together, that repairing our relationship made sense. An hour later a black sedan left me outside an apartment building on Central Park East. Black trees loomed over the street like the frontier of a savage world. A doorman greeted me and ushered me across the lobby to the elevator.

"Go right up, sir," he said. "Ms. Van Fleet is expecting you."

He pressed the button for the top floor and kept watch as the doors slid shut. A minute later they opened again onto a foyer opposite two wide, open doors.

"Nico," I called.

They waited for me amidst opulence—Harlow and Nicolette, Dr. Packer, Jones, and a handful of others—politicians I knew from the news and Wall Street moguls, popular leaders who engineered protests in minority neighborhoods, musicians, and prominent publishers—all of them regarding me with eager faces and half smiles, watching me from leather couches and silk-draped chairs. Behind them, through a wall-length, floor-to-ceiling window, sprawled the vast darkness of Central Park and the sparkling lights of Midtown and Lower Manhattan, bound by the dark stripes of the East River and the Hudson. One of Harlow's paintings hung above the marble fireplace.

Nicolette took my hand. "Come in, Ethan. It's all right. Things weren't meant to happen this way, but we'll make the best of it."

She led me to a high-backed, leather chair facing all the others in the room.

"How does it feel to remember? Do you like knowing? Does it eat away at you any less than not knowing?" Jones asked.

"What are you?" I said.

Jones smiled. "I am whatever I wish to be."

"You killed those boys, not me."

"That's true. The third boy I dragged into the darkness and devoured among the rats. Really you owe your life to Nicolette. She came to the party that night to be with you, Ethan, and if she hadn't wanted you back, I wouldn't have been following you. You'd have been beaten to death."

I looked to Nicolette. "What's he talking about?"

"I missed you, Ethan. I wanted to be with you again, but it meant you'd have to join us. Jones agreed to observe you at the party, to consider you," she said.

Jones dragged over an ottoman and sat across from me.

"This is *our* city, Ethan. We own it the way most people think they own their co-op. We possess more than half the five boroughs, though you'd never prove it on paper. We don't accept new persons lightly into our fold. We've been here since the Dutch and very little happens in this city without our influence. That kind of power doesn't come easily. It requires a hunger that's never sated and a clear sense of your place at the top of the world. There are only two types of people who interest me—the extremely powerful and the utterly powerless. Everyone else is an ignorant animal struggling to become one or not become the other. I admire your work. You're naturally drawn to those who know they are little more than cattle with no illusions of a higher purpose other than as human fodder to be ground up to keep the city running. It's what attracted you to Nicolette, made you friends with Harlow, led you to the work you do. You've built your success off the souls of others and paid them a pittance for their time and when you've risen above them, they'll remain in the gutter, like maggots brushed from your sleeve."

Jones rose and walked through a nearby arch. The others followed him, and Nicolette guided me after them into a room dominated by a wide dining table set with delicate china and gleaming silver utensils. Slender candelabras flanked the table. Jones lit the candles at one end, while Harlow attended to the other. An oversized, oblong platter occupied the center, its silver cover reflecting our faces like a funhouse mirror. Tiny opals of condensation bejeweled the lid where steam leaked out from beneath it. The diners seated themselves and Nicolette gestured for me to take the place beside her. Jones set his hand on my shoulder.

"The city is our bounty, Ethan, an endless source of nourishment for those strong enough to accept it. It changes you, of course, but the power is intoxicating. You'll see the world in ways you never imagined you could. It all becomes crystal clear once you join our feast."

Jones removed the shining cover to reveal Hink's naked torso arranged on the tray, his limbs severed neatly and removed at the joints, his head tilted back as though he were staring upward toward the heavens. The smell of raw flesh and coppery blood made my head swim.

"Devourer or devoured. All of us are one, until inevitably we become the other or die. Those who understand this thrive."

The diners attacked the platter, slicing away chunks of Hink's grimy flesh and sliding them onto their plates. Someone uncorked a bottle of wine and poured. All around the table, the feasters' eyes became wide, black hollows and their mouths grew feral, baring ragged, yellow teeth. Nicolette set a generous portion of Hink's chest on my plate. I stared at her distorted face and wondered if some part of me had sensed it lurking beneath the surface all those years ago when we first met.

"We did all this for you, Ethan, for us," she said.

I looked down at the warm meat. Nicolette had gone without a word and left me with two years of emptiness—all the time during which I'd learned to see the things beneath people's skin and taught myself to survive on what I could siphon from the world around me. The knowledge threatened to swallow me. The others picked away at Hink's skinned ribcage.

Nicolette's eyes pleaded with me. A warm tear trickled down my cheek.

"It's hard at first, but everything will be fine when you accept the world for what it is."

My stomach raged to be fed.

My soul ached to embrace Nicolette once more, but it was for the Nicolette of my memories that I yearned.

I shoved my chair back, toppling it to the floor, then ran into the next room, struggling against unwanted cravings. Nicolette followed and stood by me. Her watery eyes reverted to normal. Pity and loss drifted across her face as I fled.

I've seen Nicolette only once more, glimpsed her, vibrant and alluring, rolling by in the back of long, black car, window down, on Eighth Avenue where I huddled in a doorway for the night with a filthy blanket draped over my shoulders. I never returned to my apartment. I tried to leave the city that night, but when I tried to buy a ticket on the next departing Amtrak from Penn Station, the police grabbed me. They led me away as a feeling of intense horror came over me at the idea of seeking a new place in the world, knowing that the perverse hunger that slept inside me would follow me anywhere I could run.

The tide from City Hall turned against me then. I spent two years in prison, convicted of manslaughter. After my release I took to the streets, afraid to become anything more than another filthy, anonymous soul, safe in squalor and darkness. They could have ended me after that night, sent me away for the rest of my life or had me killed and wiped out all trace of my existence, but there is meaning in the fate that they designed, a message intended to soften me, and I'm afraid that if I ever struggle to be more than raw fodder, they will come for me again and present me with the feast for a second time.

And my hunger has grown.

Red Mami

A tall, white stranger—a *trenja* from a faraway land—smiled sadly and threw us bottles of water. They glistened as they flew over the gravel path between the orange mesh fences, off limits to all but the *dohktas*, who came in only to examine us or take us away to *hospitu*. On our side, men caught each bottle then passed them out until everyone had one, but our men didn't smile at all. No one in our little tent-and-canopy village did unless they passed three weeks with no Ebola and left to go free back home. The rest rode stretchers to *hospitu* or walked there leaning on a *dohkta's* shoulder. The *dohktas* wore yellow suits over their whole bodies with blue gloves, cello-wrap headdresses, gauze masks, and plastic eye shields. The ones they sent to *hospitu* had no reason or strength to smile. The *fiva* burned in them. Their bodies shook with aches. Soon they would bleed.

This morning, the yellow-suits took two to *hospitu* and opened the gate to freedom for a white-haired *grani* leaning on a crooked walking stick, but she didn't smile. Her sons, daughters, grandsons, and granddaughters had all gone to *hospitu* while she waited.

Some scratched lines in the dirt to count the days the yellow-suits must watch them. I came to this fearful place too scared to think of counting, asking only where my Mami and Dadi had gone. No good daughter forgets to worry about her parents.

At my village, Dadi worked in the fields or sifted for diamonds in the muddy runnels outside the big company mine. My Mami cooked and sewed. After school, I did my work and the work my older sister, Olivette, had done before a motorcycle ran her down in the road last year. My brother, Barrie, came home from Freetown for her funeral to comfort my parents, but in a week he returned to his work there. A cloud of sadness hung over our *os*, and it only deepened the day Dadi came home burning with the *fiva*. Mami tended to him until she caught it too. Then they burned together, and when they bled my uncle called the *dohktas*.

Men came to our *os* in yellow suits with wands tied to silver barrels on their backs. They woke me from bed and sprayed *meresin* on all the walls and floors to kill the Ebola. The beds of my Mami and Dadi lay stripped bare. A fire blazed behind our house. Greasy smoke twined into the clear sky. I asked the yellow-suits if Mami and Dadi had gone to *hospitu*, but none would say, and uncle stood far away from me, frowning in silence. The yellow-suits sent me on a truck with others from my village to meet the tall white *trenja*, the water bottle man with bright eyes always wet with unshed tears. He greeted us from a distance, talking a little *Krio*, but mostly English. One of the *mamis* told her tiny *bobo* he came from a distant place where kangaroos hop and ostriches run, and the *bobo* laughed and said maybe the *trenja* would bring one hopping out from a tent. His *mami* laughed too, the last good laugh I heard since coming here.

Every day, the yellow-suits take our temperature with a fancy pen they press to our foreheads and shine lights in our eyes and down our throats. Some try to hide the *fiva*, but they only vex the yellow-suits. The sick must go to *hospitu* before their blood comes. If you get too close or touch one who bleeds, the yellow-suits start over counting your days. Before I came here, a man who took secret care of his *misis* after she began to bleed started his days over when the yellow-suits found out. After I arrived, they released him home with tears on his cheeks.

I opened my water bottle and drank. The yellow-suits fed us well, even brought us ice cream cups and bananas boiled in spices, but I missed the sweet cakes I made with my Mami. They had been Olivette's favorite, the first thing we learned to cook. Here we ate mostly rice and cassava leaves or stew with peanuts, slept on mats or cots, and relieved ourselves in a wooden latrine that stank so ugly I buried my face in the crook of my arm when I had to go.

Outside the fences, men unloaded boxes from trucks furred with orange dirt. Down a hill, shaded by trees, *hospitu* waited for the sick, and armed soldiers saw to it everyone obeyed the *dohktas*. Beyond it trucks and motorcycles spun brown manes of dust from the road to Freetown. I wished I could hop the fences, jump into a truck, and let it carry me to Barrie, who promised to show me the city when I grew older. If Mami and Dadi could not take me home, I wanted to go to him when I left the camp.

In the mornings, the young *mamis* tended the children and sang, but the little ones never danced. Even the youngest sensed the fear, like I did, and the weight of the sullen, quiet stares of the men who helped when they could but mostly looked lost with no work to do and their hands so clean. They prayed to keep themselves busy, lined up on prayer rugs and bowed east or sat in circles and crossed themselves.

New faces came. Familiar ones left. Many from my truck went to *hospitu*.

I asked a yellow-suit who took my temperature how many days I had left. She promised to check but never gave me an answer.

That night, the bleeding woman walked through our camp.

A truck engine woke me, and I saw her. My heart beat so fast I feared it might crack open my chest, but I couldn't look away. She visited many of the others, one at a time, standing or kneeling by them. Man, woman, child, any of us, all of us, she stroked their hair or held their hand, smearing blood on whatever she touched. She walked nude, and blood ran down her dark skin from scalp to foot as if an invisible man emptied slaughterhouse buckets one after another onto her head. Her eyes glowed white through the deep red. Blood slicked her shoulders, ran between her breasts, and dripped from her nipples. It poured down her belly, legs, and feet, and trickled into the dirt. I had never seen so much blood. She wore it like a second skin. I held my breath wishing she wouldn't notice me, and when I blinked she disappeared like a piece of a dream trapped in the corner of my eye.

After that, she came back every night.

Some nights she sang in a soft, cooing voice, and blood bubbled and sprayed from her lips. She looked beautiful when the moonlight shone on her bloody skin, her large breasts, her wide hips and strong thighs, and all her curves. Beautiful and terrible, with a body like all my friends and sisters wished for to attract a good husband. Olivette had begun to look like that before the motorcycle mangled her. I wondered how she passed the guards and the yellow-suits, if she had escaped from the *dohktas*, but mostly I feared her bloody touch and the yellow-suits counting my days all over because all the ones she visited went to *hospitu*.

One night when voices from *hospitu* woke me, the bleeding woman knelt by an old man. She held his hand while he tossed and turned. Noticing me, she watched me with wide mother's eyes. She smiled, but with no mother's smile, all knotted with worries and love, but a little one's birthday smile, eager and blissfully greedy. I rubbed my eyes and blinked, but this time when I opened them, she remained. She came to me. The blood rippling over her body sprang from the top of her head. Clots clung to her close-cut hair and slid down the sides of her face. She sang a whispering song. I didn't understand the words. I held my mouth shut, afraid I might scream and wake the children sleeping around me.

Her smile grew, showing me teeth outlined with black blood. She blew me a kiss the way my Mami used to do. Then she vanished.

From the far side of the tent, a man stared at me. Some in the camp spoke of him in whispers. They called him *pickin solja*—child soldier. He had fought in our civil war before I was born, a boy forced by warlords to kill with gun and knife. Women pitied him for what he suffered, but they also feared him. Some of the men, especially fat, sweaty Musa, took women in the night, covered their mouths, and dragged them to a dark corner to have their way. The *pickin solja's* stare frightened me more than the bleeding woman's stare. I pretended to ignore him, lay my head down, and gazed on the half-moon nested in thin clouds, feigning sleep until dawn, listening for footsteps that never came.

In the morning, I searched for the woman's bloody prints but not a drop of her blood remained.

The yellow-suits came and sent three to *hospitu*. A boy not much older than me, whose *mami* cried on the other side of camp, the old man whose hand the woman had held in the night, and a *johmp-johmp* woman, who had lain with many men. The yellow-suits shined a light in my eyes and poked a flat stick against my tongue, took my temperature, and patted me on the back. A few more days, one said, but they said that every day. My stomach ached and cramped like I might vomit, but I said nothing, afraid they might send me to *hospitu*.

The *pickin solja* came to me by the fence.

"Why were you staring at me last night?"

I shook my head and avoided his eyes.

"Come, now, tell me. Were you even awake?"

I shrugged. He squinted like my teacher when I forgot my homework.

"Maybe you were staring at someone else?"

Again I shook my head.

"Keeping secrets can protect you. People don't always understand stories, even honest ones, especially if they don't want to hear them. How old are you, *titi*?"

"Thirteen," I told him, hitching my hip out, trying to sound grown up.

He chuckled without smiling. "Be grateful you are still a child at your age. Many in our country grow up much sooner than you. Secrets can become heavy for young ones. Share your burden with me if you want. You can trust me. We have a secret in common, I think. We both see the woman who wears blood, don't we?"

My mouth opened, but fear locked my voice inside me. The *pickin solja* only nodded.

"My name's Foday. We can talk when you're ready."

The *trenja* arrived then with water bottles piled in a large bucket. He shouted a bright "*Aw de bodi?*" and the men answered, "All well!" as they lined up to catch the water. The *trenja* looked like a big man, one much too important to throw bottles, yet he did so every day, calling across the gravel path, joking with the men, trying to remember all our names. The people pitied him as he pitied us because none of us could do anything but wait.

Foday handed me a bottle. Some of the women glared at us. Their gazes followed him as he walked away, big cats stalking prey, then snapped back to me as if they'd caught me stealing. Their eyes made my skin crawl. I drank my water in a shady corner by myself.

A woman called Claudetta warned me not to talk to Foday: "The *pickin soljas* did horrible things to women in the war because the warlords killed those who refused to follow orders. Maybe they don't bear all the guilt but what they done made them different than other men. Some, they gone down to Freetown where the *dohktas* help them in the university. Others, they gone on to new villages for what work comes their way, but they never walk far from their past. That one, Foday, he lives in my village. In the war, he raped my aunt and killed my cousin. They gave him drugs. A man held a gun to his head while he did it, ya, but—ah, a boy younger than you! And he did those things and once such things is done, how you going to trust that man, eh?"

Another time, Musa said to me, "Men see you, a young girl, talking alone to other men, they get the idea you're looking for a man, any man, if you understand me." Tall and thick as an ox, Musa also came from Claudetta's village and handed out sweets from the *trenja* to the children, but all the *mamis* kept him away from the little ones. He smelled of sweat, piss, and mud. "I see you're a nice girl. You need a man to look out for you. Musa can do this. Would you like that?"

I didn't know what to say, but Claudetta called Musa a *bizabohdi* and chased him away.

A hot wind blew through the camp, gripping the odor of ashy smoke and burning flesh. To the west an ashy haze ascended from behind the cotton trees and spread across the cloudless sky. Every few days, a *hospitu* truck rolled out that way, stacked with cargo piled under a brown canvas cover. Wind often lifted the canvas edge, exposing piles of white bags that held the dead, ready for burning to kill the Ebola growing inside them. The yellow-suits called the dead "flowers," fat with Ebola for us to pick up and scatter, like bees spreading pollen. One would never notice until the *fiva* struck because the sickness was smaller than the eye could see.

Before the *dohktas* came, before they built the camps, before the radio songs warning all the people, many got the sickness washing the corpses of their loved ones or attending funerals. Those who traveled to pay respects brought Ebola home with them to their villages. Stories told of some folk even carrying it across the oceans to foreign lands. I wondered if the bleeding woman visited there, too.

Long after dark, the salt and copper odor of her blood awoke me, so strong I gagged. She stood by my feet, blood running, and her warm eyes curious through a wet film of red. I gasped and choked back a scream. She knelt eye-to-eye with me like my Mami did when she wanted me to remember some obvious thing. All my thoughts became questions that I had no courage to ask.

A man cleared his throat. Foday sat in his usual spot, eyes narrowed sleepily. He offered the bleeding woman a sharp grin, his teeth clean unlike hers. Excited, she walked to him. Her feet stepped on air, stirring only little waves in the grit beneath them. Blood dripped from her soles but never stained the soil. Sleepers shuddered as she passed. A *bobo* on her mami's chest cried until her mami rubbed her tiny back. The bleeding woman whispered to Foday, who shook and trembled as he replied. I couldn't hear what they said. All night the bleeding woman knelt with him yet never touched him.

In the morning, stomach cramps chewed up my insides. Foday frowned at me for staring at him. Later, while the women looked after their children and had no time for watching us, he told me, "Don't stare at me. The women will think the worst and be glad for the distraction. And some of the men might get bad ideas. Stay clear of Musa if you know what's good for you."

My throat tightened. I couldn't speak.

"Hey, you hear? You understand?"

"Why?" I forced out the word.

"They think I'm not to be trusted, and you are almost old enough for a man."

"Oh."

"You really are still a child, aren't you?"

I frowned at him. "I am who I am. Can you tell me who the bleeding woman is?"

"Let her tell you herself."

"Are we the only ones who see her?"

My words drew a dark shadow to his eyes. "Maybe others see her but keep it secret. The question to ask is *why* you see the *Red Mami* at all?"

"The *Red Mami*? Is that her name? Why do *you* see her?"

"I have witnessed much blood. Younger than you, I saw a lifetime's worth and spilled much of it myself. Men burned my village and killed my parents, and blood ran. They put a rifle in my hand, gave me a knife, sent me and my brothers to do men's work, and more blood ran. Shed by violence, blood looks a certain way to a child's eyes. Frightening yet exciting. The men with you say it's okay, it's good, it's a game to kill the enemy, like scoring a goal on the football field. They laugh and clap you on the back. The blood shows your skill and pride. But soon you see red everywhere. You see it in the dirt, on the leaves, on car windshields, in the mirror, on your hands, and you don't know who spilled it, you or your brothers or even if it's your own or someone else's. It changes your sight forever."

The yellow-suits came then. I stared at the road and counted cars rushing by and imagined leaving through the gate to freedom, going to the *os* of my brother in Freetown with the wind blowing in my face the whole way. But during my check-up, my stomach cramped tighter, aching bad. I hid my pain, opened my mouth, and sat still for the thermometer. Images of bloody feet hovering above the soil and bloody eyes in the night dark swirled in my head. Then the yellow-suit flinched and fell away from me. My mind snapped back to now. Blood from where she'd touched my leg smeared the fingertips of her gloves. She tipped sideways and landed on her rear. I held my breath. I felt no *fiva*, only painful tightness in my belly, yet blood ran down the inside of my leg to my knee.

I saw my future on a stretcher, a trip to *hospitu*, and after that—a sealed, white bag, flames licking from a blackened trench, my soul scattered in heat and smoke.

Tears flooded my eyes. I shook my head. No, no, no, no!

I leapt up and ran toward the gate to freedom. Everyone fled from my path, except for Claudetta, yammering to the yellow-suit and helping her up—and then they laughed! Or maybe cried. Or both. My sobbing blurred everything. Claudetta caught up to me and carried me back, caressing away my protests, telling me over and over I had no Ebola until I calmed down. The yellow-suit apologized. I had normal blood, she said, a woman's blood. I told her I was not yet a woman. I wished for my Mami or Olivette, or one of my aunts or cousins who had spoken to me of this day and what it meant to make new life. I had only the yellow-suits, a *trenja* with bottled water, a onetime *pickin solja*, and Claudetta.

"*Lohda masi, titi!* You have a woman's body now," Claudetta said. "Take what joy in it you can in this awful place."

Claudetta sat with me until my tears dried. She asked me about my Mami and Dadi, if they had arranged for my circumcision and initiation into the Bondo near our village. I told her about Olivette who died before her circumcision, and I didn't know where my Mami and Dadi had gone. She made the yellow-suit promise to find out. Another brought what I needed for the bleeding, helped me clean myself, and showed me how to use it.

The women and many of the men looked at me differently after that. Even Foday regarded me now with more fear than annoyance.

Visions of blood replaced my sleep that night. I saw the world through Foday's eyes, red and soaked. Blood spilling from death and life, from love and hate, from sickness. When the Red Mami arrived, I knew I didn't dream her because I hadn't slept. She sat cross-legged by my feet like my Mami used to sit with greens in the bowl of her skirt while she pulled them apart for cooking. I wondered if she looked like everyone's mami when she sat near them.

"You have blood now too," she said. "Your first. Very special. That's why you see me."

"Does your blood mean you can make life?"

Her eyes widened. The pattern of the blood running down her face changed. She crept on all fours and leaned close to me. Her whisper gurgled through blood on her lips, but her voice filled my head like a sweet echo from a deep well.

"What a question to ask! *All* blood makes life."

"Not blood spilled when someone dies," I said.

"Even that blood brings about life. It may lay in the soil to feed flies who leave their eggs to hatch maggots. Death changes other lives, so those become new lives. Blood spilled in hatred or apathy feeds other feelings that grow inside one's soul. Blood feeds all things."

"Are you here to help us make new life and save us from Ebola?"

The bleeding woman's smile softened. "*Titi*, Ebola *is* new life, and *you* help me make it."

"Ebola is death. Almost no one survives it."

"Ebola survives it. Ebola takes the tiniest parts of your blood and remakes them, creates new Ebola. Your bleeding gives birth to it to pass on to the next *Mami* or *Dadi*. All who take the sickness are *Mamis* and *Dadis* to Ebola."

"Are you Ebola?" I asked.

Her face wrinkled. Blood dripped from the tip of her nose but vanished before it hit me.

"I am *Mami*. I bleed and make new life. Only women may do this. You too bleed, but you are still innocent. You could stay innocent forever and still bring new life into the world. Would you like that? To be both woman and child

204

until the seas become deserts and the deserts fill with blood and your offspring encircle the world?"

"I don't understand," I said.

"You don't need to. That's the beauty of life. You may simply live it."

She reached her open hand toward my face, blood running down her wrist, spilling into air, into nothing. Then Foday's voice, like the crack of a gun, drew her attention.

"I have spilled blood and watched it stain the earth, and I say it brings only death," he said. "The one whose blood is let dies. The one who lets the blood out dies too. It changes the soul, yes. It leaves a festering wound. You spend the rest of your life trying to cut away the dead to keep the infection from spreading until nothing remains of your soul."

The Red Mami stood and sidled to Foday. "Then you have become something new. The same way your body gives Ebola what it needs to reproduce."

Foday shook his head. "Both are destroyed in the process."

"Only changed. Death ends nothing. It transfers life. Your soul changes inside you. You try to stop it, but your evils only multiply. What you did years ago becomes more and more of who you are. Your soul shrinks. I offer you the same. Accept my seed, become *Dadi* while some of your soul remains, and what's there now shall last forever."

Foday said nothing. He only stared at Red Mami, his cheeks brightened by streaks of tears reflecting the distant light from *hospitu*. Red Mami gazed at me again, then at Foday, and then stepped away into shadows, her whisper falling to us on the breeze.

"One must choose."

Foday turned away to hide his tears. The night passed, and the sun rose. The *trenja* brought water. The yellow-suits examined us and took some to *hospitu*.

In the afternoon, Musa seized my arm, clasped his hand over my mouth, and shoved me toward the latrines. Women yelled at him; some flashed me dirty looks as if I'd invited him to grab me. His muscles crushed the breath from my chest. My heart throbbed, and my head pounded. Dim voices shouted for the guards. I screamed, asking Musa "Why?" but his moist palm muffled my words, and he only grunted at me.

I struggled for air, and then I heard nothing more. Clouds of smoke filled my sight, the scent of dirty flesh flooded my nose. I shook my head and bit down as hard as I could on Musa's palm. Blood gushed onto my tongue as he yanked his hand away. My eyes cleared enough to see a shape leap and collide with him, dragging him off me. Blood leaked from Musa's eyes. It dripped between us as I tumbled to the dirt.

Although smaller than Musa, Foday knocked him flat and kept him down, kicking his chest and face until gunfire ripped apart the afternoon. *Soljas* shouted from outside the fence and aimed rifles at Foday. He rolled off Musa and raised his hands. More shouts came, so fast I couldn't understand them. Foday retreated and then knelt in the dirt with his hands behind his head.

The guns turned toward Musa, lying near me. Claudetta hurried me away. Musa screamed and lunged for her. The guns spoke. The air around us sizzled. Clutching me against her chest, Claudetta toppled us to the ground and held me down. A chunking sound like rocks splatting mud repeated over and over then ended when fat Musa slumped unmoving.

The yellow-suits rushed in, snatched up his body, and then hurried it away.

When they saw the blood on my lips and trapped between my teeth, they looked at me with pity, and I knew they would have to count my days all over. Too shocked to cry, I sat with Claudetta and hummed children's songs. At dusk, Foday came. Claudetta said nothing against him and went to tend the little ones.

"Are you all right?" Foday asked.

"Yes. Thank you for protecting me. I don't care if the women glare and the men scowl. You're my friend."

He cringed at my words. "The *Red Mami* will expect us to choose tonight."

"Choose what?"

Foday's mouth opened, but his words remained inside. He struggled to force them out, but in the end, he only shrugged, and then walked away.

She woke me with her breath that night, its metallic aroma mixed with the odor of wet ash and burnt flesh, tying my stomach in knots. I opened my eyes to her kneeling beside me, arms outstretched as if to hug me. Beneath the blood, she looked like my Mami. Her eyes regarded me with love, hope, and expectation, all things I once saw in Mami's face. I almost returned her embrace, but Foday's voice shook away my sleep cobwebs, and the bleeding woman lowered her arms and settled back on her legs.

"We didn't choose," Foday said.

"One must," the Red Mami said. "One must choose."

"Be fair, Red Mami. Tell this *titi* what choice she makes, what you told me."

"She didn't ask."

Foday gestured, urging me, and I said, "What do you want us to choose, *Red Mami?*"

She looked at me with my Mami's face, with the expression she always wore when I surprised her with my cleverness. Faster than I could react, the Red Mami reached out and brushed my eyes with her fingertips, smearing them with blood. Everything turned red, like Foday's world, and I saw blood in and on all things, blood flowing, gushing, spilled and wasted, saved, shared, or cast onto the ground. It spread like a mat of ants, but as if a million smaller ants made up each ant, and another ten million even smaller ants made up each of those. The blood made trails from body to body in the dark, and then a single drop rose and floated into the air. It burst into a cloud of tiny red gnats, and each of those exploded into smaller gnats, and again until I no longer saw them but knew they were there. More blood lifted from the bodies and the earth, and the air filled with specks in a red haze like the smoke of the dead fires. I watched the swarm of it drift over the gravel paths and the orange mesh fences and settle onto the *dohktas*, who'd taken off their yellow suits. It passed beyond them to the *soljas* and the workers at *hospitu* and drifted farther to the road, where the wind of the cars and trucks swept it inside their windows on to the drivers, and carried it after them in their wake. Everyone, everywhere, touched by the red cloud bled. From their eyes and nose, from their skin, from their mouth, from their scalp, until they resembled the Red Mami. And Foday and I walked past them, free of our tent village, free of the blood. A car stopped at the road. I got in. It took me to Barrie, to Freetown.

The blood followed me there.

My sight cleared. I fell back on my pillow. Chest heaving, I struggled to catch my breath. Sweat broke out all over my body, and my eyes shed heavy tears.

"Ebola is already inside you, *titi*, but if you choose, you will live," the Red Mami said. "You will carry the new Ebola into the world and give it birth, your innocence intact."

I thought of Musa's blood gushing into my mouth when I bit him, and all the days ahead of me before the *dohktas* sent me to *hospitu*.

"How many will die?" I asked.

"None will die. They will become Mamis and Dadis for the new Ebola. Our children will fly where now they must touch to travel. Soon they will live in every breath, free in the air. They will reach every part of the world. You will carry them in your blood and your lungs and share them with the air from your lips. You will live to see them thrive rather than go to the smoke."

207

"If Foday chooses?"

"Then he will live, Dadi to my children, and all will be the same to you, because you won't live to see their birth."

"I wanted you to have the choice, *titi*, after you were exposed to Musa's blood today, I wanted you to have a choice to live," Foday said.

"I don't want to live if it means everyone else must die. My sister Olivette died. And no one will tell me what happened to my Mami and Dadi, but I'm certain they're dead too. Maybe I will be with them if I die. What about you, Foday? No one should choose this."

"Some choices must be made. You will understand my choice before you die."

Foday knelt beside the Red Mami. She gazed at me sorrowfully then turned her attention to him. He stretched his arms to hold her, and she pressed against him, kissed him, and then like the blood in my vision, she scattered into tiny red particles more numerous than the stars, and all of them flowed into Foday's mouth. I cried for what would come, for this not-to-be-trusted man who had saved me, and for everyone he had betrayed.

Foday touched my cheek. "It's not as it seems, *titi*. Very little in this world is."

He ran toward the fence. People jolted awake as he passed. Shouts rose as Foday crashed into the orange mesh and pushed himself over it, as he dashed across the gravel path, and thrust himself over the next fence. The *dohktas* cried out. Lights flared to life. The night filled with panic. Motors revved, and *soljas* barked orders. Foday ignored them. He ran a straight line toward their guns, waving his arms, cursing them.

When he came within ten feet, the *soljas* fired. Their bullets punched through him with eruptions of blood that splashed on the ground. A scream only I could hear sheared through the night. The ghostly shape of the Red Mami drifted from Foday's body, from his spilled blood soaking into the earth, a weeping mist that dissipated and vanished.

I watched this while the sweat poured from me. I touched my eyes and my fingers came away with the Red Mami's blood. I chose not to wait for the *dohktas*. I walked to the gate and called for them to bring me to *hospitu*.

A hint of smoke passed across my face on the breeze.

Engine noise came from the road as cars roared toward Freetown.

In one way or another, I too would soon go free.

Author's Notes

A Song Left Behind in the Aztakea Hills

One of my earliest forays into Lovecraftian fiction, "Refugees," marked the first appearance of Knicksport, a fictionalized version of where I live on the north shore of Long Island, my personal patch of Lovecraft country. Three hundreds years ago, the New England colonies governed that part of the Island so I consider it grandfathered into Lovecraft's weird New England. The town features prominently in my Lovecraftian novella collection, *The Engines of Sacrifice* and has become the hub for my ventures into Lovecraft country ever since, connecting stories in a slowly expanding sub-mythos. For "A Song Left Behind in the Aztakea Hills," I turned to the local history of Northport, one of the towns upon which Knicksport is based. In the early 1960s, Beat author Jack Kerouac lived in Northport (in several different houses during his time there) and frequented Gunther's, a Main Street bar. Gunther's still stands today, despite a fire that closed it for more than a year not long after I wrote this story, and they proudly display an article about Kerouac in the window. Baymen still go clamming out of Northport, though the business is much diminished and the bay ecosystem much altered. Some still drink at Gunther's too. Much of the story sprang from my research into Kerouac's time in the town, especially his drinking habits. There are even a few lines of dialog based on quotes from interviews he gave at the time. The bit of Kerouac-ian language near the end proved quite a challenge. Listening to recordings of Kerouac reading his work gave me the sense of the rhythm I needed to write it. What most appealed to me about this story is the contrast between Kerouac's search for spiritual grace in a material world and the horrific indifference of a Lovecraftian cosmos to all that. The story received a Bram Stoker Award® nomination.

Marco Polo

Have you ever played Truth or Dare? Depending on your age and friends at the time, the game can be goofy fun, awkwardly uncomfortable, or deadly serious. The idea for "Marco Polo," written for Max Booth III's *Truth or Dare* anthology, began with the dare posed in the first part of the story, inspired by my interest in abandoned buildings. I'm too much of a 'fraidy cat to go hunting around in their basements, but I like to wander around outside and photograph them. From there the story launched into darker territory than I expected. I most enjoyed writing the interaction amongst the kids before Henry enters the store, digging into why kids do the dumb things they do. Teenagers inhabit a twilight between innocence and adulthood with long paths laid out before them that can lead into the light or the dark, but many times they focus so intently on the immediate or on their inner worlds that they fail to see the deep, awful threats the exterior world holds for those futures.

Lost Daughters

Some stories grow into themselves. "Lost Daughters" was born as an overnight writing exercise at the Borderlands Bootcamp. For one of the activities at the workshop, each grunt receives a name randomly at the start of Bootcamp on Friday. After the main critique sessions and evening seminar on Saturday, the grunts are sent off to write a story inspired by the name for the Sunday morning session where they're printed out, read aloud, and critiqued. Little to no sleep for those Bootcamp grunts! The idea is to see how everyone implements the skills learned during the weekend. I wrote the first draft of "Lost Daughters" for this exercise. It ran about 1,000 words and went over well with the group. I liked it enough to come back to it, expand it, and eventually I sold it to an anthology, *Deep Cuts*, where my editor, Chris Marrs, provided great feedback. I further revised the story, and—I think—improved it greatly. In that regard, I suppose this is one of the few stories I've ever "workshopped." I've read it at a number of author appearances over the years because the opening grabs listeners' attention and I love the atmosphere. The original version was a simple take on a sort of modern folk myth story. The published version evolved into a tale about what happens—or might happen—when we let down those who depend on us in the ways that matter most.

Sum'bitch and the Arakadile

One of those rare stories that came to mind immediately and fully formed, "Sum'bitch and the Arakadile" popped into my head because my train was canceled one morning. I don't recall the exact details of why, but with my regular train line unexpectedly out of commission, I walked half an hour to another station in the pouring rain. Not a great morning. But I landed on the train, tired and soaked, and into my weary, frustrated head popped this piece, probably because I was too tired to overthink it. I wrote it on the train then and there but set it aside for quite some time before polishing it up and deciding to include it in this collection. I liked how the original draft turned out, but I felt it needed a few different details and some refinement to work as I wanted. Before finalizing it for this collection, I tested it out at a reading event in New York City. It went over quite well, but I'm told I flubbed the main character's accent by the end. The conviction we bring to things we are trained to believe is powerful and frightening, and sometimes they can take on an unexpected life of their own.

Mnemonicide

We have all, I suppose, suffered awful moments of regret or discomfort when terrible memories come flashing to mind. A scent or a song can transport us to another time or place, launch a train of thought that speeds off the rails into a dark abyss. Memories of betrayal or embarrassment, of cruelty, failure, and ignorance, whether we are the actor or acted upon, retain unpleasant power. They cast dark shadows over otherwise bright days. They take the wind from our sails and hold us back with self-doubt, shame, or guilt. Eventually we come to terms with them, maybe forgive others or ourselves so we can move on. Time heals. But what if you didn't have it in you for that and you found a way to simply erase those kinds of memories as if they'd never happened? What would it be worth to accomplish that, to destroy all your painful memories? Would it really make things better? What kind of person would do that? What kind of person would be left afterward? This story answers those questions. It's written in second person, an experiment I am grateful that Michael Bailey liked when he accepted it for publication in *Chiral Mad 2*. Except that's a bit of a cheat. If you read carefully, you'll see it's really more of a first-person narrative.

The Many Hands inside the Mountain

An invitation to submit to a Halloween-themed anthology instigated this story. I chose to play around with a theme from the classic E.C. Comics horror stories in *Tales from the Crypt* and its sister publications, *The Haunt of Fear* and *The Vault of Horror*: the love triangle. Almost of its own volition, the story proceeded into much weirder and darker territory than I'd expected, but in my mind's eye, I see it perfectly rendered by a dream team of E.C.'s best: Wally Wood, Jack Davis, Jack Kamen, Graham Ingels, and those gloriously lurid colors of Marie Severin. It's a very image-driven story. In this one, I enjoyed writing the character dynamics and the hubris of the young contrasted against the dark weight of the town's history—and the party scene!

What's in the Bag, Dad?

I wrote the first draft of this story for a planned anthology of carnival horror intended to have an E.C. Comics vibe. The publisher loved it, but the anthology never happened. I set the story aside and with the benefit of time realized I could do more with it than I had—one of those occasions when something not winding up published as planned works out for the best. The published story works more as a bit of historical horror fiction than an E.C. homage, but I can still hear the Crypt Keeper's voice when I read the title. I have a lot of sympathy for the characters in this one (and I hope you do too). I wish things could've turned out better for them.

The Driver under a Cheshire Moon

There are other Driver stories to be written, but this one came to me almost exactly as it appears here, bringing with it at least two other episodes of this mysterious character to mind. This story is simple, blunt, and violent, but not hopeless. It captures a particular, visceral emotion I've often felt (and suspect many others have too) while reading news stories about the horrible things done to children or the awful unanswered questions of missing children. Those things conjure a sense of hopelessness. We wonder how society allows some of them to occur, how some children slip through the cracks, or how monstrous adults walk among us unnoticed until it's too late. Maybe if there were someone out there looking out for all the ones who fall into the shadows....

Living/Dead

The title for this story plays on the fan-fiction sub-genre of "slash" fiction, stories that pair (or even group, I suppose) characters from popular fiction in unlikely romances. This story isn't slash, but the convention works well for the title. "Living/Dead" sprang from my perception that when it comes to love and happiness, we're often our own worst enemies in ways great and small and in ways we don't even understand because we lack objectivity. Whether we hurt ourselves or others do it for us, whether we let fear, despair, or complacency get in our way, there are far too many obstacles to true love to ignore it when it comes along in whatever form it takes. The other side of that is that relationships are built on trust and faith. We never fully know what's in the mind of a romantic partner, yet we entrust them with our lives and hearts, a genuine life-or-death proposition, especially here. When the feeling is reciprocated, miraculous things can happen, and love can (literally in this story) bring life.

The Last Chamber of Earthly Delights

This story marked my first work in the mythology of the King in Yellow and the Yellow Sign, created by Robert Chambers (no relation). I wrote this with a good friend in a mind, one of my editors and publishers, for a planned story collection that never came together (an occupational hazard of publishing). When writing stories in other authors' mythos, I rely on the work of the original author as a guide, in this case, Chambers' story, "The Repairer of Reputations," which introduces the King in Yellow. It's a fascinating tale of madness and the macabre, ahead of its time, and, of special interest to me, set in New York City, a place I enjoy writing about. For "The Last Chamber," I assumed the insane visions of Chambers' unreliable narrator were literally true and wrote this in that setting, fleshing out answers for many of the questions "The Repairer of Reputations" raised—but there's still a touch of madness and uncertainty there as there always must be when the King in Yellow casts his gaze our way.

Odd Quahogs

Doug Murano dropped me a line to ask if I might like to send him something to consider for the first volume of *Shadows over Main Street*, which he edited with D. Alexander Ward. The deadline was tight, but I was excited for a reason to visit Knicksport again. The theme was small-town Lovecraftian horror, and Main Street in Knicksport fit the bill. This story was written after *The Engines of Sacrifice* but before "A Song Left Behind in the Aztakea Hills," which appeared in *Shadows over Main Street 2*. It calls back to "Refugees," published many moons ago in the first issue of *Allen K's Inhuman* magazine. I had great fun writing Spencer and Big Gene (whose name is a nod to a writer friend who, though he doesn't know it, inspired Gene's combative but thoughtful spirit). As far as the story goes, Gene could still be out there on the water battling all that darkness and the cosmic horror to which it led him. Gene's fight, after all, is the kind that sadly never ends.

A Wandering Blackness

When the opportunity came my way to write a couple of stories about Lin Carter's Anton Zarnak, Supernatural Sleuth, I was not familiar with the character.

Not surprising, perhaps, since Carter apparently only ever wrote two Zarnak stories. In those two stories, though, he created a memorable pulp protagonist, his assistant, and his world—which mysteriously placed Zarnak at the same address in New York and San Francisco, suggesting the character's home existed in more than one place, perhaps even outside our typical understanding of location. The first Zarnak story I wrote, "The Keeper of Beasts," takes place in the 1930s and draws on the character's pulp elements. For the second one, I wanted to write a contemporary story, less pulp, more modern horror, and bring Zarnak into the present, as apparently he's rather long-lived if not immortal. "Blackness" is more Robert Blackapple's story than Zarnak's, and it delves into the kind of darkness that can creep into anyone's soul and ruin them from the inside out. The story received an Honorable Mention in *The Year's Best Horror and Fantasy*, 16th Edition.

Lost Boy

Few classic horror characters have so greatly influenced the genre on the basis of so little. With two television movies and a one-season TV series in the 1970s, Carl Kolchak became a horror icon. *Kolchak, the Night Stalker* streamed on Netflix for quite a while and continues to air in reruns today. An argument can be made that Carl is more popular now than when the show was first on the air—at least among horror fans. Kolchak inspired *The X-Files* and countless other supernatural investigators. Mention him at a horror convention, the reaction is usually a chorus of appreciation for the character, the original movies and series, and what he means to the genre. Created by late author Jeff Rice and portrayed by Darren McGavin, Kolchak has weathered the test of time, and in true Kolchak fashion, he's done it without changing much at all. With the exception of the failed revival with Stewart Townsend cast as Kolchak, a show more *X-Files* than *Night Stalker*, and generally disregarded by Kolchak fans, Carl has stayed in character in anthologies, comic books, and novels for more than forty years. That's the mark of a great character. He translates mostly unchanged to various settings and time periods. "Lost Boy" was my first opportunity to write a Kolchak story. As anyone who tries this will tell you, one of the hardest parts of writing Kolchak is capturing his voice, so distinctive and wry as established on the television show. In any case, I've rarely had more fun writing a character I didn't create. After I wrote this I wrote *Kolchak the Night Stalker: The Forgotten Lore of Edgar Allan Poe*, a graphic novel, which received a Bram Stoker Award®.

Picture Man

One night I got off the subway at the wrong stop in Brooklyn.

If you've ever ridden the New York City subways over any length of time, you already know how incredibly confusing it can be when construction or any other disruption of service occurs. Changes are communicated by fliers taped up around stations, and sometimes there are three, or four, or more different fliers attempting to explain changes to which trains are running on what tracks, where they're stopping or not stopping, what hours they're running, where riders need to change trains, on and on…. Often you only see these fliers after you pay your fare and go through the turnstile. In some cases, riders must go to a different line's station blocks away to catch their train. Sometimes expired fliers stay up as new ones are added, and they contradict each other. While the Manhattan Transit Authority does a fair job moving people around, it has never come close to mastering the art of telling them where they're going or how they're getting there.

I boarded a subway train at Atlantic Terminal and, confused by the crazy quilt of fliers in the station, thought I needed to change trains at another stop to get to Bay Ridge. I exited the first train to wait for a different train at a station I didn't know. I stepped onto a platform empty but for two teen girls arguing with each other at the payphone by the exit. I was at the opposite end of the platform from them and didn't think much of it until they stopped yelling at each other and both of them stared at me. Then they left. I had the platform to myself for a minute or two before a young guy entered.

A young guy holding an aluminum baseball bat.

This took place in winter, so I doubted he was on his way to a game. He didn't seem to notice me and walked toward the opposite end of the platform. I stayed put, wishing my train would show up. I jumped with the first loud bang that echoed through the station. At the other end of the platform, bat guy was now beating on a garbage can and talking to himself.

Whack. Mutter, mutter. *Whack.* Mutter, mutter.

Where the hell is my train?

Watching bat guy without looking right at him, and—oh, great, now he's moving my way, and—*whack*—taking swings at the wall. Closer. *Whack, clang*—the platform steel support column. Closer. Still doesn't seem to notice me—and then, oh, crap, he's looking right at me, watching me, not looking away, not swinging, not hitting anything now, coming closer.

215

Where the *hell* is my train?

At this point, I'm debating whether or not run out of the station, but bat guy is closer to the exit than I am. So instead, I act like I am absolutely indifferent to him and have no fear. I yawn, sit down on a bench, and do my best to look casual.

Bat guy comes closer, dragging the bat along the concrete platform. He's staring right at me, and I sense he's hesitant, confused by how I'm ignoring him. It lasts only a few seconds and then he's moving toward me again—when with a clank and rumble the train finally pulled in.

Bat guy stopped. I jumped onto a crowded car and rode out of the station.

I rode away certain that hiding my fear was the only thing that kept me from playing the role of baseball in some random guy's game. My reaction created just enough uncertainty to give him pause long enough for my train to roll in. I don't know that for sure, of course, no more than I know what bat guy's deal was, whether he was just bored and screwing around, if the teen girls sent him after me, if he was looking to put that bat to bloody use that night, or even if he was just bored and my imagination filled in too many sinister blanks, but that's the experience that inspired "Picture Man."

When I finally got to my destination I learned I didn't even need to change trains in the first place. Thanks, MTA!

Red Mami

Ebola scares the hell out of me. It's virulent, nasty, and, even with hospital treatment, fatal in more than half of cases. The Ebola vaccine isn't entirely effective. The process of the disease is right out of a horror novel, worse than the goriest horror movie. It represents mindless death that enters your body unseen, unfelt, a viral invader that turns your cells against you to reproduce itself with vigor and the sole purpose of spreading to other organisms to do the same to them.

The largest outbreak in history occurred in West Africa in 2014. Ebola killed thousands and infected thousands more. A handful of cases occurred in the U.S. and other countries where the virus isn't indigenous. I watched a compelling documentary about the outbreak and efforts to combat it in Sierra Leone, where the reality of the disease elicited not only governmental and medical responses but cultural ones too. Billboards displayed warnings. Pop songs on the radio sang of how to avoid the disease. It was a constant topic on television. The image of the infected and exposed penned in makeshift, outdoor shelters, monitored by doctors who kept their distance except when wrapped head to toe in protective clothing unnerved me. The most striking thing, though, was the spirit of the people. Their will to carry on ordinary life, their acceptance of the burden, their resolve in waiting out the disease under observation.

Sierra Leone is not a well-developed nation. Its history is marred by conflict. Added to that, traditional burial customs there, which allow for close contact between the living and the dead, were one of the factors driving Ebola infections, particularly early on before the outbreak was identified. This mindless virus preyed on its victims at their weakest moments of grief and loss.

I followed the outbreak in the news, read everything I could about it, and wondered what might happen if this mindless virus with no other purpose than to reproduce actually became conscious in some way and chose to up its game.

That outbreak ended in 2015.

As I write these author notes in the spring of 2019, the second largest Ebola outbreak in history is ongoing in the same part of Africa.

As of this writing, it has not yet shown any signs of ending.

About the Author

James Chambers is an award-winning author of horror, crime, fantasy, and science fiction. He wrote the Bram Stoker Award®-winning graphic novel, *Kolchak the Night Stalker: The Forgotten Lore of Edgar Allan Poe* and was nominated for a Bram Stoker Award for his story, "A Song Left Behind in the Aztakea Hills." *Publisher's Weekly* gave his collection of four Lovecraftian-inspired novellas, *The Engines of Sacrifice*, a starred review and described it as "chillingly evocative."

He is the author of the short story collection *Resurrection House* and several novellas, including *The Dead Bear Witness* and *Tears of Blood*, in the Corpse Fauna novella series, and the dark urban fantasy, *Three Chords of Chaos*.

His short stories have been published in numerous anthologies, including *After Punk: Steampowered Tales of the Afterlife, The Best of Bad-Ass Faeries, The Best of Defending the Future, Chiral Mad 2, Chiral Mad 4, Deep Cuts, Dragon's Lure, Fantastic Futures 13, Gaslight and Grimm, The Green Hornet Chronicles, Hardboiled Cthulhu, In An Iron Cage, Kolchak the Night Stalker: Passages of the Macabre, Qualia Nous, Shadows Over Main Street (1 and 2), The Spider: Extreme Prejudice, To Hell in a Fast Car, Truth or Dare, TV Gods, Walrus Tales, Weird Trails*; the chapbook *Mooncat Jack*; and the magazines *Bare Bone, Cthulhu Sex*, and *Allen K's Inhuman*. He co-edited the anthology, *A New York State of Fright: Horror Stories from the Empire State*, nominated for a Bram Stoker Award.

He has also written and edited numerous comic books including *Leonard Nimoy's Primortals*, the critically acclaimed "The Revenant" in *Shadow House*, and *The Midnight Hour* with Jason Whitley.

He is a member of the Horror Writers Association and recipient of the 2012 Richard Laymon Award and the 2016 Silver Hammer Award.

He lives in New York.

Visit his website: www.jameschambersonline.com.